THE THIEF

J. R. WARD

THE
THIEF

A NOVEL OF THE BLACK DAGGER BROTHERHOOD

BALLANTINE BOOKS

NEW YORK

Copyright © 2018 by Love Conquers All, Inc.

Published in the United States by Ballantine Books, an imprint of Random House, a division of Penguin Random House LLC, New York.

BALLANTINE and the HOUSE colophon are registered trademarks of Penguin Random House LLC.

Hardback ISBN 978-0-451-47521-3
Ebook ISBN 978-0-698-19299-7

Printed in the United States of America on acid-free paper

randomhousebooks.com

2 4 6 8 9 7 5 3 1

First Edition

Endpaper image by iStock/bestdesigns

Dedicated to:

You both. I can't think of

two more kindred hearts or souls.

GLOSSARY OF TERMS AND

PROPER NOUNS

ahstrux nohtrum (n.) Private guard with license to kill who is granted his or her position by the King.

ahvenge (v.) Act of mortal retribution, carried out typically by a male loved one.

Black Dagger Brotherhood (pr. n.) Highly trained vampire warriors who protect their species against the Lessening Society. As a result of selective breeding within the race, Brothers possess immense physical and mental strength, as well as rapid healing capabilities. They are not siblings for the most part, and are inducted into the Brotherhood upon nomination by the Brothers. Aggressive, self-reliant, and secretive by nature, they are the subjects of legend and objects of reverence within the vampire world. They may be killed only by the most serious of wounds, e.g., a gunshot or stab to the heart, etc.

blood slave (n.) Male or female vampire who has been subjugated to serve the blood needs of another. The practice of keeping blood slaves has been outlawed.

the Chosen (pr. n.) Female vampires who had been bred to serve the Scribe Virgin. In the past, they were spiritually rather than temporally focused, but that changed with the ascendance of the final Primale, who freed them from the Sanctuary. With the Scribe Virgin removing herself from her role, they are completely autonomous and learning to live on earth. They do continue to meet the blood needs of unmated members of the Brotherhood, as well as Brothers who cannot feed from their *shellans* or injured fighters.

chrih (n.) Symbol of honorable death in the Old Language.

cohntehst (n.) Conflict between two males competing for the right to be a female's mate.

Dhunhd (pr. n.) Hell.

doggen (n.) Member of the servant class within the vampire world. *Doggen* have old, conservative traditions about service to their superiors, following a formal code of dress and behavior. They are able to go out during the day, but they age relatively quickly. Life expectancy is approximately five hundred years.

ehros (n.) A Chosen trained in the matter of sexual arts.

exhile dhoble (n.) The evil or cursed twin, the one born second.

the Fade (pr. n.) Non-temporal realm where the dead reunite with their loved ones and pass eternity.

First Family (pr. n.) The King and Queen of the vampires, and any children they may have.

ghardian (n.) Custodian of an individual. There are varying degrees of *ghardians,* with the most powerful being that of a *sehcluded* female.

glymera (n.) The social core of the aristocracy, roughly equivalent to Regency England's *ton.*

hellren (n.) Male vampire who has been mated to a female. Males may take more than one female as mate.

hyslop (n. or v.) Term referring to a lapse in judgment, typically resulting in the compromise of the mechanical operations of a vehicle or otherwise motorized conveyance of some kind. For example, leaving one's keys in one's car as it is parked outside the family home overnight, whereupon said vehicle is stolen.

leahdyre (n.) A person of power and influence.

leelan (adj. or n.) A term of endearment loosely translated as "dearest one."

Lessening Society (pr. n.) Order of slayers convened by the Omega for the purpose of eradicating the vampire species.

lesser (n.) De-souled human who targets vampires for extermination as a member of the Lessening Society. *Lessers* must be stabbed through the chest in order to be killed; otherwise they are ageless. They do not eat or drink and are impotent. Over time, their hair, skin, and irises lose pigmentation until they are blond, blushless, and pale eyed. They smell like baby powder. Inducted into the society by the Omega, they retain a ceramic jar thereafter into which their heart was placed after it was removed.

lewlhen (n.) Gift.

lheage (n.) A term of respect used by a sexual submissive to refer to their dominant.

Lhenihan (pr. n.) A mythic beast renowned for its sexual prowess. In modern slang, refers to a male of preternatural size and sexual stamina.

lys (n.) Torture tool used to remove the eyes.

mahmen (n.) Mother. Used both as an identifier and a term of affection.

mhis (n.) The masking of a given physical environment; the creation of a field of illusion.

nalla (n., f.) or *nallum* (n., m.) Beloved.

needing period (n.) Female vampire's time of fertility, generally lasting for two days and accompanied by intense sexual cravings. Occurs approximately five years after a female's transition and then once a decade thereafter. All males respond to some degree if they are around a female in her need. It can be a dangerous time, with conflicts and fights breaking out between competing males, particularly if the female is not mated.

newling (n.) A virgin.

the Omega (pr. n.) Malevolent, mystical figure who has targeted the vampires for extinction out of resentment directed toward the Scribe Virgin. Exists in a non-temporal realm and has extensive powers, though not the power of creation.

phearsom (adj.) Term referring to the potency of a male's sexual organs. Literal translation something close to "worthy of entering a female."

Princeps (pr. n.) Highest level of the vampire aristocracy, second only to members of the First Family or the Scribe Virgin's Chosen. Must be born to the title; it may not be conferred.

pyrocant (n.) Refers to a critical weakness in an individual. The weakness can be internal, such as an addiction, or external, such as a lover.

rahlman (n.) Savior.

rythe (n.) Ritual manner of asserting honor granted by one who has offended another. If accepted, the offended chooses a weapon and strikes the offender, who presents him- or herself without defenses.

the Scribe Virgin (pr. n.) Mystical force who previously was counselor to the King as well as the keeper of vampire archives and the dispenser of privileges. Existed in a non-temporal realm and had extensive powers, but has recently stepped down and given her station to another. Capable of a single act of creation, which she expended to bring the vampires into existence.

sehclusion (n.) Status conferred by the King upon a female of the aristocracy as a result of a petition by the female's family. Places the female under the sole direction of her *ghardian,* typically the eldest male in her household. Her *ghardian* then has the legal right to determine all manner of her life, restricting at will any and all interactions she has with the world.

shellan (n.) Female vampire who has been mated to a male. Females generally do not take more than one mate due to the highly territorial nature of bonded males.

symphath (n.) Subspecies within the vampire race characterized by the ability and desire to manipulate emotions in others (for the purposes of an energy exchange), among other traits. Historically, they have been discriminated against and, during certain eras, hunted by vampires. They are near extinction.

the Tomb (pr. n.) Sacred vault of the Black Dagger Brotherhood. Used as a ceremonial site as well as a storage facility for the jars of *lessers*. Ceremonies performed there include inductions, funerals, and disciplinary actions against Brothers. No one may enter except for members of the Brotherhood, the Scribe Virgin, or candidates for induction.

trahyner (n.) Word used between males of mutual respect and affection. Translated loosely as "beloved friend."

transition (n.) Critical moment in a vampire's life when he or she transforms into an adult. Thereafter, he or she must drink the blood of the opposite sex to survive and is unable to withstand sunlight. Occurs generally in the mid-twenties. Some vampires do not survive their transitions, males in particular. Prior to their transitions, vampires are physically weak, sexually unaware and unresponsive, and unable to dematerialize.

vampire (n.) Member of a species separate from that of Homo sapiens. Vampires must drink the blood of the opposite sex to survive. Human blood will keep them alive, though the strength does not last long. Following their transitions, which occur in their mid-twenties, they are unable to go out into sunlight and must feed from the vein regularly. Vampires cannot "convert" humans through a bite or transfer of blood, though they are in rare cases able to breed with the other species. Vampires can dematerialize at will, though they must be able to calm themselves and concentrate to do so and may not carry anything heavy with them. They are able to strip the memories of humans, provided such memories are short-term. Some vampires are able to read minds. Life expectancy is upward of a thousand years, or in some cases, even longer.

wahlker (n.) An individual who has died and returned to the living from the Fade. They are accorded great respect and are revered for their travails.

whard (n.) Equivalent of a godfather or godmother to an individual.

THE THIEF

ONE

ola Morte, a.k.a. Marisol Maria Rafaela Carvalho, opened the sliding door, pulling the glass panel out of the way. Even though it was past midnight and into January, the ocean air that greeted her was seventy degrees and humid, a sweet kiss as opposed to a frigid slap. After a year of living in Miami, however, she was no longer pleasantly surprised. The kinder climate had become, like the slow pace, the palm trees, the beaches and the tides, simply part of life.

Exotic was a function of rarity, and so, as with beauty, was in the eye of the beholder.

Now, the snow-covered pines of Caldwell, New York, would be captivating and unusual.

Shaking her head, she tried to stick to the present. The "terrace" for this fifth-floor condo she shared with her grandmother was nothing more than a shelf with a railing, the sort of outdoor space added not for the functional utility and enjoyment of the owners, but so "ocean terrace" could be included in the sales description of the building's thirty units. And come to think of it, the "ocean" part was also a fudge, as it was Biscayne Bay, not the Atlantic, she was overlooking. Still, water was water, and when you couldn't sleep, it was more interesting than staring at your ceiling.

She'd kitted out the two-bedroom, two-bath place about three years ago, buying setups from Rooms To Go because they were priced right and someone else had done the thinking about throw pillows and color combinations. And then for her "luxury" "ocean" terrace, she'd hit Target and scored two yellow-and-white lawn chairs and a coffee table. The former worked fine. The latter had a translucent plastic top with what had turned out to be annoying waves in its surface. Nothing sat flush on it.

On that note, she parked herself in the chair on the left. "Full moon tonight."

As her voice drifted off, she stared across the nocturnal vista. Directly in front of her, there were a number of short houses, old ones built in the forties, and then a series of crappy T-shirt shops, bodegas, and cantinas between her and the beach. To say that she and her *vovó* lived in Miami was similar to the terrace-false-advertising thing. They were actually on the northern knife-edge of the city limits, well away from the mansions and nightlife, although she was willing to bet that in about ten years, this down-market neighborhood was going to get a glitzy overhaul.

Fine with her. She'd have a great return on her cash investment and—

Oh, who was she kidding. They weren't going to be here for more than another year.

She had another bolt-hole in California and one in Toronto. After they cycled through those, it was going to be somewhere else.

For her, there were few requirements for establishing a home base: cash purchase, Catholic church within blocks, and a good Latino market close by.

As a breeze rolled up and played through her newly blonded hair, she sat forward because it was hard to stay still. The repositioning didn't last, and not just because the top railing now blocked the view of the bay. Easing back, she tapped the heel of her flip-flop, the metronome of restless energy only bearable because it was her own foot doing the up and down, and, at least theoretically, she could stop it.

To say that memory was a lane you could walk along, a path to follow, a linear progression you embarked on from start to finish, was way off base. After this past year, she had decided it was more like a piano keyboard, and the musical notes her mind played in the form of moving-picture images were a pick-and-choose determined more by the sheet music of her mourning than the well-founded logic of her decision to leave Caldwell.

For example, if she were rational about things, she would be focusing on what it had been like to come home one night and have those attackers abduct her as her grandmother roused and started to come down the stairs. Then she would recall her trip up north in the trunk of a car. Yup . . . if she were smart, her brain would be projecting a slide show about her taking a lit flare and stabbing it into the eye socket of the man who yanked her out of the back of that sedan. She would picture herself getting shot in the leg as she had tried to run away through the forest, and then remember the cell with the bars in the underground level of that torture camp.

She would visualize with precise detail the thug with the two-toned face who had stripped her and tried to rape her—until she had twisted his nuts and beat his head in with a heavy chain.

And finally, she would see herself dragging a dead man across the floor to try to use his fingerprint to open the way out. And when that didn't work, she would retrace her steps as she returned to the basement and pulled that two-toned attempted rapist's arm through the bars of a cell so she could take a kitchen knife and cut the hand off at the wrist.

How about recalling the successful use of that still-warm thumb on the keypad to open the steel door? Or bursting out of that hellhole wearing nothing but a parka and the blood of the two human beings she had killed?

But nah, those were not the notes her cerebral Steinway played.

As tunes went, the one that her brain kept on repeat was altogether different and far more destructive.

Even though it was certainly sexier—

"Stop it." She rubbed her eyes. "Just *stop*."

Above the landlocked bay, over the breakwater rim of North Beach, the moon was a great silver plate, its illumination hazy and tickled by wisps of clouds.

Assail's eyes had been like that, silver with a deep purple rim.

And she guessed they still were, assuming he was alive—although with the kind of life he was leading? Drug lords were in risk pools over and above the generic ones like cancer and heart disease.

Not that she had judged him for his choice of business—come on, her profession as a burglar was how she'd ended up in that trunk.

Such odd, hypnotizing eyes he'd had. Like nothing she had ever seen, and no, that was not romanticizing on her part. As with his strange name, and the accent that she couldn't quite place—was it German? French? Romanian?—and the mystery that surrounded him, he had been what other men had never come close to: irresistible. With hair so black, she'd assumed it had been dyed, and a widow's peak on that high, autocratic forehead, and his powerful body and sex drive, she had often felt that he was a figment from some other world.

A deadly presence.

A gorgeous predator.

An animal in human skin.

Between one blink and the next, she saw him the night he had come to rescue her from that camp—but not as he had approached her with open arms and a calm voice just as she had run out of that steel door, all wounded and disorientated. No, she remembered him a short time later, when he had somehow met her at a rest stop some twenty miles down the highway.

She had never understood how it was possible that he had stayed behind as his cousins had driven off with her—and yet Assail had caught up with them as if he could fly.

And then there was what he'd looked like. His mouth had been covered with blood as if he had bitten someone. And those silver and purple eyes had shone brighter than this moon in this southern sky with the light in them so unholy, it had seemed the stuff of exorcism.

Yet she had not been afraid of him—and she had also known at that moment that Benloise, her captor, had not lived. Assail had somehow killed her kidnapper, and in all likelihood, his brother, Eduardo.

It was the way of the business they had all been in. And the way of the life she had been determined to leave after she had healed.

After all, when you were held by madmen and prayed to God to see your grandmother again, and that actually happened? Only a fool didn't keep their end of the bargain.

Hello, Miami.

Sola pushed her fingertips into her forehead and tried to get her brain off the well-worn path it seemed determine to process and re-process—even though it was a year later, for godsakes. She couldn't believe she was so fixated on a sound decision that she had made with her own survival at the forefront.

Nights were still the worst. During the day, when she was busy with such high-level endeavors as grocery shopping, and going to mass with her *vovó,* and constantly looking out from under the brim of a baseball cap to see if they were being followed, she managed better. But with the darkness came the haunting, the ghost of a man she never should have slept with tormenting her.

She had long been aware that she had a death wish. Her attraction to Assail was confirmation of that, and then some.

Hell, she didn't even know his last name. For all the spying on him that she had been hired to do, and then that which she had done on her own, she knew almost nothing about him. He had a glass house on the Hudson that was owned by a real estate trust. His two closest associates were his twin cousins, and both were as mute as brick walls when it came to his personal details. He'd had no wife or children.

At least not around him, but who knew. A man like that certainly had plenty of options for companionship.

Shifting to the side, she took her old iPhone out and looked at its black screen. When she woke the thing up, there was a picture of the beach from back right after she had arrived here.

No texts, no missed calls, no voicemails.

For a long while, she had had these regular hang-ups from a restricted number.

The intermittent calls were the only reason she'd kept the phone. Who else would be reaching her on it except for Assail? Who else had the number? It wasn't the phone she'd used with Benloise or any of her shadowy business, and the account was under an alias. He was the only one who had the digits.

She really should have left the thing up north and canceled the service. Clean cut was best. The safest.

The issue seemed to have resolved itself, however. Assuming Assail had been the one calling, he'd stopped—and maybe it wasn't because he'd found his grave. He had probably moved on—which was what people did when they got left behind. The whole pining-away-for-a-lifetime thing only happened in Victorian novels, and then usually on the woman's side.

Yeah, no Mr. Havisham going on up north. No way—

Another memory took her back in time, and it was one she hated. Even after Benloise had ordered her off the trail, she had followed Assail out to an estate, to what had appeared to be a caretaker's cottage. He hadn't gone there for a business transaction. No, it was for a dark-haired woman with a body and a half, and he'd taken her down onto a sofa like he'd done it before. Just as he'd started to have sex with her, he had looked directly at the window Sola had been watching him through—as if he were putting on the show for her.

At that point, she had decided to pull out of the surveilling and had resolved never to see him again.

Fate had had different ideas, however. And had turned her silver-eyed drug dealer into a savior.

The sad thing was, under different circumstances, she might have stayed with him in that glass house of his. But in the end, her little deal with God had superseded that kind of fantasy.

Getting to her feet, she lingered at the rail for a while longer, wondering exactly what she hoped she would find in the view. Then she turned away, shut herself back in the condo, and kicked off her flip-flops. On silent, bare feet, she whispered through the living room area and went into the kitchen. Her grandmother's standards were such that not only could you eat off the floor, you could toss a salad in any of the drawers, roll your bread dough out inside the cupboards, and use the shelving to cut your steak on.

The tool kit was under the sink, and she got out a full-sized hammer.

The iPhone went into a double Ziploc bag—setup on her way to the door and she disengaged the alarm before exiting into the corridor. The fire stairwell was down on the right, and as she strode over to it, she listened out of habit, but not necessity. The people in the building were elderly, and what little she saw of them confirmed she had chosen the right unit. This was the land of snowbirds who didn't have the money to fly up and back for the spring and summer, so the building never emptied out.

There would always be nosy witnesses, even if those eyes and ears were not quite as sharp as they had once been. And her fellow residents represented a complication that people coming after her would think twice about.

Plus, as always, she had a compact nine with a laser sight on her. Justincase.

The stairwell was cooler, but no dryer than the great outdoors, and she didn't go far. She put the phone in its little plastic bag–coffin on the concrete floor underneath the coiled fireman's hose and checked one last time that there had been no calls.

Then she drove the hammer down once. Twice. Three times.

That was all it took to destroy the phone.

As she went back to the condo, she turned the loose pieces over in her hands, the two baggies keeping things together. Tomorrow morning, she would go online from a secured computer and cancel the service, her last tie, flimsy though it was, cut forever.

The idea that she would never know what happened to Assail was almost as bad as the reality that she would never see him again.

Letting herself in once more, she resolved to go to bed, but was drawn back to the view of the water and the moon.

She missed the man she shouldn't have ever had as if he were a piece of her soul, left behind.

But that was the way of it.

Destiny was such a thief.

TWO

oc Jane checked her watch and resumed her pacing. As she went back and forth in the concrete corridor outside her main exam room, she was very aware of her own heartbeat—which was a little odd considering she was, for all intents and purposes, not alive.

In the back of her head, she heard Bill Murray saying, *Have you or your family ever seen a spook, specter, or ghost?*

Pretty much every time she looked in the mirror, Dr. Venkman. Thanks.

On that note, she headed down a couple of doors and stopped. Staring ahead without seeing anything, she found that she couldn't breathe right and decided that, of all the parts of her job as a trauma surgeon, what was about to happen next was something that she had never gotten good at. No matter how much training, experience, or continuing education she had, proficiency in this most vital part of her calling had not come.

And she hoped it never did.

Assail, I have failed you, she thought. *I am so sorry. I did everything I could.*

A clanking sound brought her head around. Down at the far end of the training center's long, main corridor, past all kinds of class-, break-, and interrogation rooms, the reinforced-steel vault panel that separated the subterranean facility from its multi-level parking area opened wide. Rhage, one of the Brotherhood's newest fathers, came in and stood off to the side.

The two dark-haired males who entered after him were, from what she understood, an anomaly in the vampire species. Identical twins did not happen that often and few of them made it to adulthood. Ehric and Evale had proven to be the exception to a lot of rules, however.

For example, she wasn't sure they were any more living than she was. For all the emotion they had ever shown, they might as well have been cyborgs. Such dead eyes—they had stares with all the luminosity of matte paint. Then again, they had probably seen a lot. Done a lot. And that translated, from what she had learned about war, into people who dissociated from the world around them, trusting no one.

Not even themselves.

Rhage indicated the way toward her, even though her presence was a self-explanatory destination, and as the twins walked forward, John Matthew entered as well, adding a caboose to the train.

Where was Vishous, she wondered. He and Rhage were supposed to be on transport with them?

Taking out her phone, she did a quick check. No texts or calls from her mate, and for a moment, she considered reaching out to him.

Shaking her head, she put the cell away and refocused on her job. She had to get through this conversation first, before she did anything personal.

As the twins approached, proximity didn't increase the warm and fuzzies of those males in the slightest. The closer they got, the bigger they became, until they were stopping in front of her and reminding her that immortality was so not a bad thing. They were killers, these two, and though they had extended a professional courtesy exemption to the Brotherhood's household by virtue of shared interest, she was glad she was a ghost.

Especially given what she had to tell them.

"Thank you for coming," she said.

The one on the left—the one that . . . yup, there was that mole behind the ear, so he had to be Ehric, not Evale—nodded once. And that was it from the both of them. No greeting. No nervousness. No anger. No sadness, even though they knew exactly why she'd asked them here. In all their robotic stoicism, with their black hair, and their platinum eyes, and their powerful builds, the cold-as-ices were like a matched set of Glocks, deadly and emotionless.

She had no idea how this was going to go.

"Will you excuse us?" she said to Rhage and John Matthew.

The Brother shook his head. "We're not leaving you."

"I appreciate your concern, Rhage, but patient confidentiality is an issue here. If you don't mind, maybe you could wait down by the office?" She pointed over there even though they knew perfectly well where it was. "This really needs to be a private conversation."

She knew better than to order any of the Brotherhood or the fighters off the kind of duty Rhage and John Matthew felt they were doing here. To them, she was Vishous's *shellan,* and as such, her advanced degrees and recent karate training didn't mean diddly: Even though the twins and their kin had proven loyal to the King and they had never shown any untoward behavior around her, they were still unattached males near a bonded Brother's female.

So she was going to be guarded like she was in a wet T-shirt and a pair of stripper heels.

It was ridiculous, but going Gloria Steinem on the situation was just going to delay things. Putting the very real privacy concern on the table, however, was going to get the job done. And it did.

"We'll just be right there," Rhage muttered. "Right over there. Like, no distance at all."

"Thank you."

When they were out of earshot, she said to the twins, "Would you like to talk in my—"

"Here is good," Ehric said in his thick, Old Country accent. "How is he?"

"Not very well, and I don't think we're gaining any traction with Assail's recovery." She crossed her arms over her chest and then dropped them because she didn't want to come across as hiding anything or being defensive. "His neurological functions are compromised and they are not improving. I've spoken with Havers and shared with him all of the scans as well as video of the behaviors and affects, including the change that happened about a week ago. With the onset of the catatonic state, he is less of a danger to himself and others, but that is a far distance from responsive—"

"Is it time to put him down."

Doc Jane blinked. When she'd made the transition from human surgeon to vampire healer, there had been all kinds of things to get used to. There was new anatomy to learn, new drug reactions and side effects to be aware of, a completely different circulatory system, as well as hormonal and pregnancy issues she had never seen before.

She'd also had to adjust to the race's end-of-life decisions. In the human world, sustaining life was the imperative, even when there was no quality to it. Assisted suicide remained an ethical decision to be debated, with only seven states allowing it within prescribed parameters. With vampires? It was a matter of course.

When a loved one was suffering, and there was no chance of that improving, terminal aid was rendered. Still, they were not talking about a cherished pet that had come to the end of its life cycle here.

She chose her words with care, wanting to be honest without advocating for any specific outcome. "Based on everything I have seen and all the tests we have run, I do not believe there is going to be a resumption of normalcy. We have done everything we can to support his systems in his cocaine withdrawal, but after the psychosis hit, we just . . . we've lost him and we can't seem to get him back."

In every way that counted, she was uncomfortable leaving this decision in the hands of Assail's cousins. It would be easier to trust whatever choice was made if they were upset. Troubled by conscience. Worried over whether they were doing the right thing.

With their dispositions? She had a concern that they would throw out her patient like a broken toaster. And yet, according to the vampire standard of care, she was duty bound to offer them, as next of kin, the option to terminate Assail's life now that the course of his care had reached this point of no return.

Havers, the race's healer, had been the one to bring the issue up to her, and her instinct had been to fight it—but that was a holdover from her human days. She did, however, continue to find it a potential contradiction to the spiritual lexicon of the species. In the vampire version of the afterlife, there was a belief that you couldn't enter the Fade, or what they considered Heaven, if you committed suicide. That being said, if you were lingering, and especially if you were incapable of deciding for yourself, your closest family could ease your suffering in a way that apparently got you around that provision, a loved-one loophole, as it were.

The reconciliation was evidently in the free will. If you pulled the trigger, that was suicide. If someone you loved said enough's enough? That was destiny.

Yet it was a slippery slope, especially if your next of kin was maybe angry about what you'd done to them over the holidays. Or pissed off that you'd borrowed money and hadn't paid back the loan. Or morally deficient—which was what she worried about here.

Still, Ehric and Evale had seemed to stick by their cousin, coming to see Assail regularly, receiving her updates, calling her back immediately. That had to mean something. Right?

Besides, in her heart, she knew that Assail had suffered enough. He had walked in here to detox from his drug addiction, and months later, after a roller coaster of self-harm, hallucinations, screaming paranoia, and violent outbursts, he had been reduced to nothing more than a pulse and some respiration.

"I'm very sorry." She looked back and forth between the mirror images of face and body. "I wish I had better news."

"I want to see him," Ehric said.

"Of course."

She reached for the door and hesitated. "He's still restrained. And I had to—well, you remember that we needed to shave his head. It was for his own well-being."

As she opened things wide for them, she searched their expressions, praying she saw something that eased her own conscience, that assured her this very serious decision was in the right hands . . . that their hearts were somehow involved.

The twins stared straight ahead, only their eyes moving around, their heads staying static. They did not blink. Twitch. Breathe.

Doc Jane glanced at her patient and felt a crushing sorrow. Even though her mind told her she had done everything she could, her heart regarded this outcome as a failure she was responsible for. "I am so very sorry."

After a long moment, Ehric said in a flat tone, "We will do what is necessary."

THREE

From behind the wheel of the rental car, Vitoria Benloise was impatient. So long, all this travel. So long to come to this northern state in America. Such an inefficiency to transfer her physicality from where she had been to where she needed to be.

At least the transition was over.

Up ahead, her destination appeared as an island rising up from the vast midst of the sea, the great house sitting upon its rise, a showy declaration of wealth that due to its age was "venerable" as opposed to "ostentatious."

Her brother Ricardo would have had his manse no other way. Having come from little, he had sought validation through a persistent illusion of false aristocracy and old money. No new house for him. No flashy cars. No Eurotrash ostentation.

Which she believed was what the Americans called it.

Even in his legitimate business, the one that had been but a shell for his true revenue streams, he'd had to have an art gallery. Not a construction business, no, no. Not garbage removal or cement mixing. It had to be the art.

Contemporary sculpture and painting, from what she understood, and she could guess why the exception to his preference for the aged. It was so much easier to launder money with the sale of modern offerings, as their value was more subjective than that of Old Masters and Impressionists, which had more provable prices.

The drive into Ricardo's property was a left-hand turn off this road by the big river, and she traveled up the gradual, plowed lane, taking note of the snow-covered lawn, the short stone wall holding back the tree line, the looming grand house. The mansion was larger than it appeared from down below, and as she closed in and parked by its front entry's walkway, she felt the modernist sculptures around the manse sit in judgment and disapproval of her.

It was her brother in her head. Her family, in her conscience. Her traditions, in her soul.

This was quite unseemly of her, after all. This whole thing. An unmarried woman out in the world, seeking vengeance.

Yes, it was true, the Benloise family had never been well off. Not until Ricardo had come along, at any rate. But that did not mean that there were not rules. Standards. Expectations. All of which were for the women, of course. The men were allowed to be who they were, do what they wished, carry on as they would.

Not so for a sister, a daughter.

But at least their parents were dead, and she did not care what anyone else in her family thought. More to the point, this was her chance.

She had waited all of her life for this. Thirty-five miserable years of fighting for her right to get an education, to not take a husband, to be what she wanted to be, not what others decreed for her.

She turned off the engine and got out. Cold, so very cold. She was going to hate being here, the loss of her native Colombia's warmth and humidity a thing to mourn.

Looking around, she noted that the snow had been shoveled up to the grand and glossy door, and also around to the back, all the way to the detached garage-like structure. One might be tempted to see such as a sign her brother remained alive, but she knew better.

She had not heard from him in nearly a year—and clearly, this property was held in a trust whereby its upkeep was managed as if its owner were still alive.

Money, however, was running short, and that was why she had come. For the first few months after Ricardo and Eduardo had not been in touch, she had wondered, worried, gotten concerned about her brothers. But as more and more time passed, and disgruntled suppliers had come to her with their inquiries about the business, she started to develop a plan.

If Ricardo could run a drug trade back and forth across the ocean, why could not she? And then the reality of expenses had come home to roost. Her brother had expected her to look after his various real estate holdings in South America, given that she had failed at her true calling of becoming a wife and a mother—and all that upkeep was costly. The accounts were dwindling.

No, both of her brothers were dead, and she had to do what was necessary to survive—no matter the risks.

Taking a key out of her Chanel bag, she approached the ornate, old door and slid the slender, notched length into its home. A turn, a tumble, and she was . . .

An alarm began to sound the moment the seal was breached, and she left the portal wide as she followed the noise through rooms that were dark and stuffy, navigating by virtue of the exterior lights. She found the security panel in the professional-grade kitchen, by a hardy door that she guessed opened to the outside.

The code she entered was going to work.

And it did.

Their mother's birth date, month, day, and year. Eight numbers, unknown to anybody but the three siblings. That strict, hard-driving, fervently Catholic woman had had no patience for sentiment, but Ricardo had brought her a flower on the same day each year, and uncharacteristically, she had never thrown it out.

That this was the code to his mansion was a clear tie to his hardscrabble youth. A measure of how far he had come. A defiance against the disapproval they had all grown up under.

Childhood had been a struggle, a test of endurance, for the three siblings. Then again, their mother had had to raise them all on her own, without the benefit of a husband, a steady job, a roof over their heads. Not a lot of room for extravagances or indulgence in that reality—and then there had been all the rosaries, Hail Mary's, and confessions.

But that was over now.

With the alarm silent, Vitoria's return to the front entrance was more leisurely, and she took time to measure and add up the value of the antique chairs and Persian rugs, the ornate tables and the paintings of the ancestors of others. It was impossible not to draw comparisons with how Ricardo had always seen her. As with this art and these antiques, her role in his life had been to stick where she was put, without question or objection. Her virtue was part of his illusion, a saintly sister to add another layer of curtain to hide the truth of his origin.

Her footfalls slowed and she stopped before a bronze statue that had to be a Degas. There was only one artist who could have composed and completed such a winsome, light-though-it-was-heavy object of beauty.

Perhaps Ricardo had thought of it as the daughter he had never had, Vitoria mused. Certainly a far better bet than a living breathing off-spring.

Onward, onward, to the open front door.

For a moment, she just stood there—and it was then that she realized she was waiting for a butler to appear and take her bags from the boot of the rental.

As much as she derided Ricardo for his airs, she, too, had succumbed to the habits of luxury. It was, indeed, far better to be of means than not.

She was going to need people. She could not do this alone.

Fortunately, money talked, did it not.

Planting her hands on her hips, she regarded the undisturbed snow cover of the vast, descending lawn. It was as if Ricardo had permanently disallowed all manner of deer and rodent from marring the pristine winter landscape. She would not have put it past him. Image had been so important.

With a lift of her chin, she regarded the sky, measuring the bright, full moon.

"I will avenge you, brothers," she said to the heavens. "I will find out who killed you and take care of things as you would have wished."

Her smile was slow and did not last.

In fact, Ricardo would not have wished this at all. He would have hated this whole thing. But that was his problem, not hers—and given that he was dead, he had no more problems, did he.

Yes, she would find out exactly what had happened to her siblings, and when she was done addressing the wrongs, she was going to step into Ricardo's handmade shoes.

Her future was bright as the moonlight. She was finally free.

FOUR

As Vishous took form on the terrace of his penthouse, the cold wind howling at the high altitude was to his back, pushing him, pushing him toward the glass doors. And yet he hesitated, his purpose for coming one that made him feel as though his marrow had turned toxic and was melting through his bones and flesh.

Liar.

Like the hateful secret he was embarking on, the interior of his sex den was dark. Like the haunting of his conscience, his moonlit reflection was a ghost of himself in all that glass: leather on his legs, leather on his shoulders, dark hair and a goatee, gloved right hand.

Cheat.

The last thing he wanted to do was look at himself, so he willed the black candles inside to light up, not one by one, but all at once. The insta-llumination was soft; what was revealed was not. His rough-honed sex rack, the one he had used for years, was a stained and studded piece of hardware sitting smack-center in the open living area, supplanting all manner of table and chair arrangements that would have been far more appropriate, far more vanilla. On the black walls, there was not art, but straps and chains. On the section of shelving, there were instruments. On the black floors, there was nothing on the bare wood.

Cleanup. You know.

Whore.

This was not a home. This was a factory for sexual satisfaction and expression. He'd even gotten rid of the bed he'd had for a while.

The place was also a relic. He had not visited it for how long now? Back when he and Jane had first gotten together they had sometimes come here for a little play, but compared to what he had been like before her, that had been lightweight stuff.

Turned out when he cared about the person, he wanted different things from them.

They hadn't been back for . . . Jesus, a while. Then again, they hadn't been together, sexually or otherwise, in . . . Jesus, a while.

As he went to the closest sliding door, his head hurt, but not from the concussion he'd gotten during the great warehouse battle. No, that brain damage had cleared itself up nicely, along with the bruising and other minor injuries he'd sustained as the Brotherhood and the Band of Bastards had fought the Lessening Society side by side.

Turned out those fuckers with the harelipped leader were handy.

They were also now roommates at the BDB mansion—

Am I really going to do this?

Pressing his thumbprint onto his new, discreetly mounted reader, he heard the metallic shift of the lock turning free and then he willed the door to slide open. Stepping inside, he left things wide, the winter gust barging in and ruffling the flames on all those wicks. No longer at peace, now the illumination trembled, sure as if his anxiety and unhappiness had become manifest and taken on properties outside of his heart and soul.

The walls crawled now. The shadows thrown by his table spasmed. There were things moving across the floor.

Shit, maybe that was just his conscience talking. But he had a remedy for that.

The kitchen was a stretch of never-used and never-gonna-be, nothing in the sink, the drawers, the cupboards. Which was not to say he wasn't prepared to be a good host. Four Grey Goose bottles were lined up on the counter, each of them facing label-out like bills put to right in a wallet.

They were not for his guest to drink. They were for him so he could get through this.

As he regarded these labels, he focused on the flying birds, soaring high above their little snowy, two-dimensional mountain scenes.

For a male who spoke as many languages as he did, and knew more obscure facts about the world than a *Jeopardy!* champion, you'd figure he would be less surprised by this turn of events. Then again, he hadn't expected to ever be mated. So how could he have foreseen this . . . resumption of his old life, his old ways . . . his former coping mechanism . . . rearing up to address an itch he could no longer stand and couldn't seem to scratch any other way.

Liar. Cheat. Whore.

From out of nowhere, he saw himself up in the Sanctuary, walking through his *mahmen*'s private quarters, proceeding out to the resting place of the Chosen who had had the Arrest and passed unto the Fade. He recalled reading the Scribe Virgin's departing missive, the symbols in the Old Language floating in the air as if they were mounted on an invisible flag, disappearing as soon as he had read them.

He had hated that sacred female for so long that it had become a habit, and now that she was gone, there was the strangest void in him. He couldn't say he mourned her, however—really, the only time they had gotten along had been right after she had turned Jane into an immortal. And even after that gift, their relationship hadn't stayed improved.

There was something missing from his life, nonetheless.

Two somethings missing, actually. Jane was also gone, and not just when she chose to be in ghost form, as opposed to corporeal.

It was hard to recall the last time he had felt truly connected to his *shellan.* When they had spent a day sleeping together, for example, or had truly talked, or had—

The image of the stone corridor of the Black Dagger Brotherhood's Tomb came to his mind, and he remembered Jane coming to check Xcor's vitals when the Bastard had been in their custody. Yes . . . it was then, when the pair of them had spoken about how neither of them wanted young. He'd felt such relief that they were both on the same page, that there was going to be no conflict on that subject. Now, it seemed ironic that they had bonded over a shared decision not to do what so many mated pairs built their entire lives around.

Young required a shared, common commitment, a joint connection, a partnership.

Yet he and Jane had dropped the prospect of all that entanglement like a hot potato and promptly resumed their separate, parallel, no-overlap existences: He was out in the field, fighting the war and engaging in the King's business. While she treated a boatload of patients with astonishing competence and compassion.

And never the twain shall meet.

Freedom and autonomy were something he had valued in his mating and his mate—to the point where he had assumed those inter-related aspects were mission critical for him to find any future with any one person. But all of that non-constraint, which had seemed so important, had proven to be a double-edged sword.

The flip side of the independence coin was neglect, distance . . . disintegration.

No young to worry about, yay! had turned into *Where are you? Where are we?*

At least in his mind.

Somehow, with his *mahmen* "dying," and the great massacre at that warehouse, and the addition of the Band of Bastards into the household . . . and almost every single brother he had suddenly having young . . . in the midst of that thick swill of change and confusion, he had lost the thread that had tied him to Jane, and on her side, she was too busy to notice.

Neither of them was bad or wrong.

Well, at least not until tonight. At least not until right now.

He had agonized about whether or not to check his old email account, to sift through what had turned out to be hundreds of missives and pleadings for his attention, to choose one and reach out.

And meet here.

This evening.

Liarcheatwhore.

The reality was, though, that his brain was clamoring under his skull, his demons were screaming at him, and there seemed like no end in sight to the torture. Fuck, if he didn't purge the chaos, he was going to end up in Assail's lunatic shoes.

Psychosis was an old friend, after all.

In fact, for him, madness was like a next-door neighbor who disregarded property lines now and again, not just trespassing on the land, but moving into the house.

And wrecking the place.

He had to do something or the pressure inside was going to consume him—and the fact that he didn't even think to talk to Jane about what was going on with him? It was hard to know if that was a symptom or the disease itself. Hell, maybe it was more practical than that. Her priorities were many, her time was few, and in the grand scheme of things, as this hateful war ground to its bloody conclusion, whatever that looked like, everyone was better off with her treating her patients rather than trying to save him from himself.

Division of labor and all that shit.

So yes, he would do what he knew he could to bring himself back to earth. And then when his feet were not just touching the ground, but firmly on it, he could resume life next to her.

What was his other option?

As he waited for the hundredth time for a different course of action to come to him, he was dimly aware that he was seeking an answer out of the very thing that was broken: He was looking for his fucked-up brain to provide a path out of this infidelity, even though his mind was the very thing that was unreliable.

Nothing like trying to survey a landscape with a broken compass, a flashlight with no batteries in it, and night goggles with busted lenses—

The scent of a sexually aroused female bloomed in the penthouse and he did not turn around. He knew who had arrived and was standing in that doorway that he had left open. Knew precisely what she was wearing because he had informed her what he was going to see on her body. Knew that she would be, at this very moment, getting onto her hands and knees and entering on all fours.

Knew she would wait until he gave her an order.

Vishous reached out and took the first of the vodka bottles. He opened it like a pro, but then he had had plenty of experience.

LIARCHEATWHORELIARCHEATWHORELIARCHEATWHORE—

He drank from the neck until his stomach burned as much as the center of his chest did. And then he turned around.

FIVE

ait, what are we doing here? Doc Jane thought as Assail's cousins turned away from her and walked off down the training center's corridor. What was the decision?

John Matthew and Rhage were right on the pair's exit, decamping from their leans by the office's glass door and falling into a long stride that brought them past her.

Rhage paused as the other fighter continued on. "What did they say?"

Before she could weigh the privacy issues, she replied, "That they were going to do what was necessary."

"So they're . . . ending things?"

"They were really not clear." She put a hand through her short blond hair. "I'll follow up with them later."

It hadn't felt right to press them, and besides, she was uneasy with this whole thing anyway. Tomorrow at nightfall, she'd call them and see if she could get some clarity. It wasn't like they had access to Assail without her—so she didn't need to worry about them going home-grown with a lights-out solution.

Rhage frowned and put his hands on his black-leather-clad hips. "Well, if you need them escorted in here again, just let us know."

"I will, and thanks." As the Brother went to stride off, she caught his arm. "Hey, Rhage? Wasn't Vishous supposed to be with you?"

"Yeah, he was. But he called in and John Matthew took his shift."

"Is he—well, that's fine. He's probably at the Pit."

"You know, you guys should take some time off." Hollywood smiled, his Bahama blue eyes glowing. "All you do is work. Both of you."

"That's not true—"

"I can't remember the last meal I saw you guys at." He shrugged and took out a Tootsie Pop. When he looked at it, he cursed. "Orange. I don't like orange. Then again, I got it out in the dark. Thatswhathesaid."

Doc Jane laughed. "Really."

"Michael Scott is my hero, what can I say."

Rhage gave her shoulder a reassuring squeeze and then he caught up quick to the twins and John Matthew.

Doc Jane checked her phone again, and when she saw that there was still just a lot of nothing on the screen, she mentally ran through her patient-status list. Assail was . . . exactly where he had been. Luchas was in the pool doing PT with Ehlena. No other beds were in use and she wasn't due for Rhamp and Lyric's regular checkup for another two hours.

She thought about texting Vishous and asking where he was, but an awkward, unpleasant sensation stopped her—and it took her a minute to figure out what it was.

Intrusion.

She felt as though it would be an intrusion to reach out to him, and the more she considered the tightness in her chest, the clearer things became. When had this started, she wondered. When had she begun to believe she was bothering her mate if she shot him a text?

That was wrong, she thought. All wrong.

Turning around, she headed for the office, opening the way in and going past the desk and the filing cabinets. The supply closet was off to the side, and she entered the shallow space, shuffling by all the stacks of legal pads, the boxes of pens, and the reams of printer paper. At the hidden access door in the back, she entered a code, stepped through into the tunnel—

And immediately chided herself for a lack of efficiency. Letting herself fade to ghost would have obviated all the opening and closing, but the longer she got used to being in her skin, so to speak, the more she fell into the habits and necessaries of regular mortals.

Even though they no longer applied.

Also . . . she kind of wanted to walk to clear her head.

The subterranean tunnel that linked the training center to the mansion, where the Brotherhood household stayed, and the Pit, which was Vishous and Butch's crash pad, was a straight shot of underground, the fluorescent lights on the ceiling like a landing strip that had gotten confused about gravity. As she walked along, she took her stethoscope from around her neck and put it into one of the square pockets of her white coat. Her scrubs were clean and blue, her Crocs red, her socks thick and from L.L. Bean.

What season was it, she wondered. Winter, now. It was . . . yes, January.

When was the last time she had gone outside?

Okay, that was not that long ago. In the last couple of weeks, she and Manny, her medical partner in all things whether it was surgery, general medicine, or administration, had responded to a number of emergencies out in the field downtown. But in situations like that you couldn't really enjoy the season—or even note whether it was hot or cold. Those trips were the same as going out of town for business: You might have been in New York City, but it wasn't to see a show or visit a museum or grab a gourmet meal.

No, during those times, she had been desperately trying to save someone's life: Peyton's, Rhage's . . . so many others. The wounds that the Brothers, the fighters, and the trainees got while engaging with the

Lessening Society could easily be life-threatening, and these vampires were not arm's-length patients to her. They were her family.

If she failed any one of them, she would never forgive herself.

The tunnel's exit up to the mansion was marked by a short set of steps, and she kept going, passing them by.

God, the farther she went, the more a curdling sense of dread took root in her stomach—although that didn't make any sense.

She was going home. To see the male she loved.

Why would that bother her?

Maybe it was the Assail situation. Maybe the ringing warning at the base of her neck was just generalized anxiety squirting out during a moment alone, an emotion coloring outside of the line. Yes, that had to be it. Her Hippocratic oath was running up against euthanasia and she couldn't reconcile the two.

A good hundred, hundred and fifty yards later, she came up to the reinforced door to the Pit. Punching in the code, she went up the shallow half-flight of stairs and then through a second entry—

The sound of a vacuum cleaner had her leaning around the door. Fritz, butler extraordinaire, was working a Dyson back and forth on the runner in the short hall. In his black-and-white uniform, he looked like something out of an ad for a housekeeping service that employed only English dukes.

"Mistress!" As he extinguished the *whrrrrring* noise, his old, wrinkled face smiled, reminding her of drapes pulled back to let in sunlight. "You have come back to change then! I thought you had already vacated the premises or I would not have begun thus, forgive me."

She smiled back at him so he wouldn't worry he'd done a badness.

But she was totally confused here. "I'm sorry, what?"

"Your interlude downtown with the sire." Fritz glowed like a heart-shaped nightlight. "He asked me to get him candles and libations for the two of you."

A sensation of numbing cold hit the top of her head and ran down her like water until she felt it fill her legs up as if they were boots.

"Mistress?"

"Yes, of course. I—ah, right. Of course." What was he asking? "But I'm just going to go as is."

"It will not matter to him. He will simply be glad to see you."

Jane said some more things. She didn't know what they were. And then she walked out to the front room. The black leather sofa, the foosball table, and the gym bags were exactly what she had seen in here for the last however many nights, weeks, months, years.

Vishous's bank of computers was likewise—except now, as she stared at the monitors, towers, and keyboards, she noted that everything was screen locked and she didn't have any of the passwords. Then again it never would have occurred to ask for them—or wonder what he was doing when he was sitting in his chair, brows tight, those tattoos on the side of his face pulled ever so slightly out of place.

She had always assumed he was working on his security systems, his programming, his LearnedLeague stuff.

What else had he been doing?

Or . . . who else—

Okay, Glenn Close, she thought. *Why don't you back away from the pot and the bunny until you actually know what's going on here.*

Maybe there was a perfectly reasonable explanation for what Fritz seemed to suggest was going on. Maybe Vishous was planning something for them as a mated couple and he just hadn't asked her yet.

She checked her phone. Looked around. Heard the vacuum turn back on.

Part of her didn't want to go to the Commodore because it seemed like spying. Like something a girl, not a woman, would do. It also felt . . . too real. As if her mate actually had lied by omission and was in fact meeting someone else—

Screw it, she thought. Waiting around for him to come home was just too passive.

Besides, it was, literally, the work of a moment for her to get downtown: One of the advantages to being nonexistent at will was that travel was more than a binary choice. Courtesy of V's mother, the Scribe Virgin, Jane now had ambulation, motorization, and mentalization to pick from, with the latter being similar to vampires' dematerializing: Her process of disappearing and reappearing required the same sort of concentration and will, and she could do it anywhere, anytime, with no apparent limit to the distance.

Closing her eyes, she imagined herself as a breeze, a disturbance of air molecules, a draft. Nothingness. Lightness. A pane of glass.

It had always worked in the past.

Yup. Really. It . . . had.

Yeah, well, not tonight, she thought as she lifted her lids.

Rubbing the center of her chest, she went to the Pit's door and let herself out in the event that Fritz finished with his Dyson and caught her standing there like an idiot. As she emerged into the night, the cold *woof!* of January's frigid breath made her gasp and have to collect herself.

The cottage she thought of as her home was the carriage house of the main mansion, located across the courtyard from the dour, stone mountain-on-top-of-a-mountain where the Brotherhood, the fighters, and their mates lived. She, V, Butch, and Marissa had been staying in the two-bedroom, two-bath setup since their relationships had taken root, and she had come to think of the four of them as a little family unit.

Tilting her head, she stared up at the great gray vertical expanse of the mansion. There were gargoyles along the roofline, and three or four levels of diamond-pane windows, and shadows everywhere because of the various wings, levels, and dormers.

Where else would vampires live?

Shutting her lids again, she told herself she needed to get a grip—and her self-discipline came to the rescue. Becoming one with the air, she moved through the darkness in a swirl that, when she had first started doing this, had made her stomach queasy, but now was just the same as riding in a car.

Traveling through the night toward downtown, she was no substance, all existence, her thoughts and feelings, her soul, remaining intact even as her body was ether—which meant her pain and uncertainty, her anxiety, her stress, came with her.

Off the mountain, into the hills. Through the farm country. Over the suburbs. Past the old-fashioned apartment buildings, entering the urban core of skyscrapers, parking garages, and one-way streets.

The Commodore was a high-rise right on the Hudson River, a Nakatomi Plaza–worthy show of twenty or thirty floors of steel and glass— and she landed, like a superhero, on a terrace right at its top.

"Oh, thank God," she muttered as she saw the darkened windows of the penthouse.

Vishous was *not* here with someone else. He hadn't made a decision she was going to have to do something about. There was, as it turned out, no deception, just a misunderstanding on the part of the butler and a paranoia on her side that, if she were smart and wanted to keep her mating strong, she'd use as a warning shot across her bow. She probably had been too wrapped up in her work lately—which wouldn't have been any kind of excuse for infidelity on V's part, but certainly would explain this distance she now was recognizing between them.

And if she had been feeling connected to him, she wouldn't have been so scared about all this.

Taking out her phone, she got over herself and shot Vishous a text: *Hey, off work for two hours. Let's hang!*

Cheerful. Upbeat. Positive. Not hinting that she'd lost her damn mind for an instant and devolved into insecurity. Now, she just had to wait to see what he responded.

As time passed, and she got nothing back, her heart began to beat hard again—and she thought, holy crap, it was like she was sixteen and trying to get a boy in her algebra class to ask her out.

Cupping the phone in her palms, she kept waiting, not feeling the gusts of wind or the cold, not noticing the height that made the Hudson River seem like a stream, not dwelling on the near-miss.

Okay, fine, she was dwelling on that.

But hey, this was an opportunity for them. They needed to get away and be together. Maybe they could head up to Rehv's Great Camp? She didn't think of herself as a romantic person, but that old cedar-shingled Victorian with its stone hearths and view of the lake could be just the ticket. Snow everywhere, only the evergreens offering color. No pressures or responsibilities. They could cook their meals together and sleep side by side and re-forge that which had gotten eclipsed by nightly life.

Taking a deep breath, she felt a surge of . . . optimism? Happiness? She hadn't had whatever it was in so long that she didn't know how to readily define the warm buoyancy.

And yeah, that was probably another sign she needed to rebalance things.

When a response still didn't come, she turned to face the river. The other side of Caldwell was a much quieter landscape, with low buildings that glowed instead of skyscrapers that twinkled.

Assail lived down the Hudson a little ways. On a peninsula in a glass house.

Or at least *had* lived there.

What was she going to do about him . . .

Light bloomed from behind her, and she wheeled around, putting a smile on her face. V was here and this was an opportunity—

She frowned. Behind the glass doors, the interior of the penthouse was all wrong. Instead of black floors and all kinds of her mate's kinky stuff, there was a calming interior of grays, the furniture modern and thoughtfully scaled and placed.

Ruhn, Saxton's mate, walked in from a hallway, proceeding to a kitchen that was all black granite and brushed-steel appliances.

In her upset and distraction, she had gone to the opposite side of the building.

Before Ruhn saw her and she had to explain what the hell she was doing on his terrace, she disappeared.

This time, she knew immediately she was in the right place. Too bad it was clear she'd wrong-timed it.

One of the sliding glass doors to V's penthouse was wide open in spite of the cold, and black candles flickered all around the bald space's interior, illuminating not only his sexual equipment, but the male himself: Vishous was sitting on his sex rack, his lower legs hanging free, his head down as he stared at his phone. He was in his leathers, which was a stupid relief, but his powerful upper torso was bare and she wondered who had taken his customary muscle shirt off.

So he'd gotten her text.

Or another from someone he was more interested in hearing from.

Abruptly, Jane was aware of her palms becoming sweaty and her heart pounding and her stomach churning.

This is not us, she thought. *We don't do things like this to each other.*

V's head lifted and turned toward her, his brows frowning.

For an instant, all she could do was absorb the sight of him. He was not one to ever be defeated. Between his intelligence, his physical brawn, and his incredible reflexes, he was an attacker, an aggressor, a beat-the-system, win-the-game, vanquish-the-foes source of superiority in the world. Not tonight. His broad shoulders were tilted into his chest, and exhaustion was like a stain in the air around him.

His diamond eyes were dull with guilt as they focused on her.

Jane started backing up even before he shifted off the rack and came forward.

"No," she said into the wind. "No . . ."

SIX

The knock on Sola's bedroom door was soft, but she came awake like a heavy fist was trying to splinter the thin wood. "*Vovó!*"

A shaft of illumination pierced the darkness, making her think of a lightsaber. "There is people here, Sola. Come, get up and get dressed."

Sola reached for the gun on her bedside table as she looked at the digital clock. Three a.m.? "Where? Who—do not open—"

"I am cooking now. Come."

Cooking? "*Vovó,* who is—"

The door closed firmly, and Sola was up-and-out less than a second later, the fact that she had finally crashed fully dressed a stroke of luck. Out in the cramped hall, she flipped the safety off of her nine and kept the weapon behind her back as she padded down the cheap carpeting.

The smell of sautéing onions was so out of context that she decided this was a dream. Yup, she was going to round this corner here and walk into her grandmother's kitchen and see a non sequitur at their table for two. Lady Gaga or Leonardo DiCaprio or, hell, Leonardo da Vinci—

Sola stopped dead. Across the linoleum, sitting on the pair of cane chairs, were two men she'd been convinced she would never see again.

Her first thought, as identical sets of eyes swung in her direction, was that the chairs were not going to hold all that weight for long—but Assail's cousins solved that problem by rising to their feet. As they bowed low in her direction, it was bizarre—but also what she was used to them doing whenever she walked into a room.

Dream, she told herself. This was a figment of her imagination.

"You," her grandmother ordered to the one on the right. "You go and get chair for my Sola. Go."

The six-five stretch of muscle and banked aggression trotted off into the living room like a retriever sent for a tennis ball, returning with an armchair instead of something lighter. Then again, if you'd asked him to pick up a quart of milk, he'd probably bring the whole Publix back to you.

"'Scuse me," he said as he came up behind her.

As Sola moved out of his way, she wondered how her grandmother could so calmly be dicing red and yellow peppers.

"I need to wake up," Sola muttered. "Right now."

"Sola, the coffee." Her grandmother nodded to the machine. "You start."

She gave things a minute to wakey-wakey, and when the scene wasn't replaced by her rolling over and cracking an eyelid, she decided she had to go with it for the time being.

"What are you doing here?" she asked the twins as they resettled in those structurally unreliable chairs.

It was nearly impossible to tell them apart, but the distinction was made as the one on the left spoke up.

"We have come for you."

That would be Ehric. Evale, the armchair-retriever, would never have volunteered to speak. He was as frugal as Scrooge with his words.

"Assail," she whispered.

"Coffee," her grandmother demanded.

She fell in line with the order, Sola's hands shook as she reengaged her gun's safety, tucked it away at the small of her back, and went to get the Maxwell House. After she had made quick work with the Krups, she took a seat on the armchair.

"Tell me," she said. "Where is he."

Ehric was a male first and foremost. So as the human woman sat down on the chair his brother had provided unto her, he could not help but catalog her beauty. She was not frilly nor silly. No, no, his cousin, Assail, would not have picked one of those. Sola's eyes were direct upon his own, her body tense as if she were ready to spring—not away from conflict, but toward it.

And there was a gun holstered at her waistband.

Ehric smiled a little, but that didn't last. It never did with him.

She was blond now, and he resolved that his cousin would not approve of the change. It was not an unpleasing shade, not brassy or frizzed, but it did not suit her dark eyes or the memories of her natural brown. The hair was shorter now, too, cut around her ears and shorn up close to her neck.

It was a wise choice if she were looking to disguise herself.

But no, Assail would prefer her as she had been a year ago, and at least her face was, as always, strong-featured yet smooth of skin and sensual of lip. And her simple clothes were the same, too, the leggings black and the hooded sweatshirt navy blue with no logo or image upon it.

Her lithe, long body beneath the soft folds was something he refused to let himself assess, out of respect not just for his cousin, but for her. Ehric liked her. He always had.

"Well?" she demanded roughly.

When he and his brother had materialized below her lodgings, he'd wondered the best course of their approach—and wished they could make a proper announcement of their presence during the daytime with a rap on the door and human-like greeting at a human-like hour for visitation. At this point, however, he was already counting down how much time there was until dawn's early light threatened their lives with the sun.

In the end, he had resolved unto a mental intrusion, one for which he felt guilt, but nevertheless had proceeded with. He had not engaged with Marisol. No, he was unsure of their reception with her, and her participation was vital. Her grandmother, Mrs. Carvalho, had been the better choice. With suitable concentration, and inner apology, he had connected with the elder woman's mind and roused her from her sleep, summoning her unto the terrace so that she would allow them entrance not just into the building, but the home she shared with Marisol.

Indeed, Assail's female might well have denied them, but never the matriarch. She had a soft spot for them.

"Forgive us for intruding," Ehric began, "but we are in need of aid."

Marisol's voice lowered as if she didn't want her grandmother to hear. "I am no longer in that line of work. And if your cousin wanted something, he should have called me and saved you the trip."

"He is not able to travel the now."

The woman frowned. "Why? Actually, never mind—just ask me what you need to so I can tell you no."

"We want you to come see Assail."

The woman looked back and forth between them. "I can't do that. I won't do that, I'm sorry. He knows why I had to go—you two know it, too."

Ehric glared at her, but kept his voice soft. "He was there for you. When you needed . . ." He glanced in her grandmother's direction and was reassured by the older woman's concentration on her foodstuff preparation. "When you required a . . . friend . . . Assail came unto you. He did right by you and you need to make good on that debt."

"I didn't ask him—" She, too, glanced at her grandmother. "He did what he did by choice. I never asked him to help me—"

"You would be dead now—"

"I saved myself!"

The grandmother shot a look over her shoulder, and that was enough to readjust the volume on their argument.

Ehric sat forward. "You owe him. And we need you to help him."

As he stared at her, the woman burst up and went to the coffee machine. As it had yet to finish its cycle, she stood before the unit, tapping her foot. When at last it was through, she took all due care with mugs and pouring.

"Do you guys still take it black?" she muttered.

"Yes, we do."

She brought them over the coffee and sat down once more. Clearing her throat, she said, "I'm really sorry, but I'm never going back to Caldwell." Now she stared at Mrs. Carvalho pointedly. "You understand. As much as I might be . . . grateful . . . to your cousin, I can't get involved with his business—"

"Why we have come unto you is personal." Ehric tested the coffee and found it more than acceptable. "He is not well. And it is our hope that you can provide him with—"

"If he's sick, he needs to go to a doctor—"

"—a reason to keep fighting."

Marisol stiffened. "Fighting? What are you talking about?"

Ehric had prepared for this inquiry. "Cancer. Assail has got the cancer."

The lie slid off his tongue as easily as the truth would have choked him. This human had no reason to know that she had been rescued and later bedded by a vampire. And if he told her that Assail was suffering from cocaine-withdrawal dementia, that was not just less likely to elicit sympathy, but he might well have to provide some manner of explanation as humans, evidently, did not respond to sobriety thus.

Cancer was a different story. No matter that vampires could not get the disease; it was a scourge to humans.

"Oh . . . God," Marisol whispered.

"He is too proud to ask you for aid, of course." Ehric had to look away. "But we are his blood. There is naught we will not do to secure what future he may have."

"I am not . . . I am not anything to him."

"In that," Evale spoke up, "you are misconstrided."

"Misconstrued," Ehric amended. "And that is why we are here. We want you to come to his bedside and . . . inspire him, in the way only you can."

When she opened her mouth as if to argue, he wearied of the protest and put his hand up. "Please. Do not waste our time or pretend ignorance when you know precisely why you, of all people, would matter to him."

Abruptly, the woman fell into a silence that seemed to compress her body, and he knew he had to give her space to feel most properly her emotions: Further commentary by anyone would just give her opportunities for defense. She, and she alone, was going to decide this course.

As the silence continued, Mrs. Carvalho placed plates before him and his brother, the food upon them so fragrant, he closed his eyes, lowered his chin, and breathed in the aroma.

"You have honored us, Mrs. Carvalho." He turned to the grandmother, who had gone back to her stove. "We do not deserve such a feast."

"Eat." A gnarled finger pointed to the table. "Too thin. You are too thin. I make you more."

Ah, her tone. Clipped, disapproving, accented with the unfamiliar. But her eyes were a-twinkled, and he knew that even as she kept a physical distance from them, she embraced them both with her food, welcoming them with a love that he had certainly never known.

Orphans, after all, were by definition unfamiliar with a *mahmen*'s heart and hand in their lives.

Putting his fork to its very best use, he found that the eggs were mixed with marvelous spices, and as he began to consume them, another tantalizing scent wafted up from the stove.

"What kind of cancer?" Marisol asked.

Ehric reached out to the center of the wee table and took a napkin from a holder. After wiping his mouth, he said, "It is of blood origin, and of recent and very virulent duration."

"Where is he being treated? St. Francis?"

"He has availed himself of private physicians." She would recognize Doc Jane and Manny, and he'd cross that bridge when they got to it. "The treatment he is receiving is top-notch. There is no better, I can assure you of that."

"How long . . ." She cleared her throat. "How long does he have?"

"It is hard to say. But he suffers. Greatly."

There was a long period of silence, punctuated only by their eating.

"He stopped calling me," Marisol blurted.

"He has been in touch, then?" Not a surprise. And then Ehric became concerned. "Did he tell you aught?"

"He didn't speak to me. He just hung up, but it was him, I know it was. And then the calls stopped."

"Yes."

More plates arrived, this time with something made from corn. And another thing of potato derivation that he recognized from that which Mrs. Carvalho had frozen for them before she left. The grandmother did not join them. She began to wash her dishes at the sink, and he knew better than to offer to help. Up in Caldwell, during their cohabitations, he and Evale had asked but once to be of any aid in her kitchen endeavors and she had been offended sure as if they had cursed before her.

It was not until he and his twin had finished their second and third servings that Marisol finally spoke.

"I'm really sorry," she said. "I can't go back there. You have to understand. Even for him, it's not safe for us up in Caldwell—"

Mrs. Carvalho interjected with sharp words in their native tongue, and the granddaughter bowed her head as if it would not do that she disrespect her elder with any disagreement. Still, Ehric knew by the line of the younger woman's chin that she would not relent.

"We can keep you safe," he offered. "Both of you. You have our word of honor that naught will befall either of you."

The grandmother spoke again, her hands on her hips, her wrinkled face drawn in disapproval.

Marisol got to her feet. "No. It is not safe. Maybe I can FaceTime with him, or something. Or talk to him on the phone. Or—"

As Ehric rose from his chair, Evale followed that lead. "I understand. Forgive us for bothering you."

"I wish I could help." Marisol crossed her arms over her chest. "Seriously, if the circumstances were different, I—"

"Madam," he said unto her grandmother. "You have paid us much grace and respect with this meal. We shall hold on to the strength it gives us and use that gift in your honor."

Evale murmured an affirmation as both of them bowed to her.

When he straightened, Mrs. Carvalho had her hands tucked up under her bosom. She appeared by turns delighted by the honor they paid her and frustrated by her kin.

Turning to Marisol, Ehric bowed to her as well. "We shall not tarry herein nor bother you again."

Marisol opened her mouth as if to speak, but he walked away, proceeding to the door. As he let himself out, he held the exit wide for his twin.

"Do not say it," he muttered as Evale paused in the doorway. "Stay silent."

As always, his twin was content not to speak.

SEVEN

Abruptly, Vishous looked up as he sensed Jane's presence. There, he thought, there in the darkness, in the cold wind, she had come.

He jumped off his rack, his heart beating hard. Without setting eyes on her, he sensed her emotions—and knew she had found out somehow.

"Jane," he barked as he strode over the bare floor.

Out on the terrace, she was in her ghost form, nothing but an indistinct hologram of herself in her white coat, scrubs, and her Crocs. With her blond hair and her wide, dark green eyes, she was at once achingly familiar . . . and something from a different, earlier incarnation of his life.

When did this separation happen to us, he wondered.

"What have you done," she said in a low voice.

Raw pain, the kind that threatened his balance, lit off in his chest. "I didn't fuck her. I didn't touch her."

"Why . . ." She put a hand over her mouth. Then dropped it. "Vishous, why?"

As a gust tore through the empty space between them, he heard himself say, "I don't know."

"You don't . . . you don't *know*?" As her anger started to come out, her brows dropped low, her hard stare the sort of thing he accepted like a dagger to his chest that he'd well earned. "You meet another woman— female, whatever she is—behind my back and you don't *know* why you did it? You're the smartest person I have ever met, and even dumb people know why they cheat."

Vishous shook his head. "I didn't cheat."

"Where's your shirt."

"I didn't mean for this to happen—"

"You most certainly did. You asked Fritz to bring liquor here, and someone else clearly showed up."

"I told you, I didn't touch her—"

"Bullshit! And please spare me the denials. I won't believe you. Why should I"—she pointed to all the glowing candles—"when I get to have this lovely picture in my mind for the rest of my life? So romantic, Vishous. I hope she was properly impressed—"

"You left us."

Jane recoiled and then glared at him. "Excuse me?"

"You left me even though you didn't go anywhere."

"What the hell are you saying," she snapped.

"I never see you. We are never together. You are more worried about your patients than—"

"Wait." She put her palm into his face. "Are you *seriously* spinning what you just did like it is *my* fault? Oh, grow up—"

V's voice exploded out of chest. "After the warehouse fight, I was all fucked up in your clinic with a head injury and you told me you would be back! You were going to get medication for me—but as you walked out the door of my patient room, you know what I said to myself? She's not going to come—"

"I sat beside you while you were unconscious! For two hours!"

"—back, and you *didn't*."

"You checked yourself out AMA! When I returned, Ehlena said you'd left!"

The two of them were leaning toward each other, screaming into the wind, faces contorted, fists clenched—and in the back of his mind, he felt a sadness that this was what they had come down to: Betrayal. Hurt. Anger. It was the flip side to everything that he had thought they had. Everything he thought they were.

This was the kind of argument that wiped all the good parts away, he thought. Permanently.

Jane slashed her hand through the cold air that neither of them paid any attention to. "I took excellent care of you—"

"How long," he ground out.

"What?"

"How long until you ended up back in my patient room." When she looked away and crossed her arms over her chest, he nodded. "An hour, right. Maybe longer. And while you were sitting at my hospital bed, while I was out cold, were you giving orders to Ehlena? Consulting with Manny? Tell me, how many patients did you manage to triage or treat during those two hours when you were supposedly taking care of me."

Her forest-green eyes shot back to him. "Don't you *dare* deflect this onto me. I wasn't the one making a date with someone else."

"What I did was wrong, I admit it. But I didn't follow through on it. I couldn't. And even though that's no excuse—"

"Damn right it's no excuse! You're a liar now. You're a liar forever to me—"

Without warning, a truth came out of him. "My mother is dead. Have you noticed that? Have you stopped to think about that at all?"

She was momentarily nonplussed. "What does the Scribe Virgin have to do with this?"

Vishous shook his head slowly. "You never once asked me how I felt. You never even asked me how I found out she was gone."

Jane looked away again. Swung her eyes back. "I didn't think it bothered you. You kept going like it was nothing. You hated her."

"You never asked, is the point."

Jane rubbed her face with what looked like exasperation, scrubbing, scrubbing. "Vishous, listen, you are not the easiest person to read, and you don't do emotions. It's like you're blaming me for one of your core characteristics. How was I supposed to know—"

"I was in a warehouse with my brothers and the Bastards. I was in a fucking melee that could have ended a fuck of a lot differently than it did. You never asked me what it was like. You never sat down with me—"

"It's Brotherhood business! You guys don't talk about that stuff, ever!" She threw her hands up. "You need to look at this from my side. You're knocking me for abandoning you when all I've done is take my cue from you. You never talk about fights with me. You don't tell me about the war. You disappear behind those computers like they're camouflage you're hiding in. What am I supposed to do? Sit across from you on the sofa and do needlepoint until you deign to ask me to get you a snack? Screw that 1950s crap. If you'd wanted a house pet, you should have gotten a cat."

"Whatever, Jane. You come home after being at work for fifteen, eighteen hours straight. You're half dead, dragging, cross-eyed. I put you in bed after you fall asleep on that couch for more days than you're choosing to remember—"

"Those patients are not strangers. Those people I'm treating are your *family*."

"You're my *mate*. Or at least you used to be. Lately, you've been less than a roommate."

Jane narrowed her eyes. "Do you want to consider, for even half a second—if you can spare the time in the middle of your epic rant here—what it would be like for me to lose one of those Brothers or fighters on my watch? To not take care of them well enough? To make a bad call even if I don't always have all the information or the answers? You are out battling the Lessening Society, but I'm on cleanup duty, and I would much rather be a shitty fucking wife to you than a bad doctor for them when they're dying."

V crossed his arms over his chest and nodded. "You've made it very clear where your priorities are. I'm very familiar with them."

"And you've handled not getting your way *so* admirably. If you had things you wanted to talk about, why didn't you just bring them up?"

"Check your texts."

"I never ignore you when you hit me up."

"You sure about that?"

"Yes. I *always* get back to you."

V stared down at her and felt absolutely, positively nothing like himself. He had no idea how he had morphed into this cesspool of confusion and anger, the steel dagger he always had been turning into a plastic butter knife. All he was certain of was that he wasn't going on like this anymore.

He was not a beggar. He was not a pussy. And he was not a victim in this circumstance—neither was Jane. They were two people who had gone separate ways, a thousand incremental choices made over time taking them further from their relationship rather than deeper into it.

His dumb decision had just turned the lights on the landscape, and all this emotion they were both feeling and releasing was the result of them finally catching up to where they had been for quite a while.

"I've got a scream, Jane." He pointed to his head. "In here, I've got a scream and I'm going insane. It's too much for me to hold in, and in the past, I've known what I can do to help me get through until it quiets down. It sure as fuck isn't talking, and you know what? You're the only person I would ever say any of this to. I'm scrambling to keep in my own skin and I'm not proud of it—I fucking *hate* this. But I have to function. Do you understand? I can't let Wrath and the Brotherhood down. I have to go out there and fight and be alert and get my fucking job done, and this"—he jabbed his finger into his cranium—"needs to fall in line. I didn't touch her. When it came down to it, I couldn't do it, not because it was morally wrong, but because I *want* to be with you. Hate me for making a bad decision out of desperation if it makes you feel better, but I didn't fuck her and I'm never doing it again."

Jane studied him for the longest time. "What you did or didn't do doesn't matter to me. Because as far as I'm concerned, you're a free male as of right now."

As Jane heard the words come out of her mouth, there was a part of her that was shocked. She hadn't expected to go that far, but her emotions were way out in front of her brain, the anger, the frustration, the pain, so great that it took over.

"You don't mean that," Vishous said remotely.

In the silence that followed, she studied his face and found the familiar features to be foreign to her, as if the upset had caused a kind of amnesia. His cropped black hair, his white irises with their blue outer rims, the tattoos at his temple, the goatee were all the same . . . and yet she seemed to recognize none of his details.

I don't know you anymore, she thought.

"I am going back to work," she said.

"Of course you are."

She jabbed a finger at him. "I am *not* the bad guy here."

"And neither am I."

"Then why are all those candles burning in there. And while we're at it, nice shirt." She eyed his naked chest, the circular scar on the pecs signifying his membership in the Brotherhood. "Next time you attempt to convince me you haven't been with another woman, try not being half naked."

"Jane. We need to talk this out."

"We just did. There is nothing else to say."

When he reached out to her, she took a sharp step back, and the sensation of something penetrating her flesh made her look down at herself.

She had gone through the glass panels that ran as a safety railing around the edge of the terrace. In all the upset, she had become ghostly enough to find the spaces within the molecules.

"Go then," Vishous said coldly. "Bury yourself in work. If you ever come up for air and want to talk, you know where to find me."

And there it was, she thought, the condescension and reserve she knew so well. Vishous was back behind his gates, holed up and encapsulated, removed even as he stood right in front of her.

"You're so damned superior," she muttered.

"I'm the son of a fucking deity. You want me to be average?"

She stared past his shoulder at all those lit candles. Those "toys" of his. That rack. "Just so you know, I wish I had never treated you back at St. Francis. I wish I had been off that night when you came in."

"Well, that's one last thing we can agree on then. Cheers to us."

They both turned away at the same time, he to go back into his den of iniquity, she to disappear.

For a moment, it was tempting to just let herself drop, to call her corporeal form into being fully and allow gravity to do its thing, grabbing her and snapping her down to the pavement. But the impact would only matter for however long she kept herself intact. As soon as her hold on herself lapsed and she became invisible, she had to believe she would be back to non-normal.

Or perhaps she would warp on contact with the ground. Or maybe her exterior would crack and fly apart, leaving her ghostly core uncovered.

She wasn't going to find out. Of all the things she would never allow herself to do, at the top of the list was getting broken by a man. A male. Whatever.

There was pain, yes. Disappointment in spades. A sense that this was either a bad dream or a case of her destiny having followed the wrong set of MapQuest directions.

But she refused to let this sink her. V was being utterly unreason-able, unfair, and had his head up his ass if he thought he could blame her for their problems.

As she traveled back to the Brotherhood compound, her first thought was to go to the training center and get right to work. There were always drug orders to put in and records to update and then that appointment with Layla and her young. But instead, she landed herself at the Pit's front door and hoped that Fritz was finished with the rugs.

No such luck.

When she walked in—or rather through—the entrance, she caught the old-fashioned, vaguely minty spice of Spic and Span, and sure enough, the *doggen* had switched his black jacket for a full body apron and was up to his elbows scrubbing the kitchen sink.

"Mistress!" He seemed confused as he turned to her, yellow rubber gloves held up at the elbows as if he were a surgeon about to go into a patient's chest cavity. "You are back?"

"Just to pick up a few things. Don't mind me."

Fritz bowed so low, his jowls nearly brushed the tops of his polished black shoes. "I could have packed for you if you two are staying over-day—"

"Don't worry about a thing. The floors and kitchen are much more important."

His smile was of relief and pleasure, making the lie worth it. The truth was, she didn't care about the floors or the kitchen. The roof or the chimney—did the Pit even have a chimney? It was no longer her concern.

"I'll just get my things," she murmured.

"Mayhap I shall just help you—"

"No." She recast her tone. "This is private."

"Oh, but of course, madam." The butler blushed a little. "I shall carry on then."

"Thank you, Fritz. As always."

While he happily resumed his scrubbing, she marched down the hall like Joan of Arc, all loaded for bear. When she got to the doorway of what had been her bedroom, she didn't even hesitate, she went over to—

Jane slowed. Stopped. Stared at the bed with its messy lineup of pillows and wrinkled duvet. There was a quantum physics textbook on one bed stand, his not hers, and a glass half filled with water, hers not his, on the other.

It was impossible not to think of the day before, when she had filled up that tumbler in the kitchen and come down here as she always did.

You rarely knew when you were doing something for the last time. No, that realization usually came later.

After she'd gotten her H_2O, she remembered sitting on her side of the bed and hanging her head because she had been so exhausted. Her shoulders and the back of her neck had been on fire from tension, and her hamstrings had been aching from her having been bent over Tohrment's lower leg. He'd popped his Achilles tendon again and she'd had to fix it in surgery. Pretty normal course of things—but for the fact that what should have been no more than an hour had taken three because of a bone anomaly and tons of scar tissue.

She had flopped back and tried to hold herself corporeal because she'd been hoping V would unplug from his computers and come and join her. In the end, the tantalizing peace that fading out offered had proven irresistible, and she had let herself go, disappearing so that the only trace of her was a dent in those covers, the place where her weight and her body had once been.

"Yeah, because I was helping his Brotherhood," she muttered as she went to their closet and grabbed a duffel.

She took stuff out of the chest of drawers without paying much attention to what it was. Then again, her wardrobe mostly consisted of scrubs . . . and more scrubs. Bras and underwear were the only other things she needed. In the bathroom, she grabbed her toothbrush and her tube of Crest.

He used Colgate.

See? They never should have gotten together in the first place.

On that note, she stalked out of there, proceeding down into the underground tunnel, returning to where she was both needed . . . and wanted.

EIGHT

The following day at around eight a.m., Sola walked to her neighborhood market with a grocery list her *vovó* had insisted be filled. It was good to feel like there was something she had to do. Something that was normal and uncomplicated, but necessary nonetheless.

Distraction was key. Otherwise, she was going to start packing and head for Caldwell.

Which would be a really stupid idea.

Entering the store, which had as much in common with a Walmart as a horse and buggy had with rush-hour traffic, she was embraced by her heritage. In the cramped little space, all the aisle markers, the price listings, and the labels were in Spanish. Overhead, Latin music murmured softly, more like a pleasing scent in the air than anything registering in the ear. And the patrons all had dark hair, dark eyes, and tanned skin like her.

Well, she would have had dark hair without the dye job. God, she hated the blond. Next month, she was going as a redhead, damn it.

Checking the list, she read her grandmother's scribbles as if they were her own, the quirky construction of the vowels and consonants indecipherable to others, easy for her.

She was going to need—

Habaneros . . . locotos . . . pequins? And a ghost pepper—which you could get here even though it was of Indian derivation rather than South American?

Was her grandmother trying to kill her through capsaicin?

"I saved you some plantains," a male voice said in Spanish.

Sola glanced over her shoulder and forced a smile. The guy coming up to her was holding what seemed like—yes, actually, they were a really good-looking lot of plantains, and they were on her list, too.

"Thanks," she replied.

"I will get you a basket." He hurried over to a stack of them by the door, popping free the top one. *"Here."*

As he held out the yellow plastic holder with its double handles, Sola pulled the bill of her baseball cap down lower. It wasn't that he was skeevy. He was a nice young Latino guy, who had a gold cross around his neck, friendly eyes with thick lashes, and a good shave and haircut. He had probably lived in this neighborhood his whole life, and either his father or his uncle or maybe a cousin owned this business. Naturally, he was looking to get married and have kids with a nice Latina girl because that was what the women in his family would be pushing him to do. And undoubtedly, he would take over the running of the shop after the generation above him passed.

There was absolutely nothing controversial, scary, or threatening about him. And he was staring at her with respect—and hope.

You have no idea who I am, she thought.

Sola accepted the basket. *"Thank you."* What she wanted to say was, Stop it. *"But you don't need to save things for me."*

"You always buy them on Tuesdays."

Did she? She needed to fix that. Predictable habits were bad news for the likes of her.

"I'll just find what's on my list and get going."

As the screen door creaked and banged with another entry, she measured the man who came in. Forty. Loose jacket. Dark sunglasses. Could have been law enforcement. Or a drug dealer. Or a regular Joe getting his lunch on the way to his work.

"Can I help you with what you need?" The supermarket guy nodded down at her slip of paper. *"If you want me to ever bring you things, I can do that, too. We have a delivery service."*

"No, I'm good. Thanks."

Loose Jacket Man walked by without seeming to notice her or check her ass when he thought she wasn't looking. But that didn't mean anything. Maybe this was Benloise's crew finally catching up with her.

Sola fell into step a little distance behind him and watched the fall of that jacket, looking for signs of a shoulder holster. When he paused by a display, she popped her list up and re-traced her grandmother's writing with her eyes. Perfect timing—she was in the canned-tomato aisle.

When the man continued on without pulling anything off a shelf, she resumed the trail.

He ended up in the refrigerator section, grabbing two pre-made, microwavable chicken tortillas and a Coke. He left money next the register, calling out to her friend with the baskets and the plantains in Spanish. Then he was gone.

She took no deep breath of relief and there was no easing of her tension.

This was life now. Anywhere she went.

Doubling back, because she had missed a lot of stuff during her skulk, she got everything and then went to check out at the counter. The young guy came over and first processed the man's lunch purchase; then he started scanning in bar codes, moving the boxes, cans, and cartons, over the reader.

"We have a lot of regulars," he said. *"My pop, he owns this place, can remember their fathers and grandfathers."*

"Loyalty is good."

"We're getting more and more new faces, though. People are moving in from other places." He looked up with a smile as if he were hoping she would fill in her particular blank. *"Where are you from originally?"*

"Nowhere." She got out her billfold and tried to estimate how much it would be. *"I'm not from anywhere."*

"I was born here, but my parents, they came over from Cuba. Oh—I have a coupon for these." He leaned down under the counter—

And she went for her gun, tucking her hand into her jacket.

Stopping that instinct before she blew his head off, she forced herself to keep in control. And sure enough, he popped up with a battered old folder full of colorful flyers, instead of a weapon.

"It's okay," she said as he started going through the pages. *"Really."*

He glanced up. *"I'd like to help."*

"I'm kind of in a hurry."

"Oh. Okay." He shrugged and put the thing away. *"Busy day ahead?"*

She made a show of inspecting the lottery-ticket selections behind him, the rolls of tickets lolling out of their vertical slots like dog tongues in August. *"Have you ever sold a winner?"*

He nodded and smiled. *"We had fifty dollars last week."*

"Outstanding."

When everything had been added up, she pushed her money at him and bagged for herself as he made change. Then she was out of there with a quick bye.

She was going to have to find another place to shop, and that sucked because his market was so close and had really good—well, plantains, among other things.

On the street with her plastic bags of her *vovó*'s list, she walked fast, searching the faces of every person who came toward her as well as the pedestrians across the street and those behind her. There was no fear for her, though. No paranoia, either.

Okay, fine, maybe there was a little paranoia. Bottom line, she was living out that last scene of *The Sopranos,* waiting, waiting, for the end to come from an unexpected angle—only there was no Journey sound-track and she had a better hairline than Tony had had. Waistline, too.

Going back to Caldwell was *not* going to help any of this reality, she reminded herself. The people who were after her weren't going to grant her a mercy pass because she was up there on a humanitarian mission. They were going to look at her conscience as a stroke of luck for them.

Assuming they hadn't found her already and only had yet to reveal themselves.

By the time she stepped out of her building's elevator on the fifth floor, she was feeling no better about anything. Not Assail. Not the shadows still thrown by the life she had lived. Not—

As she opened the door to the condo, she stopped and cursed.

There was a suitcase by the armchair that had been briefly relocated earlier. As well as a duffle bag, a pair of winter coats, two sets of gloves and scarves, and her grandmother's pocketbook.

"*Vovó*," she groaned.

Her grandmother came out of the back, where the bedrooms were. "We go now. Drive through. Get there eight tomorrow morning if we no stop."

"No."

"You right. Closer to ten."

Her grandmother had changed out of her housecoat and was in one of her handmade dresses. She even had hose and short-heeled pumps on. Her hair had been curled and sprayed, looking like a washed-out version of Sally Field's *Steel Magnolias* brown football helmet, and yes, there was lipstick involved.

"This is not a good idea, *Vovó*." Sola let the door close itself behind her. "It's not safe in Caldwell."

"They will keep us safe."

Sola looked around the condo, taking in all of the anonymity. Then she stared at her grandmother with hard eyes. "You know what kind of man Assail is. You know his business."

"And."

As those old eyes glared right back at her, she wanted to curse some more. But she knew better. And she should have known "criminals" and "against-the-law" were relative terms to her *vovó*. The woman had a long history with people who were less than on the up-and-up.

Make that loved ones who were not all that law-abiding.

Fine, time to bring out the big guns, Sola thought.

"He's not Catholic."

"He will convert."

"*Vovó.*" She shook her head. "You need to stop this. Even if we help him—and honestly, what can I do for someone who's terminal?—he and I are not going to get married or anything."

"We go now. Why we talking?"

The old woman bent down, draped her winter coat over her arm, and picked up her pocketbook.

Jesus, Sola thought. Now she knew what people had to deal with when they crossed her: Brick. Frickin'. Wall.

She closed her eyes. "I made a vow to God. I promised Him, if He saved me, if I got to see you again, I would leave . . . that life . . . forever."

"Assail, I called. I called him that night when you were taken. He came when I needed him. God brought you back to me through him. So now we go. We help who helped us. That is the way."

Sola shifted the plastic bags of groceries around to relieve the pinching of her hands and fingers. When that didn't help, she put the weights down on the floor.

"I don't know if I can protect you up there. Or protect myself."

"And I say they will take care of us."

Will you forgive me, Vovó, she wondered. *If something goes wrong, will you forgive me?*

Will I forgive myself?

"You are all that matters," Sola said hoarsely.

Her grandmother came forward. "We will go. It is God's way."

"How do you know that?"

The smile that came back at her was old, and wise, and very beautiful. "I, too, prayed. To the Virgin Mary. I prayed you see Assail again, and then God sent those men to our house last night. We will leave now. Come."

With that, her grandmother, who not only had no driver's license, but couldn't reach the pedals on anything other than a tricycle, headed for the door.

"Bring the groceries with the suitcases, Sola" was the command over her shoulder.

NINE

It was a little after ten o'clock two evenings later when Vishous materialized into the alleys of downtown, re-forming in the lee of some crappy-ass walk-ups on the east side of the city's armpit of skyscrapers.

By a stroke of luck, the normal rotation schedule had not required him to be on deck the evening before, so he had managed to isolate himself from everyone for a good forty-eight hours, crashing at the modest ranch Layla had lived in during her estrangement from the household. V had not contacted anyone, not even to ask Fritz to bring him food and drink.

Learned that lesson well enough, fuck him very much.

And hey, Arby's had been good enough back in his bachelor days, and it was good enough now.

As his time to calm the fuck down had come to a close, there had been a part of him that had debated going off the grid and pulling a permanent relocation. Shit, there were plenty of places to disappear to if a male wanted to not get found. In the end, however, he decided he wanted to fight more than he wanted to be in a pussy's retreat.

On that note, the Hummer he was looking for came around a street corner like a predator stalking dinner, its headlights off, its running lights glowing softly, the steam coming out of its tailpipe curling up orange and red. As it stopped in front of him, the passenger door opened, a long leg with a shitkicker at the end landing treads-deep in the dirty, packed snow.

Butch O'Neal had been a human for a good thirty and a half years, give or take. Now the former homicide detective was not just a vampire, but Wrath's own kin: One of the few survivors of a "jump-started" transition, his body hadn't just gotten taller, but had filled out like he was shooting up steroids and pumping iron like Ahnold in the good ol' days. Compact as a bulldog, mean as a snake in a fight, loyal as any good Red Sox fan had to be, he was the brother Vishous had never had.

And the bastard knew too much.

"Thanks for the ride, Q—what? Yeah, I'll text." He leaned back into the SUV a little farther. Laughed. "Too right."

The cop shut the door, banged his gloved fist on the quarter panel, and stepped aside as Qhuinn's second armor-plated SUV rumbled forward. The first one had been car-napped in front of a CVS—when the brother had left the keys in the ignition. Talk about your engraved invitation for a drive-off.

V lifted a hand as the vehicle went by. And then he started the countdown in his head. Three . . . two . . . one—

"So." Butch jacked up his leathers even though they were already cupping his sac like a jockstrap. "How's you."

"Let's go patrol."

"Where you been?"

"Out." Why in the fuck couldn't he have lived in a cave all these years. By himself. "I'm done with this conversation, true."

As V started stalking down the center of the street, he looked up at the windows of the grubby walk-ups on both sides. Every single one of them had the drapes drawn, and most were darkened. Those at ground level had iron bars locked on, and none, absolutely none, of them would be opened in the event of a scream, or a gunshot, or a holler.

In this neighborhood, nobody asked questions, made eye contact, or got involved in business that wasn't their own.

Which made him think about the only thing the Lessening Society had in its favor. Those soulless bastards who were remote-controlled by the Omega didn't want human involvement in the war any more than the vampires did. So the field of engagement, by mutual, if unacknowledged, agreement, was always here in the land of—

"You usually text if you're gonna be out," Butch said from behind him. "And we were supposed to play pool last night."

When V didn't respond, the cop whistled under his breath. "So Manny's right."

Vishous stopped and swung around. "About what."

The cop shrugged, those hazel eyes annoyingly steady. "You and Jane okay?"

"Perfect. Why."

"You know, you have an interesting way of posing a question without actually using a question mark."

"That's because I'm trying not to encourage a response."

"So you guys did have a fight."

Vishous crossed his arms over his chest. Because it was either he locked that shit down or he was liable to throw a punch—and the cop technically hadn't done anything wrong.

"What did Manny say?"

"That Doc Jane has been in a release-the-Kraken mood since the night before last. And she's sleeping in a patient room."

"She's fine. I'm fine. We're fine."

"Isn't that a nursery rhyme? Or is it from an ad for an antidepressant? I get the two confused." When V just stared at the guy, Butch shrugged. "All I'm saying is, if you need—"

The flash of movement was an in-and-out the corner of the eye thing, an almost-missed, was-it-real-or-Memorex stutter in the pattern of shadows at the opening of an alley. But Butch saw it, too, the cop shutting up and turning in that direction.

They both put their hands into their open leather jackets, where their arsenals were, and took cover behind the shell of a car that had no windows, no doors, no trunk and no hood.

It was like holding a coat hanger up to play hide-and-seek. But beggars. Choosers. And all that bullshit.

Except . . . there was no scent of a *lesser* in the air. Nothing human, either. Then again, the wind was coming from behind them so no help on that one. And yet . . . no, there really was a presence in that alley's black hole of no-see.

Off in the distance, a stream of obscenities was answered by a volley of yelling, but the highly intellectual and rational exchange was a good block away and who gave a crap if humans wanted to fuck each other up. It was one of their few core competencies.

"I saw something," Butch muttered. "I swear."

Vishous looked the street up and down, and then refocused on that dark area. "I'm going in there."

"I'm calling for backup—"

"Don't bother."

Walking out from behind the wreck, he did nothing to shield himself. If whoever was in there wanted a piece of something? Then he'd be more than happy to give them a fucking slice.

The cursing that followed him was in a Boston accent—and all those "friggin"s and "idiot"s were spoken too close for V's comfort. Glancing behind himself, he shook his head at the cop and pointed for the guy to get back—

A knife came slashing at V's face, and he ducked and spun to avoid the blade. With a quick jerk, he grabbed the weapon and got control of it, pitching the thing out of range. And that was when he saw . . . a shadow.

But not one thrown by a figure. One that was freestanding, free moving . . . and aggressive as fuck—

The strike on his upper arm was like a punch from a fist full of bee stingers, at once focused and diffused, ringing throughout his body in the shiver-pain of a thousand poisoned needle sticks.

Instantly compromised, V tripped over his feet as he fell away from an attacker he could not comprehend—but before he hit the ground, Butch caught him and dragged him back.

V's only thought was to get back on his feet. Fight whatever the fuck it was. Take control of the situation.

No go, maestro.

His body was epileptic-uncoordinated, his joints failing to work right, his limbs floppy except for where they were randomly rigid. And his brain was no better, his thoughts scattered and full of hiccups.

As his hearing came and went, he was aware of a gun sticking out in front of him. It was the cop's weapon; Butch had somehow managed to get him back to the car-sieve while outing his forty at the darkness—

That gun started going off, the autoloader doing its thing with a flash of light at the tip of the muzzle every time a bullet discharged. *Pop! Squeeeeeeeee.*

Pop! Pop! Squeeeeeeeeeeeeeeeee.

V frowned in the midst of his delirium. What was that sound? What the hell—

As the stinging sensations began to fade, Vishous became able to properly focus, and what he saw, he couldn't explain.

It definitely appeared as if a shadow, as generic as any that fell at his feet, had declared itself free of a source object and was floating forward with another dagger. Extensions of the whole would snap out at Butch, sometimes with the weapon, sometimes without it, the stabs and punches brutal and accurate. But at least the bullets drove the entity back.

And with each slug that hit, the shadow made that high-pitched squeal, as if a child's balloon were being pinched at its aperture with air coming out of the mostly closed neck.

Vishous ordered his hands to find the pair of guns in his hip hol-sters, and although it was like trying to command someone in a language they didn't speak, eventually, his appendages complied. And just in time. As Butch's clip ran out, the shadowy form rushed at them, and V lifted his weapons into shooting position. Discharging both weapons at nearly point-blank range, he emptied everything he had into the fucking thing.

Bang! Bang! Bang! Bangbangbangbangbang—

*Squeeeeeeeeeeeeeeeeeeee*EEEEEEEEEEE—

No more kid's balloon. Now that sound was like tires skidding on asphalt, the treble ringing at such a high pitch that V stopped hearing the noise and was conscious only of a stinging pair of headaches at the sites of his eardrums. And then a sonic *boom!* was released—

Everything went quiet except for his and Butch's ragged breaths.

"What the fuck was that?" the cop said.

Deep in the alleyway from which he'd ordered his shadow soldier to attack, Throe, forsaken son of Throe, fell back against something, he knew not what. The piercing pain at the center of his chest was what he imagined a heart attack felt like, pressure compounding at his sternum such that he had to look down at himself. But no, there was no wounding, no source of blood on his fine camel-hair coat.

He thought perhaps one of the bullets from the Brothers' guns had impacted him? With trembling hands, he tore wide the lapels and then had to fumble with his suit jacket and tie, getting them out of the way. Naught marred his fine button-down shirt, however, the silk as pristine as it had been when he had dressed at sunset.

Forcing his lungs to expand with cold air, he wondered what had injured him and lamented the poor showing in the fight. He had come to this unexalted part of town with one of his growing army of fighters, his obedient shadow by his side, tethered to him without leash or lead, bobbing along in servitude. He had been in search of what he had eventually found: members of the Black Dagger Brotherhood or the Band of Bastards.

Indeed, as the former's interests had always conflicted with his own, given his quest for the throne, and the latter were now his enemy even though he had been with them for centuries; there were many enemies to choose from.

As he had waited with his pet, he had taken comfort in the presence beside him, one born from his blood and shadow as directed by a ritual his Book had provided him. This was to have been the big test as up until now, the tasks he had ordered the handful he'd brought into being had been of far lesser challenge.

The murder of his dead lover's ancient and decrepit *hellren*, for example, had hardly been a difficulty.

No, his primary goal in making this army was not the eradication of the Lessening Society, which had plagued the species for millennia. Rather, he wanted the heads of the Brotherhood and the Bastards on stakes and Wrath the Blind King's body to be set afire before the wide-eyed citizens of the race, who would then be motivated to gather behind a true leader.

Himself.

Throe massaged his chest. He had been so sure of his success, but now he wondered. Mere bullets had driven his entity back from its target until it had been destroyed—

He looked down with a frown. The strange pain had come unto him exactly when the shadow had been blown apart. Was it possible . . .

As he tried to breathe long and slow, he found the agony was unfading, and knew he had to depart with alacrity. The Brothers were casting off whatever injury the shadow had caused them and reemerging from behind the picked-clean remnants of a car.

They were focusing on the alley where he stood.

Did they know he was here?

Stumbling into a retreat, Throe bid his legs to make good time, but the ringing discomfort in his sternum and a lack of oxygen hindered him. As he proceeded through the filthy snow and slush, he tried to will himself to dematerialize to safety, but his sensory input was too high and the spike of adrenaline that came with being too exposed made things worse.

Faster. He tried to go faster.

At least they would never know it had been him. Yes, his ambitions had been well-expressed, but who could guess he was receiving help from such an unknown, unknowable source?

His Book was not the Omega. Or at least it had not revealed itself as such.

Indeed, it was a beautiful mystery to him—

Frowning, he slowed. Why had he never wondered what the Book's origins were . . . Book's . . . origins . . . were . . .

Like an engine stuttering to a halt without gas, his thoughts stopped, no further cognition occurring.

Abruptly, Throe looked over his shoulder and cursed at the fact that he had allowed his enemy to close some of the distance: The Brothers were breaching the mouth of the alley, and though the one known as Vishous, the taller and goatee'd of the two, seemed to be limping, neither of them appeared to be overly compromised.

If they caught up with him, they were going to kill him.

TEN

As Ehric sat at the counter in the kitchen of Assail's glass house, his mood had scrummed down into vile territory. He had been so sure that his cousin's woman would respond favorably to an entreaty on his behalf.

But instead, he found himself here on this stool, continuing to stare out at the lit drive, watching all of the absolutely-no-cars coming up to the back of the mansion.

"Would you care for aught?"

He shifted his focus away from that which had proven so persistently disappointing. Markcus, the freed blood slave, was standing by the sink, his thin body strung with tension, his youthful face and ancient, haunted eyes cast in shades of worry and concern.

In reply, Ehric wanted to bite the male's head off. But not only was that unfair, it was cruel. Markcus was not like the others in the household, to war bred and trained. On the contrary, he was but an orphan in this world, and as he had only recently been freed by Assail, the male required the sort of kindness and patience that debauched mercenaries were typically unfamiliar with.

Ehric passed his eyes over the black slave band that had been tattooed around the male's throat.

"No, Markcus," he said roughly. "I am well in hand, thank you—"

The cell phone next to him went off with a vibration that sent the
unit on a wander across the granite. When he saw who it was, he cursed,
but answered.

"Healer," he intoned.

Doc Jane, as she was known, hesitated. "Ehric, how are you?"

"I am well, thank you." He had never understood the wasted time
of pleasantries. But he did not wish to offend the female who had tried
so hard and for so long with his cousin. "And you?"

"I'm good." There was a pause. "Listen, I wanted to follow up on
our meeting of the night before last about Assail. I left you a message
yesterday?"

"I did not receive it." And by that, he meant that he had not listened
to what she had recorded. "Forgive me."

"That's all right. I, ah, I don't want to pressure you in any way, but I
would just like to clarify where you and Evale are with respect to your
cousin? I'm afraid I wasn't clear on whether or not you had made a decision."

Unable to stay still, Ehric got up and walked out into the open seating area that faced the river, the vast space populated with furniture
that his cousin had purchased with the home. As no lights were on, the
sofas and chairs, tables and lamps, were nothing but shapes and shadows in a palette of blacks and grays, the decor doing nothing to improve his utter lack of optimism.

Verily, Assail's condition had been weighing on him for weeks now,
and he did not relish being the decider of the male's fate. Yet he could
not bear the suffering.

"Hello?" the healer prompted. "Have I lost you?"

Stopping up at the great glass expanse, he stared out at the snow-
covered lawn that terminated at the shore of the Hudson River. Across

the sluggish waterway, the city of Caldwell's dense urban core was an uneven pattern of vertical lights that were static and horizontal ones that moved.

"No," he muttered. "You have not lost me."

"Would you prefer to take no action at this time? There is no rush."

"Other than the hell he is in." Ehric paused and reminded himself that males did not express weakness—except then his mouth moved anyway. "I hate the prison he is in. He is the last who would wish to be immobile, trapped in a body he cannot control. You say he has no brain waves . . . but what of his soul?"

The healer sighed with regret. "No, you're right. He has been suffering, and his quality of life is . . . poor to say the least."

"I thought perhaps I had come up with a solution. Alas, I fear that is not true."

"What kind of solution?"

"It matters not." As he fell silent, he waited for another idea to come unto him. "We are at the end of things, aren't we."

"You have as much time as you and your brother need."

"If I were in that condition, I wouldnae favor indecision."

"He doesn't appear to be in pain."

"Do you know that or just assume that?" When she didn't immediately answer, he nodded even though she couldn't see him. "So you are not sure."

"His scans lead us to believe that—"

"It is time. Enough with this. Evale and I will leave now and come unto you. We will do what must needs be done, and be there when he . . ." As his voice cracked, he cleared his throat. "We will not desert him in his last moments."

"I can appreciate how hard this is for you," the healer said grimly, "and I'm glad—well, not that any of you are in this situation, but that you clearly appreciate its gravity as you do. I have been struggling myself with his case."

Indeed, the sorrow in her voice was something that comforted him—as it suggested he and his brother were not alone in their grief.

The female continued. "While you arrange to come in, I'll get everything ready—"

"Wait." He closed his eyes. "What does . . . what happens at the end?"

"We are going to give him morphine to ensure he feels no discomfort. And then I am going to stop his heart from beating."

"He won't feel anything?"

"No."

"Are you sure?"

"In this, I am absolutely sure."

As Ehric reopened his lids, he saw that his twin had entered the room behind him. In the glass, Evale's reflection was still as a mountain, the light from the kitchen turning his body into a looming shadow.

"We shall leave the now," Ehric told the healer. "And meet transport as soon as they can get to us."

Vishous penetrated the alley's throat with his guns up and his instincts on high alert. His body, unfortunately, was logy and uncoordinated, as though his blood had turned into rubber cement and his bones were struggling to hold his weight. But goddamn it, he was going to find out if there were any more of those shadows.

"You ever seen anything like that before?" Butch asked in a low voice.

"Nope."

"Heard about something like—"

"Nope."

"Read about—"

"What do you think," V snapped.

The cop cursed. "You know what, I'm going to dub in a 'yes' at this point because I am totally freaked out by the idea you have no clue what that was."

Breathing in through his nose, V caught a lingering scent in the air, and he stopped. Frowned. Turned to the right.

"What is it?" Butch demanded.

Sniffing like a bloodhound, Vishous closed in on the alley wall. "Cologne. Fresh. And there's vampire under the shit. Someone was just here."

Butch leaned in and sniffed the building's flank like it had mortar made out of cocaine. "Acqua di Parma. Expensive stuff. And yeah, it was a male who's one of us. Maybe a member of the *glymera*? But what would they be doing in this part of town?"

"No blood, though."

"So that shadow didn't get them."

Vishous removed the lead-lined glove from his curse and lifted his deadly, glowing hand up. Willing illumination from the center of his palm, he lit the entire alley for the distance of four blocks.

No one was there. And the snow was so packed and ice-covered that a retreat wouldn't leave any prints—although considering it had been a vampire, they would have dematerialized to get away.

Unless the entity could consume a mortal?

"I don't like any part of this," V muttered as he lowered his palm and re-gloved.

As the wind swirled and changed directions, coming at his face, he sorted through the complex, interlacing layers of scents, a job challenged by the cold because it tamped down the smells' intensity: There was garden-variety city-nasty, which was a combination of human feces, rot, and generic decay . . . your typical gas and oil fumes . . . an electrical burn from somewhere . . .

Nothing remotely *lesser* or vampire-ish.

Whoever it was had left.

"I've smelled that before." He nodded to the wall. "I just can't frickin' place it. No . . . wait. I think . . ."

Taking out his cell phone, he sent a text. The reply was instantaneous, and the response he was after nearly as fast: In less than a minute, two huge fighters appeared. The one with the harelip and the scythe on his back was Xcor, leader of the Band of Bastards, mated of the Chosen Layla. Next to him, his soldier Zypher was just as big, but preferred guns to big knives.

Which was a minor strike against the male. Then again, V had been making daggers for a couple of centuries, so he was biased toward the steel.

"Greetings," Xcor said. "What is the—"

Instantly, the male's head cranked toward the alley's wall. And then he stepped in close.

"Throe," he growled as he inhaled.

ELEVEN

ix stops.

Sola and her grandmother made six stops on the fourteen-hundred-mile, thirty-six-hour-long trip. Other than that, they had steadily moved north on the highway system, through the never-gonna-frickin'-end, long-and-thin of Florida, into Georgia and the Carolinas, and finally up to the almost-theres of Maryland, Pennsylvania, and New Jersey.

The idea that they could have come in to Caldwell's zip code at ten in the morning had been craziness. Especially given that, after some thirteen hours of driving, she'd had to get out from behind the wheel and grab a crash of about six hours at a La Quinta. But then they'd kept right on going after her sleep, and man, she'd enjoyed a shot of thank you, Jesus triumph as they'd finally passed into New York State. Talk about your premature celebrations. There had still been hours to go at that point, and by the time she'd battled through Manhattan traffic to shoot out the other side, she had reached the cold-storage suffering part of any long trip.

It Was Never Going To Be Over.

Like all things, however, the rule of beginning, middle, and end applied to their travel and signs for Caldwell had started to appear, like the lights of a rescue plane to someone who had been Tom Hanks–stranded for the longest time.

"We are here," her *vovó* said as the Northway made a turn and the city's bridge over the Hudson River appeared like the promised land.

Or, at least, the land of less-likely-to-get-a-DVT-blood-clot-in-your-leg-because-you-can-finally-get-out-the-car.

"Yes, we made it."

There was only a moment of relief, however, that balm to her aching neck and stiff shoulders immediately replaced with an OMG. She had no idea what was going to happen when they got to Assail's: For one, they were not expected. His cousins hadn't left her with a way of getting in touch. And then there was the unknown of Assail's condition and the shock of seeing him after a year.

Why hadn't she thought to get a phone number from Ehric? Then again, she hadn't seen this turn of northbound events, had she.

As she took herself and her grandmother over the bridge to Caldwell's quieter side, she looked to the left, searching for Assail's glowing glass house on its peninsula. She couldn't see anything but tiny clusters of lights on the shore, and God knew, his big place lit up like the Kennedy Space Center at night.

Maybe he was at a hospital? She had no idea where he was being treated.

After they came off the bridge, she took the first exit and then the turnoff for the peninsula's road was a split from a curve that narrowed things down considerably. Finally, she passed that little hunting cabin, which was the last structure before Assail's mansion.

Now her heart began to beat hard, the beautiful, transparent house appearing like the bird's nest of a Swarovski finch.

But yup, everything was dark inside, which didn't exactly inspire confidence. Although at least, as she rolled around to the garages in back, there were lights on in the kitchen and someone was standing at the sink.

"You stay here," she ordered her grandmother as she stopped the car and ran a check of her gun.

Nine times out of ten, she deferred to her elder. Okay, fine, nine and nine-tenths out of ten. But when it came to physical safety, she was always going to be in charge and her grandmother recognized those instances.

"Lock up," Sola said as she got out and shut the door.

She waited until there was a *thunk* sound that meant the car was secure. Then she walked over to the rear entrance of the mansion, her running shoes squeaking in the snowpack, her breath coming out in puffs of white, her sinuses humming and her ears tingling.

Ah, January in upstate New York. You might as well have been on the arctic circle.

Especially when you'd been living in Miami.

Before she could knock or otherwise make herself known, the back door opened and she gasped. The dark-haired man standing before her was half the size Assail had been, with the arms and legs of someone who was starving to death. Or dying.

"Assail . . ." she whispered.

"May I help you?" a voice she didn't recognize asked.

Wait—what? Okay, no, that was not Assail—which was a relief. "I'm a—I'm a friend of Assail's. This is still his house, right?"

"Yes."

When nothing more was offered, she cleared her throat. "May I see him?"

"He is not here."

"Where is he?"

"Who are you again?"

Sola glanced back at the road-grime-covered car and saw her grandmother sitting there, buckled into the passenger seat, her pocketbook clutched to her bosom. Thirty-six hours. Sola had driven that poor old woman thirty-six hours in a car that had the shock absorbers of a cardboard box and a heater that smelled like an electrical fire if they were going over sixty miles an hour.

All that for, *Who are you again?*

Ehric and Evale had come down, hadn't they? She and her grandmother couldn't possibly have had an identical bizarre dream.

"If Assail's not here, are his cousins available," she said, her voice growing strident.

"They have just departed."

"Can you reach them?"

The man shook his head, and he took a step back, as if he were uncomfortable keeping the door open and not just because it was letting cold air into the house. "No. They are—it is private business. Please come back another time—"

She caught the heavy panel with a strong hand and looked the guy right in the eye. "You get on your phone, right now, and you tell Ehric I'm here. And then I'm going to help my grandmother out of that car and escort her in here. She's eighty damn years old, we've been on the road for a day and a half, and she's not staying in there one goddamn minute longer. Are we clear?"

And if he didn't do what she said? She was going to pull her gun on him. She was done with the games and utterly over being polite.

Not that she and Emily Post had ever been besties, anyway.

TWELVE

Five minutes. Maybe less.

Within five minutes, Sola and her grandmother were in the house, using the ladies' room, and getting the kinks out. And two minutes after that? Ehric and Evale came through that back door like they had been shot from a cannon.

The two men stopped dead when they saw her, as if they were shocked that their request had been actualized.

"You're here," Ehric said in a strangely flat voice.

"Yes." She glanced at his twin. "Where's Assail?"

Ehric bowed so low, he nearly kissed his heavy combat boots. "Let me take you to him."

"Which hospital? I'll drive myself." She glanced at her grandmother. "*Vovó*, let's go—"

"I stay here." Her *vovó* took off her coat. "Bring me the groceries from the trunk. I send him for more things."

As she pointed at Evale, the man assumed a look of messianic zeal, and Sola debated putting her foot down. But Assail's cousins had never been anything less than respectful, and besides, it didn't seem fair to drag her grandmother to a hospital and ask the woman to wait around while Sola tried to inspire a dying man. That could be hours.

Evale spoke up. "She will be safe herein. Markcus and I shall protect her."

If Markcus was the thin guy over in the corner, it was hard to believe he'd be much help in a fight. Then again, like Evale was going to need any? He had more guns on him under those loose clothes than he had fingers and toes.

"Okay," she said to Ehric. "Let's go."

The man nodded, and as he headed for the mudroom and the garage, Sola glanced at her grandmother, giving the woman one last chance to change her mind. When her *vovó* simply went for the refrigerator to check for staples, Sola started off in Ehric's footsteps.

As she passed by the guy's twin brother, she said in a low voice, "She's older than she thinks she is."

Evale snapped a hold on her arm, stopping her. Eyes that were the color of a blue diamond bored into her like stakes through her skull.

"You take care of my kin, I take care of yours."

Sola's chest tightened, and in that moment of connection, she realized how alone in the world she was. She had never felt as though she had help keeping herself and her grandmother safe and alive—because she trusted no one, out of necessity. And yet this killer in front of her? He had just given her the kind of vow that made them . . . almost family.

"Thank you," she said roughly.

He released his vise grip of a hand and bowed. And then she was walking out on legs that were wobbly.

In the garage, there was a blacked-out Range Rover she knew all too well. It was the SUV she'd ridden in after the abduction, and the sight of the thing took her back to that horrible night.

"Which hospital is it?" she said as she went around to the passenger side.

"You've been there before. It is where we took you."

"Oh, right." Even though she had few memories of the place. Shock'll do that to a girl. "How far out of town is it?"

"Not far. But we have to pick up someone first."

As she got in, she felt for her gun. "Do I know them?"

"Do not worry." Ehric glanced over from the driver's side. "I will not let ill befall you."

Actually, that's my job, she thought. *But thanks.*

Ten minutes later, they pulled into a strip mall, headed around the back, and a man stepped out from behind the mountain of snow that had been cleared from the parking areas. He was blond-haired and—yeah, wow, really good-looking. Wait . . . she recognized him from before.

As the guy walked over, Ehric stared across at her. "Please remove your hand from your weapon. He is our escort or we will not be allowed to pass. If he senses your aggression, things could get . . . complicated."

Sola slid her hand back into view, but kept her palm on her thigh. "Who are these people?"

"Friends."

File this under birds of a feather, she thought as she re-measured the blond's enormous size. And P.S., why couldn't she hang out with normal people who had normal jobs?

The man popped the door, bent himself like a pretzel to squeeze inside, and filled the entire back seat as he unkinked his bends. "How we doing, people? Hey, Sola, I don't know if you remember me. You were pretty out of it when I saw you last. My name is Rhage, and I'll be your deadweight for this trip. Please keep all trays in the upright position and the swearing to a minimum. In the event I get carsick, I will request a transfer to the front seat, driver or passenger is fine. And if the lady wouldn't mind giving me her weapons, we can get moving."

As she twisted around to look at him, he gave her a winning smile, his brilliant blue eyes so stunning, she was momentarily struck dumb by their color. It was almost as if they were backlit, somehow? But she wasn't fooled; good looks and charm aside, if she didn't pony up the metal, he was going to lose that easygoing facade quick as a camo sheet being pulled off an anti-aircraft gun.

"I'd feel better if I kept it," she muttered.

"I'm sure you would. But then you aren't going to my facility. So what's our choice? And by the way, if we get in there and I search you, which I will, and I find anything you didn't disclose? We're going to have some problems, the three of us—problems that are going to be difficult to solve amicably. Have I made things clear enough?"

He smiled again. And waited, as if he didn't care what her decision was, either way. Her choice was going to determine what he did, and he took no ownership over whether the outcome was A) "amicable" or B) "bust a cap in your ass."

Ehric shifted in his seat and started handing over his weapons. "It does not apply solely to you," he said. "And I trust them."

Sola watched the show, coveting the man's pair of forties. As well as his switchblade, and his—were those throwing stars? And a . . .

"Excuse me," she cut in. "Is that a grenade?"

Ehric looked at the compact, palm-sized bomb in his hand. "Why, yes. It is."

As that was passed back, like it was nothing more than a Halls Mentho-Lyptus being shared between cold sufferers, she knew she was solidly in drink-the-Kool-Aid-or-get-off-the-ride land.

"I really don't want to do this," she muttered as she got out her nine and handed it over. "I mean . . . really."

Annnnnnd twenty minutes later, they were out far from the city and its suburban skirting, traveling on a two-lane road through a forest of evergreens, passing by yellow reflective signs with deer leaping on them and nearly no cars.

"Oh, yo! Turn this up!"

The man named for the Hulk's primary emotion shot his arm out between the seats and hit the volume just as they slowed and bumped off the asphalt onto a pair of deep ruts in the snow and underbrush.

"—you're face-to-face with greatness and it's strange—"

Sola cranked around, and the guy took it as having an audience, flexing his biceps and singing to her, every word perfect and on pitch as if he had done this a million times before. ". . . It's nice to see that humans never change . . ."

They began to bounce up and down over divots and dips, the music swelling as big-and-blond sang his heart out. ". . . What can I say except yooou're WELLLCCCOMMMMMME!"

Sola blinked and looked at Ehric—who was bobbing his head to the beat like a dad riding tight in an Odyssey at carpool. As her brain tried to assimilate the *Deadpool*-meets-Disney extremes, it was impossible not to wonder why she kept falling down rabbit holes—although at least this one had a soundtrack she could stand. If it were *Frozen*? She would have killed herself.

Rhage tapped her shoulder like he wanted the attention back. "My kid loves *Moana*. We watch it all the t— What has two thumbs and pulled up the sky?"

When he got to the "this guy," his leather jacket opened and she checked out a matched pair of daggers that were strapped, handles down, to his enormous chest. He had disappeared all their weapons into somewhere, and God only knew what else he was packing under his—

As Ehric slowed to a stop, she glanced out the front windshield and frowned at a decrepit old farm gate that was wing-and-a-prayer'ing it at the job of keeping anyone from heading farther on the lane. Clearly, they were just going to plow through the thing—

The old gate broke apart and moved in two halves out of the way, its structural failings clearly an illusion. And as they continued on, there was soon another . . . and another . . . and still others. With each succeeding barrier, the fortifications became newer and stronger, the ruse of no-security, this-is-nothing-special fading away.

Wonder how many hidden cameras are in those trees? she thought, as they slowed again for a twenty-foot barrier that looked capable of keeping a velociraptor in place.

"Are you guys with the government or something?" she asked.

The guy in the back seat was now busy singing "Can't Stop the Feeling," so he didn't answer, but he probably wouldn't have even if there had been low-level elevator Muzak going on—

Wait . . . something was wrong with the landscape, everything blurry, with the pine trees indistinct vertical blurs and the ground smudged to the point she couldn't pick out the bald bushes or boulders or fallen trunks anymore. Was it fog? Except how was that happening in the dead of winter?

Pulling the sleeve of her heavy fleece over her hand, she rubbed her window, but there was no condensation on the glass. And leaning in closer did not help, either. God, the stuff was so thick, the headlights were illuminating a distance of no more than ten feet ahead. Past that, it was impossible to find any kind of focal point—

Holy Moses.

The last gate was a massive, military-worthy installation of concrete slabs, iron pinnings, and barbed wire. And as soon as they went through it, everything around the SUV became crystal clear again, the descent into an underground tunnel smooth over an asphalt road that had been professionally laid and maintained. Down at the bottom, a multi-level parking area appeared, and Ehric took them over to a reinforced steel door.

Yes, she thought. This was where Assail had taken her after the abduction. This was where she had been treated.

"We are here," Ehric said as he hit the brakes.

Before Sola could unscramble herself from events a year old, the entrance to the facility swung wide, a blond woman in a white doctor's coat bracing the weight open.

Sola recognized the doctor instantly, and that was when the trembling started. What was her name . . . Jo? Jules?

With a shaking hand, Sola opened her door. "Hey, Doc."

The woman smiled. "Hey there, yourself. You're looking well."

Jane, she thought. They called her Doc Jane.

"Thanks." Sola went over and felt an absurd impulse to hug the female as if they were friends. Which they were not. "I feel good."

Liar. As the time she had spent in the clinic came back, she felt her inner Fiona Apple come on, all sorts of deep emotion warping her consciousness in ways she did not appreciate: She remembered arriving here, bloodied, bruised, and with a gunshot wound, Assail by her side. She had been seen by this doctor, assessed medically, and patched up. How long had she stayed? She couldn't recall.

Everyone had been perfectly nice and professional, and all she'd wanted to do was see the last of them.

Doc Jane nodded a greeting at the men and then addressed Sola. "So Ehric's told me you'd like to see Assail?"

"Yes." She cleared her throat. "I don't know how I can help, but . . . that's why I'm here. Yes."

Stammer much?

The doctor put her hand on Sola's arm. "I'm glad you came. Let's go down to him."

As Sola stepped into a long corridor that was wider than a train tunnel, Doc Jane asked, "Tell me, how much do you know about his condition?"

"I know that he is dying."

Ehric joined them. "We're hoping that she will inspire him."

"Miracles can certainly happen," Doc Jane said. "And I am open to anything at this point."

After the blond guy with the Disney tracks came inside, they went forward in a group, their footfalls echoing throughout the concrete hall. The men said a few things, Doc Jane answered, and Sola heard nothing of it. She was too busy looking around, trying to get her bearings, and praying that she kept her shit together when she saw Assail.

He had to be in really bad shape.

They went by many closed doors, none of which had any signage. And at one point, she could have sworn she smelled popcorn, like there was a mess hall or a break room somewhere close, but then the doctor was stopping.

"I want you to be prepared." The woman smiled gently. "He'll know you're here, I promise you. Just talk to him as you would normally, he'll hear you—"

"Wait, he isn't awake?" Sola asked.

Doc Jane glanced at Ehric. "No. He's not conscious."

"Oh."

"Are you ready?"

Sola stared at the door they'd halted in front of. It was such a generic one, the flat metal panel painted a soft gray, and yet her tangled emotions turned it into an obstacle course that was miles long.

Do it, she told herself. *Go on. You drove for a day and a half straight to get here.*

"This is harder than I thought," she heard herself say.

"Do you want some extra time?"

What was really going to change, though? "No. I'm ready."

Doc Jane opened things slowly, and at first, what was up ahead in the small, bare room didn't calibrate. The hospital bed was expected, and so were the beeping machines, but what she saw underneath the thin blankets was not . . .

"Assail," she choked out.

Stumbling forward, she caught her balance just before she fell, and then she simply stood there, unable to move.

If she hadn't been told it was him, she would not have found one . . . feature . . . that was Assail's in the patient lying, bald and shrunken, in that bed. His skin was white as snow, his cheeks hollow, his cracked lips parted as he barely breathed—

As Sola became aware of a pressure on her own mouth, she realized she had put her palm to her face to keep her reaction in.

How had this happened? she thought. How had he gone from being that healthy, strong man . . . to *this*?

Then again, cancer was a fucker.

"Talk to him," Doc Jane prompted quietly, before raising her voice. "Hello, Assail. You have a visitor."

As if he were a hundred years old in a nursing home.

Sola lowered her hand and tried to find something, anything, to say.

"It's still him in there," Doc Jane whispered. "The physical body may seem different, but the soul remains the same."

"Oh, God . . . what do I say?"

"If you were lying there, what would you like to hear?"

I love you. You are not alone. I am not going to leave you. As her heart pounded and she felt sick to her stomach, those three simple sentences went through her mind over and over again. *I love you . . .*

Back when he had been healthy and she had been centered, when time had seemed like a river without beginning or end, it had been so important to keep herself from saying those words. Now? Impending death wiped out all that self-protection and that illusion of choice and free will, giving her a courage she had lacked.

Forcing herself to go around to him, she reached out to take his hand—

Frowning, she looked back. "Why is he restrained?"

"It was for his safety and ours—"

Without warning, Assail's lids popped open and he looked at her— and Sola gasped. His silvery eyes were dilated so wide, there was no color around the pupils, and the sclera was red, as if his skull had filled up with blood and drowned out the white.

As he stared through the pain of his suffering, he began to pant, his hollow chest pumping up and down and his arms rising against the binds that kept them in place.

Sola took his hand and squeezed his cold fingers. "Assail? I've missed you."

His mouth moved as if he wanted to speak, but nothing came out.

Instead, his response was a single crystalline tear that formed in the corner of his eye . . . and dropped silently onto the pillow.

"Assail," she begged. "Can you stay with me? Don't go now. Stay here with me for a little while?"

She had no idea whether he could see out of those eyes, but the doctor was right. He knew it was her. He absolutely knew she had come.

THIRTEEN

"You're hurt, my man."

Instead of responding to Butch's co-dependency, V leaned forward between the front seats of the Hummer. "Yo, Q, this piece of shit go any faster?"

Qhuinn shot a glare over his shoulder. "We're doing seventy in a forty-five. And I just blew through two red lights. This is not the Millennium Falcon—what else do you want."

"Cut through the park up here. Just punch over the curb and plow through the bitch—"

"Next time, you drive. Until then, shut up."

Sitting back, V crossed his arms over his chest and refused to meet the cop's annoyingly steady stare—which was being beamed across the backseat like a laser. Instead, he glared out at the small, chic shops they were tooling by. When his upper arm burned, he repositioned the damn thing, and then had to move it yet again.

So yeah, fine, the cop might have a point, but V wasn't going to see what was doing with his biceps, that was for damn sure.

At least not in front of witnesses. Besides, there was no blood—and the sleeve on his leather jacket wasn't even broken. So what could possibly be wrong under there?

As his cell phone went off, he checked the text and hid a grimace as that arm of his let out another holler. "Wrath is ready for us."

"Everyone's coming in?" Blay asked from the passenger seat up front.

"Yeah, even the Bastards." V put his phone away. "So can you drive faster there, Grandma?"

Qhuinn bared his fangs in the rearview mirror. "Put a patch on, asshole, if you can't handle being without your nicotine."

As Qhuinn turned up the Guns N' Roses, V wanted to lob a fuck-off with plenty of spin on it at the brother, but it was hard to argue with the logic. He was, in fact, pissy because he was jonesing for a cigarette, and by the way, he couldn't wait until Qhuinn got off this rock kick he was on. How about some Bryson Tiller, FFS.

Butch elbowed him in the wound, making him hide a groan. "Take this," the cop said.

As V's vision checkerboarded on him, he grabbed whatever the cop was offering. Wait, Nicorette?

"When did you start this?" V asked as he popped a piece of gum out of its plastic tile.

"About a month ago. I won't smoke in front of Marissa, it's too nasty. But you know, old habits die hard, and lately, I've been stressed the hell out."

V put the square in his mouth and gave his molars a workout. The taste wasn't bad, but it wasn't Wrigley's, either. What mattered was that after a little bit, he did feel considerably less like playing target practice with their driver, true? And yeah, sure, he could have dematerialized to the Audience House, but Butch, as a half-breed, couldn't ghost out, and V never felt right about deserting the guy during transports.

"You got any more of that?" he asked.

"Sure. Take another if you want."

As Butch sent a flat of the things in his direction, V popped every piece out and put it all in his mouth.

"Pay you back," he said around the basketball-sized wad in his mouth.

When Butch didn't reply, he glanced over at his roommate. The guy was staring at him in utter disbelief.

"What."

Butch shook his head slowly. "You are about to fly off the face of this planet, my friend. There's enough nicotine in that to take down an elephant."

"I'll be fine," he muttered as they turned onto a street with mansions on both sides.

Wrath's Audience House was halfway down, the yellow Federal set back on its snowy yard like something out of a catalog for fine china and crystal.

Qhuinn pulled into the drive and went all the way back to the detached, two-story garage. As V got out, he looked at those windows on its second floor and remembered taking the three humans who had tried to kill Ruhn up there. Saxton, the King's solicitor, had more than adequately *ahvenged* his love, something that had been a surprise. Lawyers tended to be better with the pen-across-the-page than the dagger-across-the-throat, but motivation was the key to everything—and thanks to Saxton, those humans had not come down for breakfast, as the cop liked to say.

V had enjoyed his job that night, for real.

Approaching the mansion's rear door, he jumped ahead and held things open for the cop, and Qhuinn and Blay, then the four of them passed through the kitchen and went out to the front of the grand house. Except for some *doggen* vacuuming upstairs, the place had emptied out at the King's command, the civilians rescheduled, the receptionist dismissed.

For what was going to be discussed, there could be no witnesses.

Just as they came into the open foyer, V pared off and hit the loo that males used, locking himself in the one-stall room and stripping off his jacket to see what his arm looked like—

Oh . . . *fuck.*

No reason to lean into the mirror for a closer look. The snake-shaped wound that ran from the top of his left shoulder down past his elbow was the color of a neon bar sign, glowing ruby red in his tan skin.

Naturally, his first impulse was to poke it—okay, *ow.* There was no blood, though, the epidermis not so much broken as singed—like he'd been lashed with a hot chain and gotten a third-degree burn.

Jane should take a look at—

Nope, he corrected himself. Not an option. Besides, he was a medic, he could take care of himself.

Starting the faucet, he grabbed a hand towel and wiped the wound off with some soap and hot water. When he was done, he pulled his jacket back on and checked the sleeve again. The leather was truly intact. So damned weird.

He thought about the interaction with that shadow entity, reviewing its approach, the altercation, the extermination. It was bad that he didn't know what the thing was, but there was something so much worse than the no-familiar.

Much, much worse.

Leaving the bathroom, he went down to where all the conversating was, entering the dining room and picking a place out of the way for a couple of reasons: No, he didn't want to talk about the attack until everyone was here—he was going to do it once and only once. More than that, *no,* he didn't want to explain to anyone else who might have noticed why he and Jane were not holding hands and skipping together wherever they went. And NO, he didn't want any commentary on this bulging wad in his cheek.

So yeah, he far-cornered it and kept to himself.

The dining room was typical Darius, elegant, old school, classy. It was also essentially empty now. Its handmade table, which had been long as a bowling alley and glossy as a mirror, had been moved out, along with dozens of chairs and two sideboards the size of SUVs. The only things left of the former way the house had functioned were the big-as-a-lawn rug and the chandelier, which hung, like a galaxy, in the center of the space.

A couple of armchairs had been angled toward each other in front of the marble fireplace and the desk of the King's solicitor was off to the left. Every night, civilians came and went, taking their time with their leader, seeking blessings for matings and young, judgments on disputes, and guidance about matters small and large. It was the Old Ways in the modern world, Wrath stepping into his father's practice after so many eons of not having any contact at all with those he ruled.

And this meant the Brotherhood and its affiliated fighters were now functioning once again as the King's private guard. Even though the vast majority of males and females who were seen here were perfectly law-abiding, no one was taking chances with Wrath's life. Two of the brothers were always on site with him, with everybody else ready to come at a moment's notice.

When you considered the rotation necessary to give brothers a night off, the fact that the training center needed to be manned, and then all the guarding here? Even with the addition of the Band of Bastards, they were short-staffed covering everything—especially given that the Bastards couldn't guard Wrath by law, and they weren't used in the training program, and the trainees were too green still to be of much use. Add in some injuries?

V thought about that shadow out on the streets and felt a ripple of unease that was about as characteristic of him as the urge to bake bread. Paint by numbers. Crochet.

We need more fighters, he thought. Xhex and Payne were going to have to come in on this.

As he started to mine his brain for more people they could pull into service, Abalone, First Adviser to the King, arrived, and so did Saxton. And then there was a quieting, the heat under the boil of chatter turned down.

When Wrath walked in with George, his seeing-eye dog, the King's looming presence was the sort of thing that changed the energy in the room sure as an electrical storm. But he wasn't alone.

Oh . . . great, V thought. This night kept getting better.

Lassiter, the fallen angel, that male with the silver blood, the sunshine fetish, and the hideous taste in clothes and television, was a grim shadow of his usual jackass-self, his blond and black hair braided down his back, the gold at his throat and wrists the only thing that was glowing on him.

Fuck. He was looking like someone had just broken the news that *RHONJ* had been canceled.

Wrath and George went over to the armchair on the right of the open flames. As the King sat down, the golden retriever curled into a ball at his shitkickers, the dog tucking his muzzle into his long tail.

"So," Wrath said in V's direction. "I hear you met a new friend tonight."

As everyone looked at him, V went to cross his arms over his chest, but thought better of it because of his wound. "I'm not the one who needs to be talking here."

"Passing the buck," Wrath muttered. "Not like you."

"The details of the attack, I can go into," he said. "But they're not the problem. The main issue is . . . it's not the Omega, is it. It is not from the Lessening Society." He focused on Lassiter. "Otherwise, you wouldn't be lookin' like that, would you."

Back at the training center, Jane couldn't believe that Assail was conscious. His eyes did appear to be focused on Sola, however, and he did seem to be listening to the woman, but given those brain scans? Jane was looking for signs that this was reflexive.

The longer he stayed "aware," though, and the more he followed the subtle shifts of Sola's head as she spoke with him, the more the evidence suggested a miracle had in fact happened—and so Jane stepped away from the hospital bed. She didn't go far, however. The violent outbursts could come on without warning, a lesson hard learned, so given this unforeseen and un-assessed change in neurological status, she wasn't taking any chances. God only knew what Assail was capable of.

He definitely seemed to recognize who was with him, though. His eyes were locked on Sola, her mere presence beside him doing what all their medicine had not been able to. She had brought him back— except for how long?

Jane glanced over her shoulder at Ehric, who was standing just inside the door. Guess the cyborg wasn't so removed after all: A sheen of tears was brightening his eyes, the flush of his emotion turning his face red. He had been right to bring the woman here.

He had done the right thing.

Yes, she thought as she turned back to the couple. This was the miracle that love could bring, the soul reaching out of a broken body to connect, perhaps for one last time, to its other half.

I had that once, she thought with a lump in her throat. *I knew that bond . . . I have held that blessing and gift in the center of my chest and it warmed me.*

As sorrow came to her sure as the shadow of death, she told herself to go back to the anger she'd been stewing in since she'd left Vishous on his penthouse's terrace.

Righteous indignation was where she needed to stay. This sadness was dangerous.

A gasp from the bed got her attention—

Just as she looked up, Assail kicked his head back on the pillow and started to seize, his arms jerking against their ties, his legs kicking at their restraints under the blankets.

"Step back," Jane ordered Sola.

As the other woman jumped out of the way, Jane hit the *call* button and lunged for a bite guard, which she forced between Assail's front teeth. The anti-epileptic meds were right by the bed, the needle preloaded with a benzodiazepine, and she grabbed it, and put the drug directly into the IV.

"What we got?" Manny said as he rushed in.

"Just administered the lorazepam." Doc Jane checked the heart rate on the monitor. "It should kick in quick—"

The blood-pressure alarm started going off, indicating a critical drop.

"Everyone out of the room!" she barked.

Ehric didn't have to be asked twice, but Sola shook her head and pressed herself against the wall. "I am not leaving. Do not make me go."

Jane cursed, but didn't argue. She had other things to worry about. "Damn it, he's got a heartbeat so we can't shock him."

"We're going to lose him," Manny muttered as he readjusted the IV drip. "If this keeps up, he's not going to—"

"Give me the epinephrine." She looked at Ehlena, their nurse, who had come in. "Give me the goddamn EpiPen."

As Ehlena went for the handoff, Manny put himself between them. "Jane, you're moving fast here—"

"You think this is trending in a good direction?" She pointed to the monitor with a jab of her forefinger. "He's going to die on us—"

"He can't handle that epi."

"You're wrong. This is what I've done before with him—give me that." Jane ripped the pen out of Ehlena's hold. "I know what I'm doing."

Epinephrine could be administered through the IV line either in a series of pushes or as a continuous infusion with D5W. But she didn't want to throw him back into a seizure, either—and she had been through this with him. Intramuscular was the only safe option when he seesawed back and forth between coma and spasm.

With the EpiPen in her hand, Doc Jane pushed Manny aside, ripped the sheet free, and exposed Assail's withered thigh. With his weight loss, the skin was loose around the shrunken muscles, and she grabbed as much of the thigh meat as she could, pinching up a pad of a target. Then she popped the top using her teeth, drove the pen down, and sent that epinephrine into his system.

Dimly, she recognized a scent in the air. Something like dark spices. But before that could really register, his blood pressure took another dip downward.

She looked at Ehlena. "Give me another pen."

"You're going to kill him," Manny snapped.

She looked directly at her partner. "He's going to die anyway. But I'll be goddamned if I'm going to sit on the sidelines and do nothing about it. Ehlena, get me another pen!"

FOURTEEN

As Vitoria got off the Northway at downtown Caldwell's Third Street exit, she felt her jet lag ease off. The sight of the city's shimmering towers rising so high into the night enlivened her.

Yes, she thought. This was why she had come, this commerce, this population, this just-north-of-Manhattan metropolis that would feed her ambitions, not starve them.

The traffic was light on the roads, given that it was nearly midnight, and after following a series of one-ways, she located the correct avenue and . . . there it was. Her brother's art gallery.

The building took up an entire block, its contours bold and proud, its exterior covered in brushed steel with blackened panes of glass, big as barn doors, set into the walls.

Benloise Art Gallery was spelled out in capital letters backlit by a neon blue glow.

Turning onto a side street just before the gallery, she pulled around to its rear, where signage delineated where the staff parked and deliveries were made. After she killed the rental sedan's engine, she fumbled to get the keys disengaged from their insertion point—and was reminded of how much she despised driving herself. Opening her door, she extended a Gucci stiletto—

Slush, like a cold, oozing hand from the grave, grasped on to her foot, seeping easily through the satin strapping and causing her to glare down at what should have been clean pavement. Instead, the ground cover appeared to be a combination of motor oil, city sludge, and snow that was past its expiration date.

She glanced over at the pair of rear doors, one of which read STAFF ONLY. It seemed a mile away, and she considered re-parking herself closer to it. But no, that was too much work, she decided. Besides, these shoes were from last season. Shifting her other heel, she threw out a hand to steady herself—and landed the bare skin of her palm on the cold exterior steel of the car.

As she recoiled and shook off the burn, a stream of vile Spanish, unfit for her brother's sister, left her lips. The past couple of days, however, had been a trial. She had had to unpack her own clothing; her bed had not smelled fresh; there had been no one to draw her bath this afternoon; and she had had McDonald's for a repast.

At least she had liked the fries.

But she had hated everything else. Her hardscrabble youth was a long-faded memory not just due to time, but circumstance. When one was used to being waited on, transitioning to self-sufficiency, no matter how transitory she intended the state to be, was an unpleasant awakening.

And there had been other problems, too. She had called the gallery to inform them she was coming in, and an annoying woman, Margot Fortescue or some such, had been highly resistant to the idea that things were going to change. The Benloise family was back, however, and yes, although Ricardo and Eduardo's absences had permitted things to run themselves, that time was over now—

The door to the building opened and a large shape filled the jambs. "I didn't think you was gonna show," a male voice said.

"How perfectly articulate of you," Vitoria muttered into the cold.

"Huh?"

Madre de Dios, she thought as she pulled her St. John wool coat closer. Could he be any more stupid?

Then again, one didn't expect ground beef to have an elevated command of the English language—something that had taken her a master's degree to achieve. And she wasn't hiring him for his grammar, was she.

As Vitoria made her way around the car, she picked and chose her footings as if her life depended upon it—and one slip might well be a mortal event given all the ice. Why had she worn these shoes? It was so much colder up here than she had packed for, her Chanel woolen suit and this coat as flimsy as two sheets of tissue paper against the chill.

"You are Streeter, then," she said as she finally arrived at the entrance.

"Yeah."

With the light streaming behind him, it was impossible to see his face. But she approved of the size of his shoulders and the fact that his waist was not that of a heavy drinker. What she didn't appreciate was when he failed to move.

"Are you going to step aside," she demanded.

"Why you here?"

"I told you on the phone. I am Vitoria. This is my brother's business and so it is mine."

"He didn't tell me you was coming. He ain't told no one nothing for a while now."

"Get out of my way," she snapped. "We have business to discuss—unless you're making too much money currently to know how to spend it all."

Streeter didn't hesitate for long. And he complied because that was what men like him did. They were like backhoes, in this regard: power in need of direction, motivated by cash. Left to his own devices, as he no doubt had been since Ricardo or Eduardo had last called him into service, he was liable to have devolved into an inanimate object that was having trouble covering his bills.

As she entered, he shut the door behind them, and she looked around. The back of the gallery was much as she expected, a high-ceiling'd space with exposed electricals and ductwork that hung like stalactites from open metal rafters. Larger installations awaiting their time out where the patrons milled about were like passengers lined up to board a bus, some in packing crates, others draped with cloth. Cubicles for minions were arranged between filing cabinets, the office equipment and silent phones sleeping on the off time. A break area with a table, coffee maker, microwave, and mini-refrigerator was to one side.

Streeter locked them in together. "How'd you get my number?"

"I know all of my brother's employees." Or rather, she had remote-accessed the gallery's server about three months before and gotten the information then. "And how to reach them."

The man came into the light and crossed thick arms over his chest. His nose had been broken a couple of times and his skin was marked with acne scars.

Disappointing, really. His body contours had suggested their association might have been multi-layered.

"You will take me to my brother's office, where we will discuss your employment."

"I get a paycheck just fine from UPS."

"And you are satisfied with your standard of living? Possess all that you would choose to own?"

There was only a brief pause, during which he no doubt considered the specifications of the latest American muscle car. "Mr. Benloise's office is upstairs. But it's locked and I don't know the code. Nobody been there since he dint come in no more."

"Lead the way," she said dryly. "I will have no trouble getting in."

After entering the gallery space, they crossed over to an unmarked door which revealed a set of stairs that were unmarked and uncarpeted, little more than a steel ladder painted black. As they ascended, with him in the lead, she noted that the walls on either side were likewise matte black and the motion-activated lights that came on were inset into a ceiling that was the same.

At the top, she put her body between the keypad and Streeter, and entered her mother's birth date. As the lock slid free, she shot a glare over her shoulder.

"My brother would not appreciate the way you are looking at my legs. I am also armed and a very good shot. You can get rich or get buried. Tell me, what is your choice."

Before he could move, she outed the nine she kept hidden in her coat and shoved it right into the man's crotch.

As Streeter gasped and defensively went to grab the weapon, she took out her second nine and placed it to his throat.

"Do not doubt me. Ever," she said. "I have no attachment to you whatsoever. You live or die, it matters not to me. If you are useful, however, you will benefit greatly."

There was a tense silence. And then Streeter muttered, "You are so his sister."

"Did the dark hair and eyes not give me away?" she drawled. "People back home always say that Ricardo and I have the same-shaped face, too. Now apologize."

"I . . . I'm sorry."

She gave him a moment to truly absorb his reality. And then she stepped away and pulled open the door. As she entered her brother's office, lights came on sequentially, illuminating a long, thin chute of a space . . . that culminated in a raised platform upon which a grand desk had been placed like a jewel box upon a bureau.

There were no computers. No files. No clutter upon the smooth expanse. Just a lamp and an ashtray for her brother's cigars. And two chairs only, Ricardo's and that of a visitor.

On the approach, sadness choked her, images of her and her brothers coming one after the other, from their shared childhoods and then later, when they had been adults. Ricardo had always been the one she respected, much as his dictates had smothered her. Eduardo had been fun, however, a buffer between her and their eldest's clashes.

Gone. All gone. And with their presumed passing, she had lost a bit of herself, as well.

But that would not stop her.

Stepping up onto the platform, she turned to Streeter and leaned her weight back against the desk. "There are employment reports filed on all of you. My brother Ricardo was quite meticulous about these things." And this was true for the real employees and the hired thugs. "Yours were quite exemplary. That is why I contacted you, as I am looking for a personal guard and will pay well for it."

"What are we talking about for cash."

"I will pay three times what you were earning with Ricardo."

"I'm in."

"Good."

Vitoria smiled and glanced around the barren room. Then she focused on him. "Now, tell me, what do you think happened to my brothers."

"It's the bonding."

As the Brother Rhage spoke up, Ehric looked across the training center's corridor. The pair of them were outside Assail's room—and he was trying to ignore the arguing he could hear through the closed door. "What?"

"That scent. Can you smell it? I can. It's his bonding for that woman—good call bringing her in."

"We'll see how successful it is."

With a curse, Ehric paced up and down, but didn't go far. The healers were still having an angry exchange and he wondered what in Fate's name was being done to his cousin.

The Brother tapped the outside of his perfectly straight, perfectly proportioned nose. "Nah, when she came into the room, it woke him up. She did what nothing else could."

"She sent him into a death rattle is more like it." Ehric rubbed his eyes. "I had thought she might revive him with less trauma."

"Love will bring him through. And then it'll all be cool."

"Your optimism is not something I share. And even if it does work, she will have to return to Florida."

"Why?"

"She does not know."

"That he lives here? I don't get it. I thought she was—"

"What he is." Ehric looked back at the Brother. "She does not know he is a vampire."

Rhage frowned. "That's not necessarily a deal breaker. My Mary didn't know what I was and it worked out—well, it took a miracle. But they do happen."

"'Tis all a moot point, if he dies the now—"

The door opened and Dr. Manello came striding out. "It worked. I can't believe it, but it worked. For the moment, he's back to being stable."

Ehric all but jumped into that hospital room, except then he stopped dead. Indeed, his version of "it worked" was his cousin sitting up and asking for some pudding. Manello's idea was clearly more along the line of a heartbeat and some respiration, and yes, one could put paid to that: Assail was lying back on that pillow, still tied down, still the color of the white sheets, still with his eyes closed.

But he was breathing on his own and that little graph of regular beeps suggested his heart was doing its job correctly. Or at least correctly enough so no alarms went off.

Doc Jane and the nurse were at Assail's head, talking quickly, nodding and pointing to the machine readouts while they traded syringes.

Ehric looked at Marisol. The human woman was all the way in the far corner, her body shrunken in on itself, her eyes so wide she was nearly an anime version of herself.

He went over to her. "What may I get you?"

After a moment, her stare shifted to his face.

Something passed between them, something unspoken and powerful. And the next thing he knew he was opening his arms and she was in them like a sister.

"I don't understand," she said as she turned her face toward Assail. "This happened so fast. How much longer can he hold on?"

"I don't know. I believe no one knows that. And let us not speak of it the now or here."

"You're right." She pulled back a little. "I'm glad you came down and told me. I'm glad I'm here for him, for however long he has."

Ehric nodded. "My cousin picked the right female."

Marisol grabbed his arm and squeezed. "I'm not leaving. Not until it's over. Just so you know."

Ehric sagged in his own skin. "Thank you."

Doc Jane came over and nodded to the door. "Let's talk out there, okay?"

Ehric went across and held the way open. As the females filed past him, he glanced back at the nurse, who was adjusting something on one of the monitors. Then he focused on his cousin. Assail had always seemed indomitable, the sort of male who was so controlled and had such strength of purpose that whole armies might well fall before him, not because he was royalty, but because he would will it no other way.

And now there was naught left of him save a balded shell.

So this was the evil that death wrought, Ehric thought. It was the ultimate emasculator, rendering even one such as his cousin into a decayed shadow of what he had been, the essence departed with rind left to rot.

I shall take myself before I e'er allow this, Ehric thought. *To hell with the Fade.*

He would go unto *Dhunhd* before he conscripted himself to disintegrate until his heart stopped. Or better yet he would die with honor, protecting those he loved in battle—which now numbered three, he realized: Evale, Assail . . . and this human woman.

For loyalty shown unto his blood was loyalty earned.

As he joined the females, Doc Jane cleared her throat. "There's no easy way to say this. But in spite of his brief return to consciousness, nothing really has changed. I'm not suggesting you take action tonight"—the doctor put her palms out toward him—"I just want to align your expectations. With the scans as they are, it is impossible—"

"He looked at me," Marisol said in a steely tone. "He looked right at me."

"Or he opened his eyes," Doc Jane countered gently.

"No. You're wrong." Marisol went back to the door. "I'm going in there. Don't bother saying anything else to me. I know he saw me."

As the woman disappeared back into the room, Ehric had to smile. "He chose someone just like himself. She will not take no for an answer, Healer."

Doc Jane shook her head sadly. "It's not up to her, unfortunately. And I fear his body and brain have already made their decision."

Ehric thought about all the time he had spent in this underground facility, all the nights, even some days, too. As much as he wanted to believe otherwise, he knew the doctor was right.

"I have brought her up here to say goodbye, then."

Doc Jane put her hand on his forearm. "I'm really sorry about this."

In an inexorable advance, exhaustion curled like a boa constrictor around his body, squeezing, squeezing, squeezing his breath and energy from him. "This is a nightmare, the ending of which is the only thing worse than its middle."

"I wish I could have done more," the healer said. "Just don't feel rushed, okay? You and Sola and Evale take your time. We're keeping him as comfortable as we can."

Ehric looked over at the door. "I will not allow this to continue forever."

FIFTEEN

$\mathcal{M}$arisol . . . *Marisol!*

As Assail screamed the name of his female in his head, he floated above his body, sure as if his consciousness were a separate entity from its corporeal confines, a kite of self aloft in existential winds, tethered unto the flesh by an invisible string—that was held in his Marisol's hand.

Her presence was what had pulled him back down here, to this hospital room in which he had watched over his body for how long? Her arrival here, unexpected, joyous, a miracle, had been a calling siren he had followed back from the foggy netherworld he had been transitioning into.

Marisol! he said again.

He was directly above her, hovering like a thought yet to be spoken. Why could she not hear him?

As he tried again, she lowered a hip upon the high mattress and brushed a tear from her own eye.

Do not give up on me, he told her. *For you, I will come back . . . do not let them kill me.*

When she started to cry in earnest, he smelled the tears and shifted around such that he could watch her. He wanted to have arms to hold her, a chest to pull her in against, a body to protect her and serve her with.

Instead, he was nothing but spirit.

"Oh, God, Assail . . ." She sniffed and took one of his tethered hands in her own. "I wish I had known. I would have come sooner. Is that why you were calling me? Why didn't you talk to me when I answered? Why didn't you tell me?"

Reaching out, he brushed her cheek—

Marisol jerked her head up and looked directly at his ethereal self. But then she shook her head as if to clear it and refocused on those parts of him that were in the hospital bed.

"I would have come right away."

How did he get back in there, he thought. His body was like a house he was locked out of, and no matter how much he wanted in, he couldn't get through the door.

"I have missed you so much." She leaned forward and snapped a tissue free from a box, pressing it against her own cheeks. "I have been down there in Miami, staring at the bay at night . . . wishing you were with me. I didn't expect you in my life. I never expected . . . you."

Marisol, he moaned.

"I should have told you before now, I should have said something . . . but I was afraid to. I've never . . ." She cleared her throat. "I never thought I would feel like I do . . . it just wasn't supposed to be this way for me."

As her thumb rubbed slowly back and forth on his hand, the stroking resonated through him and he tried to feel every nuance, and use the sensations as an entry point.

"People like you and me, we don't have happy endings with picket fences and dogs and kids." She breathed in deep. "That is never the future for us. Still, if it had been just me, I maybe could have stayed after Benloise was killed. I might have been able to—but my grandmother must come first. I can't risk myself because without me, she has nothing—and I have to take care of her."

I understand, he said to her. *But she was always welcome to be with us. I would never have asked you to choose, and I would have taken care of you both.*

"You took off before I could say goodbye to you. That night she and I left, I looked for you in the house, but you . . . you'd left."

Untrue. He had hidden in the shadows behind his house and witnessed her departure in private. He had not trusted himself not to beg, and even though it had been agony, he respected that she had her own course to choose and steer.

But it had destroyed a part of him to see her go.

As she continued to murmur to him, and tell him about her condo down in Miami, and her grandmother, and the Catholic church they attended, he kept trying to will himself back into that body of his . . . to animate that flesh . . . to gain access once again. Pushing, pushing, pushing, he sought to regain entrance into that form that had clothed his soul.

He had never understood that there were two parts to the living.

And only one part to the dead.

He did the now.

Yet the harder he tried, the angrier he became, and that seemed to work against his efforts. With his temper rising, he could feel less of Marisol's touch, smell less of her scent, hear less of her voice.

". . . prayed for us." Marisol smiled sadly. "Can you believe that? My grandmother, she prayed to God that we would be reunited, and then your cousins came to me."

Bracing himself, Assail marshaled every resource he had, his vantage point shifting until he was face-to-face with himself, his closed eyes and shaved scalp and pale complexion horrible reminders that any physical attractiveness he might have had was now gone.

Now! he ordered himself. *I must return now!*

But there was too much resistance. It was as if a force field surrounded his flesh, and the harder he pushed against it, the stronger it became. There was pain, too, as he threw himself metaphysically at the barrier over and over again, an electrical shock as if the effort were causing static friction.

Eventually, he lost the energy to keep going and drifted back.

This is not to be, he realized. *This is not—*

"So I should have told you this before," she whispered. "But . . . I was afraid. I didn't trust you, I didn't trust myself . . . sometimes I wonder how much of my leaving Caldwell was really about you . . ."

What, he asked. *What are you to tell me?*

"I love you, Assail. I love you with all that I am and all I will ever be, and if you die tonight or tomorrow or the night after, I just want you to know that you will always be with me. Right . . . here."

And then it happened.

As she touched her heart, a marvelous peace overcame him, and instead of fighting his way back into his earthly home, he moved as a light breeze into the spaces between his cells, filling up that which had been emptied, enlivening that which had been on the verge of demise . . .

The croaking sound was so soft, Sola wasn't sure she had heard anything— or maybe she had made the sound? There was so much pressure in her chest and constriction in her throat that her every inhale and exhale was an effort.

"I love you," she said again—because as sad as this situation was, it felt good to let the secret she'd kept out—

Click—cough.

Sola recoiled. "Assail?"

Those eyes of his were open once again, the red and black depths at once scaring and reassuring her.

"Are you back?" she said, leaning up to him.

She brushed her free hand over his forehead, as if his once thick and beautiful black hair still existed. "Hi."

Her voice was wavering and her body was shaking, but she didn't care. He was with her for this split second—and she knew without medical advice that this could be over at any moment.

"I'm right here."

Click . . . click . . .

He was trying to communicate, his tongue moving in his dry mouth.

"Shh." She smiled at him—in what she hoped was a halfway normal fashion. In reality, she was bracing herself for another seizure, and a rush of medical people coming into the room, and a horrific sorrow that it was all over.

"No, don't try to talk. There'll be time for that. You have all the time in the world."

As she spoke the lie, it was for the both of them. Otherwise, she would be bursting into tears—

His hand jerked in hers, and she squeezed it harder. "I'm right here."

She stroked his face. Pressed her lips to his forehead. Smoothed his brows.

"Stay with me," she said tightly. "Please don't leave me . . ."

Assail started shaking his head, yet his eyes were sticking with her and no alarms were going off—so it was not a seizure. No, he was communicating with her, she realized.

"You're going to stay?" she whispered.

When he nodded, she started to cry, her tears falling on his cheeks. "Good. That's good . . ." Sola smiled. "I've missed you."

Staring into his face, it didn't matter that he'd lost his hair, or that his eyes weren't right. It didn't matter that he was in a hospital bed and his body had shrunk to half its size.

Love transformed him back into the man she knew.

To her, he was beautiful no matter what he looked like.

SIXTEEN

"It is not for me to say."

As Lassiter let that no-comment fly, Vishous considered the merits of pulling a haymaker on the fallen angel in front of everyone and their uncle.

On the fuck-yes side: The Audience House's dining room was definitely big enough for V to get a good running start at it; Lassiter more than deserved a punter for lesser infractions ranging from hogging the remote to those zebra-print, David Lee Roth–from-1985-wants-his-pants-back leggings; and, as V was the son of a deity, there was a chance that he would survive the retaliation that would inevitably come to him.

Not-so-hot-idea side: Wrath was probably not going to appreciate this meeting devolving into a cage match; Lassiter had tricks up his sleeve that would hurt like a motherfucker; and it wasn't going to get that angel's mouth flapping.

If he didn't want to say shit about those shadows, nothing was going to open that piehole of his.

"What's that supposed to mean?" V demanded around the wad of Nicorette in his mouth. "Do you know what the fuck they are or not?"

As the Brotherhood and the Bastards went Wimbledon on the situation, all heads swinging back to Lassiter as if they were waiting for a line-drive response to that lob, Vishous looked over at Wrath. The King's brows were down behind those black wraparounds, his massive body overflowing that armchair like he was an adult in an infant's car seat.

Hard to read where the brother was with this sitch. Maybe he was pissed off. Maybe he had gas. More likely, he was waiting to see what happened next.

But yeah, no, there wasn't any V-beat-his-ass-for-me vibe coming off him.

Goddamn it.

Refocusing on Lassiter, V drawled, "Come on, angel, tell us what you know."

Lassiter shook his head, his bizarrely beautiful eyes steady as an anchor at the bottom of the sea. "I cannot interfere in this. It is not my business to change any course before you."

V chewed harder and recognized that yes, a monster buzz was coming on. Either that or he was stroking out from frustration. "Why are you trying to sound like fucking Morpheus. Flo from Progressive is more your style."

"Enough," Wrath snapped. "V, tell us what happened."

As V started talking, he narrowed his eyes on the angel, challenging him to step in. "Butch and I were working our territory. An entity came from out of nowhere and attacked us. It was a black form, elastic, capable of extending portions of itself like it was rubber, but hard as steel when it hit you. It was also armed with a pair of conventional knives."

"Were you injured?" Wrath asked.

"Nope. Not at all." As Butch coughed at the lie, V kept right on going. "I killed it—or destroyed it, whatever—by shooting point-blank at the entity. The thing squealed like a motherfucker—then it was gone. No residue. No smell. No . . . nothing." He paused. "Anything you'd like to add, angel?"

Lassiter showed no reaction at all. He just stood there in the corner, away from all the fighters, the glow of the gold on him giving him a halo that made V uneasy.

Something was going on here.

"If you're not going to contribute anything," V snapped at the SOB, "then why are you here."

"Shut up, Vishous." Wrath's black sunglasses swung around the room. "I'm not going to ask if anyone else has seen this shit. I'm damn sure it would have come up in conversation. Clearly, the Omega has a new weapon."

"I don't know that it's the Omega." V winced as he got a hand-rolled out of his pocket and his biceps bitched about it. "Maybe something else is at play here."

"Based on what?"

As V lit the end with his Bic, it was hard to inhale around the Nicorette, but he managed. "Didn't smell like a *lesser*. Didn't read like the Omega—I can sense that evil. Butch can, too. The telltales just weren't there."

"I don't know what it was," the cop said. "But at least you could shoot it."

"I say we double up on guns," Tohr interjected from next to Wrath. "We need to load everyone up with extra munitions."

"Too bad Assail's down for the count," someone muttered. "That shit he got us was sweet."

"Can we find out who his contacts were?" somebody else asked.

"Those cousins of his must know—"

"There was one other thing." As all eyes returned to him, V exhaled. "There was someone in the area right before the attack. Ain't that right, Xcor."

Xcor, who was standing with his boys, bowed to the King. "My former second in command, Throe. He was there."

"What the fuck are you talking about?" Wrath demanded.

"I smelled cologne in the alley the thing came from." V shrugged. "And the scent of a male. Xcor came when I called and ID'd him."

There was a bunch of frickin' chatter at that point, which Wrath put to rest by whistling through his two front teeth loud enough to make the chandelier twinkle.

"Xcor," the King said, "your boy have any access to special tricks? Anything we need to know about him?"

"He was, and I believe will remain, an aristocrat," the Bastard replied. "So other than social manners he did not require during his tenure with us, he has no special skills that we did not teach him."

"So it was a coincidence," Tohr said. "Throe just happened to be in that part of town?"

"Maybe he's doing drugs," someone said.

V just kept on staring at Lassiter. Something wasn't adding up.

And not just about Xcor's little friend and that dark shadow.

As a wave of trippy dizziness hit him, he shook his head to clear it— and then looked down at the hand-rolled. Chewed a little more on the basketball between his molars.

And wondered exactly how much nicotine he had in his system.

Time to add some alcohol, he decided. The second this meeting was over he was going to tamp down this head rush with some Goose and enjoy some good-night-Gracie.

What he wasn't going to do was go back to the Pit and see how much Jane was not there.

Nope. That simply didn't bear thinking about.

The patient room Jane had been using as a crash pad was a generic one for non-criticals. The bed was standard-issue hospital stuff, with an inclinable head and liftable foot, and every time she laid down on it, she was reminded that they probably should upgrade their sheets and pillows.

As she closed herself in, she ran out of gas and stood there like a dummy, staring at the wrinkled covers. All things considered, she had worked this perfectly, her exhaustion such that the instant she got prone, she should pass out. There was only one problem. Every time she closed her eyes, she saw Sola and Assail's love for each other, and she had a feeling those memories might just win over passing out.

Heading into the bathroom, she didn't turn the light on because she did not want to see herself in the mirror. Hot water, not her reflection, was what she was after, and she leaned into the narrow shower stall and got the spray rolling.

Her Crocs were happy to be kicked off. Socks were stripped. Then her scrubs hit the floor. Even though all of that took a minute and a half, it felt like an hour until she was under the warm rush, tilting her head back and getting her hair wet.

So yes, ghosts did take showers. If they wanted to—and sometimes it felt good to pretend she was normal . . . to make like she had to wash her hair for it to look good, had to clean her body, had to exfoliate, for godsakes.

There was a reason for rituals. When you were lost in your own life, they provided a false structure, like paper walls for your house of cards, the illusion that things were predictable and safe sometimes the only thing that got you through.

Grabbing the Biolage, she got too aggressive with her squeeze and ended up with a palmful of shampoo, but she wasn't going to waste it.

Not like doing this at all wasn't a waste in the first place—

As she slapped the load on the top of her head, the knock on the outside door was loud enough so she could hear it over the falling water. "Yes?" she called out.

"He's awake again," Ehlena answered.

Jane pulled the curtain back and stuck her head around. "Assail is back?"

The nurse leaned into the room and smiled. "He is! And he's not having a seizure. He's taking water."

Jane pushed dripping suds back into her hairline. "I'm sorry . . . what?"

"You heard me. Through a straw."

"Oh, my God, that's fantastic—but do not remove the restraints. We've got a long way to go. I'm coming right out—"

"No, it's fine." Ehlena swept a chill-out hand through the air. "Take your time, I'll let you know if there's an emergency—"

"They need me—"

"Jane. It's fine. I'll come and get you if anything happens. Enjoy your shower."

Jane closed the curtain sharply and started to rinse the shampoo. "I just need a minute!"

Jumping back out, she rushed to dry off and get her clothes on again, nearly leaving without putting on her socks-and-Crocs. Running down the hall, she—

Pulled up short.

Manny was standing outside of Assail's patient room with Ehlena. But he wasn't smiling.

"What's wrong?" Jane asked. "Is he arresting? Let me see—"

"No." Manny stepped into her way. "You don't need to go in there right now."

Jane frowned. "I'm sorry?"

"You and I are going to take a little walk. Ehlena is going to stay here and monitor things. If we're needed, she'll come get us."

"What is this about?" Jane looked back and forth between them. Then shook her head. "Whatever, I'm just going to check on—"

Manny put a hand on her arm. "I've checked everything. He's conscious. His vitals are stable, if a little on the low side, and he's still restrained. There is no reason for you to go in there. You'll only be interrupting them."

Jane opened her mouth. Closed it with a grind. "I don't see what the problem is."

"And that is precisely why you and I are going to talk."

Manny steered her in a circle and led her away from the clinic—and with each step, the compulsive need to go into that patient room and just . . . *do something* . . . made her want to scream.

"This is ridiculous." She glared at her partner. "I mean, what is this, an intervention?"

"Yeah, as a matter of fact, it is."

As she faltered, he swept her along, forcing her to keep up or get dragged. And then they were all the way down by the pool, Manny opening the way into the humidity and warmth. He let her go first, and she was so pissed off, she walked ahead with hard footfalls, crossing over the tiled anteroom and entering the pool proper with its lofty ceiling and Olympic-sized lanes.

She wheeled around on him. "Are you saying there is something wrong with my patient care? I'm a goddamn good doctor and an even better surgeon. You have nothing to complain about—"

"There is no nice way to say this, Jane."

"What the hell are you—"

"You've lost your objectivity." He put his hands on his lean hips, his handsome face serious. "You're down here too much—you've worked yourself into a state past exhaustion, and sooner or later, you are going to make a mistake."

For a moment, all she could do was stare at the man like he was a stranger. And yet he wasn't one. He was still the big, tall, dark-haired guy she had been in the trenches with for years, Hawkeye to her Hunnicutt.

"I cannot believe I'm hearing this from you," she snapped. "You're working all the time, too."

"I take breaks. I sleep with my wife. I see her every day—"

"Do *not* make this about Vishous. Don't you dare turn this into a personal issue—"

"It *is* a personal issue, Jane. As well as a professional one."

"Whatever, I am doing important, necessary work here. I give everything to my patients and you know it—"

"You're giving too much. That's the problem." He put his hand up when she went to cut him off. "No, you're going to listen to me. And then when I'm through, you can tell me to fuck off, if you want. But you're going to shut up and hear me out."

"I don't believe this," she muttered.

"Believe it. And do you honestly think you're the first physician I've had this conversation with? Huh? Really? I was departmental chair at St. Francis before I came here. I've gone the rounds in this ring with a shit ton of people like you and me. You need to take some time off before you make a bad call and never forgive yourself."

Jane went to run a hand through her hair and discovered it was wet from the shower. Probably still had some suds in it. Who cared. "Listen, we are short-staffed and you know it. It's only you and me and Ehlena. The Brotherhood and the fighters can get hurt at any time—"

"And that's what they make phones for. Jane, I'm telling you, as a friend and a partner, that you need some perspective. And then maybe you and Vishous can finally—"

"Wait, hold up here." She leaned forward with anger. "Did he call you and ask you to do this? Because that is *bullshit*, Manny. Don't you dare take his side in this out of some kind of guy code—"

"Side? I'm not taking anyone's side—"

"Did he tell you he cheated on me? Huh? Did that come up?"

Manny recoiled. "Jesus, Jane."

"Guess he neglected to mention that, huh."

"Vishous and I haven't talked about this—"

"Whatever, you men always stick together. I just expected more from you after everything we've been through together."

Manny looked away, to the aquamarine water that was still. When he refocused on her, his face was cold and his eyes were flat. "You know what, we're done talking, you and I."

"Good. Can I go back to work now, *sir*?"

"No, you can't."

"Excuse me?" Jane cocked an eyebrow at him. "You're not in charge. I was here before you."

"Wrath is in charge. And unless you take twenty-four hours off, I am prepared to go to him and tell him that in my professional opinion, you are unfit to function as a physician at this time. Your choice, and make it now. Either you leave or I have you removed."

"I have done nothing wrong!"

"Maybe in your opinion, but I am not comfortable with how fast you moved in there with Assail. You were flying around that room, grabbing syringes and using them without checking—"

"I filled those myself! I knew what was in them!"

"There is a reason we double-check things. What if Ehlena or I had switched them out for something else."

"But you didn't!"

"How did you know that?" Manny also leaned forward on his hips. "You and I run this place together, and we have to be each other's oversight. There's no Patient Care Assessment Committee checking on outcomes, no hospital Board of Trustees we're accountable to, no Joint Commission coming to inspect us and make sure we have, and are observing, best practices. It's you and it's me, and we need to police ourselves."

"Ehlena doesn't have a problem with me."

"Who do you think raised this in the first place."

Jane shook her head and stared at the tile, tracing the pale blue and black pattern. Then she started to walk away.

"Fine," she said over her shoulder. "You want this place to yourselves, have at it, genius."

SEVENTEEN

After Streeter left the art gallery, Vitoria locked herself inside and went to her brother Eduardo's first-floor office. She didn't have to ask which one it was. It had a gold-leafed door.

As she went to enter the code that had worked on everything else, she worried it would not function here. Eduardo had had his own ways of doing things—but she needn't have worried. This was, after all, Ricardo's establishment, and therefore he would expect to be able to get into every space under its roof.

Also, at the end of the day, their younger sibling had always done what he was told.

Opening the door, she walked into the pitch-black room, and instantly, lights flared from brass sconces.

"Oh, Eduardo."

No minimalism here. No, it was Versace everything, lush with animal prints and gold accents, the desk like something a French royal would have had made in the eighteenth century. And talk about your messes, although not because the office had been sacked. Eduardo had been obsessive only about math and money, not neatness: There were papers everywhere. An adding machine with tape drooling out of its printer onto the floor. Three phones, cockeyed with one another. Pens here and there. A coffee mug with an inch of dehydrated stain at the bottom.

The modern padded leather chair that Eduardo had sat in was turned about and facing the exit, as if he had bolted up and left the room in a hurry. Or perhaps risen with alarm due to an intrusion.

No windows. No closet. Air that was so musty, she wanted to sneeze.

Heading around, she braced herself as she looked at the floor behind the desk. No body there, however—and someone would have smelled that a year ago, anyway.

She had almost expected to find him here.

When her two brothers had gone into business together, they had been a poor pairing on paper, the elder so disciplined and decisive, the younger so flashy and exuberant. The only thing they had in common was trust born out of familial connection—which was necessary in a line of work wherein the legitimate law could not be used to govern interactions and contractual arrangements. Still, there were limits to brotherly love.

In truth, when Ricardo had first disappeared, she had wondered if the brothers' relationship hadn't concluded in the old way, with a grave.

But now? With Eduardo's office so obviously untouched and looking like he had left in a hurry, perhaps called to aid? It seemed more likely they had both been killed by someone else.

Or someones.

Sitting down in that soft chair, she stared over the year-old receipts, the bills . . . the notes written in a leather journal that was lying faceup, a whore with her privacy exposed.

Oh, yes, Vitoria thought as she picked the thing up. This was what she was looking for.

Everything scribbled in the little book was in a Spanish dialect shorthand that she recognized from their youth. Smart. It would require a native speaker who excelled at codes to decipher it.

And what did you know, Eduardo, greedy as he was, kept precise notations on things, both the drug deals and—guns, too? Interestingly, they had diversified into arms.

Profitable. Smart.

She turned another page. And another. And another, going backward from the last entry. There was nothing about art; then again, that was the front of the house's operation, the ruse for the rest, so all those deals were processed and accounted for properly by trained staff with adequate transparency. She had seen the reports herself when she had gotten server access.

Ricardo had set all that up so well, the business had functioned without him for the last twelve months—

Oh, good man, she thought. Eduardo included names in here and numbers of contacts on both sides of the table. As well as pricing and delivery locations. This was perfect—yes, there had been a lapse in supply, but there was no reason to think competitive pricing for cocaine and heroin couldn't bring back customers who had once been loyal.

The laws of a free market economy applied to the drug trade, after all.

Going back to that final entry, she reread the notation about a delivery on the river to someone named . . . Assayl . . . ? Must be misspelled. That name certainly appeared often, however.

It would seem logical to start with whoever that was and see if it led anywhere. If that was the last meeting? Maybe Assayl was the killer

Or perhaps another "client."

During her meeting with Streeter, the man had maintained he knew little about her brothers' disappearance, and she believed him. Considering the kind of people Ricardo had done business with, both on the abroad side for the importers, and the U.S. contingency for distribution, it was wholly conceivable that her kin had been disposed of in such a discreet way that nobody would find the bodies. But the lack of a message was odd. Typically, there would have been something sent to the family back in South America, a photograph of the bodies, a gruesome memento.

A threat that the trail should be left to grow cold or further unpleasantness would ensue.

Yet there had been nothing sent to her. And as neither of her brothers had ever married, she was their next of kin.

Looking up at the ceiling, she imagined her brothers working here, Ricardo on top, figuratively and literally, doing the strategy and the deals on the second floor, Eduardo tallying everything down below in his Studio 54–meets–Neiman Marcus cave.

And then something had interrupted the flow.

What, though—

As her new burner cell phone rang in her coat, she took it out. "Streeter."

"How'd you know it was me?"

"You are the only person to whom I have provided this number. Have you forgotten something?"

"Yeah. I dint think of it till I got home. I had this friend of mine. He worked for your brothers, too. His name was Two-Tone 'cuz he had this birthmark on half his face. 'Bout the time your brothers got gone, he and me was out and he said he was leaving on assignment the next day. He never come back."

"Tell me more," she murmured, sitting forward.

"He said he was takin' care of someone. You know. Takin' care."

"Where? Here in Caldwell? Or at the West Point house property?"

"No. Somewhere's else. He said he was goin' outta town, up north someplace."

"Can you remember an exact day?"

"It was like, the week of my birthday. That's why we was out."

As the man worked on a precise date by drawing all kinds of complex mental notes on an imaginary calendar, Vitoria kept track of the numbers as she waited for the tally to be completed.

"Yeah, I remember now," Streeter concluded. "It were that Wednesday."

And look at this, she thought. The final entry in the middle of the journal was the day after.

"What else can you tell me?"

"That's all I got."

"Do you have access to your friend's abode?"

"His what? Hey, I don't go like that—"

"House," she snapped. "Can you get into his house?"

"Yeah."

Although she didn't know why she was bothering to ask. So much time had passed.

"Go there. See if you can find anything. I want to know where he went and with whom."

As she ended the call, she glanced around at the desk. She was going to have to go through every sheet of paper here—and also at the mansion. Ricardo had had a lot of files there, all handwritten in Spanish as if he didn't trust computers very much.

Her brothers' secrets were going to be her own.

'Lo, the best-laid plans of mice and vampires.

Vishous was distracted and buzzing out of his skin as he walked into the Pit. Somewhere between him resolving not to end up here and the meeting at Wrath's Audience House breaking up, he'd been tasked with doing a search on social media for any mentions of shadows jumping out of alleys and attacking people.

Not the kind of thing he could do easily on his phone.

As he shut the door behind himself, he listened to all the quiet and thought . . . God, the place was so empty. And as he went forward into the living area, everything was so neat, no duffel bags crowding the base of the foosball table, no medical journals facedown in mid-article on the couch, no open boxes of cereal on the counter of the galley kitchen.

Fritz had obviously been by. But more than that, no one had really been living in the living room. With Jane and him both avoiding the place, and Butch and Marissa happiest when they were in their bedroom together, there wasn't much going on to mess shit up.

Shrugging out of his leather jacket, he grimaced and ignored his aching arm as he went to his liquor cabinet by the kitchen sink and pulled out a nice big Goose. Popping the top off the vodka, he drank from the open bottle—

The coughing fit left him with drool down the front of his muscle shirt.

Nicorette didn't mix with liquor. Go figure.

As he spit the fist-sized wad of gum out of his mouth, however, he decided that that was more a space issue.

Yup, this time, as he took a pull, everything went as planned, the vodka heading down into his gut smoothly, his other addiction taking the wheel.

Going over to his computers, he took off his weapons and his damp shirt. Then he sat down and signed in to three of his Four Toys. Security-cam feeds popped up on one monitor, the Internet on another, and a blog he had been following on the third.

Damn Stoker hadn't been posting much on her site—which was the outcome V had engineered, to quote Rhage.

After Vishous had wiped Miss Jo Early's feeds of all the vampire links she had been putting up and commenting on, and then scrubbed her short-term memory, that little threat had been neutralized. Sort of. He and that woman were probably going to have to cross paths again. She was about to have a big problem in her life, and he hadn't decided how to handle it yet. He'd wanted to bring the trouble up to Wrath, but then this shit with Jane had hit and . . .

Whatever. Jo Early was about to learn firsthand why she was so fucking interested in vampires, and he supposed he hadn't mentioned it to anybody because he was still debating whether or not to get involved.

Miss Early was a half-breed, the product of a human and a vampire, and she was about to go through the change. She didn't know it yet, however. Or he was assuming she didn't because there was no sign she had reached out to the species—and by law, if a half-breed surfaced, the King had to be told.

So what to do. She was going to die without help.

Hell, she was going to die anyway in all likelihood—and V was hardly the Good Samaritan type. The problem? She would probably seek medical help when she collapsed—or end up in the back of an ambulance on a siren-run to St. Francis's ER because someone else called 911 on her behalf.

Which would lead to medical tests that would show all kinds of anomalies, fuck them very much.

God, humans were such a fucking pain in the ass, and the only reason coexistence with them was possible was because they thought vampires were a myth. Hard evidence to the contrary was not a good thing. If the war with the Lessening Society had been a bitch? Going rounds in the ring with Homo sapiens was going to make that shit look like a cakewalk—

Down the hallway that led to the bedrooms, the door up from the underground tunnel swung open.

"—goddamn know-it-all—"

Jane entered like she was in a bare-knuckle argument with someone—except she was alone and talking to herself as she disappeared into their room.

Her room. His room. Whatever.

Vishous slowly stood up from behind his computers.

Sounds that suggested she was pulling things from out of drawers with the delicate touch of a professional wrestler were the background to more of that muttering. And then a couple minutes later, she came out with a duffel bag on her shoulder. She had changed from her scrubs into a pair of blue jeans and a Patagonia jacket, and she marched forward as if she had no idea he was there.

That changed quick. As she came up to the archway into the living room, she stopped dead and looked at him with a startle that had her jumping back.

He put his palms up. "Sorry. I'm here."

Her eyes shot to the front door. Then she took a deep breath. "That's fine. This is your house. It's not a big deal."

There was a long pause, and as he stared at her, he decided he'd never seen her so exhausted. Her blond hair was a mess, there were dark circles under her forest green eyes, and her shoulders were sloped. Given all of that, he was surprised she was wasting energy on being fully corporeal. Then again, she was clearly pissed off at something and probably wanted the satisfaction of stomping around.

Ghosts just hovered.

"How are you," he said cautiously.

"Okay, and I'm going."

Closing his eyes, he cursed. "Can we please talk?"

"We just have. See you later—wait, what is that?"

Vishous popped his lids. "What's what?"

"On your arm. What the hell did you do to yourself?" She dropped her bag and clomped over to his computer desk. "That's a nasty wound—it looks infected."

He had no interest in anyone checking out his pretty new piece of body art—not even her. But if it served to keep them both under the same roof for a little longer? Fine. He'd play patient to her doctor.

Funny how all that anger he'd felt when they'd argued at the penthouse was gone. In its place, he felt hollow. Which made sense. She'd taken something of him with her when she'd announced she was out of his life.

Turning his shoulder toward her, he shrugged. "It doesn't hurt."

Jane bent in, her brows going tight. "When did this happen? A couple of nights ago?"

"No. It was more recent than that—"

As he hissed when she touched the wound's tail end, she gave him a bored look. "I thought you said it didn't hurt."

"Maybe a little."

"Come on. Into the bathroom." When he just stood there, she grabbed his wrist and pulled at him. "Let's go. I'm not leaving until this is taken care of."

Fine, he thought as they went down the hall to their—his, hers, whatever—room. Hopefully they could talk while she—well, there wasn't anything to clean. But maybe she had some ideas to reduce the swelling, though.

God, who in the hell would have thought that talking would be a goal of his with a female. Then again, Jane had always been different.

And because of that . . . she made him different.

EIGHTEEN

"Okay. Yup. I love you, too, *Vovó.*"

As Sola ended the call, she handed the cell phone back to Ehric and stretched her stiff shoulders. The two of them were outside Assail's room, standing together in the corridor, and she was careful to keep her voice low. Assail had fallen asleep, and she didn't want to disturb him.

Although that was assuming he was just asleep and not gone again. There were no alarms going off, however. And as long as she couldn't hear that horrible, shrill beeping and medical staff wasn't rushing down like police to a break-in, she had to believe everything was okay. For this moment in time.

"Thank you," she said to Assail's cousin. "I just wanted to make sure my grandmother was okay and knew the plan. And they took my phone away."

She wasn't going to bother to ask why he got to keep his. At this point, that kind of stuff was way down her list of things to worry about.

The man bowed low. "I will see to her myself as soon as I arrive home. And again, you are safe here, I promise you. I too would stay, but you are far better here with him than I."

"I'm fine now that I've spoken to my grandmother. It sounds like she's been cooking all night. Will you try and get her to go to sleep? I failed, but hey, maybe you could give it a shot."

Ehric smiled. "I shall endeavor to be persuasive in that regard."

The big blond man with the hostile name came out of a glass door and walked down to them. "We ready to go?"

"Thank you," Sola said to Rhage. "For bringing me here."

The guy unwrapped some kind of lollipop—a Tootsie Pop, yup that's what that was—and put it in his mouth. "I'm glad you brought him around. Now keep him with us, you hear? We need him."

Sola narrowed her eyes as she wondered, *For what? Drugs?*

Were these his dealers on the street? She didn't think so. They didn't seem the types to take orders from anybody—and besides, why would they be hanging around a hospital?

"I'll do what I can," she murmured.

As the two walked off, she watched them go, putting her hands in the pockets of her fleece and leaning back on her heels. Her brain was telling her that so much of this didn't make sense, but in the end, Assail's condition was the only thing she was prepared to get thought up about.

One thing she had learned from being on the wrong side of the law? Don't make other people's crap your own.

Pivoting around, she re-entered the room and immediately looked at the monitoring machines. Nothing was going off, and Assail was lying there peacefully. Her first impulse was to wake him up to see if he was still alive, as if he were an infant in a crib. Instead, she settled for watching his chest go up and down.

He had suffered so much, she thought as she looked at his bald head and too-thin body. Cancer was such a bitch, and the only thing worse than the disease was what the doctors did to you to try to get you to beat it.

A soft knock on the door brought her head up. "Come in?"

Ehlena, the nurse, leaned into the room. "Hi, there. I'm sorry to bother you, but if he's able to feed, we'd like him to."

Perfect excuse to wake him, she thought.

"He's asleep right now, but—" Sola glanced at Assail and smiled. "Oh, wait, his eyes are opening." She went around and took his hand. "Hey."

As his stare locked on to hers, his mouth moved.

"You're saying hello to me, aren't you." When he nodded, she smiled some more. "Yup. I can read you like a book."

Ehlena came over. "Assail, we'd like you to have Ghisele come in so you can take her v—"

When he shook his head sharply, the nurse went quiet and Sola braced herself for another seizure. But then he just looked at Ehlena as if he were trying to communicate with her telepathically or something.

"Yes, well . . ." Ehlena cleared her throat. "Okay, anyway, Sola, we'd like to change his catheter and do some things that we'd prefer to offer him some privacy around. Do you think you could head down to the break room and have a bite to eat? We'll need about twenty minutes. It's the fourth door on the left."

"What about food for him?"

"And we'll get him some food, yes."

As Assail squeezed her hand, she smiled at him. "I'll be right back. Soon as they let me."

He smiled at her as best he could, and then she was stepping out into the corridor again—

"Oh, excuse me," she said as she bumped into a woman who was trying to come into the room.

As Sola moved back, she thought . . . *Wow, what a robe.* The thing was white as a cloud, floor length, and had more swing than something out of Ginger Rogers's closet.

And, ah, wow, what a female. She had blond hair—the real kind, it seemed—and perfect features, and was so tall, even Sola had to look up some.

"No, it is my fault," the woman said with a bow. "Pardon me. But I have been summoned—"

Ehlena opened the door. "Ghisele. Hi, let me introduce you to Sola. She's Assail's female."

"It is my pleasure to serve," the woman said as she offered another bow. "Will you permit me to present him my—"

"Come on in, Ghisele." Ehlena pulled the woman inside and looked at Sola. "She's another nurse here. She works with us."

And then the door was shut in Sola's face.

Where did they hire their staff from, she wondered. The Miss America pageant?

Shaking her head, she went for a wander and thought about the woman's accent. There were a lot of English-as-a-second-language folks around the facility, and that was comforting. She was used to hearing all different kinds of accents—although she couldn't quite place the origins here. Then again, she was primarily familiar with variations on South American dialects.

She found the break room without a problem and checked out the vending machine, which was—bonus—free: No dollars were required to drop the bags of pretzels and Doritos or the Snickers bars and the Milky Ways. And then there was the Coca-Cola–branded drinks unit, which had everything from soda to Gatorade to lemonade in it, all free for the taking. There were also displays of fruit, sandwiches, desserts— and even microwavable Hot Pockets.

All free.

Okay, maybe this was a university?

Strange, very strange.

Her stomach wasn't interested in food or drink so she tucked into a cup of coffee and a donut; then she went back out into the hall and found the ladies' room—which turned out to be a locker situation with all kinds of showers, sinks, and toilets. And oh, my God, bonus: They had any toiletry you'd ever want. Deodorant, hairspray, brushes, makeup, Tums, Advil, Band-Aids . . . it was like an entire CVS was set in pretty little baskets along a wall-length counter that ran above the basins.

There were even sealed toothbrush packs.

Rarely had she ever enjoyed fluoride more.

Re-emerging minty fresh, she wandered down to the far end of the corridor, where they had entered from the parking area, and then she went all the way in the opposite direction to a glass door that housed some kind of office. Then down-and-back. And once more.

This time, as she passed Assail's room, Ehlena came out with the other nurse, who seemed to be holding her arm to her midsection.

"Everything okay?" Sola asked.

"Perfect." Ehlena smiled. "You're welcome to go back in."

"Okay. Thanks."

Sola frowned as the other two walked off together, their voices low as they spoke. But then she opened the door and—

"Oh . . . my Lord."

Assail was sitting up in the bed, his eyes alert, color back in his face. And as he focused on her, he smiled in a shy, but very alert way.

"Well, hello, beautiful," he said in a soft voice. "You are a sight for sore eyes."

As Marisol stood in the doorway like she'd seen a ghost, Assail cursed to himself. The Chosen Ghisele's blood had been so pure—and he hadn't fed in so long in the midst of so much physical stress—that the roaring strength coursing through his body had jumped him weeks and weeks ahead in his recovery.

All in the time lapse of . . . twenty-three minutes. According to that clockface over there on the wall.

If she had been a vampire like him, she would have understood immediately and rejoiced. With her being human, it was impossible to explain unless he revealed himself—

All at once, his brain shorted out, the thoughts that had been traveling in an orderly fashion on a train track of neurons disintegrating.

Nothing existed in his mind, at all.

"Xxxxx?" Marisol came over, her face worried. *"Xxxxx, xxxx'x xxxxx?"*

Her mouth was moving and sounds were reaching his ears, but he couldn't decipher the syllables.

He was able to recognize the expression on her face, however: She was concerned and asking him what was wrong. Yes, her eyes were worried, and she was leaning in, and she was talking some more.

"—call the nurse? Should I?"

With the same abruptness that everything had gone out of phase, cognition came back online in his brain, her words making sense to him once again, his mind processing reality as it should.

"No," he said. "No, please don't call them. I just got . . . fuzzy for a moment."

"Are you sure?" She took his hand and stroked it. "I can just—"

"You're blond now."

She reached up and touched her short hair. "I hate it. But it's necessary, I don't want to be identified—well, anyway. It's a change."

For a moment, he thought about the fact that she was on the run—and hated that she would not let him take care of her. Maybe that would change now, though. Maybe she would stay here with him after he recovered.

When he went to lift his hand to touch her, the binds on his wrists jerked his arm in place, and he tried to lower things back down discreetly so she couldn't notice—he didn't want to have to explain why he had needed to be strapped down. He didn't want her to think he would ever hurt her.

But he remembered why he had to be restrained. He recalled feeling the maggots under his skin, the burning, churning, restless twist of all of them itching at him, biting at him. He had scratched at his skin to get them out, to shake them free . . . then he had bitten at his arms—

As echoes of the hallucinations became so vivid they threatened to take over, he willed himself to stay in the present with Marisol. To see her, scent her, hear her. To feel her not just as she touched him, but in his heart and in his soul.

His bonding for her was what had rewired his neurological damage. He knew without a doubt that Marisol's presence was the reason why that which had failed to function was now approximating normalcy: Males of the species were so locked in with their females that they were capable of great feats of strength and power on their mate's behalf.

And that included a return from madness, evidently.

Still, he hated for her to see him like this.

Marisol sat on the bed next to him and stroked her warm hand up and down his forearm. As she did, he frowned at his pin-thin limb, the muscle so withered the skin was loose.

"Ugly."

"What?" she asked.

"I am . . . ugly."

"Not to me." She shook her head. "Never to me."

When her eyes circled his head, he had some vague memory of Doc Jane coming in with a shaver. Why had they taken his hair—oh, right. He'd been ripping it out, convinced that it was worms inside his skull. He'd been so freaked out, he'd chewed his bindings free so he could claw and tear at the black lengths until he was bleeding from wounds.

Yes, that was why they had had to shave him. And afterward, they had shown him a mirror to prove to him there was nothing there—and he had calmed down when he had seen it had been removed.

That had been back when they had tried to reason with him in the psychosis.

"I am so sorry," he said hoarsely. "I didn't want you . . . to come back to this."

"I'm here. That's all that matters."

"My brain . . . is sick."

"We don't have to talk about that now if it upsets you."

"It's sick."

"Is that . . . where the cancer is?"

Assail frowned, wondering if he was having another out-of-phase moment. But then . . .

"What did Ehric tell you?"

"Not any more than that." She shook her head. But I don't need details if you don't feel up to it."

"I'm sorry," he said again. Although this time, it was for the lie he would not correct.

How could he? He had just gotten her back. To explain that what had landed him here was intrinsic to him being a vampire was the last thing he wanted to confess. She would be properly horrified at what he was, and he would lose her again—and this time, nothing would ever return her unto him.

"I love you," he said urgently. "I was trying to tell you that before. When I couldn't speak."

Her beautiful, dark stare widened with surprise and then glowed with happiness. "So that is what you were saying to me."

"Yes."

"I thought . . . well, I'm glad to hear the words." She stroked his face. "They mean everything."

Fates, her eyes were lovely, rimmed with lashes beneath the arches of her brows. And there was color on her cheeks, the flush of joy making her seem younger, freer . . . more alive than ever he had seen her.

As a wave of post-feeding exhaustion came unto him, Assail desperately wanted to continue talking, to be reassured she and her grandmother had been safe in Miami, to discover how the year had gone for them both.

"Did you bring your grandmother . . ." That tiredness rose up through his bones and began to drag him down in earnest. "Tell me . . . you brought Mrs. Carvalho."

"I did, yup. She's at your home now. With both of your cousins— and there was another man there? A young guy?"

"He is . . . family friend. Staying with us. You . . . can . . . trust. . . . him . . ."

As he gave in to a yawn that cracked his jaw sockets, his eyes started to close. "Don't leave?"

"I won't," he heard her say as he drifted away. "I'm not leaving you, I promise . . ."

NINETEEN

hen Jane had come to get her things from the Pit, she had not intended to get anywhere near Vishous—but most especially not a half-naked V, in the bath of their former married . . . mated . . . whatever . . . bedroom. But she was first and foremost a doctor, and when she saw something that looked as though it was going septic, she was not going to let her personal bullshit stand in the way of treating a patient.

And whatever this was on his arm was nasty.

Under the lights at the sink, she inspected his skin. The wound was puffy and bright red, and he hissed again as she touched even the healthy, normal-colored areas around it.

"How did this happen? Did you run into something rusty? Were they using an old crowbar when they attacked you?"

When there was no answer, she looked up. Vishous was staring at her with those diamond eyes of his, his face drawn in lines of regret.

Do not get sucked in, she told herself as her heart kicked in her chest. *Don't you dare forget where you found him, on that rack in that penthouse.*

"Well?" she prompted as she stepped back. "What was it?"

"Nothing."

She rolled her eyes. "Fine, be a tough guy—even though it might help me diagnose your infection. But you're going to let me open that up and clean it out. Then you're going on antibiotics. Maybe even through an IV."

Although considering she'd just been kicked out of her own damn clinic, she was going to have to get Manny to help with that. A referral, no less.

Jesus *Christ,* she hated her life right now, she really frickin' did.

V pointed to the cabinet under the counter. "There's a suture kit with a scalpel under—"

"I know, I put it there."

Along with a paramedic kit worthy of an ambulance. As she muscled the load up and out onto the counter, he moved aside—and was smart enough not to offer to help. See? He truly was Albert Einstein with fangs.

"I don't want any lidocaine," V said as she began lining up the sterile gauze, the saline rinse she was going to add some antiseptic to, and that suture kit.

She paused and looked over her shoulder. "This is going to hurt."

"Good."

Cursing under her breath, she told herself to just let it go. This pain thing of his was none of her business, and besides, if she were honest? She wanted to hurt him a little.

After gloving up, she surface-cleaned the area with Betadine and then tested the wound with her forefinger. "We've got to get the pus out."

Taking the scalpel, she went to the base of the wound, inserted the blade vertically, and went with the contour for about a half inch.

The muscles all over V's torso tightened in response, and she tried not to notice how spectacularly he was built. No fat, anywhere. He was just hard strength under smooth, tight skin, an animal more than anything she had ever seen in human men.

Focus, Jane—

"What the hell?" she muttered.

Nothing. No infection. There was absolutely no oozing, no smell, no anything. She tried a little higher on the wound. And higher still. But no matter where she tested along the ten- to twelve-inch length, there was nothing that would suggest a bacterial invasion that was being fought off by his white blood cells.

"It's more like an allergic reaction," she concluded. "The inflammation and irritation. What the hell did this to you?"

"I don't know. And that is the honest truth."

Jane glanced up his broad pectorals to the jut of his chin and his goatee. "You didn't see what it was?"

"No, I saw it all right. It attacked me and Butch. I've just never seen anything like it before."

Jane straightened. "It wasn't a *lesser*?"

"Nope. No one knows what it was, true? That's what I was doing when you came in. I was about to search the vampire groups and see if anyone else has ever run up against one of those shadows."

Fear, like a fire alarm, rippled through her.

And it was strange—and perhaps V's point, not that she was interested in admitting he had a valid one—that it was only at this moment that she realized his mother, the Scribe Virgin, was truly gone. Because Jane's first advice, her initial response, to the idea there was an unknown threat to the species, was that he should go talk to the race's spiritual and metaphysical foundation.

V's voice went through her head, from back when they'd had it out: *You never once asked me how I felt. You never even asked me how I found out she was gone.*

Clearing her throat, Jane said, "Maybe you need to go up to the Sanctuary. Maybe the information is up there, not down here. In the library, or . . . I don't know."

Vishous rubbed his tattooed temple like he had a headache. "The volume of records that have been kept are staggering. Going back centuries."

"But they're the whole history of the race, right? And they have to be organized in some way."

"By date. Not topic. Even if all the Chosen helped me, I wouldn't be able to go through it all in any reasonable amount of time—and besides, if it's recent? No one records anymore."

"Well, there's no fixing that. But if the Chosen recorded the history, they'd remember something as big a deal as a threat like this, right? Maybe you could ask them. They're all up at Rehv's Great Camp. You could talk to them and they could at least narrow your search."

"Yeah, that's true. I could do that."

"So let's go—" She shook her head. "I mean, you. You should go."

Those eyes of his bored into her own. "I could use some help on this. If you've got some time to spare."

Jane looked down at the gauze in her hand. There was a red stain in the center of the sterile white pad.

Manny wasn't going to allow her anywhere near the clinic. And she was just going to go stay at one of the Brotherhood's properties, cooped up like a prisoner, cursing her life and her professional partners and everyone else in the process.

Or . . . she could help V with his job.

She thought of all the secret meetings he went to, all those closed doors, those rooms she wasn't welcome in, that information he never shared.

"It's fine," he muttered. "I know you're busy—"

"You sure you want me to know anything about this?"

As she spoke, there was bitterness in her voice—and she had to admit she had been hurt for quite a while now. She hadn't wanted to acknowledge this, of course, because, come on—she had her own life, and it wasn't like she could share patient details with even him. But she had felt left out of so much of how he spent his hours, how he purposed his life, how he committed himself. He and the Brotherhood were so close, they were essentially one entity, between their working relationships and their off-rotation, inside-joke, male macho stuff.

Which she didn't mind at all—as long as she felt like she and V had a connection.

"I have no problem with you knowing anything," he said.

"You sure about that?"

"What's that supposed to mean—"

She put her hand up. "I don't want to fight."

He took a deep breath, that star scar on his chest expanding out of shape and resettling. "I don't, either. And I do mean that. Hell, you'll probably be the one who makes sense of it all. You're one of the smartest people I've ever known."

Jane looked away and tried to hide the little bit of sunshine that had bloomed, unexpected and unfamiliar, on her face.

She wasn't going to tell him this . . . but that compliment meant more to her than any throwaway line about her being pretty or attractive would have.

Coming from someone like him? It was the highest form of praise she could get.

"Okay." Her voice was rough so she cleared her throat and squared her shoulders. "I'll go with you."

Even though there was a lot of night to spare, Throe settled into his bed, reclining back against pillows soft as clouds.

In retiring to his private quarters, he was following—after too long a hiatus—the traditions of his class. Back before he had been conscripted into the Band of Bastards and forced to learn to fight or die, a mansion such as this one that he had taken over, and servants such as the ones he had created, and moments like this, where one reclined when feeling not well, were part of the normal course of life.

In truth, he was already recovered from the previous night's strange chest pain. So this was out of an abundance of caution and a love of luxury.

There was also quality time to be had with his female.

Extending a hand, he put his palm on the cover of the ancient tome that had proven to be the means to his ends.

"My love," he murmured as he closed his eyes.

The Book warmed under his touch, communicating with him as it did, filling him out in ways he'd been previously unaware of being deflated, restoring his energy after the pain and depletion he'd experienced back in that alley.

Yes, he thought, as he fully returned unto himself, strong once more. He needed more time with his love and then all would be well—even if a loss of one of his soldiers had compromised him, it would be only temporary. He would make more.

As Throe lay in quiet in a bedroom properly appointed for a member of the *glymera,* his thoughts embarked on an idyll through the recent past, as if he were going on a museum tour and the docents were stopping him from time to time before certain paintings.

He recalled going into that psychic's in a bad part of town and being called unto the Book surely as if the thing were saying his name. He had been in search of dark magic, it was true—although he wouldn't have stated such at the moment. All he had been presently aware of, as he had mounted those steps to the second floor of that walk-up and found himself transported to another dimension without his body changing positions, was that he had ambitions unto the throne that were struggling to find success.

Without the muscle of Xcor and the Band of Bastards, and with the aristocracy completely castrated with the dismantling of the Council, he had seen no way forward.

"But then I met you," he murmured.

The Book had shown him how to create the shadows, the incantation requiring but a small sacrifice of his blood and some minor pain. It had been so easy, with the only fault being that each spell was a one-at-a-time.

If only there were Amazon Prime for the damn things.

As it stood, he had five—well, now four—shadow entities under his command. In order to defeat the Brotherhood, he would need so many more. A proper army.

The idea of doing that spell over and over and over again filled him with restless frustration. But what choice did he have? And they were a weapon that needed better defenses. If they could be eliminated with only bullets?

Under his palm, the Book grew cold as an ice cube, as if it were in disagreement—and he turned his head upon the pillow toward the tome.

"How can you disagree? My soldier was felled readily—ouch!" He jerked his hand off the cover and frowned. "Really? Must you."

In the back of his mind, as he sent a glare at an inanimate object, he was aware that this was all off. Everything about what he was doing felt . . . as if he were subject to the will of another. These events, these choices, this . . . path . . . was only his own on the surface—

The Book threw its cover open; its pages, no longer dusty due to use, began to flip with growing speed. And then it settled on a folio.

Leaning to the side, he looked at the ink on the page. As usual, it was nonsensical to him, but he had been through this before. He had to wait until it translated itself for his eyes, for his language . . .

He smiled, a warm glow in his chest. "I have my faith," he murmured. "And my faith has me . . ."

Across the page, the same sentence, written in the characters of the Old Language, was in all manner of sizes, the wording fitting in and around itself, forming a beautiful pattern.

"Let us not fight, my love," he whispered as he dipped his head and pressed his lips to the page. "I have my faith, and my faith has me." He caressed the page, feeling a velvet softness that was like the skin of a female. "I have my faith, and my faith has me. Ihavemyfaithandmyfaithhasme . . ."

An erection sprang forth at his hips and he ducked a hand beneath the sheets. Pushing his palm under the waistband of his silk pajamas, he gripped himself and felt a stab of lust go through him. A pumping action, strong and sure, was all he needed to find bliss as he said the words on the page over and over again—

A knock at the door lifted his head. It would be his tea. Earl Grey on a silver tray with sugar cubes and a lemon slice on the side.

The shadow he had sent to get it would wait out there until the earth ceased to exist, subject to Throe's will and not its own, for though it moved, it had not a brain of its own.

The opposite of his Book.

"My love," he said as he extended his tongue and licked up the page's ink.

The taste was like the glorious, aroused sex of a female, and as he began to ejaculate, all was right in his world . . .

And he even had good help finally. Which was so hard to find.

TWENTY

Rehvenge's Great Camp, on the shores of Lake George, was typical of the summer houses built in the Adirondacks in the 1870s. Cedar-shingled, multi-porched, and so close to the water you could spit a watermelon seed or toss your empty G-n-T's ice into the lake with ease, the estate was a gracious nod to earlier times. Especially in winter. With the steep, snow-covered mountains framing its acreage, and threads of smoke rising from its five brick chimneys, it was the kind of place you wanted to curl up in with a good book and not come out until spring.

As Jane crunched through the snow to the rear door, she had her hands in her pockets and her head down. It was so cold her ears burned at the tips and her cheeks tightened up, but she didn't want to solve the "problem" by fading out.

It felt good to be in the elements and not distracted by an emergency, and she stopped and looked up. Overhead, the sky was full of stars that shone so clearly, they were like pinpricks in a theater curtain, and the high, almost-full moon provided illumination that the winter landscape turned shades of blue.

"This is so beautiful," she murmured.

"I agree."

As she glanced at V, he wasn't looking at the heavens. He was staring at her.

And even though his expression was remote, his eyes were anything but.

With her heart starting to beat hard, she turned away from him. "We better get inside."

The door into the kitchen opened before they stepped up onto the back porch, the Chosen Cormia putting her head out. "Just in time! Scones are fresh out of the oven."

The blond-haired female was wearing an Irish knit sweater that was so big, it ended below her knees, and her smile was as beautiful as a sunrise, warm and welcoming. Phury's mate was that rare combination of kindness without the cloy, a genuinely caring person who was a perfect match to Z's twin brother—and without her, Phury would never have beaten his addiction demons.

Oh, for the love of a good woman. Wasn't that how the saying went?

Great. Now her chest ached again as that treacherous part of her, that sniveling, girl-not-a-woman, weak-ass whiner portion of her character, wondered why she had not been enough for Vishous.

Except that was some rank bullshit right there.

"Thanks," she said to the Chosen as she went in. "I am hungry."

Liar, liar, she thought as she made a show of checking out the baking sheet resting on the top of the gas stove.

After living with the Brotherhood for as long as she had, she had grown used to huge, professional kitchens. This was a much more personal-sized setup, with a reasonable six-burner Viking, and a regular refrigerator, and a potbellied stove that was throwing off BTUs like a priest handing out benedictions at Easter. And the rest of the space had been renovated with an eye toward keeping things as authentic to the period of the house as possible, the hutch in the corner an antique, the exposed beams painted garnet and gray, the old floorboards varnished, but not stained, to show their age.

"So what brings you up here?" Cormia asked as she went over and started transferring the scones into a basket with a fork and fingertips. "Your text didn't say much, Vishous—not that you ever need a reason. You're always welcome."

As V started to explain the attack, Jane took a seat at the butcher-block island and watched the happy drain out of the Chosen.

"I'll get everyone down here," the female said when he'd finished.

After throwing a dishtowel over the basket to keep the scones warm, Cormia left, her footfalls growing dim and then transitioning to overhead as she hit the second floor.

Left alone, Jane found herself trying to remember the last time she and Vishous had been together in the same room—when they had both been properly awake.

It had been back during Xcor's abduction, she decided. When she had gone to the Tomb to do an assessment on the Bastard and Vishous had been on guard duty. They had talked about how neither one of them wanted kids. Which had been a relief at the time.

Now? That accord just seemed like more distance, more separateness.

When Vishous cleared his throat, she looked up at him—and as if he had been waiting for her attention, he said, "I owe you an apology. For the way I spoke to you at the penthouse the other night. I was obnoxious and defensive."

She focused on the basket. The dishtowel on top was red, the one lining the inside was blue, and the combination made her think of the Fourth of July.

"It's okay," she said eventually. "We were both pretty upset."

"I am really sorry that that happened. The whole thing."

"You know what hurts?" she blurted. "The fact that you carved out time and made arrangements and thought about . . . someone else. It makes me feel like I'm not here. I'm not significant to you. I mean, yes, there's the whole cheating thing. But over and above the mechanics of the sex, what kills me is that you prioritized somebody—when all I want is to be seen by you. Really, truly . . . *seen*."

There was a rustle and a creak . . . and when she looked up again, he was right beside her, looming in his black leather jacket and broad shoulders, his weapons mostly hidden, his face full of sharp angles as he stood beneath the old-fashioned wrought-iron light fixture.

"I didn't want anyone else," he said. "I don't want anyone else. Just you."

As her throat got tight, she whispered, "Then why did you do it?"

"I will never forgive myself." He reached out and touched her cheek; not with his gloved hand, though. With the one that was warm and bare. "And you're right. It was not about you—until I decided I couldn't go through with it. Then it was *all* about you."

Their eyes met and held as there was more walking up above, many footsteps crossing the floorboards as Cormia gathered the Chosen.

"I'm sorry," he said in a voice that cracked. "More than you will ever know. I love you, Jane. It's always been you . . . I did a horrible, stupid, unforgivable thing. And as for the sex, I swear on my soul that I didn't touch her. As soon as she came, I sent her away. I couldn't do that shit. I could not."

She searched his face, his cruelly beautiful, tattooed face.

"You hurt me." Her voice was so rough, it didn't sound like her own.

"I know."

"Don't do it again."

"I won't." He leaned in and pressed a kiss to her forehead. "You have my word."

As he straightened, something dawned on her—and she let out an awkward laugh. Then a giggle. "Oh, my God."

"What?"

"I can't believe I just quoted *Pretty Woman* to you." She put her hands to her face and laughed more. "I was Julia Roberts, right there."

He smiled, his goatee widening. "I've never seen the movie—wait, no. Lassiter was watching it once. It's where that red-haired chick goes shopping or something?"

"That's the one. Anyway, I didn't think I would ever walk in those shoes."

V got serious quick. "I'm sorry I was the one who put you in them."

"I'm not going to say it's okay." She took a deep breath. "Because it's not."

"I know. And I agree."

As female voices grew louder, Cormia walked into the kitchen and pointed over her shoulder. "We've gathered in the living room by the big hearth because it's warmest there?"

"Good call," V said as he stepped back and let Jane get to her feet. "Let's do this."

Nothing.

None of the Chosen had heard of anything such as that shadow entity, either as they had functioned as scribes or as part of any conversation about the race.

After meeting with the sacred females, V stepped out of Rehv's old and wonderful house and held the door wide for Jane to follow him.

"I'm not surprised," he said.

"I thought for sure they'd know something."

The two of them walked forward through the snow, their breaths leaving in puffs, their boots crunching through the icy top layer to the soft stuff underneath.

Shit, he thought. There was no reason to check social damn media. If the Scribe Virgin's females didn't know about it, the Joe Schmoes on the planet wouldn't . . .

Then again, Phury had released the Chosen of their lockdown up in the Sanctuary quite a while ago. So there had been a lag between when the seeing bowls had been in regular use, and when tall, dark, and see-through had showed up in that alley.

"I guess we go back," V said as he slowed to a stop.

Fuck. He didn't want to leave, because Jane was going to pull out if they returned to Caldwell—

"What about Amalya?" she asked.

As he turned to her, he got caught up in the way the moonlight fell over her features and made her blond hair glow. Goddamn, he wanted to kiss her. Wanted to do even more to her.

"Sorry, what?" he murmured.

"She's up in the Sanctuary, still, as the Directrix. Maybe she knows something?"

"Will you go with me?"

"Ah, yeah. Sure. I think I can get up there. I haven't tried."

"I can help you." When she nodded, he stepped in close. "I'm going to have to put my arms around you."

As she stiffened, he gave her time to change her mind. But then she nodded—so he moved in even tighter and extended his reach, his leather jacket creaking in the cold.

"Close your eyes," he told her.

V didn't wait to see if she followed instruction. It wasn't necessary, anyway. He wasn't even sure why he said it; hell, maybe he was hoping she'd forget it was him. Or more likely . . . he didn't want her to see how vulnerable he was feeling.

In a slow series of movements, he wrapped his arms around her and stepped in against her.

She fit the same. She felt different. Holding her, it was as if it was the first time all over again, that moment when you had another body against your own and all your senses were in tune to the way their shoulders hit the insides of your biceps and how their head fit under your chin and what their shampoo smelled like.

Vishous had told her to shut her eyes, but he was the one closing his lids.

"Hold on to me," he said hoarsely. "Here we go . . ."

The world went on a swirl that made them the center of the universe

around which all things spun, and then there was a wave and a bump—
and justlikethat, the cold and the night were gone.

The Sanctuary was a rainbow wash of green lawn and multi-colored
tulips, its climate a perpetual spring afternoon under a milky sky that
had no obvious light source but all the illumination you could ever
want. The air was still and a perfect seventy-two degrees, the humidity
giving everything a dewy resonance without making you sweaty. Greco-
Roman–like marble structures with open loggias and arched, pane-less
windows dotted the acres, like chess pieces placed with strategy on a
board.

Vishous didn't want to let her go.

He did, however.

And as he pulled back, he felt her hands smooth over his waist—
which caused lust to spike into his body.

Even though sexual frustration was typically not a male's BFF, it felt
so good to want her again. To not just remember feeling this way, but
actually be in the sensation, the experience.

"Where do we go?" Jane asked in a husky voice.

He shook himself back into focus. "To my mother's private quarters. We'll wait there for Amalya. She already knows we're here. The
Directrix always knows when someone breaches the barrier."

As they started walking, he wanted to take her hand. He didn't want
to push her and make things awkward, though.

"God, this place is beautiful," Jane murmured. "The colors—it
makes me think of somewhere over the rainbow."

"What?"

"That Judy Garland movie—the one that was half in black-and-
white and half in color? My sister, Hannah, before she died . . . she and
I used to watch it every year. Jeez, my brain is going—why can't I remember the title? There was the dog, Toto. And Auntie Em, who she
wanted to get home to. The yellow brick road and the Scarecrow. The
Tin Man and the Cowardly Lion. Okay, this is going to drive me

nuts . . . there was that witch and those frickin' monkeys. I hated those monkeys, always gave me nightmares—they made me not want to go to zoos."

V knew what the movie was called, but he liked the sound of her talking, so he kept it to himself and let her continue to describe it as they walked over the carpet of perfectly level, golf course–worthy grass.

Up ahead, by the Scribing Temple, a high, white marble wall, so pristine it was as if a porcelain dinner plate had been stuck into the ground, delineated his mother's private space. There was no conventional door to access the courtyard. Instead, a section parted for you if you were welcome.

As they approached, striding side by side with so much still unsaid, he wondered if they would be blocked for having a bad vibe, like they were carriers of an existential stomach flu that required quarantine. Or maybe with the Scribe Virgin gone, all would be locked out—

Nope. The opening appeared, the marble that was there now not.

Stepping inside, the sound of the fountain, which was now flowing again, was like a choir without any particular music or specific set of voices; it was more an ambiance that made him think, *Ah, yes. That is good.*

The songbirds he had brought up for his mother, twice, were silent for a moment. Then they resumed their lovely songs, until the warbling tunes from those avian throats became as the twinkling, falling water, a part of a landscape so perfectly engineered to both set a mood and be unobtrusive that your shoulders uncoiled and your gut eased up and your heart, still so broken moments before, began to beat a rhythm of peace.

Jane strolled forward, the boots she had put on back at the Pit no longer crusted with snow, the grass having cleaned them off. Her coat would be making her too warm, he thought—and sure enough, she removed it and ran a hand through her short hair.

I see you, he thought. *And you are beautiful to me.*

"So we just wait?" she said as she wandered around and then stepped into the colonnaded preamble to his mother's suite of rooms. "Until Amalya finds us?"

"Yes."

"Hey, look in here. There's a bed and things—okay, well, not things really, but there is a bed." She glanced back at him. "I didn't really think the Scribe Virgin would sleep. You know . . . like us."

V shrugged. "I don't know what she did in there."

She pivoted around sharply. "*The Wizard of Oz.* That's the name of the movie. Guess I haven't lost it completely."

There was a long silence. And Vishous realized he would remember her forever here, standing in the white marble expanse, staring across at him with that parka over her arm and those snow boots.

"I've missed you," he blurted. "More than I've wanted to admit—and now that you're here with me, I can't figure out why I worked so fucking hard to avoid telling you that."

TWENTY-ONE

The following afternoon—was it afternoon? The arms on the wall clock said two and change, and it *felt* like afternoon—Sola stepped out of Assail's room so that Ehlena and that other nurse, the one with the long robe, could remove his catheter.

He had been sleeping in chunks of two or three hours, and Sola had been doing the same, thanks to a cot that had been brought in for her. With him in restraints still, it wasn't possible for them to lie together, but it was good to be stretched out and off her feet, right by him.

Ehric had been really diligent about sending her texts on the phone he'd given her about her *vovó*. Pictures, too, the snaps of the old woman at the stove, at the cutting board, pointing at Evale as if she were ordering him around, making Sola smile with happiness and relief. During the last month in Miami, she'd worried her *vovó* was slowing down, but maybe it was because she'd needed more mouths to feed, a bigger house to organize, a schedule punctuated by more than just church.

Ehlena stepped out of the room. "I think he wants a shower."

Sola jumped to attention. "Really? I mean, yay! Are the restraints off?"

"Yes." The other woman made slow-down motions. "Now, we really don't know how he's going to be. I don't want to alarm you, but his mental status could change quickly and without warning. So please be careful."

"I can handle myself," Sola said grimly. "I would hate to have to with him . . . but I can take care of things if that's the way it goes."

Ehlena reached out with a reassuring hand. "Hopefully it won't be necessary. And you know how to call us."

"So he can have a shower? I can help him with that?"

"Yes, Dr. Manello has cleared him. There's a chair in the stall for him to sit on and also a call button mounted on the wall, you'll see it. I'm just one room over if you need me."

The other nurse came out of the room, the one with the long robe, and her arm was in that same position, tucked against her torso as if she were hiding something or it hurt. But she was pleasant enough, offering that bow-thing she did and some murmured words of respect.

Sola was pleasant in response, but she didn't waste time, flashing back into that room because she had a hunch that—yup, Assail was sitting on the edge of the bed like he was about to jump onto his feet, break off a piece of his Kit Kat bar to a disco track—and probably fall flat on his face and break all of his teeth because he was too weak to be doing anything other than giving sheets a job.

"Let me help you," she said as she ran forward.

"I got it—"

"You don't got shit—"

Except he did. He stood up and didn't wobble, his body solid on those thin legs, his breath hitching only a little, his hands splaying out as he balanced on his own.

"Look at you." Sola smiled, and had to blink back tears. "Next thing you know, you'll be doing laps."

"May I have your arm?"

"I was hoping you'd ask."

Sola let him set the pace, and although he shuffled like a little old lady, she didn't care. The idea that there was progress, any sort of forward motion—natch—out of the death throes he'd been in the night before was good enough for her. Yes, she realized he was still terminal, and she was going to have to keep facing that reality . . . but for as long as she could, she was going to stay in this present. Anything else was just too hard to think about.

"Okay, so I'm going to start the water," she informed him as they entered the loo. "And you're going to park it on this nice toilet right here—let's put the seat cover down. Excellent. Good work. Now let me get the shower going."

As he sat where she told him to, Sola extended an arm into the tiled stall and cranked the stainless-steel handle most of the way to the engraved "H" at the top of the fixture. Then she turned back around—

Assail was no longer sitting down. And he was not by the toilet.

He had moved to the sink and was staring at himself in the mirror.

With a shaking hand, he reached out to the glass and touched the reflection of his hollowed cheek, his too-prominent brow, his lips that were loose.

"The water's almost warm," she whispered. Even though it wasn't. "Come on, let's get you under the spray."

But Assail just stood there, staring at the image of what was clearly a dying man.

When his knees started to go, she caught him by throwing an arm around his frail body. He weighed far too little, but she didn't allow herself to dwell on that.

"Sit," she said as she helped him back down onto the closed toilet seat.

Then she kneeled in front of him. As his eyes welled with tears, she felt so powerless.

"It's all right," she murmured as she snapped a hand towel off a rod. "Just let it all out."

Folding the terrycloth in half again, she pressed the softness to his face—and then somehow, he was in her arms, leaning on her for strength, his body collapsed onto her.

In slow circles, she moved her palm around the prominent bones of his back and rib cage. "I've got you," she whispered in his ear. "Cry it out, you'll feel better—"

A knock on the door stiffened him and he lifted his head in alarm as if he were terrified that anyone but her would see him as vulnerable as he was.

"We're fine," Sola said sharply as she urged his head back down and protected him. "Do *not* come in."

Ehlena's voice was muffled through the closed door. "Just checking. I'll give you guys privacy."

"Thank you."

After a while, Assail lifted his head as if it weighed a thousand pounds. And before he could speak, she wiped his face. "Let's do the shower later—"

"I never thought . . ." He cleared his throat. "I never thought I would come back. I thought I had lost me forever. I'm so scared, Marisol. What if I . . . I don't want to be lost again."

She would have given the world to be able to tell him he didn't have to worry about that. But she was not going to lie to him.

"I'm not leaving you. However much time you have, I'll be here."

With trembling fingers, he touched her hair, her cheek, the curve of her jaw. And then he lingered at her mouth, running a feather-light stroke across her lower lip.

She knew exactly what he was asking.

"Yes," she said. "As soon as you're able."

Staring into Marisol's face, Assail desperately wanted to be with his female. He wanted her naked and underneath him, his body sexed up and penetrating hers, the two of them orgasming at the same time.

Unfortunately, that seemed like a distant country, reachable only after a treacherous, exhausting trip. But he would get there. He had told the Chosen Ghisele to come back in another eight hours. She was feeding from the Brothers to keep her own strength up as she provided him with what he needed, and maybe after another feeding he would lose the paranoia he would backslide again.

Every time he took that Chosen's vein, he progressed by leaps and bounds.

But 'lo, how he wished it could have been Marisol's blood in him.

For a moment, Assail entertained that fantasy, except then he refocused. With his madness only so recently dissipating, he didn't like to get too lost in memories or daydreams. In both cases, such vivid thoughts took him away from the touch-taste-see-hear of reality, and the dissociation terrified him.

He'd had enough of that to last a lifetime.

"Let's go back to bed."

"I want to be clean," he countered. "I just want to feel . . . clean."

As if a good shampoo and soaping would wash this nightmare away.

"All right," Marisol said as she got to her feet. "Let's do this."

He absolutely despised the way she had to help him stand up, and he'd learned his lesson with the mirror over the sink: As she aided him with taking off his hospital johnny, he did not look down at himself.

No, thank you. He wasn't going to like what he saw there any more than he'd enjoyed his face or bald skull.

And damn it, he wanted to stand on his own underneath the spray, like a grown male should, but with the heat swirling around because of the hot water, he could feel his blood pressure dropping. So the chair it was—

"Oh . . ." he sighed. "This is wonderful."

"Too hot? Too cold?"

"Perfect."

Leaning back and resting his bald head on the tile wall, he let the amazing rush cascade down his flesh.

"You want me to wash you?" Marisol asked.

"Oh, yes," he said. "Please. That would be most gracious of you."

Embarrassed by how little he could do for himself, he fell back upon his aristocratic manners, as if politeness could somehow make up for his weakness. Yet Marisol didn't seem to judge him at all—or hold him in lesser regard. In fact, she smiled and seemed to enjoy helping. And she was gentle with the washcloth on his hypersensitive skin.

It felt so good to have her hands upon him. He didn't want it to end. "All finished."

"Brush my teeth?" he murmured drowsily.

"Absolutely."

She came back with a toothbrush preloaded with paste, and that he did himself. Then the water was off, dripping loudly in the stall.

Marisol wrapped him in thick towels and together they got him back onto the bed. As he sagged against the pillows, he realized it was more exercise than he'd had since Dr. Manello had come and picked him up from his house to come here for his detoxing—

Assail took his female's hand urgently and spoke in a strong voice. "No more drugs."

She blinked. "Okay. I can tell the doctors you don't want any more—"

"No. No more cocaine. Ever." He shook his head emphatically. "I will never do it again. I should never have started using, and then it got away from me. It nearly killed me. That is an evil drug, and I am e'er rid of it."

Sola leaned down and smiled. "That is good to hear."

As she grew serious, he had a feeling she was thinking about his dealing. "And I'm getting out of the business, too," he said. "It's not for me anymore."

"Wait . . . you're going legitimate? As in, completely legitimate?"

Assail frowned as he considered his past pursuits. Ever since he had come to the New World, he had been hell-bent on making money— because that was what he had always done. And he preferred the black market because he hated paying corporate taxes, and moreover, he had enjoyed thwarting the human legal system. But unless the stock market had collapsed during the time he had been off the planet, he had more money than he could spend over the course of his centuries-and-centuries' long lifetime.

There had never been a need, actually, only the drive.

A compulsion for winning.

Except, now, after what he had been through over the last—had it been weeks or months?—he found himself not wanting any part of such pursuits. Hell, he'd already shut down his drug business to get out of that messy problem of having dealt to the *Fore-lesser*. He'd had plans to import and sell guns and munitions, but really, what for?

"There will be no more of that for me, Marisol."

As tears sprang to her eyes, he assumed they were from happiness. But then he wasn't so sure.

"That's good news to you," he prompted. "Is it not?"

"Of course it is." She seemed to collect herself. "It's the news I've wanted to hear."

"Lay with—"

As his thoughts abruptly stopped, and he had nothing but a blank space in his head, he panicked. This was how it had been going, however, these little hiccups in cognition creating the proverbial sound of crickets in his skull . . . and then resolving themselves.

Marisol was speaking unto him, and he tried not to become agitated when he couldn't properly interpret her words—

"Lay with me," he blurted. "Lay with me? I'm all right. I swear unto you. I just have these . . . little interruptions. They always take care of themselves, though."

She stayed where she was, staring at him as if she were trying to diagnose him like a doctor. But something must have satisfied her, because she nodded and got up on the bed gently. As she stretched out beside him, he rolled in toward her. They both took a deep breath, and he would have willed the lights off if he'd had the strength.

"I will be better in the morning," he mumbled. "I just need rest."

"Of course. It will all . . ." She exhaled slowly. "In the morning, all will be well."

Something in her voice wasn't right, but as sleep strengthened its hold on him, he contented himself with dreams of a future where they were together. Here. Miami. The Old Country. It didn't matter.

But yes, he was going to follow her lead and get out of the life.

Fates, why hadn't he decided to retire sooner?

TWENTY-TWO

"A word with you, if I may?"

The following evening, Vitoria looked up from her brother Eduardo's desk—and thought about getting her gun out. "How did you get in here?"

"The door was ajar."

The woman standing just inside the office and speaking in that autocratic, I-win-the-game voice, was all angles: Dark hair cut blunt at the chin and flat-ironed straight as a set of drapes. Anorexic body dressed in an avant-garde black suit with asymmetrical lines and shoulder pads out of Alexis Carrington Colby's wardrobe. And the nose job and brow lift made her appear to be in dramatic lighting even if she wasn't.

Miss Margot Fortescue. The one who had proven so resistant to everything, especially when Vitoria had informed the gallery's staff first thing at nine a.m. that she would be taking things over. Fortunately, the others had been warm and open. Then again, exactly how many high-end art galleries did Caldwell have? Even snobs had to be employed.

When they were the salespeople as opposed to the buyers, that was. Such a world of difference.

Vitoria sat back and resolved to make sure she shut things firmly behind herself in the future. "What may I do for you?"

Miss Fortescue closed the door sharply. Then again, she no doubt did everything with a punctuation of some sort.

"I would like some proof of your identity."

This was said as if it were meant to shock. Dismay. Cause a fluster.

And so when Vitoria made no response at all, Miss Fortescue's left eyebrow, which had been drawn on as if it were part of an architectural rendering, twitched. "Well?"

"Life is full of unrequited desires." Vitoria smiled. "We must learn to adjust to being disappointed—"

"We don't know who you are. You could be anyone. Eduardo and Mr. Benloise didn't tell us they had a 'sister.'"

That last word was uttered with a tone that put its definition more along the lines of "thief" or "interloper" than familial relation of a female extraction.

As the woman's eyes settled on the desk, her expression became remote—and that was when all became clear. Ah, yes, Eduardo had been engaging in a bit of fun with this paragon of precision and disapproval, hadn't he.

Vitoria smiled. "Clearly, you were just not significant enough to merit information about our family. That happens to mere casual or business acquaintances."

Miss Fortescue planted a hand on the blotter and leaned in. "I know what else got sold around here. I know what Eduardo was keeping track of—"

"Do you often find yourself overstepping bounds? Or do you simply lack the self-awareness to recognize them in the first place. I think perhaps the latter informs the former."

The woman seemed nonplussed. But she recovered presently. "I could bring down this whole lie. Eduardo told me things, and when the two of them stopped coming in here, there was a lot of talk. I kept quiet, but that may not last."

Vitoria sat forward and linked her hands on her brother's journal of notes. As her burner phone started to ring, she let it go to voicemail. "This is an art gallery. My brothers sell art—which I believe is your reason for employment here?"

"I know about that little book." The woman pointed to what Vitoria was covering. "I know what's in there."

"Tell me something, has my brother gotten in touch with you recently?" When there was only stony silence: "Yes, that is what I thought. I'm afraid you are less amusing than your cheerful attitude and dress suggest."

"They say he's dead."

"Who is 'they'?" When there was no reply, Vitoria shook her head. "You know so much less than you maintain you do—and I imagine it can be disappointing when one's position is less exalted than one assumed." Vitoria made a show of looking at her watch. "Is it six o'clock already? Closing time."

"I want proof of who you are."

"Yes, you've made that clear. However, what I would be worried about, were I you, was whether or not I will have a job in the morning."

"Are you threatening me?"

"Not at all." Getting to her feet, Vitoria came around the desk. "Why would I fire someone who has just suggested that my brothers were engaging in illegal activity? That deserves a promotion. Now, off you go, and I'll lock up behind you."

"So I'm thinking Amalya is not going to show."

As Jane spoke, Vishous looked over at her. The two of them had spent all day in the courtyard, lounging on the marble floor of his mother's private quarters, propped up against the lip of the fountain. It was typical of the Sanctuary that not even the stone made your ass fall asleep. Even after all these hours, they might as well have been stretched out on a pair of Wonder Bread loungers.

"I guess not." He rubbed his hair. "She knows we're here. I mean, that's the way it's always worked."

In fact, he had half expected the Directrix to magically materialize from out of his mother's private bedroom and announce that she was the chosen one, the handpicked successor to the Scribe Virgin.

That shoe hadn't dropped yet, though. And as for Amalya's no-show? It had meant he and Jane had talked for hours and hours about absolutely, positively nothing that was hard stuff. They had stuck well away from her work, his work, their distance. Instead, they had covered things like Assail's recovery, Luchas's progress, the Lessening Society's disintegration, the *Dhestroyer* Prophecy—and Right vs. Left Twix, Super Bowl predictions, and the theory of Atlantis.

That last one had been because they had also gotten into a quote war over the original *Ghostbusters.*

"I'm sorry I never asked you," Jane said softly.

He refocused. "What?"

"About losing your mother."

There was a pause, and then her eyes locked on his own. As the silence stretched out, he knew she was inviting him to talk . . . deliberately giving him space and attention.

V brought his knees up and propped his gloved hand on one of them. Flexing the fingers, he pictured the thing without a covering. "You know how when you go out at night, you look up and expect to see the sky? And when you do, it's this combination of something that affects you, because it can be cloudy or clear, raining or snowing . . . and yet it is totally impersonal? The sky is at once dispositive and irrelevant—and that's what she was like. She was always there, and I don't know; maybe she tried the best she could to connect with me and my sister. But she sucked at relating to people." He looked at Jane pointedly. "I get that from her." Then he shrugged. "So that's what it feels like for me on a personal level. But then there's also the other, more important shit. I feel like the race is exposed, and I don't like that. There's too much weird shit happening at once. I mean, she disappears, and we're coming down to the end of the war—and then I run into that shadow in the alley? I don't fucking like it, true? We're at a crossroads, and sometimes the new direction doesn't improve things. It lands you right in the crapper."

Jane nodded. "Makes sense to me."

As she said the words, there was a loosening in V's entire body, a relaxation of muscle he hadn't been aware of tensing.

"Do you think also . . ." Jane cleared her throat. "Do you think maybe you're disappointed that things between you and your mother didn't get fixed? That as long as she was alive—or whatever she was— there was a possibility that sometime, way down the line, she might be who you needed her to be? But now that's gone."

"I didn't need shit from her."

"Everyone needs something from their mother. It's the way it works."

When he smiled, she said, "What?"

"No one ever disagrees with me. But you."

Jane looked down at her own hands, her brows getting tight. "Not one of my virtues, huh."

"Actually, it's a part of you I love most."

When she glanced at him in surprise, he leaned in quick and kissed her on the mouth—even though he shouldn't have. Then to cover up the faux pas, he jumped to his feet and extended his hand.

"I guess we better go."

Jane got up on her own, leaving his palm in the breeze—another thing he loved about her. She would never need anything from him or any male. Any female. Anybody. Jane took care of herself—and had so much competence left over, she could take care of everyone else, too.

"Do we get back the same way we came here?" she asked roughly.

"Yeah, we just focus and—"

With a quick shift, she fit herself against his body, wrapping her arms around him and holding on.

Vishous closed his eyes and embraced her, tilting his head down so that his nose was in the sweet warmth of her neck. "I can't say I'm sorry."

"For what?" she whispered.

"Kissing you."

Before she could reply, he sent them back down to earth.

He wished that they could have stayed in the Sanctuary alone, though. Forever.

TWENTY-THREE

"*I* want to go home."

Assail was sitting up in his bed with a rolling tray full of food in front of him, his eyes alert and back to normal, the whites as bright as they should be. And as Sola stood with Ehlena and Dr. Manello, she was at once excited and full of dread at his demand.

If he were terminal, he needed to be here. So that if something happened, it could be handled by people trained to, you know, handle those things.

"Hello?" he said. "Will one of the three of you respond?"

Sola looked at the other two and figured this decision was way above her pay grade. She was more support. Showering. Toothbrushing.

But it was hard not to want to get him away from this clinical environment, even if it was only for a little bit. He had been taken off all the monitors and the IV. The catheter was long gone. And other than a couple of pills, the purpose of which she didn't know, he was mostly not being medicated. Whatever acute episode had been brought on by his cancer treatment had passed. For now.

"Well?" he insisted. "You just put me in how many machines over the last six hours, and you yourself said that my brain is functioning within normal limits. So what is the problem."

Sola had to smile. With each passing hour, he was turning back into the man she had known and been bristled by. Assail had always had an autocratic way about him, as if he had spent his entire life giving orders and having them followed without question. It was irritating, and sexy—depending on whether she agreed with him on the issue or not.

"Have we all forgotten how to speak English?" he drawled. "Or am I having one of my phaseouts again?"

"Let's talk about these—what do you call them?" Dr. Manello put his hands in the pockets of his white coat. "Phaseouts?"

"Oh, no, you don't." Assail wagged his forefinger back and forth. "I'm not falling for that. You're looking for an excuse to keep me here."

And then they were all staring at her.

Clearing her throat, Sola said, "As long as you tell me what to watch out for and when to call, I'm happy to be there to care for him. And I always have nine-one-one—"

"Actually," Dr. Manello cut in, "I'll give you a number to phone. We can be to you in the blink of an eye. It's best to keep in touch with us directly."

"So is that a yes?" Assail's eyes were like lasers on the doctor. "Are you letting me go?"

"I have one condition," the other man said. "Myself or Doc Jane gets to come out and do regular visits."

"So I'll see you next week then." Assail smiled. "I'll pencil you in."

Sola had to look away. These comments he made, like getting out of the drug business, or putting anything on a calendar, reminded her that he was not in a position to set long-term plans of any kind. She wasn't sure whether it was delusion, denial, or part of his brain problems, but sooner or later, reality was going to be a crushing blow—and she hated that for him.

Dr. Manello made a *pshaw* movement with his hand. "You're cute. Try every twelve hours—no, make that eight."

Narrowing his eyes, Assail spoke in a *Masterpiece Theatre* tone. "Must you."

"Yup, I gotta. Unless you'd prefer to continue to enjoy our luxurious five-star accommodations here?"

"Fine." Assail crossed his arms over his chest. "I shall welcome you with bated breath."

"That's the spirit."

When the medical staff stepped out to arrange for an ambulance— or whatever, maybe that Range Rover—Sola excused herself.

"I'll be right back," she said to Assail.

Out in the hall, she called after Dr. Manello. "I'm sorry, can I grab you for a second?"

The man turned around and smiled. "What can I do you for?"

"You're sure this is okay?"

"Yes, I am. We can get there fast if something happens, and the brain scans are looking good. You're going to be there with his cousins, and they can control him until we arrive."

Ask him, she thought. *Ask him for all the ugly details of the diagnosis and treatment.*

And then she should raise the truly awful questions that gave her the most anxiety: *How long does Assail have? Is the end going to be bad? Are you certain you've done everything you can?*

Dr. Manello put his hand on her shoulder and squeezed. "It's going to be okay. Besides, getting him out of here will do him good. Ehlena's calling Ehric right now, and as soon as he finds an escort in, they'll be here."

Sola refocused, moving away from what terrified her to the things she could control. There would be time, when she was stronger, for the hard conversations. *Get him home and settled,* she told herself.

"You'll give me his prescriptions?" She cleared the lump in her throat. "Or do I have to go to a CVS or something?"

"We'll give you everything. Not to worry."

• • •

The doctor was true to his word. Within half an hour, Ehric arrived in the Range Rover and Sola got a goody bag of pills with detailed instructions and all kinds of telephone numbers to call. And then Assail walked out of the facility on his own, refusing assistance from the medical staff, his cousin, even her.

It was clearly a matter of pride, and as he struggled with his head held high and his jaw tight with effort and concentration, she had to blink away tears. But he made it all the way to the parking area and into the back of the SUV without a slip, fall, or help-me.

The big blond man was once again their escort, and as Sola settled into her rear seat next to Assail, he smiled at her from the front. "Nice to see you again. Glad it's under these circumstances."

"Me, too." She glanced at Assail and tried not to worry over how pale and exhausted he seemed. "It's good to go home."

And then they were heading out. She didn't pay much attention to the gating systems or that strange fog this time. She was too busy watching Assail.

After a short recovery time from his exertion, he began to glow with happiness as he looked out the window—and she tried to get in touch with that emotion. The sad truth that they were bringing him home to die, however, was too overwhelming for her—to the point where she almost wished they could turn around and go back to the clinic.

This resurrection of his was but a flare, not a true fire source.

God, the seesawing was exhausting, she thought. One minute she couldn't wait to get him home; now she wanted to return to the hospital . . . heaven knew what she would be feeling or thinking next.

"Look at the snow," Assail said as they emerged onto the country road. "So much of it has fallen."

His face was full of wonder, as if he were a child, and he sat forward in his seat, focusing on the headlights and the road. When he reached behind himself and started patting around, she wasn't sure what he was doing—until their hands brushed and he held on to hers.

Closing her eyes, she rested her head back and felt the subtle bumps of the ride, the heater blowing on her ankles, the warmth of his palm against hers.

I don't know how to do this, she thought. *I don't know how to . . .*

"We're here!"

Sola jerked herself awake and looked around. They were on Assail's long driveway, his glass house glowing with light up ahead—like it recognized its owner was finally back home.

As they came around to the garages, the door in the middle trundled up, and Ehric pulled them inside. No one moved until the panels were lowered back into place—and the instant those heavy sections landed, everybody got out at once.

Evale threw open the way into the mansion, the man's face both tense and hopeful.

Assail refused help and did not stop smiling as he shuffled over to his cousin. "Miss me?"

Evale went down the shallow steps and closed in, his arms stretching out and embracing his family. Quiet words were spoken and Sola looked away to give them privacy.

"Oh, man, who is cooking in there?" Rhage said.

Sola took a deep inhale and, sure enough, caught all kinds of her grandmother's magic. "My *vovó*," she replied. "That's who's at the stove."

"She's obviously a genius."

"I would agree," Sola said as Assail motioned for her to come in with him.

Hand in hand, they walked through the mudroom and then they were in the kitchen. Her grandmother didn't look up from the skillet she was using.

"Wash hands," she commanded gruffly. "Time to eat."

It was her *vovó*'s way, of course—love shown through effort, rather than words. And Sola had to smile a little—especially as she saw the table set for five, and the thin guy she had threatened with her gun pouring water into glasses. He straightened as he looked at Assail, and then paled as if he were going to pass out.

"Markcus," Assail chided, "let's not become emotional. I'm home and going to be fine."

Sola closed her eyes and had to remind herself that that was probably the best attitude for him to take. Positivity was a good thing.

Assail went over and gave the young man a hug, and then Rhage was over by the back door. "As much as I want to stay, I've got to catch you all later. But you take care, and call us if you need us."

"We shall," Assail promised as he went to the sink and began to wash his hands. "Thank you as always for your service."

"Good deal."

The man gave them a wave and walked out into the night. Guess he was being picked up by someone, Sola thought.

"Are you sure he shouldn't wait in here?" she said. "It's really cold."

Assail shook his head. "He will be fine."

Platters of food came out of the oven where they had been warming and were carried by her *vovó*'s strong hands to the table. And Ehric and Evale washed up at the bar sink across the way and then got into their seats as if they were good little children ready for lunch at school. Markcus joined them, and Assail led Sola over to a vacant seat, which he pulled out for her.

It was sometime around then that her grandmother stopped moving and just stared at Assail. Her expression was frozen, but her eyes were not. They traveled around him, noting . . . everything.

He hesitated after he scooted the chair in under Sola's butt.

"Sit," her *vovó* said as she pointed to the head of the table. "You will eat much now."

Assail flushed, but followed orders, planting himself in the chair. And then Sola's grandmother approached him with a grave expression. Putting her hands around to the back of her own neck, she removed a slim gold chain that had a small medal hanging off of it.

"This is St. Raphael. He will protect you and heal you. You will wear this and no take it off."

She transferred the necklace to Assail's throat and switched to Spanish, offering a prayer for Assail's health as she took his face in her old, beautiful hands.

Sola rubbed her eyes as they teared up.

"Now, you eat," her *vovó* snapped. "All of you. Too thin!"

As her grandmother headed back for the stove, she gave Sola a quick, hard hug. And then Assail's cousins began passing the food around. The man himself simply looked down at the medal, however.

Sola cleared her throat. "Don't worry, I won't let her make you convert."

"This is very kind of her." Assail glanced up. "Very kind indeed."

"There's more where that came from." Sola accepted a platter of enchiladas—and realized she was starved. "We have a saint for everything."

He turned toward the stove. "Mrs. Carvalho?" When the woman looked over, he lifted the medal. "Thank you. I am honored."

"Eat. We go to mass at midnight—"

"*Vovó,* I don't think that is a good idea—"

"Yes," Assail said. "That is perfect. We shall go, indeed."

And with that decided, he began to pile his plate high, that special smile on his face making him seem renewed from the inside out.

After a moment, Sola resolved to just go with it. She had no idea how much time they had together, so she was going to damn well enjoy every second she had.

To do anything else was a foolish waste of a gift she had never expected to receive.

TWENTY-FOUR

Assail started with *sopa de fubá,* which was a spectacular combination of collard greens and sausage in a thick broth. Then he moved on to three servings of the *feijoada,* a mix of smoked ham hocks over white rice—with plenty of *pão de queijo* on the side. Dessert was something they called *sobremesa de banana com queijo.*

Banana pudding.

He wasn't the only one who put the goods away, so to speak. Everybody, including Marisol, ate like it had been a year since their last meal. And when they were done, they all pushed their chairs back and just sat there, the effort of moving any farther away from the table too much like work.

But Assail had something on his mind, something that he could wait no longer for.

Looking over at Marisol, he said, "Will you please help me to my room upstairs? I should like a shower and a lie-down before we go to church, and I shall require help."

Marisol nodded and got to her feet. "Let me just clear first—"

"No," Mrs. Carvalho said sharply. "I will clean. Then I will rest as well. We leave here at eleven-twenty. I no want to be late."

Assail stood up. "Allow me to reassure you, madam, that your grand-daughter's aid will be that of a necessary nursing function only."

"You are good boy. Now, go! Out of my kitchen."

"You have honored us greatly with this meal."

This caused all the males to get up and bow low to the diminutive, white-haired elder, and the flush that hit Mrs. Carvalho's lined face told him that they had pleased her—although she would never say as much.

"Enough of this ceremony," she muttered as she turned the sink on and got out the Ivory dish soap. "Off you all go."

Ehric and Evale followed instruction to the letter, taking their stomachs in hand as if they were carrying boulders at waist level, and disappearing down below to their quarters. When Markcus hesitated, Assail had to do him a favor.

Putting an arm around the young male's shoulder, Assail said quietly, "Go and rest."

"Are you sure?"

"This is an argument you will never win. And we shall find other ways to serve her, I promise you."

As Markcus nodded and followed the descending example set, Assail was free to hold an arm out to Sola and use the excuse of his physical condition to draw her close.

Underneath the soft, thin scrubs he had been given to wear home, he was already partially erect, his sexual drive awakening and resurrecting him even further, the need focusing him and giving him an urgency that was very familiar. He did pause, however, as they rounded the corner to the sleek stairs and he saw into his office.

"What is it?" Marisol asked. "Do you need to sit down?"

"I spent many hours in there." He pointed through the open doorway, to the slice of hall light that penetrated the darkness and landed on his desk as if it were a portent. "So much time and effort."

"Come on," she said gently. "Let's not think of anything right now. Let's get you another shower."

He allowed her to direct him to the ascent, and he was surprised by how weak his legs were. Even with his weight loss, they struggled to carry him up the stairs.

It was dark in the master bedroom, too, and he willed the dim lights on—

"You installed motion detectors?" Marisol said.

"Ah . . . yes. I did." He was going to have to watch that. Vampires didn't have to use light switches. "Look at this place. I am . . . back."

The room was circular and had windows all the way around, the view of the winter landscape extending for miles. Paneled in a buttery burled walnut, everything glowed in the soft illumination, the sleek, contemporary decor a non-competing background to that incredible night horizon.

"I never thought I would see this again." He went over and stared out at the river, the distant mountains, the city across the water. "I appreciate this all so much more now."

"Listen, you don't have to go to church. My grandmother is from the old school, and very devout, but that doesn't mean—"

"Oh, I will go." He turned around to his Marisol. "I am not familiar with your customs, but I would like to learn them."

"So you're not Christian? Not that it matters to me."

"No, I am not." Crossing the distance between them, he stepped in close to her and put a hand on the side of her neck. Rubbing his thumb over her jugular, he murmured, "So tell me, do they offer a forgiving of sins? For I am afraid I lied to that good woman downstairs."

Marisol's eyes flared and then her lids got heavy. "What did you lie to her about?"

"I don't want a shower." He stared at his female's lips, watching them part. "And nursing is not what is necessary from you right now."

Marisol leaned into his body, her hands going around him. "I think we can get this absolved."

"Do you? That is good news, indeed."

Tilting his head, he brushed his lips on hers, and the contact caused a bolt of energy to shock through him. So soft, so warm . . . so vital. It had seemed like a lifetime since he had kissed her properly, and the feel of her mouth made his world spin.

"Oh, Marisol," he breathed.

He took things slowly, relearning the contours of her lips, asking and being granted permission for entry. Together, they backed up to the circular bed, and as they lay down, he dimmed the lights further.

He did not want her to see too much of him. Far better for her to rely on recollection; it was a more attractive picture.

"So you have a remote, too?"

Assail lifted his head. "What?"

"For the lights."

Damn it, he was going to have to be more alert about these things.

By way of answering her, he kissed her some more, sweeping his hands down her arm and onto her rib cage. She was liquid gold beneath his touch, arching into him, her body hidden by the veil of her clothing and nevertheless awe-inspiring. And the more he touched her, the thicker the scent of her arousal grew—and soon he became stuck between wanting to hurry to be inside of her . . . and wanting this to last forever.

Easing back, he looked into her dark eyes and brushed her short blond hair back. He missed its natural color, he decided. His Marisol was an uncontrived beauty, too purposeful and direct to fuss with things like makeup trends and products that would add nothing to what already shone forth. But she was sublime in any way she came unto him.

As if she knew what he was thinking, she took the bottom of her fleece and the T-shirt under it and swept the pair up and over her head.

"Marisol . . ." he moaned.

Her breasts were just as he recalled, perfectly sized and covered not with lace, but with a simple cotton-cup bra. With fingers that trembled, he stroked over her collarbones . . . down to her sternum . . . and then up the edge of the bra, first on one side, then on the other. Her breath caught and released as he did so, her nipples hardening and showing themselves.

There was a front clasp.

Which, in his current frame of mind, was a clear sign that the Creator was a benevolent force in the world.

"I have to see you," Assail groaned as he released the fastening.

The cups fell off to the side and he gasped as he ran his palm down the center of her body. His mouth was a greedy seeker as he pleasured her, sucking her tips in and giving himself up to the sounds she made, and the taste of her, and the fact that that scent of her sex was making his head hum—in a good way.

She was wearing blue jeans and he took his time stripping them and her panties off her long, muscled legs. His hands traveled the length of her, stroking her as he went back to attend to her breasts. And he stopped only when she tried to get under the loose scrubs that covered him.

"I don't . . . I want to keep those on," he said in a rough voice.

"All right. But not on my account."

He shook his head, thinking about what he'd seen in the mirror at the clinic. "How can you say that?"

"Because it's you." She smiled up at him, and touched his face. "It's still you."

"Fates, Marisol, there is so much more that I want to do with you—but I do not know how long I'll have my energy."

"Don't worry. Anything with you will be amazing."

A sudden wellspring of emotion made him tear up, but that was so not sexy. Just like his body, his bald head, his . . .

And yet Marisol was lying back in his pathetic, scrawny arms, staring up at him as if he were a god.

That was love, was it not.

When he couldn't speak and didn't move, her brows tightened. "What is it?"

Assail cleared his throat. "There are so many ways to tell someone that you care for them."

"Yes"—she stroked his face some more—"there are."

Marisol brought him to her mouth, pulling him on top of her. As he settled between her thighs, he could feel her heat, and he fumbled to get the waistband of the scrubs down over his erection. His sex kept getting in the way, however, the one thing on his body that had not been subject to shrinking size.

Thank Fates.

"Goddamn it—"

"Here, let me help—"

The two of them went for the tie on the scrubs like the thing held the key to the gates of paradise, their hands tripping and tangling, him leaning back until he fell off of her. Sometime along the way, the absurdity of it all hit him and he started to laugh—and then she joined in.

"What did you tie this with?" she said. "A winch and a crane?"

"Scissors!" he a-ha'd. "We need scissors!"

"Where?"

"Bathroom?"

Marisol scrambled naked off the bed, and he twisted so he could enjoy the view as she went into that bathroom on a mission from God. He had an impulse to will the lights on over the sinks to help her, but he caught himself. Besides, watching her naked body move was the most beautiful dance he'd ever seen, whether it was in the light or the shadows.

When she came back, triumphant, he smiled. "You know, I suddenly am glad I didn't do a bow."

Marisol straddled him at his thighs. "I won't hurt you."

"I know. And I can assure you, I am enjoying this."

Placing his hands behind his head, he had a momentary lapse as his palms got a tactile reminder that he was now bald—but then she was using those sharp, steel scissors on the tenacious fabric knot.

"This is a huge turn-on," he drawled.

"I agree." She winked at him. "Almost got it—there!"

As she stretched to put their rescuer on the bedside table, he took the opportunity to find her nipple with his lips—and she ended up dropping the scissors just short of goal.

"Do we care they're on the floor," she gasped.

"No," he said around his mouthful.

This time, when he went to push the scrubs out of the way, they went without a problem, and Marisol sat back.

As they both looked at his erection, he said dryly, "May I just point out that my weight loss appears to have had no effect on that portion of my anatomy?"

Marisol laughed, and then she took him in hand—and now he was the one gasping and rising up for more of her touch.

"Please . . ." he groaned.

"I couldn't agree more."

Straddling his hips again, she angled his arousal . . . and sat down, impaling herself in the most marvelous way.

Assail's eyes rolled back, and his body drank in the sensation of completeness. "My Marisol . . ."

It was true, Sola thought as she began to move up and down. Assail had most definitely not lost any girth or length. He filled her and then some, the stretching so incredible, the possession so total, her body was alive in the pleasure.

But she was gentle with him. She kept the rhythm a slow rocking— it was more than enough, though. And he was right there with her, moving to the pace, his arousal sliding in and out of her, the friction so good, it made her pant.

"Marisol . . ." he said again, his fingers biting into her thighs. "Oh, *God* . . ."

His orgasm reverberated up through her and she was not far behind, her own release rippling outward, coloring her with a joy so great she wanted to weep.

When they both stilled, she was careful to settle herself off to the side, so she wasn't directly on his body—and she was going to remember the happiness on his face for the rest of her life. He was resplendent, transformed, younger and more vital than ever.

It was hard to say who wrapped whose arms around the other first, but what did it matter. Next thing she knew, they were lying heart-to-heart, her head tucked into the crook of his arm, the heat drifting down from the ceiling keeping her warm even as her naked body cooled on top of the duvet.

"Assail?"

"Yes," he murmured.

"You don't have to convert."

"What?"

She inched back. "If my *vovó* goes on the hard sell tonight, I just want you to know that I accept you exactly the way you are. We don't have to be the same to be together."

"That is good to know." He brushed her mouth with his fingertip. "But I am not worried."

"My *vovó* can be persuasive."

"She approves of me, already." His smile was as she remembered, sexy, a little dark, very appealing. "After all, she and I are alike. We both appreciate the way things should be done."

"This is true."

"Shall we shower the now?" he said. "I can help you with the soap."

"You can?" Actually, that sounded like a great idea. And not only because she liked being clean. "You would help me? Well, what a kind gentleman you are . . ."

Leaning in, she kissed him. And kissed him some more.

Eventually, they made it to the hot water. But it was a while.

TWENTY-FIVE

As Jane stepped through the supply closet and into the training center's office, she checked her watch. Eight p.m. It had been twenty-four hours since Manny had kicked her out. Well, twenty-four, more or less.

Just exactly how precise was he going to be?

In the corridor, she found herself fiddling with her scrubs as she went down to the clinic rooms. She always kept clean sets of the tops and bottoms in her room at the Pit, and as soon as she and V landed back on earth, she'd excused herself, had a shower, and changed into her second skin of loose-and-cotton-and-blue.

When she'd reemerged, V had been strapping his weapons on, getting ready to head out into the field with Butch again. As she'd left, he'd stared at her as if there were things he wanted to say or do, but wasn't sure where the new boundaries were. She felt the same way.

About him . . . and her job.

She'd ended up giving V an awkward goodbye wave—and had no idea what was next for them. Did they meet up at Last Meal? Or . . . text? Or . . .

God, she felt as though she were dating her husband.

And while she was covering unknowns, she wondered whether Manny was going to kick her out again or force her to—

"Hey."

Jane stopped short and looked up. Speak of the devil: Manny was in front of the main examination room, the door slowly shutting behind him as if he had just walked out.

"Hey, yourself." She cleared her throat. "How we doing?"

When in doubt, she figured, go with the open-ended: that could cover her situation, the patients on deck, the weather . . . anything.

"We're good." He shifted a legal-sized pad of paper from his right to his left hand. "More importantly, how are you?"

"Good. Yup. Just fine."

Cue the weird pause. And then she abruptly decided she was too tired to worry about pride.

"I'm really sorry I got into it with you," she blurted. "And you're right. I do need to take a breather and get on a better schedule. I have lost all sense of perspective, and even though I had, and always will have, the best interests of my patients at heart, I've potentially compromised care by being over-involved and exhausted."

Manny exhaled with relief. "I'm so glad to hear you say that. And listen, I didn't mean to come across like it was an intervention. I just didn't know how else to handle it."

"You did the right thing."

"Well, along those lines." He put up the pad. "Tada! Our new schedule."

She leaned in and then smiled at the scribbles. "Okay, you have a doctor's handwriting. Has anyone mentioned that before?"

He frowned and turned the paper back around. "I felt like I did better keeping it all caps and printing?"

"I think I got the month right. January?"

"Um . . . actually I started it in February."

She laughed and came around to stand beside him. "So tell me what we've got."

He pointed out things in the little boxes he'd made. "Both of us work nights. Then we alternate days sleeping here. So we'll have plenty of coverage when the Brothers are out in the field, but when the sun is up, only one of us is on. And if there are no acute cases here, then we both go back home. Every seven days, though, each of us gets a whole twenty-four hours off—and it syncs with the day rotation. See?"

She nodded, her stomach unclenching. "You know, this is going to work."

"There's one other piece, though." As she looked up, he seemed braced. "We're going to have to hire another nurse—and another surgeon."

Jane opened her mouth. Shut it.

Told herself to think before she spoke.

"You're right about the nurse." She nodded. "It's not fair that you and I have time off, but Ehlena doesn't have that option. Another surgeon, though?"

She pictured working with someone like Havers night in and night out—and was very sure she was not up to that rash of superiority: Undoubtedly, any vampire who was a trained doctor would come from the *glymera,* because it was considered a job only aristocrats were allowed to aspire to.

Wait . . . was there even another physician in the species?

"Hear me out." Manny put his palm forward. "We could go to an every-other-day schedule then. And more hands means less stress."

"Provided they're good hands. Do you have somebody in mind? I'm not even sure there's anyone but Havers?"

"I haven't gotten that far."

"Well, I want to be in on both hires."

"I wouldn't have it any other way. So you'll support me as I take this to Wrath?"

Crossing her arms over her chest, the loud, screaming voice in her head that said, *No! This is mine!* suggested she was still too close to things. Sure, Vishous had built out these facilities for her, and she and Manny had established all the practice standards, and figured out the ordering procedures, and taken care of each and every case that had come through the system they'd set up.

But she needed to be about the patients, first and foremost.

And her desire for control, in this instance, felt a lot like squatter's rights run amok.

"Yes, I will support you." She nodded firmly. "All the way."

"I know this is hard, Jane."

She laughed in a short burst. "The truth is, this place, this work we do down here, it's my baby."

Funny way to put it, she thought.

"I mean, it's all I have." She frowned. "Hold on, what I'm trying to say is—"

Manny put his hand on her shoulder. "I know exactly what you're talking about. And I just want to get us into a sustainable, marathon-type situation here. We've been sprinting for too long, out of necessity. Now, it's time to change our paradigm for the future."

"I agree. So when do we go talk to the King?"

"I'll make the appointment and we'll go together."

"Just let me know."

It was hard not to view Manny taking the lead on making a staffing schedule as evidence of a failure on her part to police herself and everyone else. And God, she really hated the idea of bringing other people on staff. But she needed to adapt. She *would* adapt.

Besides, when was the last time, before the previous night and day up in the Sanctuary, that she and Vishous had spent any period of time together?

She hadn't given any weight to the idea she'd abandoned him. She'd always just thought of her job and her patients—and that was the point, wasn't it.

"Anyway," she said sharply. "How were things while I was gone?"

"Good, good. I released Assail."

"You did?" *That was my patient,* she thought. "I mean, he continued to improve?"

"He was prepared to march out of here on his own if I didn't let him go. Scans all looked good. Functioning was good. I sent them away with the anti-seizure meds, and told them every eight hours or so, you or I were going to come out and check with them over the next week." He smiled at her. "And on that note, I figure you'd want to take the first round on that, am I right?"

"You are—"

Ehlena came running out of the exam room. "We've got two down in the field. Gunshot wound and a broken leg."

"Motherfucker," Manny said. "I'll get the surgical van."

"What's the address?" Jane asked. "And who is injured?"

"Trade and Twenty-first. It's Vishous and Butch. Phury called it in."

For a split second, Jane felt the world spin. Then her training and experience refocused her. "I'll go out ahead and stabilize them."

Sometimes life came at you fast.

Death, too.

As Vishous dragged his useless lower half backward into a doorway, he was cursing the hell out of his left shitkicker.

Not that it was the boot's fault his foot was ninety degrees off angle.

Although actually, the shitkicker *was* kind of responsible. When he'd gone and done a running tackle on that *lesser* who'd been shooting at Butch, V'd expected a ground game. The surprise? The fact that the slayer and he had gone on a pummeling roll that had taken them out of the alley and directly into the path of an Uber.

Brakes slamming. Humans freaking out in the Ford Explorer. Lots of skidding on the snow and ice.

The *lesser* had taken the brunt of the impact on the hood and grille, but V had somehow managed to get his left leg tangled in the front spoiler—courtesy of the bulk and the steel toe of his shitkicker.

Snap! Crackle! Pop!

He couldn't feel anything down there so he didn't know whether it was an ankle dislocation—yay!—or a compound fracture—boo!—but either way, he was out of commission when it came to upright ambulation.

And he was scared as shit about Butch.

"What we got, Phury!" V called out again.

When there was still no response, Vishous sat forward and tried to see what was going on around the corner. His brother had been busy erasing the memories of the humans in that car, and no doubt calling for backup.

Stop fucking around with those humans, he wanted to scream. *Get to Butch!*

He had no idea what shape his roommate was in, and he couldn't see down the road far enough to get any intel on that. What he did fucking know was that the goddamn slayer's pistol had discharged a number of times before V had taken the undead off the vertical, and there absolutely was the smell of vampire blood in the air.

The cop must have been shot.

"Goddamn it, Phury! Talk to me—"

From out of nowhere, an image of his Jane formed, sure as if his mind was placing a call to the universe and summoning her—

"What have we got," she said as she knelt before him.

V recoiled. "Huh?"

"Your leg. Are we a dislocation or a fracture?"

"Are you really here?" But then he kicked his own ass. "Don't worry about me! I got this—Butch is shot over there! Go!"

She met him in the eye for a split second, as if she were assessing him. And then she nodded once.

"I've got him. Don't worry. No matter what it is, I'll handle it."

Then she dipped down, kissed him quick and hard, and took off at a dead run.

As he watched her go, a feeling of total pride and security overwhelmed him nearly to the point of tears.

Whatever problems he had had with her focus on her job, he wouldn't have wanted anybody else—not Havers, not Manny, not even himself—going to treat his best friend's gunshot wound. Butch could not possibly be in better hands—

A soft shuffling sound overhead brought his attention up to the fire escape above him, and he flared his nostrils, breathing in deep.

"Sonofa*bitch*," he muttered as he went for his gun.

Before he could shout a warning that they had company, a *lesser* dropped down on top of him from the iron latticework that went up the side of a building, the heavy weight compressing his spine from the back of his neck all the way to his ass. Courtesy of the impact, his broken/dislocated/whatever'd foot decided to wake up and get talking, and the pain was so great, he blacked out for a split second.

Which was all it took for the slayer to get the gun from his grip and start the fucking party.

TWENTY-SIX

itoria made the trip back from Ricardo's West Point house to Caldwell in under twenty-five minutes. Then again, at this late night hour of ten o'clock, there was little traffic to speak of, and she was already refining her route and discovering shortcuts. As she drove along in her rental car, she hummed to the Latino station she had found on the radio, her manicured forefinger tapping on the top of the wheel.

She was not returning to the gallery, however.

No, no. Instead of getting off at the second exit for downtown, she stayed on the highway. A few miles farther north, she removed herself from the interstate and entered a part of the city that was technically suburban, but in terms of architecture, more akin to the financial district with its modernist houses made from concrete, steel, and great panes of glass.

This made so much sense, she thought as her old-fashioned map's directions took her deeper into the land of people who preferred to spend their wealth on ugly things to fill cold, barren spaces.

It was absolutely perfect.

After some manner of recalculation, the house she had come in search of was located through the maze of streets—and its location on the very edge of the community's homogeny was logical as well.

Vitoria drove past the address once . . . made a fat circle by taking a series of left-hand turns . . . and then passed it again.

The abode was two-storied, with an open room to one side that was all glass, and some manner of wings out to the back. Compared to the others, it was much smaller and on a lot that wasn't quite as well planted or illuminated, an almost-there as opposed to an I-have-arrived.

If it were a plant, one would hope to water and repot it over time so that it could grow into fruition to match the others around it.

But that was not the way real estate worked. And once again, it was as she had expected.

Finding an appropriate place to park was something worth considering seriously, and she settled on a small park a quarter of a mile away. Before exiting the rental, she put the hood up on the black parka she had donned and slipped her burner phone into a pocket with a zipper.

As she got out, she looked around without moving her head. The night was so cold, casual pedestrians were staying indoors, and the few-and-far-betweens who were out with their dogs were tucked into their bodies and glaring at their four-legged friends.

Vitoria strode off, backtracking to the house.

She entered onto the property via the road behind it, slipping through a stand of evergreen bushes that had been clipped into a horizontal wave pattern.

No dog fence, but she could have guessed no pets.

As she halted and surveyed the house, she thought . . . oh, how she loved all that glass. So much to visualize before she broke in, so much helpful information.

And there it was . . . there was what she had come for: Yes, the homeowner was on the premises. And drinking a glass of white wine in a black silk robe.

Vitoria stayed where she was, watching, waiting. When no one else appeared, she closed in, crossing over the lawn in the shadows because the house was lit from within, not without.

The garage had an exterior door on its far side, and in another stroke of luck, she did not have to pick a lock. The thing gave way like a good host, allowing her access into a two-car space, which had only one vehicle—a four- or five-year-old white Mercedes—parked directly in the center.

This was just getting easier.

There were three bare wooden steps to the steel door leading to the home's interior, and as Vitoria went up them, first, second . . . third, she curled up a fist in the black leather gloves she'd put on.

Knock, knock, knock.

Then she stepped back down onto the poured concrete floor and waited, making sure she was off to one side a little.

The door swung open, the figure in the black robe with the glass of pale wine backlit by the lights of the hall behind.

"Hello?" came the impatient demand as the homeowner patted the wall beside them for the light switch. "Jonathan? Did you forget your key—"

Vitoria pulled the trigger on the gun in her hand, discharging three bullets that were silenced beautifully by the suppressor she had screwed onto the muzzle's tip.

Miss Margot Fortescue's arms jerked up, that wine thrown over her shoulder in a splash, her feet tripping over themselves as she fell backward.

Vitoria leapt onto the top step and caught the door, holding it wide.

Miss Fortescue was gasping like a fish, her perfectly pale skin going paler as her blood pressure began to fail, her hands clawing at the gray tile she was on. The slippery robe had fallen open and there were three spots of blood on the white silk nightgown beneath.

Vitoria angled the gun and pulled the trigger three more times, drilling more slugs into that chest, even though she was certain she had accomplished her goal with the first trio.

No more movement after that. No gasping, either.

The door was weighted to close on its own, but as she didn't want any noise, she guided it into place silently.

Then she left as she had come in, rounding the Mercedes and exiting back into the yard. Jogging over to the wavy hedge, she stepped through the bushes—

Stopping short, she did not move.

One of those dog owners and his animal were walking down the street on the other side, the pair moving fast, the owner because he was cold, the standard poodle because he was energized, perhaps by a recent defecation.

Vitoria got her gun back out of its holster. She would much prefer not to use the weapon again, as killing potential witnesses could become an exponential thing, with bodies piling up like cordwood. She would do what she must, however.

If the pair were lucky, the dog would not scent anything. Would not look over and start barking. Would not cause the owner to investigate the source of canine engagement.

And wasn't that the theme of the evening, Vitoria thought. Keeping to oneself and one's own business was, in so many situations, the very best way of ensuring one's long-term health and well-being.

TWENTY-SEVEN

Jane hated leaving Vishous wounded and down on the ground, but she knew he was safe in that doorway—and unlike a gunshot wound, what was going on with his leg was not terminal. Plus he was lucid and his color was good.

Moving quickly, she ran out to the road and bypassed the carload of humans Phury was erasing . . . then jumped over a slayer who was writhing in a pool of black blood . . . and finally penetrated the darkness of the next alley over to find Butch.

"Hey there," a familiar Bostonian voice said. "Fancy . . . meeting you here."

She stopped and spun around. "Where are you?"

"Behind the trash cans."

Rerouting, she rushed over to a lineup of metal bins. The cop was sitting upright against the brick, his legs kicked out in front of him, one arm hanging loose, the other grabbing on to a wound that was somewhere up and to the left of his sternum.

Jane shifted her medical backpack off. "How's it going, roomie?"

"Good, good." Butch smiled weakly. "I'm making vacation plans for the spring. Think I'll take Marissa to Fashion Week, and—" He groaned as he tried to move. "Fuck."

"Let me have a look." He allowed her to remove his protective hand and she immediately took a deep breath of relief. "Okay, I believe we're a lot more shoulder than I initially thought—"

The sound of shots ringing out twisted her around. Out in the road proper, as the SUV drove off, Phury had his gun up and was racing into the alley Vishous was in.

"Oh, shit, V!" she said. "That's where he is—"

"I'm good to go!" Butch grunted as he started to stand up. "I'm coming, V—"

Jane shoved the cop back down and held him there. "You are going *nowhere.*"

More shots. And then Phury stumbled back into the road. He was shouting at an attacker Jane couldn't see as he fell to his knees.

Then, like something out of a horror movie, his torso took impacts that jerked him like a puppet, his mane of glorious hair blowing back as he collapsed into the snow.

Jane jumped to her feet and went for her phone. "Stay here—"

"I'm coming, too!"

As more bullets sounded out in a series of pops, she jabbed a forefinger at the male. *"Stay. There."*

Allowing herself to fade from her corporeal form, she ran directly into the line of fire. The lead slugs that were flying out of the alley V was in passed right through her, leaving ripples as if through water, her non-flesh registering the penetrations and exits in dull flares of heat.

Jane skidded in the snow and dropped down to Phury. Vishous was first and foremost on her mind, but she had to be professional—and triage rules had to apply.

As she reached out, Phury gasped and went to fight her off, his flailing arms going through her ghostly form.

"It's me," she said urgently, dropping her face close to his own. "It's Jane."

As he calmed down, she tried to see what was going on with the gunfight. There was more shooting, and she didn't know whether that was good, because Brotherhood backup had arrived, or bad, because other *lessers* had and V was dead.

"I'm hit," Phury said as he scratched at his leather jacket and tried to rip it open. She helped him with the zipper, and then—

"Thank God," she muttered as she got a gander at his bulletproof vest.

The thing had done its job, catching the bullets and holding them from his flesh. But there still could be internal damage—

The slayer that shot out of the alley was running as if its non-life depended on it. Black blood was pouring out from its throat, a geyser tapped, but the bastard was still up and rolling. And it was armed.

Focusing on Phury, it lifted the gun in its hand, pointing the muzzle at the Brother's head.

Bulletproof vests only worked on the places they were covering. A shot to the cranium was lethal.

And then, just before the *lesser* pulled its trigger, Jane saw the unbelievable.

Vishous was up on his feet and somehow walking out of the alley. He was bleeding down the side of his face and dragging his body, but he was pissed off and fully engaged in the fight. Hell, he even had daggers in both his fists and the snarl of a beast for an expression.

As things went into slo-mo, Jane had a moment of total pride in her mate. Even injured, he was fighting to protect his brother—and prevailing.

But then it was a case of one, two, three, all at the same time.

The *lesser* pulled his trigger.

Jane made herself fully physical to block the bullet.

And Vishous threw both of those blades.

• • •

Assail would have preferred to be the one driving to the church. As a male, he felt as though that was his duty. His two female companions, however, took a different opinion of tradition—and so he was in the Range Rover's passenger seat whilst Marisol had the wheel.

At least he had a lovely view to enjoy. In the glow of the dash, his female's profile was so beautiful, she arrested him completely, stopping everything but his heart. Even with that baseball cap pulled low, he enjoyed the curve of her cheek, the lushness of her lips, the column of her throat above her parka . . .

In fact, he could not look away. But at least he was causing no offense. Out of the corner of his eye, he caught her grandmother smiling in the backseat—and his Marisol glanced his way every now and again, her blush a charming, secret gift.

Yet all was not perfect for him.

Shifting in his seat, he did not like the way his cashmere coat hung off him in folds, even though he was wearing a full suit underneath. And he had disliked the sight of the suit even more, that which had been tailored to fit his proper form dwarfing him the now, turning him into the son trying on the father's clothes.

As he thought about his weight, he murmured, "I am already looking forward to your next meal, Mrs. Carvalho."

"Big breakfast," the grandmother said. "Very big."

"This is good. I have much to regain."

"You have been sick."

This was uttered as if it were a form of absolution, a pardoning of that which was, in other circumstance, an intolerable offense.

"You both could not have come along at a better time," he murmured.

'Lo, how he wanted to reach across and take Marisol's hand, especially as she shot him a smile. But he had to be discreet out of respect to her and her grandmother.

Some ten minutes later, they were pulling into a parking lot beside a grand cathedral that reminded him of the ones built by humans in the Old Country, its buttresses, peaked Gothic arches, and ribbons of stained glass taking him home in ways too intense and internal to bear for long.

"Quite a beautiful church it is," he commented as Marisol halted them in one of the spaces.

There were fifteen other cars parked in a lot big enough to handle a hundred, and the vehicles were all huddled close to the walkway leading around to the front.

As he got out, he opened Mrs. Carvalho's door, extending his hand forth to help her down. Shutting things up, he offered Marisol's grandmother his elbow, and the lady took it, wrapping her arm through his.

They waited for Marisol to come around, and he loved that look on his female's face. That slight smile.

"Ready?" she said, her breath white in the cold night.

"Let us go—oh, madam, the curb." He helped her grandmother up to the sidewalk. "There we are."

As they proceeded over that which had been heavily salted, he looked up at the cathedral's towering height. The structure was maintained in beautiful condition, nothing faded in its grandeur, the interior lighting showing through the stained glass and turning the pictorials into jewels.

"Do they always do midnight rituals?" Assail asked.

"It's a mass." Marisol glanced over her grandmother's white head at him. "It's called a mass. And this cathedral does them on Thursdays and Saturdays each week, as well as on certain holidays. Caldwell has a very active Catholic community, and with so many people doing first and second shifts, these services offer working folks times to worship they wouldn't otherwise have."

The sound of voices behind them had him looking over his shoulder. A man and a woman were walking along in their wake, both burrowed into their coats and talking softly. As he regarded them, it was strange to realize that for as long as he had lived amongst humans, he had never spent much time with them. Yes, he had had business dealings, of course, but not anything of any leisurely pursuit.

Although, to be fair, he had not had much leisure to pursue in any kind of company.

The doors of the church were heavy and carved, and out of habit and manners, he went to jump ahead to open them, but Marisol got there first. Which was probably a good thing. He was not very strong, and just from the walk from the car, he was breathing hard.

Inside, he found himself in a vast entry room with red carpeting and dark wooden walls and stone plaques inscribed in Latin.

"The coatroom is over here," Marisol murmured.

When they reemerged without their outerwear, he found himself fiddling with his baggy suit and the tie that was the only thing holding his loose collar against his neck.

"Marisol," her grandmother said, "you must take off the hat. You cannot wear it."

"*Vovó*, I have to."

The two switched into their mother tongue, the argument hushed and quick. And then Mrs. Carvalho made a grunting sound and walked forth.

The baseball hat stayed on, and yes, it did hide most, if not all, of Marisol's face—but how he hated the reason she had to wear it.

"Come on," she said, tugging at his hand.

The worshipping space was magnificent, with a lofty vaulted ceiling, marble statuary, and a polished stone floor that went on forever. Hundreds of wooden pews in six sections of tight rows progressed down to an altar that was set beneath a glorious mural of the Christ enthroned. And indeed, the seating was so vast that the thirty people in front did little to fill out things.

At Marisol's prompting, they settled over on the left, a couple of rows back from the last one that had anybody in it. As they got themselves arranged, with Marisol in the middle and him on the aisle, he took a deep breath.

Considering where he had been of late, it was an unexpected miracle to be in this incredible place.

And then the organ began to play, its deep basses reaching into his chest, its ringing highs . . . reaching into his soul.

I am home, he thought.

Although that was about who he was with, rather than where he was.

TWENTY-EIGHT

cross town, at the head of the alley, Vishous screamed as he saw Jane go from translucent to fully corporeal just as that fucking slayer started shooting.

"*No!*"

She was right between Phury and the shooter, protecting her patient, his brother, with her very body. And as the bullets went into her, the daggers V had thrown with perfect accuracy went into the *lesser's* back.

Filled with terror and rage, Vishous threw himself into the air, his dislocated ankle tripping him up, his momentum more than overriding that. The tackle was short of his target so he curled in a ball, rolled the extra distance, and then locked on to the *lesser's* head with both his hands.

He twisted so hard, he popped the skull off the tip of the spine, nothing but ribbons of skin and sinew holding the thing on.

There was so much more pain he wanted to give the soulless bastard, except he had to get to Jane.

Leaving the undead body, he scrambled through the snow to his *shellan,* who had fallen on her back. As he reached her, she lifted her head and looked down at her body. There were tufts in her Patagonia jacket where the bullets had gone through.

Her breathing was all wrong—short, tight, fast.

"No . . ." he moaned. "I'm not losing you again—"

She was mouthing something to him as her eyes met his—blood spattering her lips, her skin too pale. "Love . . . you . . ."

Then she was disappearing into thin air—

"Jane!" He wrapped his arms around her.

"Oh, God," he heard someone say. "What did she do? What did she do . . ."

In Jane's place, there was something in his hands . . . bullets. The bullets that had been in her had fallen into his palms.

"What did she do!"

He jerked his head toward the male voice. Phury was staring at him with horror, the words coming out of the male as if he felt responsible.

Vishous patted the snow where she had been. Her blood was there, staining the dirty white red . . . but she was—

"Jane!"

He screamed her name. And then with no answers and nothing but stark terror in his soul, he flipped over and launched himself at that slayer. He attacked the carcass even though it accomplished nothing, ripping with his fangs and tearing with his hands, foul, black blood covering him—until a brilliant pair of headlights flashed into his eyes and some force popped him off his prey.

Thrashing, kicking, biting, he went wild, fighting against everything and everyone around him—

The punch was perfectly placed on his jaw, a floater that hit him like an atomic bomb. Instantly, his body and brain went limp, although he was still conscious as his head lolled on his neck, a school yard's tetherball.

His will came back online immediately, his need to *ahvenge* his love a force too great to be denied—but those arms and legs of his refused to follow any commands. He just hung there like a scarecrow in the arms of one of his brothers, *lesser* blood dripping out of his mouth, his clothes torn, his breath so hoarse and loud it sounded like a windstorm.

At that moment, he realized what the fuck was up with losing his mother.

He didn't mourn the female. He didn't even think she had been particularly good for the race. No . . . it was more that she was the one who had given him his Jane back.

With the Scribe Virgin gone? He'd been terrified that the magic or whatever the fuck it was that kept Jane in her state of ever-existence was going to be compromised. The shit failed and who did he go to?

No more anyone to pray to. No more anyone to demand that magic keep going.

And what do you know. Fate, the little bitch, had seen fit to place him in exactly the position he had been so terrified of that he hadn't even wanted to acknowledge its existence.

The dog didn't see Vitoria.

So the owner lived to die another day.

Back in her rental car, she took her time and obeyed all traffic laws as she drove out of Miss Fortescue's neighborhood and got back on the Northway. She was not returning to the West Point house, however.

Her old-fashioned map took her to her next destination—because GPS could be traced on car systems and phones—and she was even less impressed than she had been with her first stop in terms of architectural significance and desirability. This rough, lower-middle-class neighborhood was cut up into lots the size of index cards, the houses sitting upon them single-storied and in poor condition. Most had doors and windows covered by bars and chain-link fences around their yards with the cars inside the barrier.

Streeter's house was seven in and on the left, and as she pulled up and stopped, she thought that both places she had gone tonight matched their owners: Miss Fortescue's was an aspirational poseur, an outsider looking in on the world of great wealth and desperately wishing she could afford that which she sold. Streeter was a tough thug and did what he had to in order to survive.

All things considered, Vitoria would take a hundred of the latter before she crossed the aisle for the former.

After she texted him from the burner phone, she waited with little patience. He didn't keep her long.

The man emerged dressed in black from head to foot, the hood on his parka likewise pulled down low over his head and face. He paused to lock up and then strode out toward her, his eyes fixated on the trampled path to the gate in the chain-link as if he were a man that resolutely stuck to his own business and left others alone.

Vitoria got out from behind the wheel. "Have you had any alcohol or drugs tonight."

"I smoked a joint at five."

"You're driving." She walked around and got in the passenger seat. "I will sleep on the way there."

"Okay."

Streeter took the seat she had been in, and then they were off, traveling out of his neighborhood and getting on the Northway.

"Tell me again the story," she said as put her hands in the pockets of her parka and crossed her snow boots at the ankles.

"Two-Tone told his old lady—"

"Please do not refer to any woman like that. Or I shall have to start calling you Short Dick. Continue."

He looked over, the light from a passing streetlamp illuminating his surprise. "Ah, his . . . yeah, whatever she is . . . let me in their place. She thought he been on the lam, and that I knew where he was and was keepin' it from her. When I told her I ain't about that shit, she let me go through e'erthing. She still thinks he comin' home."

"And then what." Vitoria shut her eyes and let Streeter's perfectly fine voice and perfectly awful diction and grammar wash over her.

"I made her try to remember the last night she saw him. See, she'd took him to the bar where I saw him later. He was real good about not drinkin' and drivin'."

"Noble of him," Vitoria murmured, laying her head back and tilting it toward him.

"She said he got a phone call on the way. They was fightin' and he took it and she got hella pissed off. While he was on with whoever it was, he was talkin' about meetin' up with a guy in a hour and then something on the southern side of Iroquois. She thought it was Iroquois Avenue, which is like, across town. She said she heard him say 'half a mile' see a drive, and that they had to pick up a package first."

Streeter passed a semi on the right, just before the highway narrowed down to two northbound lanes. "She thought he was meetin' up with a female, but he told her she was crazy. She dropped him off at the bar, told him to fuck off, and then she tried to call him. He never answered the phone again, and that was it. So I was thinkin' about it. Lived here all my life. Never heard nobody talk about south side of Iroquois Avenue. What the fuck she thinkin'." The man looked over. "But that's what I was tellin' you. There's an Iroquois Mountain. And it's got a south side for sure. Then I remembered. Back when I was workin' for him, I overheard Mr. Benloise mention something about a safe place up north, a place where things could be hidden. He said it was almost to the border. That's where Iroquois is."

"I hope you are right."

Five hours one way was a big investment of time. But she would sleep up and back, and make some progress with her jet lag.

And she better get some rest. Tomorrow was going to be a busy day at the gallery. She wanted to be on hand bright and early when the police showed up to ask their questions about the mysterious murder that had taken place the evening prior, poor Miss Margot Fortescue being found by her housekeeper/boyfriend/girlfriend/whoever, shot execution style in her back hall.

By a professional.

"Wake me when we are near," she ordered. "And stop speeding. I do not want the police to pull us over."

As Streeter nodded his acceptance of the order, Vitoria closed her eyes again and smiled. Ricardo would not have approved of any of this tonight, most especially how she had dispatched his salesperson. Oh, the reasoning behind the assassination was sound, and something with which he would have agreed. But his sister? With that gun? Murdering a woman in that brazen, yet calculated manner?

Except she hadn't only studied English during those years he had been away.

The dark arts lessons she had taken had cost two to three times over their going rates: As a female, she had had to convince men to teach her how to shoot, how to fight, how to kill, and as Ricardo's sister, she had had to keep everything highly discreet. If he had found out? He might well have shot her himself.

But thanks to time and practice, she had become very good at solving her own problems. If she could use a Streeter, she much preferred to do so. If one such as he was not available, however? Or if it was a special circumstance that required a personal touch?

She did it herself.

TWENTY-NINE

As Jane became conscious, she jerked upright and grasped at her chest. There were tufts in the front of her parka, holes that bled white feathers, but as she took a deep breath, the suffocation was over. The pain was gone, too.

She was only partially corporeal, however.

Looking around, she recoiled. The snowy alley had been replaced by rolling green grass and vibrant blooming flowers and buildings that looked like they belonged in Caesar's Rome.

Why was she in the Sanctuary?

"Vishous?" She got to her feet. "V?"

Okay, so was she dead . . . or was this a cosmic restart kind of thing? Like, an existential return to sender that provided, if she "died," that she got rebooted back to where the Scribe Virgin had stayed?

Turning in a circle, she surveyed the landscape. She was smack in the middle of the gorgeous field, halfway between what V had told her were the Chosen's dormitories and the Reflecting Pool.

A feeling of panic flooded her circuits, but she got over that quick. Collecting herself, she figured she better bite the bullet and—

Hardy-har-har.

Not.

Yeah, it was going to be a while before she used that expression again.

At any rate, she probably needed to try out being fully present and see what happened. Unzipping the parka all the way, she took the thing off and stared down at herself. Using her will, she called upon her body to come forward fully, even as she braced herself for pain.

Except there was none. She felt just fine as she came totally into her flesh—which meant one of two things: She had either died and this was the afterlife or she really was immortal.

As she remembered how the gunshots had happened, she worried about Vishous. She could recall so clearly how he had held her, his face wild with horror, her physical pain getting between them, cheating her out of things she wanted to say to him.

And then it had all gone dark.

She had to get back to him, back down to earth. So she could tell him she was all right.

Thinking about how he had transported them here, she didn't have a clue exactly what he had done. She had just held on to him and let him do the work, that body of his something at once familiar and exotic as the reality had spun around them.

Whatever. She could do this. Closing her eyes, she held her parka against her chest and, on the theory that getting in or out of this realm was just the same as moving herself from one zip code in Caldie to another, she willed herself to up-and-out.

When it didn't work right away, she cracked her neck, took a deep breath, and gave it another shot.

After the third try, she cursed and realized it was not that easy.

Was she stuck here until someone happened to come along? Shit.

Deciding to be proactive, she started walking across the tranquil landscape. Surely, she'd run across Amalya, the Directrix, or a Chosen who had come up here to rejuvenate themselves . . . somebody, anybody.

Except what she found instead were her own regrets. And man, did they start talking to her.

"What the hell was wrong with me?" she said to the grass. "Why did I waste all that time?"

It wasn't that treating her patients was unimportant. It was more that she had spent hours between cases fiddling around with paperwork and non-urgent things that she could have delegated. Why hadn't she headed home? She could have been with V. They could have been together.

Or if he'd been on rotation, she could have been sleeping. Binge-watching *AHS* or *Stranger Things* on Netflix.

But no, she had been obsessive about being rightthereincasesome-oneneededher . . .

Like phones didn't work on the Brotherhood mountain? Like someone couldn't have come and found her? Like maybe somebody else could have handled a low-level trauma—

Her cell phone. She had her damn cell phone with her.

Taking it out, she went to hit Vishous up—"Damn it."

Okay, she was so not surprised there was no reception for calls or texts. Duh. Like Verizon covered other worlds? Or the Sanctuary was in-network?

Back to plan A. Which was to walk around until she found someone.

God, she just needed a way to tell Vishous she was okay.

Sola prayed so hard for Assail to be healed in that cathedral that afterward, on the way home, she realized she'd made her forearms and elbows sore from pressing her palms together. And perhaps she had been wrong to ask what she had. She had been told, many times by many different men and women of God, never to pray for specific outcomes, but instead to ask for God's will. The trouble was, she had a problem with that. To reduce things down to an absurd metaphor, she kind of felt like that was going to an aunt who had always gotten you socks for Christmas and telling her, *Hey, do what you want.*

She'd just offered a little specificity, a small bit of direction, is all—

Abruptly, she winced behind the wheel, and thought, *Oh, wow, I did not just old-maiden-aunt our Lord. Really. I did not—*

"So, Assail, what religion?" her grandmother asked from the backseat.

During the awkward pause that followed, Sola looked out the window to the heavens and nodded in God's general direction. Clearly, her *vovó*'s question was payback for that wisecrack.

And I love socks, she thought. *Socks are good, they keep your feet warm, they come in different colors. I am very grateful for all the socks I have in my life, socks that You have chosen to give me—*

"Marisol?"

"Sola?"

As the other two both said her name, she jerked to attention. "I'm sorry, what?"

"Socks?" Assail asked. "You just spoke of socks—"

"Do you need socks?" her grandmother cut in. "I get you some more. Everybody, they need the socks."

At least this got her *vovó* distracted off the religion track. "Sorry, I was just mumbling to myself. And I'm good on foot coverage, thanks."

"I get you more," her grandmother said. "Assail, answer question."

Sola closed her eyes. Then refocused on the road. She wanted to tell him he didn't have to reply at all, but—

"I am agnostic, Mrs. Carvalho. Although the mass was certainly moving."

"You will go again with us, but next time to our church. You will meet Father Molinero—"

Sola shook her head and looked into the rearview. "We cannot go back there, *Vovó*. Not an option. I told you that already."

Her grandmother's eyes lowered, and as sadness came over her aging face, Sola wished that the woman would come back swinging, as was her usual style. Defiance was life; defeat was death.

"We can keep going to the cathedral, though," Sola said as they got to the end of the bridge and she took that first exit to go down the Hudson's shoreline. "Right?"

Assail was all over it. No hesitation: "Absolutely."

Her grandmother recovered quickly. "Then next time, you meet Bishop Donnelley. He will bless you."

"A request, if it is not too much?" Assail turned to look into the back seat. "May we please attend the midnight masses? You will find I am a night owl."

"I like that better, too." Sola nodded. "That works for me. Fewer people."

"I no care when we go as long as we do."

Sola glanced in the rearview mirror again. Her grandmother was sitting back with satisfaction, that smile on her face the kind of thing that she would have hidden if she had known anyone was seeing it.

Taking a hand from the wheel, Sola reached across the seat. When she clasped Assail's palm, he glanced over.

I love you, she mouthed.

Assail lifted his free hand and pressed his fingertips to his lips. Then he extended his arm and put them to her mouth.

"I love you, too," he said out loud.

As Sola blushed, she could have sworn she heard her grandmother laugh softly. But maybe she imagined it.

Then again, her *vovó* had always wanted a good Catholic boy for a grandson-in-law, and if Assail kept this no-more-drug-dealing, going-to-church thing up? She might just get what she had prayed for.

Abruptly, Sola lost her levity.

Yeah, that might happen . . . if Assail lived long enough. But what were the chances of that, she thought sadly.

THIRTY

Up in the Sanctuary, Jane had no idea how much time had passed, was passing, whatever. It could have been ten minutes or a thousand years, and she had the sense she would feel the same. In this respect, minutes in this sacred place seemed to be like its horizon, having no beginning and no ending: No matter how far she walked, she never seemed to be able to get to the forest ring that encompassed the landscape. Every time she thought she was finally going to go into it, everything double-backed on itself and spit her out at the opposite side with the trees to her back. It was enough to make her crazy.

Well, that and the fact that there was no one around.

And the other irritating thing? She had been wandering for how long, and yet her feet weren't tired, she wasn't thirsty or hungry, and she didn't have to pee.

Yes, okay, fine, she realized it was insane to bitch about the fact that she wasn't uncomfortable—or having to squat in one of the Scribe Virgin's flower beds like a camper in the woods, for godsakes. But it seemed further confirmation that she didn't exist, and that made her feel lost and alone more than her lack of company.

To that point, she kept herself fully corporeal. Kind of like she was middle-fingering the whole I'm-not-really-alive thing.

Oh, God, she prayed Vishous wasn't doing anything to hurt himself.

To keep from losing her mind with worry, she set a route out for herself, her need to make order of her situation and her surroundings asserting itself even though it was hardly necessary. What, like somebody from the afterlife was going to show up here with a clipboard and be all, *Wait, you missed the Baths, and your speed of ambulation past the Temple of the Sequestered Scribes was .2 mph slower on your third lap.*

When had she gotten to be so tightly wound?

Discipline, always her friend, had morphed into a brittle hold attaching itself indiscriminately to everything, and its invasion had clearly been incremental, the sort of thing she hadn't noticed as it had taken over.

Until what should have been a virtue had strangled her.

She'd always had a healthy confidence in herself and her skills. And she'd earned that self-esteem, damn it. But now that she thought about the focus she'd been bringing to her work, she saw, thanks to this involuntary, but kind of critical, time of reflection, that she'd equated her obsessive-compulsive efforts with her patients' salvation.

Hell, with the security and safety for all the Brothers and fighters in the war.

As if she were the only thing that stood between them and death.

Rhage had been right to challenge her on how long it had been since she'd attended a First or a Last Meal, and now she knew why she hadn't been going to them: That long dining room table with all of its males and females, families and children, were no longer friends to enjoy.

They were disasters waiting to happen.

She didn't see Z smiling with his family. Instead, she pictured him getting shot in the gut on the field and bleeding out, with her going there to treat him and having to open him up. But what if, instead of finding both of the bleeders—which in that case, she had—she fucked up, missed the secondary nick in the inferior vena cava, and he died right there?

Well, then, he wasn't at that table anymore, was he. And Bella and Nalla? Their lives were over. Because Jane hadn't done her job well enough. Nalla literally had no father for the rest of her nights and days and Bella was brokenhearted forever. Family ruined.

Or hey, how about when Beth went into labor. Placenta previa. Came to the clinic on a stretcher, and instead of Jane getting L.W. out and doing that emergency hysterectomy successfully, she botched the removal of the uterus so the patient bled to death.

In that case, Wrath's life is over, he fucks off the throne, and the entire species loses its leader. The Brotherhood is never the same, and courtesy of the trauma, they go out the next evening and several of them are killed in the field because they're suffering and in mourning.

There were too many examples to count. Layla with her babies. Peyton, the trainee, shot in the head. Xcor. Rhage.

Every one of them had ended up in her care in the last year. Or had it been two years?

The problem was, she wasn't working on arm's-length patients, ones who had no relationship whatsoever to her own family: Fucking up under normal clinical circumstances was horrible enough—hell, she knew doctors who made honest mistakes on the job and never, ever got over it. But to have that happen to someone you loved? Saw every night? Laughed and cried with, lived your life with?

There was a reason people did not treat their nearest and dearest. And yet for her it was the very definition of her job.

No wonder she was going nuts.

She stopped, looked around—and decided maybe all that was just a moot point now. Did she even have a future? Or was she going to be stuck in this dimension forever?

And what about Vishous? He was going to blame himself. Somehow, he would find a way to feel responsible for her choice to shield Phury, and that was going to lead to disaster.

As Jane's heart began to pound with all the things she didn't know and couldn't control, she focused on what was in front of her so she didn't lose her damn mind.

It was a while before the temple's contours and dimensions properly registered. The white marble structure was the smallest on the campus that she had seen, taller than it was wide with, unusually, no open windows. Actually, it looked like a vault . . . or a tomb—

Without a sound, the one side of the panels that served as a door opened outward.

"Hello?" she said. "Amalya?"

As she went over and mounted the steps, she was so ready for some help, some answers . . . some relief—and in the back of her mind, she recognized that this was what her patients had to feel like as she came to them.

"Hello?" She pulled the heavy panel wider and peered in. "Oh . . . my God."

It was Ali Baba's cave, she thought with wonder as she entered the thirty-by-thirty square. Everywhere she looked there were gemstones—and not in a Jared Jewelers or a Shane Co. kind of way, the sparklers one-offs with plenty of space around them. No, this was *The Goonies* . . . this was some straight-up One-Eyed Willy right here, with dozens of bins filled with what certainly appeared to be gem-quality sapphires, rubies, emeralds . . . diamonds. There were also amethysts, opals, citrines, and aquamarines—pearls as well. And all of them were the size of thumbnails or larger.

The wealth represented was incalculable, and so incomprehensible, she just went from bin to bin, staring down at the largesse with marvel. She didn't dare touch any of it, although she wondered how the stones would feel, sliding cool and smooth, through her hot hands.

And there were other things in the vault, too—although it was a while before she paid them any attention. In a series of marble and glass display cases and shelves, there was a strange assortment of non sequiturs, from revolvers that looked as if they were from the Revolutionary

War period to fossils to—was that a meteorite? There was also a bowl that was encrusted with gems. A scepter—

Jane stopped in front of one of the last cases she came to and frowned. Whatever object had been there was gone now, although the glass wasn't broken. But you could definitely tell there had been something in there because the outline of a large square had been singed into the red velvet underneath.

Like it had been radioactive.

Or claimed by an evil hand.

Down on Earth, on the shores of the Hudson, Assail slipped free of his bed and pulled a robe on in utter silence. Marisol was naked in his sheets, her body tucked in tight, her now-blond hair on his pillow. She would only be able to stay another hour or so before he had to wake her and send her down to the basement in order that her grandmother would find her in the morning where she should be. But he didn't want her to leave. He preferred her right where she was.

As he stood over her and watched her breathe, he began to feel like something out of Mr. Stoker's universe, the vampire hovering, soulless and hungry, above the fragile human life he intended to suck dry.

That was what she was going to think of him if she ever found out what he really was. Indeed, he despised lying to her—which was ironic considering he had quite comfortably uttered falsehoods to both fools and family his entire life—but he feared her reaction to the truth even more.

Troubled by much, he forced himself away and went down the stairs to the first floor, shutting the doors behind himself.

There was another reason for that, apart from wanting to keep things quiet.

As he faced off at his office, ripples of unease tingled through his torso, and it was a while before he entered and crossed the distance to his desk. Sitting down in his padded chair, he placed his hands on the blotter. If he were to turn on the PC—which he did not—he could access his accounts, check his portfolios, look at the rising level of his fortune, and perhaps feel a concomitant buoyancy.

Or perhaps not. His wealth didn't seem as important to him as it had been.

Bracing himself, he swiveled the chair with his feet and opened the top drawer on the left. Inside was a dark brown glass vial about the size of a Life Savers roll.

He'd had smaller ones at first. Then larger ones had become needed. Toward the end, it nearly had been necessary to pack a suitcase.

Assail's hand shook as he reached out and picked the vial up. It was empty of cocaine, nothing but a fine residue inside. Not a surprise. During that last week or so, he'd been hitting the coke so hard, he'd put a hole in his septum.

Rolling the circular container back and forth on his palm, he marveled at how an inanimate object with almost no intrinsic value could strip him down to his bones like a grenade going off at the end of his wrist.

He waited . . . waited . . . to see if the urge came upon him.

When it did not, he had a moment of euphoric freedom, a soaring sense of victory that he had bested his foe, vanquished the demon—and yes, his beautiful damsel was, in fact, upstairs in his quarters. But then a cautionary sense bettered that delusion. It was easy to resist the temptation when he was at peace and relaxed. The trick was going to be when he was not.

He put the vial back in the drawer and closed it up. He wasn't sure why he was keeping the thing, and didn't want to look too closely at that. Was it as a grim reminder of all that he had put himself through to keep things on track? Or as a placeholder for when he fell back into his addiction?

Assail could not bear the answer because he did not trust himself.

And it was upon that realization that he turned on his computer, the blue glow coming up on the monitor like illumination from a fire. His passwords came back to him with ease—which was a relief—and thanks to the bull market, he supposed he was pleased at where things were.

Whilst going insane, he had made money.

Sitting back, he tried to ascertain if he was tired. There was soreness in his muscles, which had grown unaccustomed to movement. He was vaguely hungry, but disinclined to the effort required for a remedy. He was also a little cold.

The silence in the house washed over him, and for some reason, all the quiet seemed oppressive, robbing him of the happy relief he had been feeling ever since he had had the restraints removed from his wrists and ankles.

Ever since he had come back to inhabit his body.

Was this all there was to life now? he wondered. Sitting passively in front of his computer, watching numbers change due to forces he had no participation in nor control over?

He did not want to return to the chaos and mania of his addiction or his illegal business. But with no other options for how to spend his time, he felt an existential version of color-blindness, the world lacking a certain vividness and depth. Of course, as a bonded male, he would live for his female, it was true. But there had to be more than him becoming another piece of furniture in this sleek room.

Marisol would not find much to respect about her *hellren* in that case.

Assail opened the drawer again. Next to the vial was an untraceable cell phone, and as he went to turn it on, he thought, but of course, the battery had gone dead.

Maybe it was a sign, he thought. After all, if he was out of the business, why would he need to access the phone he had used for it?

An unsettling sense of void caused him to proceed. The charger was plugged into the outlet under the desk, and as he got the cord and gave the phone some juice, he cradled the Samsung flip phone in his hands. It was a while until the thing woke up. And whilst he waited, he considered putting the cell back in the drawer or maybe throwing it away. In the end, however, he opened its lid, and found there were four voice-mails.

Putting in the password, the oldest message came up first, and it was one he had long saved.

"I received your message. I am prepared to see you for coffee. Be well, my friend."

Eduardo Benloise. Responding to the directive to meet in a code previously agreed upon. And when Assail and his cousins had intercepted the man at the appointed location? The assumption on Eduardo's side had been that it was for the delivery of a million dollars in cash—and as the man was greedy and liked to hide things from his older brother, he had been more than happy to come unaccompanied and without any in his organization knowing.

Except no money had changed hands. Instead, Eduardo had been o'ertaken against his will and placed, with little more consideration than one would use on a parcel post, in the back of Assail's Range Rover, a lever to be pulled at the right time.

Assail had kept the message as a reminder that he had done Marisol right.

It had been a sad tie to her and their relationship.

The second message was a hang-up from two weeks ago, a misdial. The third as well.

The fourth, however, had been left earlier in the current day, some twelve hours before. And it was a female voice with only the hint of an accent.

"Good afternoon, sir. I am calling from the Benloise Gallery in reference to your purchase dated December twentieth. Our records show that there has been a delay in fulfillment, and we would like the opportunity to discuss this matter at your convenience. If you have already been in contact with us, please disregard this phone call. Thank you."

Assail frowned and replayed the message. Twice.

Yes, she did indeed have an accent, and was covering it up very well. Her "r"s and the lilt were not quite right.

She was South American.

And to what purchase was she referring?

No number had been provided on the message, but that was unnecessary. It was in the phone's call log.

"Assail?"

At the sound of Marisol's voice, he looked up. She'd come down the stairs and was heading in the direction of the kitchen.

He put the phone back in the drawer and shut things as far as he could with the charger still plugged in. Then he got to his feet.

"In here, my love."

Her footsteps were quick but soft on the turnaround, and as she came up to the open doorway, she hesitated. "Why are you in the dark?"

"I was just checking my accounts." He indicated the monitor. "I am pleased to report that I can afford to pay for gas and electricity for at least the next year. Maybe the year after."

"Oh . . . good." Marisol coughed a little. "Ah, I was worried when I woke up and you were gone."

As he held his arms out, she came forward. She had put the shirt he had worn to church on and her bare legs were beautiful.

"You mustn't worry about me." He pulled her in close and kissed her sternum, right over her heart. "I am well indeed."

"Do you want to come back to bed?"

"Hmm . . . yes." His hands traveled down to her hips, and before he knew it, he was under the hem of his shirt, her bare skin warm and smooth.

"Should we go back upstairs?" she said huskily.

"I want you here."

He eased her back against the desk and then urged her to sit upon it, pushing his keyboard and an ashtray out of the way. When his monitor almost went off the far side, he didn't care.

Willing the door to the office shut, the light from the hall was cut off and darkness took ownership of the room except for that pool of blue light—

Shit, he thought. The door. He shouldn't have closed it with his mind. However, at least Marisol, in her state of increasing arousal, didn't seem to notice.

"You're going to have to be quiet," he drawled as he rested both sets of fingertips on her thighs. "You mustn't disturb anyone."

"How do you know you're not the one who'll be gasping?" she countered.

"Because this is not going to be about me."

With that, he jerked out the second drawers on both sides of the desk and spread her legs, putting her feet on the ledges he had made for her. Then he sank down onto his knees.

She started to pant before he even began stroking up the inside of her thighs.

"Remember," he said as he brushed his lips on one of her knees. "You wouldn't want to wake anyone up."

Sweeping his hands toward her core, he did not touch her. Yet. He unfastened the lowest button of his shirt. And then the one on top of that. And then the next . . .

He wanted to go all the way, but in the unlikely event someone knocked, or worse—and unheard of—walked in, he needed to spare her modesty.

The shirttails were terribly accommodating as he parted them and moved them out of the way, the twin swaths content to stay back on either side of her hips.

And there she was, bare and wide to him.

"Mmm," he purred as kissed his way from her knee to the edge of what was becoming so very aroused for him.

Looking up, he smiled. She had braced her hands on the blotter and was leaning her body back, but keeping her head forward so she could watch him.

Assail extended his tongue and was done with any preamble. He licked up the center of her, flicking the top of her sex. Then he sealed her with a kiss.

The groan she tried to stifle made him smile, but then he had work to do. Sucking her in, then licking at her, he took his time, enjoying the feel and taste of her, the warmth and the rush—and greedy for even more, he spread her knees farther apart, his hands locking on, squeezing.

The lapping sounds were loud in the silence of the room—and so was her breathing. And both got their volume turned up as he started flicking at her, his tongue a darting, dancing tease that had her hips jerking back and forth as she rode his face.

When she came, her palms squeaked on the blotter and she went into an arch that banged the monitor into the wall.

He gave her no time for recovery, though.

Such a cruel taskmaster he was.

THIRTY-ONE

On the leather couch at the Pit, Vishous came around to the sound of an ESPN *30 for 30*, the announcer giving the background on a piece about . . . Ric Flair, the old-school wrestler.

V opened his eyes with an effort disproportionate to how much his lids weighed. Fuck. He'd used less energy bench-pressing in the damn gym.

The foosball table was the first thing he could properly focus on. The wide-screen TV behind it was the second. The third was the two males standing in the kitchen, their bodies close together, their heads leaning in, their conversation at such a soft whisper, he could hear nothing of it.

Butch and Rhage each had a drink in their hand: The former was rocking a tall glass of something that was brown, but most definitely not of the Coke/Dr Pepper/Pepsi variety. The latter had a mug the size of a bathtub, and V knew without sniffing the air that that was Swiss Miss without the marshmallows, made with milk, not water.

Still, all of these details about where he was and who and what was around him were not relevant. They were more pass-throughs for his brain, the thin mint, not the entrée.

Pain was more the point of his existence, and as his state of consciousness picked up more and more steam, memories of holding Jane in his arms and losing her again, hit him sure as if a slayer were standing above him and beating him with a lead pipe over and over until his skull did not so much cave in as get pulverized.

Whatever drug they had given him was wearing off by inches, not yards, and he was frustrated with this—although why exactly, he wasn't sure. Sobriety was just going to mean more suffering.

Jane, he mouthed. *Jane . . .*

When there was a hot streak down his cheek, he wondered who was dripping candle wax on him—

A pair of bizarrely pupil-less eyes popped in front of him so unexpectedly, he jerked back, his head bouncing off the leather cushion behind him.

Lassiter was the last person in the fucking world he wanted to see, the blond-and-black horror with the big mouth exactly what the doctor did not order.

"Shut up," V mumbled. "Go 'way—"

The angel put his forefinger up to his lips. *Shh. All is well.*

Jane is gone! V wanted to scream. *She is fucking gone and I don't give a fuck about you or anybody on this—*

Lassiter reached out and put his hand on V's forearm. *Shh. All is well.*

The fuck it is!

As the male squeezed, V looked to the kitchen and wondered why Butch and Rhage weren't acknowledging their unwelcomed visitor. Then again, the pair of them were as sick of the Lassiter show as he was—

All at once, the world went on a spin around him, as if he were a funnel and everything was draining into him.

The next thing he knew, he was surrounded by green grass and milky sky as he lay flat on the Sanctuary's lawn. And for no good reason, he wondered why he was always landing on the grass now, instead of inside his mother's private quarters. Before, he had always arrived in that courtyard.

Maybe because she was no longer here? Whatever.

"Lassiter," he croaked. "What the fuck is your problem."

Sitting up, he rubbed his eyes and discovered he was in front of the Treasury . . . and the fallen annoyance—angel, that was—was nowhere to be seen.

After a moment, he noticed that the door to the vault was open—which was wacked. That thing was always closed.

V got to his feet and ambled over because he couldn't think of anything else to do in the midst of his agony, and besides, he was nominally curious as to whether his legs would hold his weight. Huh. They did.

When he got to the doorway, he almost didn't look in, but something told him to shift his eyes—

There was a figure across the way, its back to him, its head down as if it was looking at something in a case—

Short blond hair. Lithe body. Female. Very female—

"Jane," he groaned, thinking it was an apparition that had showed up to torture him.

Except it turned around on a spin.

Shock on a familiar, beautiful face made the world spin again.

"Jane!"

Even though this had to be the cruelest joke Lassiter had ever played, V went with it, racing across the shallow space and slamming his body into what certainly appeared to be his *shellan's*.

"Vishous?" she said, as if she were equally confused.

He palmed the back of her head, and closed his eyes, and as he kissed her, he prayed that this was not some figment of his imagination, a product of grief meeting the drugs they'd given him.

"I thought I'd lost you," he said hoarsely.

As he spoke the words, he realized that was true not just with her getting shot, but with the distance that had grown between them.

Jane's arms squeezed him hard, as if she knew he needed to feel that. "Never," she returned through her tears. "You'll never lose me . . ."

"What are you doing here?"

"I don't know. I don't care right now—just kiss me again!"

As Jane held on to her mate with desperate strength, she knew she was probably making it hard for Vishous to breathe, but she needed visceral reassurance that she was alive and so was he.

Oxygen was just going to have to take a backseat for a minute.

"Oh, God, I thought you were gone," he mumbled, his voice reverberating with emotion. "I can't believe you're here. What happened? Why are you—shit, I . . . don't have a fucking clue what I'm saying."

Pulling back, she looked up at him. Then she had to touch his face, running her fingers over the tattoos on his temple, and his cheekbones, and his goatee. His diamond eyes were shining with a love so great, she was humbled and full of regret.

Why had they ever wasted the time they'd been given? Why had they lost track of each other at all? How could they have let that happen?

"V," she cut in urgently. "I'm so sorry I got so wrapped up in my work—"

"What? What are you—no, I'm sorry I was a fucking asshole." When she tried to speak again, he shook his head. "Can I kiss you again? Please, just let me—"

Without missing a beat, she threw her arms around his neck and pulled herself to his mouth, her heels lifting from the floor. Their mouths met once more and the sensation of soft on soft rocked her to her core.

"Please," he groaned. "Please, I need you."

She knew exactly what he was begging for, and she didn't hesitate. Backing herself up until she felt the wall, she went for the waistband of her scrubs, loosening the bow and letting them fall to the floor. Her boots were a tougher sell on the whole get-off-me thing, but she managed to cross that finish line with the one on the left and kicked it across the Treasury. And that was all she needed to get half her bottoms off.

V took care of his own pant-problems, nearly ripping his fly open, and then she was back to hanging off of his neck and he was pulling her legs around his hips—

His penetration was so fast and deep she yelled. And then she didn't know what the hell she did—and she didn't care.

Vishous was dominating by nature, a force in the world that wasn't to be denied. And he had sex in exactly that way: He pounded her furiously, his body clapping against hers, the structural integrity of the marble wall she'd put her back against the only reason they were still standing.

And even that was a "maybe" instead of a "definitely": At the rate he was going, he was liable to fuck her right through the stone and out onto the lawn—and she loved it. She loved the near-violence, the knife-edge of pain, the sense that she had walked into the woods and found a snarling beast and laid herself down so it could take her.

He was the out-of-control that she otherwise didn't let into her life. And she had missed this. She had missed him.

As she began to climax, the tears rolled down her face. The awareness that she had let this connection go made her panic—because what if she had lost it forever? What if she had ceased to exist in the middle of that road? Or worse . . . what if she had just kept going as she had been with work being the most important thing in her life and everything else slowly fading away.

And it was not just her. There were things Vishous had to work on, too. Things he was going to have to change.

Then again, true love required so much more than the boy-meets-girl stuff—and mutual attraction was the easy part: Life did not sit back politely and not interrupt the conversation between two souls united. It wasn't a properly raised lady of leisure with a soft voice, ordering the staff to bring canapés for the hungry. No, it was more like a cocktail party of guests where some of them you were happy to welcome into your little clutch of two . . . and others were drunken frat boys who tripped, fell, and vomited on your collective feet.

Vishous eased up on the pumping. "You're crying. Oh, fuck, I hurt you—"

"I'm just glad we're together." She sniffled as he wiped her tears with his thumbs. "And all I want is more of this."

"Me, too." He kissed her. "That's what I want, too."

The pain in his face, in those diamond eyes, was a window into the depths under all that cold, calculating intelligence, and she knew the vulnerability wasn't something he showed even his Brothers. This was a gift to her, a testament to what he felt for her, the foundation of their relationship that thankfully hadn't crumbled, but only been partially obscured for a short time.

"I left you," she whispered. "I didn't meant to, but I did."

"I left you, too." He shook his head. "I'm at fault—"

"No, you were home a lot of days when I was at the clinic—"

"When was the last time you came in and I didn't have a drink in my hand?"

Jane opened her mouth. Shut it.

"Exactly," he said as he brushed her hair back. "I've been drinking every second I wasn't in the field since my *mahmen* hit the road. And even before that, with the war cranking up and the shit with Xcor, I was constantly the one volunteering to be on deck. I've been getting eaten alive by work, too. That is not just on you."

"How do we make sure this doesn't happen again?"

V rolled his hips, his sex sliding in and out of her and making her moan. "We stay connected. That's how."

She had to laugh. "I can live with that . . ."

As he started moving again, entering and retreating, entering and retreating, she tightened her legs around his backside.

"I can live for that," she amended as they both began to orgasm.

THIRTY-TWO

itoria woke up as the car's velocity changed, the steady hum of sixty-eight mph dropping in volume as Streeter decelerated to get off at an exit that read Iroquois Mountain Reserve. Talk about a change in landscape. Gone was the crowded sprawl of Caldwell; in its place, there was nothing but snow and mountains.

No lights of inhabitation, no cars or trucks, nothing but miles of frigid wilderness.

The isolation was unexpectedly intimidating, reminding her of some of the remote places in Colombia that she never wanted to visit. Whether arctic tundra or rain forest, she was not one to venture too far off the beaten path, as it were. If their car broke down out here, for example, who would help them?

Streeter looked over at her, and his expression was remote. "You're awake."

"We are here. Why didn't you rouse me?"

"You're up now," he muttered.

"What is wrong with you?" If he was not hardy enough to drive them this far on short notice, he was not going to fare well as her primary support. "What."

"I just got a text from a buddy of mine. He works security for the gallery during after-hour shows."

What a nice reminder he could read. "You shouldn't be texting and driving."

"Margot Fortescue was found dead in her house by her boyfriend."

Vitoria made a show of frowning. "She's that one who thought she was running things. Rather rude awakening I gave her today. What a pity."

"She used to fuck your brother. Did you know that?"

"Which one. And watch your language, would you." She unzipped her coat. Her gun was in there. "I am a lady. My ears are delicate."

"Eduardo. She used to be with him." Streeter glanced across the seats again. "Did you kill her?"

Arching a brow, Vitoria feigned a recoil. "Me? Dear God, what are you thinking? Of course not. Why would I care whether she was alive or dead?"

"Margot knew things. That's all. I just wondered whether that shit—er, stuff, came up when you was talkin' to her or something."

"Not at all. I will admit that she doesn't like me—well, *didn't* like me. But it appears as if that will no longer be a problem. Not that it was much of one to begin with." Vitoria sat forward as a sign entered the illumination field of the headlights. "We are getting close. Four miles. Do you know which way is south?"

"It's the direction we came from."

As they continued on, she stared out at the mountain that was peaking high above the tree line off in the distance. "Tell me, what kinds of things did Margot know?"

"'Bout this side of the business. She knew that there were other things being sold by your brothers. But I don't think she knew deets."

"And how did you find this out about her?"

"Two-Tone fucked her a couple of times. She made like she was on the inside track or some sh—stuff. He didn't tell me no more than that."

"What a paragon of virtue the woman was." Vitoria pointed forward. "Slow down here."

Streeter hit the brakes as they came up to an intersecting road marked by a large wooden sign that read Iroquois Mountain Reserve.

"This way," she ordered.

He hit the gas like the good little delegatee he was, but soon enough, forward motion was impossible. No more plowed passage. Whoever was responsible for snow removal stopped at the foot of the ascent.

"It's impassable," Streeter said. "We can't go no more. This ain't gonna work—"

"We proceed on foot."

He turned to her. "What?"

By way of answer, she leaned across, put the engine in park, and extracted the keys from the ignition.

"We walk."

"Are you crazy?"

"I have gear for us both."

As she got out of the car, the cold was downright daunting, but that would be cured readily enough. The mountain, on the other hand? Craning her neck to look up to its snow-covered peak, she was far less confident of tackling its elevation.

A half a mile, she told herself. They had to go only half a mile up.

Walking around to the trunk, she opened things up and took out the two pairs of snowshoes she had found in her brother's vast garage—which hadn't been half of the treasure trove she'd discovered therein. So many useful things. And there had also been a Bentley Flying Spur and a Rolls-Royce Ghost, both appearing to have been as meticulously maintained as the mansion.

She was looking forward to the transportation upgrade starting tomorrow. But those cars were not what one used to go out into the night, looking for bodies. No, this was her rental's last duty.

"Put these on." She threw a set of the snowshoes at Streeter as he joined her. "The harnesses are adjustable."

"I ain't walking nowhere on those."

"We will make good time."

"I'm a smoker."

"Of course you are. Now stop making excuses and let's get properly clothed. I have ski gloves and down jackets and snow pants, and other gear to aid us."

After some further grumbling on his part, they prepared themselves properly and started off, her in front, him trailing behind. The shoes proved to be a brilliant last-minute supply grab on her part, allowing them to travel across the surface of the snow as they began an ascent on the broad flat clearing that was the road. With the landscape draped in white, the moonlight that showed through the sporadic cloud cover made headlamps unnecessary, but they each had one just in case.

Progressing along, it felt good to be outside, her breath leaving her mouth and rising over one shoulder, smoke from the chimney of her body.

Behind her, Streeter was wheezing. But the exercise would do him good—and if he died, she would just leave him where he was and let him be found in the spring.

"Tell me, Streeter," she said. "Why?"

"Huh?" he gasped.

She stopped and twisted around. He was about ten feet back, and as he came up to her, his face was bright red.

"Did you honestly think I killed her?"

It took a while before he had enough air to answer her. "J-J-J-Jimmy was who called me. His brother . . . CPD. . . ."

"Jimmy's the one who's a gallery security guard?"

"Yeah." More with the breathing. "He said he was pickin' up . . . his paycheck . . . and you was in Eduardo's office . . . he saw Margot go . . . in there. When she came out . . . she looked pissed."

Vitoria smiled, even though she was most displeased. The guard had a cop for a brother? Damn it. "I can assure you, if something happened to that woman, I had nothing to do with it. Come, let us continue."

· · ·

Up in the Sanctuary's Treasury building, Vishous was standing strong in his shitkickers, one arm up against the marble wall and the other around his female to hold her in place at his hips. He felt like he had gotten over an illness, kicked off a rare case of human flu that had jumped the lines of the species and come knock-knock-knockin' at his immune system's door. With the symptoms gone, he felt renewed, some kind of shooting star–Disney shit going on all around and inside of him with the rainbow and unicorn brigade not far behind.

"I don't want to let go," he said.

"You must be getting tired of holding me up."

"Nah." And even if he was, he didn't care. "But you've got to be uncomfortable."

He gently set Jane back on the floor and then they just looked into each other's eyes.

"So I guess I got the answer to the question I didn't want to ask," he murmured.

"What was that?"

V searched her face. "I'd worried about whether you'd still be around after my mother left. You know, whether the magic or whatever it is would still work. And it does."

"Yup." Her smile was radiant. "I'm still here."

As his eyes watered from all the fucking feels, he wanted to cut them out of his skull with spoons. "I am so glad no one else can see me like this, true?"

"Your brothers love you."

"I love them. But when it comes to shit like this, I prefer my sandbox with only you in it."

She leaned in. "Does this mean I don't have to fight with anyone to play with your toys?"

He got serious. "That's exactly what it means. You know that, right?"

"Yes, I do." She stroked his face. "I honestly do."

V cocked a smile. "And along those lines, can you just dub in, in your head, all kinds of Tonka, I-got-a-big-bucket, you-can-pull-my-stick commentary right now?"

"You got it."

After they laughed, they spoke quietly for a while, and it felt so incredible to just be normal—which, hell yeah, could happen between a ghost and a vampire.

On that theory, who else could the two of them be "normal" with?

"So should we go back down?" Jane asked as she pulled the loose leg of her scrubs back on. "Everyone's got to be worried."

"Yeah. Sure." Except after he buttoned up his fly, and she put her other boot on, neither of them made any move to leave.

To kill some time, V glanced around at all the bins of gemstones. "You know, I've never been in here before."

"I couldn't *believe* all these jewels."

"It's the wealth of the race."

She shook her head. "How did it get up here?"

"Who the fuck knows."

"And did you see the revolvers?" She pointed over her shoulder toward a set of antique guns. "And what do you suppose was here?"

With a frown, he shuffled over to a marble case that was empty. Something had been set within its velvet-lined interior, however. There was a rectangular singed spot in the middle of it.

"What the hell?" he muttered.

"V, you're limping. I think we need to check out your ankle."

He glanced over his shoulder and lowered his lids. "Can we do an internal exam?"

"On you or me?"

"Both."

Jane laughed as she joined him in front of the vacant case. "Weird, right?"

"It was a book. I'll bet it was a book. Even though there's no identification on the exterior."

Then again, it wasn't like this was a museum with little brass plaques explaining what everything was and where it came from.

But whatever. Not his problem. For all he knew, his *mahmen* had found a misplaced comma on one of the pages and fried the tome in a fit of fury.

"Come on, my female," he said as he took Jane into his arms. "Back to the land of the living. My brothers are no doubt marshaling a search party for me at this very moment."

Jane was smiling at him as he up-and-outed them to the other side, materializing them to the mansion's dour entrance. And as he let them into the vestibule and shoved his mug into the security camera, he kept his arm around Jane.

Fritz started to open the way in, but Vishous finished the job, shoving the heavy weight wide to help the old *doggen* out—

Sure enough, all of the Brotherhood was milling around and arming themselves like they were about to head off to find his sorry ass before dawn made shit too late.

All eyes swung toward him, and as he saw the surprise and shock on those familiar faces, a load of aw-shucks hit him hard.

To cover that up, he gave 'em a sly grin. "I'm back, bitches—miss us?"

There were some shouts and then people were coming up and there were hugs and other malarkey that, under normal circumstances, made him want to scratch. Not tonight, though. Not tonight. After everything he had been through with Jane, and all that he had both lost and found, he wanted to hold on to his true family, to this moment, to this place in life he found himself. Sure, the war sucked, and the future was unknown, and danger was all around, but with Jane at his side and his brothers and the fighters of the house coming up and embracing him? He couldn't help but think it was all going to be okay.

As Fritz announced he was going to go gather Last Meal for everyone, and the brothers headed to the bar for celebratory drinks, Vishous put his arm back around Jane and kissed her on the mouth.

Leaning into her ear, he whispered, "I want to rechristen our bedroom."

"So do I. How long do we have to stay?"

"Dinner, no dessert."

"Deal."

He was following the crowd into the billiards room when something had him look over his shoulder.

Lassiter was standing in the far corner of the foyer, his face grim, his eyes intense. There was absolutely no fooling around to the guy. No laughing. No joy, either.

A warning tightened V's shoulders and shot down his spine into his ass. Something was just not right here, he thought. But he couldn't put his finger on it.

"V?"

As Jane spoke up, he shook himself—and the fallen angel disappeared into thin air.

"Are you okay, V?" she prompted.

"Yeah," he said, turning back to the poolroom. "S'all good. It's all . . . perfectly fine."

No doubt it was only the aftershocks of everything making him paranoid. The angel was probably upset that *Stranger Things* Season 3 had been delayed or some bullshit.

All Lassiter really cared about was himself and TV.

THIRTY-THREE

The dawn was beginning to hint at its arrival with a blush of pink on the horizon when Vitoria determined that they were on a fool's chase. She, along with Streeter's failing set of lungs, had mounted the foot of Iroquois and progressed, as instructed, what had to be over a half mile. Or two. Or twelve. Yet no lane, or even the offshoot of a trail, had appeared.

As Vitoria stopped, she did some panting herself—and knew a frustration that was so deep, she was cursing in Spanish in her head.

"Go . . . back . . . ?" Streeter wheezed.

She looked all around and saw nothing but this singular snow-covered road that continued farther up toward whatever was at the peak—picnic spot, observatory, park ranger station.

There was a desire to blame the intel Streeter had brought to her, but that was counterproductive. And this was a lesson learned. Her desire for a given outcome had colored her analysis of the information and led them on this wild-goose chase.

A waste of time and energy.

"Yes." She allowed one, single curse in her native tongue to escape her lips. "Back to the car."

Resuming the lead, she made a little circle and continued along, putting one snowshoe in front of the other over the track they had made. And though there was some relief that came with a downward course, her anger did not permit any appreciation of the aid.

Perhaps it was best for her to abandon the search for the bodies of her brothers. If she were honest, the reason she wanted to find them was not so much the closure and burial, although she would feel she had done a right and dutiful thing if she could put them in proper graves. No, she was desirous of the knowledge that they were well and truly gone. That she didn't have to worry about her reinstating the business only for them to miraculously show up and steal her future away—

Vitoria slowed and then halted.

"What?" Streeter groaned behind her.

Well . . . there it was. The cut-through they had been looking for, the lane so narrow and unmarked that she had missed its appearance on the ascent due to the snow's masking properties: It was only thanks to this different viewpoint that she could pick out the break in the forest, the hole in the evergreens.

"We have found our drive," she announced.

Success gave her a burst of energy, and it certainly improved Streeter's respiration. The pair of them made quick time through the manmade tunnel in the forest and then there it was. Yes, this had to be her brother's bolt-hole: The structure was single story and unadorned, only a row of thin windows just under the roofline allowing light into the interior. A snow-covered car was parked off to one side and there was a petroleum tank the size of an outhouse cozied up to the opposite flank.

Although none of that was what told her it was Ricardo's.

The door was the telltale. It had no handle, no knob, just a security keypad that offered a choice of either a numerical grid or a thumbprint reader.

If this were just a hunting cabin in the woods almost at the border of Canada, why would you need such security?

Vitoria went forward, the *piff, piff, piff* of the snowshoes loud in her ear. She had never been much for premonitions, but as she came up to the door, she had one that was very clear.

Bad things happened here. Very bad. Although . . . not recently: the snow cover was utterly undisturbed by tire track or human print, and God knew that snow-impacted car hadn't been driven anywhere in quite a while.

Before she attempted the numerical lock, she paused and looked to the heavens. After offering a prayer in Spanish, she put in their mother's birthday—

The shift of the lock was automatic, and as if forces from the other side of the grave wanted to urge her entry, a release of interior pressure pushed at the door, causing it to open a crack.

Vitoria clicked on her headlamp, the beam a bright, burning blue that hurt her eyes until they adjusted. Extending her hand, she opened things wider, that shaft of light from her forehead penetrating the dense dark.

"Whattaya see?"

She didn't bother answering Streeter. Bending down, she released the snowshoes and stepped free of them. "You stay here," she told him.

"No problem."

As she put one foot over the threshold, she turned . . . and her headlamp illuminated a severed human hand that lay on the floor, just inside the door, like something one might find in a gag gift store. The shriveled fingers were curled up around the palm and frozen in place, the decayed flesh gray and white.

It had been cut off cleanly.

"Be on guard," she heard herself say.

"Yeah. Okay."

As Streeter answered, she frowned and realized she'd uttered that to herself. Forgetting all about him, she went in farther and closed the door most, but not all, of the way. God knew she wasn't about to take a chance on getting locked inside . . . except there was no need to worry. There was the same keypad and thumbprint reader on the interior—

That was what the hand must have been used for, she thought. Someone had escaped from here, getting free of her brother's vengeance by cutting that hand off and using its print. Because they hadn't known the code.

Taking a deep breath of air that was as cold as that of the outdoors, she smelled mold and must, but not the telltale sweet stench of mortal decay. Then again, given the layer of dust on everything? Nobody had been in here in a long time—so whatever bodies there might be had gone through their decomposition process already.

She saw the boots first. Then the legs, long legs encased in blue jeans that were stained—so this was not either of her brothers, as neither Ricardo nor Eduardo ever wore those kinds of pants. The male torso plugged into the denim was clothed in a loose sweatshirt, and there were hands at the base of each arm. So this was also not the one whose fingerprint had been used for escape.

As she inspected the grimacing face, she winced. The man had been in great pain as he had died, his gray, frozen visage bearing a stunning wound in one eye's socket.

A burn, she thought. Someone had stabbed him in the eye with a torch or a flare.

Moving her head around, she inspected the interior and found nothing surprising: Galley kitchen, tiny bathroom, cots to sleep on. There was a minor degree of inhabitation debris like wrappers for food-stuffs and soda cans, as well as some weapons, so she guessed they had been here for a time before the ruckus had occurred.

Training the headlamp higher, she noted those narrow windows all the way at the top of the walls. Smart. One wouldn't want anybody see-ing inside—

Across the way, there was another door, one more akin to that of the entrance than the bathroom.

Vitoria stepped over the body and proceeded over to what turned out to be a stairwell down into a cellar. As her beam penetrated the black hole, something skittered out of the way at the bottom, and she began her descent cautiously, putting her gloved hand on a railing that was bolted into the wall.

There was a slight smell of death halfway to the lower level, the awful perfume the kind of thing that activated the most ancient part of her brain, triggering thoughts of stopping, turning around, leaving immediately. Which she refused to do.

At the bottom, she stopped and looked around.

There were three cells directly ahead, and there was a body locked in one, its arm extending out through the bars, the hand missing. The head of the man had been badly beaten in, with a pool of dried blood around it, all facial features unrecognizable between the damage and the decaying.

Vitoria took a deep breath. More blue jeans. It wasn't either of her brothers.

Turning around, she—

"*Oh . . . dear God,*" she said in Spanish.

As she hastily made the sign of the cross, her stomach clenched and then heaved—and she had to cover her mouth or throw up.

A corpse was splayed against the far wall, hanging by chains that had been locked on its wrists. The male was naked, the head lolling to the side, a trail of long-dried blood running from one side of the neck down the chest to the leg, a wound of some sort in the abdomen.

She knew it was Ricardo by the hands and the pattern of hair.

But she had to be sure.

Walking forward, she shook so badly her teeth rattled together and her hands slapped against her hips. And when she leaned to the side so the beam flashed upward to the features of the face, she began to cry. The dried-up eyes were open with horror, the mouth distended as if Ricardo had cried for help that would never come, the flesh horribly wrinkled and falling off in strips because he had been dead for so long yet no one had come for his remains.

For all of the violent things Ricardo had wrought on others, for the many deaths he had caused, directly or indirectly, for the rigid restrictions he had put on her, there was plenty to justify this terrible, lonely, painful demise.

Yet as she stared at the decayed remains of the face she had known all her life, she thought not of all the bad things. She remembered the vases of flowers on their mother's birthday: Though she was before the body of the man, she thought of the soul of the child.

She would mourn the latter, for that was the one she had the most in common with: all those hard, early years of poverty that had been the kiln to Ricardo's ambitions had served the same purpose for her. They had been dirty and hungry together, mocked in the street as they begged, beaten, and chased away.

As emotion overcame her, there was a temptation to fall apart. To sink to her knees and wail. To throw her hands up in a scared defeat and return to safety back in South America.

This was what she had come here for, however. A slate wiped clean—and Eduardo was dead, too. She knew that without a doubt. If someone had done this to Ricardo, then the other had been killed as well.

Vitoria had wanted a revolution. So she needed to be able to stomach the bloodshed.

As she forced herself to go back upstairs, she tripped at the first step—but upon none of the others. Up at the top, she cleared her throat a couple of times and breathed through her nose. For some reason, she wanted the smell out of her nostrils before she went outside, as if that would dim the memories. Or perhaps she was trying to catch her breath. Or . . .

She couldn't think straight. But she needed to start doing that immediately.

Striding to the door that was still only slightly ajar, she said roughly, "Nothing."

Outside, Streeter pivoted around, his exhale of cigarette smoke floating up to the brightening sky. "No?"

She made what she hoped was a negatory sound and closed things up behind her. Before she put herself once more in her snowshoes, she checked to make sure the locking mechanism had engaged.

"So this was a waste of time," he muttered.

"Yes. It was."

If he had known her better, or been paying closer attention, he might have noticed her voice was hoarse. And her hands were shaking. And she was breathing hard. But he was too self-involved, and that was perfect.

Clipping herself back into the snowshoes, Vitoria set off once again, at a faster pace than before.

She had no choice but to leave the bodies, even that of her brother. It was better for her to pretend she knew nothing and be sought out by law enforcement if things ever came to that. Which would be a very long while, if at all. This outpost was totally secluded and secure, and she and Streeter's tracks would be covered by snow soon enough—

"I'm sorry."

Vitoria looked over her shoulder without breaking stride. "For what."

"Bein' wrong. Wastin' your time."

Now she lost her rhythm. "It's okay. Do not worry yourself about it. We all make mistakes."

"Thanks, boss."

"You are welcome, Streeter."

As she continued on, she tried to distract herself with plans to continue following up with more of those names in Eduardo's journal. But it was hard. Ricardo's throat had been torn open, for godsakes.

What kind of animal did that?

THIRTY-FOUR

ometime after sunrise, Jane had her face in a pillow. Her naked body was flat on the mattress, and her legs were spread, and there was good reason for both. A huge weight was on top of her, moving, penetrating, the rhythm like waves in the ocean at high tide. Her hands were held down, big palms pressing on them, keeping her in place. Fangs, sharp and delicious, were sunk into her shoulder, the bite deep.

How Vishous managed to be in all those places at once was something to ponder—at a different damn time.

Bumping her butt against him signaled what she wanted and he was right on it, releasing his fangs, and lifting his weight off her so that she could get up on all fours. As soon as she was set like a table, V was back on her, his body so much bigger that he became a cage around her, one arm planted next to her, the other coming under her torso, between her breasts. His gloved hand locked on her collarbone and she got herself good and braced.

The pistoning force was so great that without his hold on her, she would have been thrown into the headboard—but fortunately, her male was strong enough to keep the pace and her in one place.

Holy hell, they were probably waking Butch and Marissa up with the bed banging like this.

Something to apologize for later.

Jane wasn't going to waste a moment of time on anything but what they were doing. There was just such joy in giving herself up to the experience, laying down her inclination to dictate, anticipate, plan, and execute—and letting go. The trust she had in V was the conduit; the love was the connection. And there was also the knowledge that, at least when it came to her, he was willing to do fair turnaround. He would give himself to her in any way she asked or wanted—

An orgasm lightning'd through her, hitting her sex like the crack of a whip, and as if he had been waiting for that, V's pelvis clapped forward once, twice . . . three times. After that, it was all inside of her, his erection kicking as he filled her up.

Then it was the great collapse.

When her eyes were able to focus, she looked at the clock. 8:38 a.m.

"You are the best alarm clock in the world," she said.

V's laugh was low and a little evil. "No hitting my snooze button, huh."

"Nope."

"Pity."

They rolled over and spooned, and then she had to motivate. "So here's the plan," she said. "I go and do this check-in at Assail's, and then I'm back for the rest of the day. Ehlena's covering at the clinic, and Manny and I are on at nightfall."

"I like this new schedule."

"Me, too. And I wouldn't be going anywhere now if we weren't running those checks on him still."

She twisted around and kissed Vishous, and then slid out from his arms. Heading for the shower, she was smiling, and she made a point of turning on the bathroom light. There, in the mirror, was the happiest version of herself she had seen for a long while, and she wanted to enjoy the view.

"I'm going to meet Payne in a half hour," V said from the bed.

Jane leaned back out into the bedroom. "You are?"

"Yeah." He put his arms behind his head and crossed his legs at the ankles. "You know, to spar. In the gym."

"You're going to talk to her about your mom, huh."

His eyes shifted away. "We figured if we did it this time of day now, we could have some privacy."

"I think it's a really good idea."

"Mary's—you know, Mary's going to be there."

Jane popped her brows. "Really?"

"I was the one who suggested it."

Jane smiled some more and then paused to appreciate the sight of Vishous's enormous, naked body, lying on that messy bed like he was a lion in the sun.

Those diamond eyes swung back around to her. "Take a picture," he drawled, "it'll last longer—and you can keep it in your pocket while you're gone, to remember me."

"You're pretty unforgettable."

"You'll make me blush." He eased onto his side. "Do go on."

His sex lay on his thigh, shameless, half-erect, and as she looked at it, the thing hardened even more.

V slipped his hand down and palmed himself. "Can I get you all messy again as soon as you're out of the shower?"

"You are—"

"Hungry still. I have a couple of months to make up for, you know." Stroke up. Stroke down. "Plus I like the idea of you out in the world with me in your panties."

Jane laughed. "How about you do my back in the shower?"

"I thought you'd never ask," he said as he jumped out of bed. "We have enough time for me to do your front, too, if we're quick about it, true?"

•   •   •

Forty-five minutes later, Sola was pacing around Assail's kitchen. Doc Jane, as folks called her, had arrived just a little late, the woman apologizing profusely as she came in through the garage door.

Doctor and patient were currently in the vast living area, their soft voices unintelligible. Sola had wanted to be in there with them, but she thought it was important for the two to have a little privacy. Plus she didn't trust herself not to break down. It seemed inconceivable that Assail would do anything other than continue to improve, get stronger every day, be here next week and the month after and the year after that.

She could swear he was becoming better by the moment. The trouble was, feelings were a response to reality. They didn't dictate it—

As the door up from the cellar opened, Ehric and Evale filed in. The two brothers were half-asleep, their hair sticking up in exactly the same way, as if not only did they look alike, but they slept the same.

"Anything?" Ehric asked as he went over and sat at the table.

"Not yet."

"Your grandmother is still sleeping," he said as he rubbed his face. "We were very quiet."

"I'm glad." Sola paused by the stove. "I worry she's on her feet too much, although good luck trying to get her to lie down."

"We will ensure her list of groceries is filled," Ehric murmured. "At nightfall, and not before."

"Good plan."

As Sola resumed pacing in her socks, Evale started going through the cupboards.

"Can I help you?" she offered, even though it wasn't her kitchen. And she wasn't a cook. And she didn't know shit about anything at the moment.

"I am looking for the peppers."

"The stuffed ones? They're in the fridge."

"No, the little ones—ah, yes. Here."

The guy took a package over to the counter, and she didn't pay much attention until he started to put something in his mouth—

"No!" she barked, throwing her hands out. "Stop!"

Assail's cousin froze with a ghost pepper just about to drop in a piehole that would never be the same. "What's wrong?"

"Put that down and wash your hands! That'll make you sick!"

He frowned and regarded the shriveled piece of hotter-than-evil. "Are you certain?"

"It's a ghost pepper—you want to handle them carefully. They'll burn you from the inside out."

"I had them last night." He popped the thing into his mouth and started chewing. "I like them."

Sola couldn't move for a moment. But then she exploded for the refrigerator, grabbing a carton of whole milk and diving for a glass in the cabinet. There was a delay between when the peppers were taken on a oner like that, and if she could just get him to spit the stuff out and start rinsing with the milk, they might not give Doc Jane another patient to treat—

Sola wheeled around only to go statue.

Evale was looking at her with pleasant curiosity as he chewed—like he couldn't understand what she was getting on about, but he liked and respected her enough to give her space to be weird. And then he put a second into his hopper.

"Hit me," Ehric said from where he was sitting.

In response, Evale pivoted and tossed a ghost pepper across the room, tagging his brother right in the mouth.

Sola stood there with the glass of milk and played an ocular tennis match between the pair of apparently-indestructibles.

"Let me see those," she said, holding her hand out. "No, I don't want to touch one, I want to see the package."

Maybe she was confused—nope. As she got a close look at the label on the cellophane bag, it had all the appropriate warnings on it. Except maybe they were duds, like ammo that had failed or something?

A quick sniff and she found they smelled as awful as they should. Still, she took one out with her fingertips and extended her tongue. She knew better than to do a test with a full-on chew—and if she hadn't needed a distraction, she wouldn't have bothered with the verifying.

She took a lick. And waited—

"Oh, my God!" Bending down, she coughed. "How in the world—"

"Are you finished with them?"

As Evale put out his hand, she gave the package back and hit the milk. And while she was trying to calm down all the HOLYSHIT on the tip of her tongue, he and Ehric proceeded to dust the peppers one by one.

And then they snagged the other package in the cupboard.

"I do not understand how you guys can—"

Doc Jane and Assail came into the kitchen, and Sola tried to read their expressions.

"Cousin," Ehric said, "would you care for a—"

"No, no." Sola stepped in between the two. "He's good without the ghost peppers. Right? You're good. Yup, maybe later, thanks."

"What are you guys eating?" Doc Jane asked offhandedly.

"These?" Evale showed the package. "They're quite delightful."

Doc Jane nodded. "Vishous loves those. Eats them like candy."

Sola could only shake her head. "You guys are amazing."

Then she refocused and met Assail's eyes, searching for an answer. When he gave her a wink, she wasn't sure what that meant.

"Well, I'll head out now." The doctor put a backpack on. "Manny will be here after nightfall, and I think we'll have Ghisele come out to—ah, help my partner with the exam."

Abruptly, a pounding anxiety rumbled through Sola, the storm of bad energy rattling her so badly, she forgot the burn that was still on her tongue.

"I'll walk you out, Doc Jane," she said as she headed for the rear door.

"No—"

"Not that way—"

"Garage—"

The three men all spoke at the same time, with greater urgency than she'd thrown at the Great Ghost Pepper Non-Incident.

"Sorry," she said. Security concerns, of course.

Doc Jane put an arm around her. "Let's go this way."

As they headed off, Sola was aware of Assail staring after them, his moonlight eyes intense. But then his cousins were talking to him, and he stayed back in the kitchen.

Out in the garage, Jane preempted any questions. "He's doing really well," the doctor said. "I think you can start to relax a little."

Sola frowned. "But what about the cancer? It's still in his brain, isn't it? I mean, how can you say I should start to relax?"

Doc Jane almost caught her reaction. Almost. But that subtle recoil and the widening of the eyes were the kind of things that, when someone was scared to death about their loved one's future and reading every single fucking nuance about the person who knew the situation best, were as obvious as a Broadway stage actor's tap-dance and arm-circle routine.

The other woman cleared her throat. "Listen, I think you need to talk to Assail."

"You're his doctor."

"Please, go speak to him."

"About his cancer."

Doc Jane's forest green eyes shifted ever so slightly to the left. "Yes."

"Okay. I will."

Sola spoke the words with a defiance that was maybe unwarranted, but she wasn't going to worry about that as she turned away and marched back into the house. As she came into kitchen, the three men looked over at her.

"You mind if we go talk?" she said as she walked by Assail.

She didn't wait for him. And he did follow her, out into the hall that led to his office and the stairwell to the second floor.

Spinning around, she had to remind herself that whatever might be going on, he had just been critically ill and hospitalized for it.

"You want to tell me what the hell's going on," she demanded in a low voice.

Assail's handsome-as-sin face was remote. "About what, pray tell."

Sola crossed her arms over her chest. In the back of her mind, she wondered whether she was going too far—but no, her instincts told her things were simply not adding up.

"Your doctor won't tell me about your cancer. And I have a feeling that's because you don't have it."

THIRTY-FIVE

As Marisol stood before him as if she were about to enter into a bar fight—and win it—Assail felt an exhaustion that had nothing to do with his recovery. Indeed, this was the problem with lying to intimates, he thought. The untruths always came home to roost and never in a way that justified the falsity, however small or large it had been.

Because, in fact, there was never a justification to lie to someone who loved you.

"Do you have cancer or don't you," his female demanded.

Assail wished he'd had more time. But for what? As if that would change this part of things?

"Come," he said, taking her elbow. "I should like some privacy."

She jerked herself free of his hold, but she did go into his office with him. And as he shut the door, she went over to the windows that ran from ceiling to floor.

"Please do not open the drapes," he said as she reached out.

"Why. Don't like the light of day?"

"No, I do not."

"So?" She turned around. "You want to tell me what's really going on here?"

Assail lowered himself into the padded chair that was opposite all of his computers. As he propped his chin up with his fist, he stared across at her. "I am sorry you were deceived by my cousins."

She blinked, as if taking a moment to absorb the news. "So you're not terminal."

"I was. But I am no longer."

Her laugh was short and harsh. "I don't know whether to be relieved— or get my grandmother and take her back to Miami right now."

"I am sorry they chose not to be honest."

Marisol jabbed a finger at him. "Don't get it twisted. They may have started it, but you kept the lie going."

"You are correct."

When he didn't go any further, she crossed her arms again. "I'm waiting. And I want to know everything, whatever it is."

As he scrambled in his empty head to find words that made sense, he couldn't decide what was worse. Baring his weakness before her, or knowing, in the depths of his dark heart, that the real secret was one he could never share with her: He could not tell her what he was. As a rule, his species did not reveal themselves to humans—and in the very rare, *extremely* rare, case where that operating principle was violated, if the human somehow was able to accept things, they had to leave their life behind and find their way within the vampire world.

It required a complete immersion. A never-go-back.

And he wasn't prepared to ask that of her—because her grand-mother, her most important responsibility, who happened to be a de-vout, God-fearing Catholic, would either have to be jettisoned at the proverbial side of the road . . . or Mrs. Carvalho would have to come with.

And that was not going to happen. Even if Marisol could evolve into the reality, her grandmother with her traditions and her strict codes and her God was never going to get there.

Assail was not about to ruin that wonderful old woman's life.

"You have one more minute," Marisol announced, "and then I am getting my car keys—"

"I have been addicted to cocaine for a good year now." Assail took a deep breath. "And by addicted, I mean . . . vials and vials of it up my nose every night. I was a raging coke addict, Marisol. I am not proud of this, and yes, I was doing it hardcore when I was with you."

Her brows lifted. "I never saw you do drugs."

"Why would I ever have snorted a line in front of you? I wanted you—I still want you—to find me suitable as a mate. That is not the kind of behavior that creates such an impression."

"Were you . . . did you do anything intravenously?"

"No, I never used needles."

She seemed visibly relieved. "I, ah, I knew you were dealing it."

"But you didn't know I was my own customer." He focused on her socks because he was afraid of what he would see in her eyes. "When one is in a fancy suit, living in a house like this, drug addiction is far easier to hide than if one is a junkie in a cardboard box in an alley. But the reality is, both the homeless man and I are exactly the same when it comes to being crippled."

"You detoxed," she murmured.

"I did, yes. Three months ago, I went to the clinic to be medically supervised while I got off the cocaine. Unfortunately, my"—he touched his head—"my brain did not do well. I had a period of psychosis."

"Why didn't your cousins just say this?"

"Would you have come if you'd been told I was dying of insanity?" He wanted to reach out to her, but he stayed where he was because he didn't want to pen her in. "I am very sorry that you were deceived, and I do believe that you, and you alone, are the reason that I am here instead of still at that clinic. But you shouldn't have been lied to. That was wrong."

Marisol opened her mouth, but didn't speak right away. "Why didn't you just tell me?"

"I haven't been thinking correctly. And more than that . . . I was ashamed. Addiction is an ugly, nasty disease, and I didn't want you to know I was so weak as to get lost in it."

She looked up at the ceiling. Refocused on him. "So you are not dying."

"No, I am not. Not more than any other living, mortal entity." He shook his head. "And please know I am sorry. I truly am."

It was a long while before she moved toward him, and at first, he assumed she was leaving the room to go gather her things and her grandmother. But then she stopped in front of him.

Tilting his chin up with her forefinger, she stared into his eyes, and he prayed that she found whatever she was looking for.

"I'm glad you're going to be okay," she said after a long moment.

Will you stay, he thought as he put his hands lightly on her hips. *Will you still stay with me?*

He kept those questions to himself. He was too afraid of the answers.

God was so odd.

As Sola stood in front of Assail, she thought she probably needed to rephrase that, even though it rhymed. After all, she had prayed at that mass for just this kind of break in the bad news, had hoped for this unbelievable outcome, this reprieve.

But instead of jumping for joy, she was left off-kilter and feeling betrayed. Part of her told her to get off her high horse and understand Assail's and his cousins' point of view. The other half, though, was feeling manipulated.

"I hate that you've put me in this position."

He nodded. "Myself as well."

"So I guess I should just go home."

"Your home is not Miami and you know it."

"It's not Caldwell, either," she countered. "I've been here for ten years, and you know something—they've all sucked. Which is a helluva commentary considering how bad the decade before this was."

"Your grandmother is your home. Wherever she is, you are at your place of residence."

Damn you, she thought. *For knowing me.*

"Marisol, I am out of the life. I am as free as you are. I would like to start a new chapter—anywhere. Miami, Caldwell, overseas. Like you, my home is where another is, not specific to any particular zip code."

As he stared up at her, his moonlight eyes were steady and sad.

"So you're at home with your cousins." She took a step away from him. "Wherever they are you—"

"Don't be daft. This is naught to do with them."

"Watch your tone. You are *not* in a position to get pushy."

"I can protect you. My cousins and I are a safer bet for the two of you, and well you know it."

Sola narrowed her stare on him. "I've been doing a pretty good god-damn job on my own."

"Are you willing to gamble your life on that? Your grandmother's? There is safety in numbers."

"Do you really want me to stay with you only through self-interest?"

"Whatever it takes."

She shook her head. "You have no pride."

"Nope. None. Not when it comes to you."

Sola went back over to the drapes that he wouldn't let her open. Jesus, it was like living with a bunch of vampires in this house, everything buttoned up during the daylight hours. Then again, that was the way of drug dealers. Night owls, the lot of them.

Staring at the opaque fabric, because there was no looking through it, she tried on for size the idea of them moving around together as a pack, Assail, her grandmother, the two cousins, Markcus, herself.

Turning back to him, she looked at him for the longest time, weighing everything. He was right, there was strength in numbers. And he was still so weak, his body frail under the button-down that he'd tucked into those too-loose twill slacks.

In her mind, she heard him say that he was ashamed. Then she recalled when he had first opened his eyes to her and she had seen that the whites were all red . . .

Such suffering.

"Are you going to stay clean?" she demanded, even as she wondered how in the world she could trust any answer he gave to that.

"Yes. On my life, Marisol. I will never do any drug again—I have learned too well where that takes me."

Shit, she thought.

After what felt like a lifetime, she shrugged. "I catch you lying to me or doing coke, and I'm leaving. I have no interest in enabling you, making excuses for you, or pretending I will spare you any kind of a backward glance. You have one chance and that is it. Are we clear?"

Pushing himself upright, he nodded immediately. "I understand and I accept this."

"And she's going to make you convert. My grandmother does not play—and you're going to have to learn Spanish and/or Portuguese. She'll teach you it whether you like it or not."

"Marisol . . ."

When Assail's voice cracked, she went over to him and embraced his thin body. He had been through hell, and the medical staff had certainly assumed they were going to lose him—and as much as Sola would have preferred the truth right from the beginning, he was correct. She probably wouldn't have come up here if it had been just a he-isn't-coming-out-of-his-addiction or he's-lost-his-mind thing.

And that was kind of ugly to admit. Like cancer was a noble disease, but if your biochemistry had conspired with a drug to your mortal detriment then you were undeserving of sympathy, support, understanding.

"I am sorry," he said into her hair.

"Me, too. And I love you."

The shudder that went through him made her feel as though she was doing the right thing: He was relieved like that because he didn't want to lose her as badly as she didn't want to lose him.

"I will take good care of you and your grandmother," he said roughly.

Leaning back, Sola pegged him with a hard eye. "That's a two-way street. I'm not a damsel in distress who needs to be saved, I'm a partner who will help you to survive, too. If there is a price on my head, then the Benloise family has one on yours, too. You need me as well."

"Yes," he murmured. "I most certainly do."

Sola had to smile. "Guess I told you, huh."

"You certainly did. And it's a huge turn-on. You want to go upstairs and order me around some more?"

She narrowed her eyes again. "Say please."

"Pleeeeeeeeeeeeease . . ."

THIRTY-SIX

It was at about four in the afternoon the following day that Vitoria arrived at the gallery and learned she'd made a mistake. And unfortunately, she discovered her lapse of judgment in front of the police.

Striding through the rear of the building, she nodded at staff who were clustered together in stressed, chatty groups. Not much work was getting done, but she let that slide, given what was going on.

As she came out into the gallery space proper, she immediately identified the man standing in front of a balloon sculpture of a woman giving birth.

"You must be Detective de la Cruz?" she said as she walked over to him.

He turned to her and seemed relieved not be focusing on the "art." "That's right. Vitoria Benloise?"

"That is I." Yes, she knew grammatically it was "me," but she'd always felt that was too common-sounding. "How may I help you?"

He flipped opened a leather wallet, revealing a photo ID that read *Detective José de la Cruz, Homicide,* and a brass Caldwell Police badge.

Then he put out a hand. "Do you have a few minutes to speak with me?"

The man was forty-ish, and with a name like his, she liked him even though they were already on different sides of the table. Plus he had nice, dark eyes. His clothes were simple, the sport coat and open collar professional-looking, but not stuffy, and she was surprised, given how cold it was, that he didn't also have on some kind of an overcoat or parka: Even with the late-afternoon sun shining down, when she had gotten out of her brother's Bentley, she had been chilled to the bone during the short distance to the staff entrance of the gallery.

"Absolutely, Detective." She shook his hand. "What's going on?"

"I'm investigating a homicide committed last night."

"Oh, dear. Is this about Margot? I've seen the news on TV. What a tragedy! How does something like that happen in what should be such a safe part of town?"

"Actually, most homicide victims are killed by people they know."

"So scary." Out of the corner of her eye, she noted that a couple of salespeople had come out from the back and were watching. "Tell me, how may I assist you?"

"Well, I've spoken to some of the folks here already—about when Margot left work yesterday and who she might have been with. And they all told me that you've recently taken over the business?"

"I am here looking after my brothers' interests, it is true."

"You say that as if you expect them to return here. Yet it's my understanding they've been gone from Caldwell for a while?"

"They have been."

"Have you seen or had any sort of contact with either Ricardo or Eduardo lately?"

She assumed a sad expression. "No, I have not. I have been worried about them."

"When was the last time you had contact?"

"It's been months."

"And you didn't think to call the police?"

"I did back in Colombia. When they didn't do anything, I came here. It has always been my intention to reach out to the authorities if I could not locate my brother."

Abruptly, the image of Ricardo strung up and rotted in that cellar made her throat tight. But now was not the time for emotion. She was speaking to her enemy.

"Right. Of course." The detective flipped open a little notebook. Scribbled something in it with a pen. "And you've been here since when? I mean, when did you arrive in Caldwell and from where?"

"I came from Colombia four days ago. Or is it five? With jet lag, I am confused." She smiled at him. "Detective, would you mind talking to me upstairs? Privacy is best and I have clients here."

To help him understand, she inclined her head toward two women across the way. The matched pair of avant-garde rich were inspecting a work of art that was made up of shredded bedsheets draped over a taxidermied cow standing with each hoof in a toilet.

"Yeah, sure. Lead the way."

Vitoria took him through the unmarked door off to the side and up the stairs to Ricardo's office. As she went along, she channeled her walk into her hips and her ass under the theory that all assets were to be brought to bear in this situation. However, it was hard to keep things smooth. Her thighs and her calves were screaming in pain from the trip up that mountain. The two Motrin she had taken four hours ago were losing their potency.

"Here we are," she said as she opened the door at the top of the metal staircase.

"Wow." The detective went in. "Fancy."

"My brother likes things a certain way."

"Clearly." De la Cruz wandered around, even though there was little to see. "Where were we—oh, yeah. So you do expect your brothers back or not?"

She closed them in together. "I must confess I have begun to really worry. It is not like Ricardo especially to just up and leave for this long, but then again, they are men. They do what they want."

Vitoria went across and turned the guest chair in front of the elevated desk around. Sitting in it, she crossed her legs such that the slit in her skirt fell open.

"Are you okay?" the detective asked. "You grimaced there as you sat down."

"It's nothing. Just a good workout." She smiled. "I'm quite stiff from the gym."

"I should work out more." De la Cruz approached on a casual stride. "That's quite a desk. Up on that platform."

"My brother liked to make an impression."

"Liked? Or likes."

"Sorry, my English is not so good." She touched her forehead. "And where are my manners? I should have offered you coffee or tea."

"It's okay. I hit the diner before I came over here." He cleared his throat. "So you live in Colombia?"

"Yes, but we have homes in a number of places. São Paulo, Brazil, Santiago, Chile—oh, and Punta del Este, of course. My brother likes real estate, and I take care of his homes, overseeing his staffs and the estates."

"Man, you left the equator to come to Caldwell, New York, in the middle of January. No offense, you must really be worried about Ricardo and Eduardo. My wife hates it here this time of year."

"You should send her on a vacation."

"She loves me, though." He smiled and glanced down at his little pad. "Can you give me a general idea of when was the last time you spoke to either of your brothers?"

"As I said, it was months and months ago. Ricardo called me."

"How did the conversation go?"

She shrugged. "Much as usual."

"So nothing seemed odd to you?"

"Forgive me, but why are we talking about my brothers? I mean, I am happy to help the police in any way I am able, but I thought this was about the woman who was found dead?"

"Just trying to get the whole picture. Your brother Ricardo is a prominent businessman in this town, and everyone here says they haven't seen him in about a year. Your other brother hasn't been around, either, and then someone who works in this gallery was found dead last night. There just seem to be a lot of people going missing." He looked at her pointedly. "You might want to be careful."

"You are so right. I guess I never put all that together."

"But about Margot Forest."

"I'm sorry—I thought her name was Fortescue?"

"Her legal name is Forest. Did you have any interactions with her during the last couple of days since you've been here?"

Thank you, Streeter, she thought.

"As a matter of fact," Vitoria murmured, "she came to my office last night—I mean, my brother Eduardo's office—before she left. She wanted to talk about a new artist she was bringing in."

"Do you recall the name of that artist?"

She pulled a random name out of the air, one that she had overheard in the gallery. "Daymar Locust—or Locasta?"

"Oh, yeah. Someone mentioned him." Notation. Notation. "Anything else come up while you were talking with Ms. Fortescue?"

"No." Vitoria smiled and played with the hem of her skirt. "I wish I could be more helpful."

"What were you doing in your brother's office?"

"I'm sorry?"

"Why were you in there? If it was his office."

Vitoria considered the various ways to play what was coming next. There were a number of different approaches she could take, and as she went over each in turn, it was rather like cards in a poker hand, she supposed.

Eventually, she made a show of sighing. "May I be honest."

"I think you'd better be, if you don't mind me saying. This is a homicide investigation."

She moved her eyes off to the side, as if she were composing her thoughts. Then returned them to the detective. "I've been really worried about my brothers. As you must know, our culture is very different. As their sister, I am expected to wait patiently for news, rather than go find things out myself. But after a year . . . anyway, I went into Eduardo's office to see if I could find anything to explain where he and Ricardo might be. I am in an awkward position, you see. They would never approve of me interfering, and if they are alive? They will be furious at me."

"So things are traditional in your family, huh."

"Very." She deliberately hung her head, as if she were caught in a tangle. "It's part of the reason I am scared to call the authorities. If my brothers are all right, they will be furious at me for meddling in the man's world. And I truly don't want to believe anything bad has happened, but . . . what else can I think? It has always been just the three of us, since our mother died. I am not a worldly woman in the sense that I am adventurous or familiar with travel. I was terrified to make the trip here on my own, but as they are my only family, I felt compelled to come find them—I am babbling, aren't I. Listen to me."

To ensure that the energy coming off of her was correct, she pictured once again Ricardo's body, seeing his lolling head, the neck wound, the gray ribbons of flesh—and instantly, she felt genuine sadness, regret, fear.

"What do you think happened to your brothers?" de la Cruz asked quietly.

"I do not know." Her eyes went to the floor. "I truly do not."

"Are you aware that your brother Ricardo may have been involved with drug dealing?"

Vitoria whipped her head up. "I beg your pardon. He is a dealer in art. That is his business."

"I don't mean to offend you." The man put his hand up. "But I'm not sure you're aware of everything he did here."

Vitoria went to get up, but her thigh muscles spasmed in an unco-ordinated way. As she lurched to one side, de la Cruz ran over and caught her arm.

"My brothers were good men." Or at least Ricardo was. Eduardo had always been a bit of a flake. "I won't have their memories darkened with conjecture."

"You're speaking about them in the past tense again."

She pushed herself away from the detective and stumbled as she went over to the windows. There was nothing to look out at particu-larly, no vista. Just the row of 1920s-era storefronts across the four lanes of Market Street.

"Listen, Ms. Benloise, I didn't mean to upset you." There was a pause. "I just think it's time you know more, if only in case they get in touch with you. What you don't want is to get sucked into this."

"I know nothing of any other kind of business." She pivoted back around and straightened her Escada jacket. "Is there anything else I may help you with?"

"Actually, yes. Since it appears as though you've taken over opera-tions here on behalf of your brothers, I'd like your permission to view any and all security camera footage from the premises."

Vitoria blinked. And kept the curse in her native tongue to herself.

This was the mistake she had made.

She hadn't thought about any cameras. How in the hell could she *not* have thought about searching the security feeds? And what could be on them?

In rapid succession, her brain ran through the various angles. If she said no, they might force her to give them access by some kind of court order—although how they would get permission for that, she wasn't sure, as Margot had worked here, but had not been murdered on the premises. More to the point, if de la Cruz was indeed aware of her

brothers' endeavors in the drug trade, the police might well use whatever was on the feeds as a way to . . .

To what? she wondered. Ricardo was dead. Eduardo had to be as
well. And she had no official knowledge of the goings-on. Her only ties
thus far were with the frustrated suppliers back in South America, and
there was no way they would give her up: The American authorities
couldn't reach that far, for one thing, and anything that incriminated
her would incriminate the suppliers.

But if she granted de la Cruz access, maybe he could do the work for
her. She had no idea how to run computers or isolate footage—she
wasn't even sure where the feeds were kept. But both her brothers had
been notoriously secretive. There wouldn't be cameras in places there
shouldn't be.

Like up here, she thought as she glanced around the ceiling and saw
nothing even remotely camera-like.

And given that Eduardo tracked the illegal money, there would be
absolutely nothing in his office, either.

How was she going to explain her meeting Streeter after hours,
though? Except . . . no, there was nothing illegal about her seeking out
an associate of her brothers' once she got to the States. It was not illegal
to meet a man at the gallery—although if they could prove Streeter was
into the drug side . . .

Then Streeter might implicate her.

Vitoria straightened her spine. "I would love you to look at the footage. I don't know where it is, though?"

"Is there a security room here?"

"I don't know." She nodded toward the door they had come through.
"Let's go find out."

As she walked over to the exit, de la Cruz followed her—and he
stopped her before she opened things.

"I am very sorry about all of this. I know this has to be hard on you."

She made sure to picture Ricardo in that cellar of death. And as the sadness rolled off of her, she said in a voice that cracked, "I am, too. My brothers were very traditional, and that could get stifling for a sister. But they loved me very much, and the feeling was mutual. I really . . . at the end of the day, I just want to know what happened."

De la Cruz nodded. "I lost someone once. My old partner. One of the best men I ever knew, although he had a lot of demons. Big demons." Those deep brown eyes grew unfocused, as if the detective were reliving scenes from his own life. "One day, he just disappeared, and no matter where I've looked, who I've talked to . . . I've never gotten an answer and it eats me alive still."

"So you know how I feel."

"I know exactly how you feel. And I don't care whether or not your brothers were drug dealers. If they were murdered, if that's the reason they're not around, I will find out who did it and I will make sure justice is served. Do you understand? And if they were involved at the level of deals we think they were? Then they were very exposed, and it doesn't look good for bringing them back alive. The kind of people making those sort of moves put a very low value on human life, and if they're threatened in any real or imagined way, things get ugly quick."

Vitoria put her hand to her mouth and closed her eyes.

The image of her brother did not have to be summoned this time. It came forward like a specter, haunting her.

"I hate the idea they would be hurt in any way," she said roughly. "Especially Ricardo. I owe him so much."

"I'm not going to let you down."

"Thank you." She opened her eyes. "Does this mean Margot could have been . . . I mean, if there was anything bad going on—which I cannot believe my brothers would be a part of—could Margot have been in it with them?"

"We're not ruling anything out right now."

She put her hand on his forearm. "Will you please tell me if you find out anything?"

"I will, ma'am." He nodded grimly. "You have my word."

THIRTY-SEVEN

As the sun began to lower over Caldwell and early rush-hour traffic flooded the downtown streets and highway ramps, Jo Early sat at her desk at the *Caldwell Courier Journal* with her aching head cradled between her thumbs and forefingers.

Rather like you might ever so carefully keep a bomb with an impact detonator cushioned from any possible impact.

She had been getting headaches over the last few weeks, and they were growing more intense. This one, in fact, was presenting her with a new level of agony, the light-sensitivity, pressure at the base of her neck, and roiling nausea a triple threat she could totally do without.

Closing her eyes, she came to a conclusion: As much as she prided herself on being a logical person, it was very clear she had a tumor.

Or, as Arnold Schwarzenegger called it in *Kindergarten Cop,* a toomah.

Kidding aside, maybe it was an eyestrain thing. Ever since she'd taken this job as online content editor for the *CCJ,* she'd been spending long periods of time in front of a computer screen. Back when she'd been a receptionist for that real estate office, she'd done scheduling and stuff on them, but this new position was exclusively computer work—

"Do you need some Motrin?"

As a familiar male voice pierced into her ear as if it were an ice pick, she almost told the man who had gotten her this job to pipe down there, Pavarotti. But she had a feeling it was her, not him.

Opening her eyes, she stared up at Bill Elliot's earnest, hipster face. "I swear, I cannot shake this migraine."

"Do you need to get your eye prescription checked?"

"I don't have glasses."

"Maybe you need them?"

Yup, Bill was the reason she had gotten this job, and he and his wife, Lydia, had opened themselves and their home up to Jo even though they were only in their mid-thirties. Then again, marriage and a mortgage were far greater separators between age groups than a couple of calendar years here or there.

It was like the difference between an eleven-year-old who hadn't yet gone through puberty and someone who was fourteen and going on their first date.

A lifetime.

"I'll make an appointment." She sat back and rolled her shoulders. "You leaving for the day?"

"Almost. Do you want to go check out that warehouse with me tonight or no?"

"I would love to." She looked at her monitor—and then promptly glanced down at her desk as the thumper in her skull got worse. "But I'm in no shape to go anywhere."

"Troy might come."

"I wish I could."

Bill pulled on a coat and then tied a red scarf around his neck. "Let me know if I can get you anything?"

"I will. And if you find something at that site, call me."

"You got it." He smiled. "I hope you feel better."

As the guy walked off, Jo got to her feet and looked around. The open newsroom was nearly empty, phones no longer ringing, people gone from their cubicles, everything grinding down.

How had the day passed so fast? she marveled as she headed for the ladies' room in the far corner.

The *Caldwell Courier Journal*'s headquarters had recently gone through an extensive remodel—or so she had been told by every single reporter she'd met on her first day on the job. The multi-storied brick building, which had housed the paper since 1902, had had a total redo, although not for any good reason as far as the staff felt.

Like a lot of dailies in medium cities, the *CCJ* was dying, its page count and ad revenue getting smaller, its stories growing shorter, its middle section now *USA Today* instead of any content generated in Caldwell itself. In the previous year alone, two senior editors, seven reporters, and all three proofreaders had been let go, and the renovations had been done so that the footprint of the newsroom could be shrunk accordingly, with the freed-up space being rented out to—surprise!—a technology start-up.

The mood around the place was grim, and the fact that Jo had been hired at all had been a miracle. Still, they had wanted someone cheap and young to take care of their online stuff, and she fit the bill. Her degree in English Lit from Williams had been a nice little bonus for them, something her superiors might have boasted about if anyone had cared what newspaper people thought anymore. Which they evidently did not.

As she went across the newsroom, she decided that at least the decorators could have chosen a different color than gray. Sure, that was the hue of the decade, but with the layoffs and the one-foot-in-the-grave-other-on-a-banana-peel vibe, being surrounded by carpeting the color of asphalt, cubicles done in old porridge, and walls that matched a corpse left in the cold was only adding to the depression.

In the bathroom, which was done—surprise!—in gray, she splashed her face with lukewarm water and couldn't decide whether it was a good or a bad decision. After she dried the water off, she looked at herself in the mirror, half expecting one of her pupils to be dilated. Or half her mouth to be on a droop. Or maybe some kind of twitch to be working out an eyebrow.

Nope. She was the same as she always had been with her red hair and her green eyes and her pale skin. But she felt wrong. She felt all . . . wrong.

Over the past few weeks, her body had started to betray her on all kinds of levels. Night sweats. These headaches that made her flinch at light and sound. Hunger for weird things at strange times, like bacon and chocolate at three a.m.

Of course, the good news was that she lived with a bunch of stoners, so not only did they have Oscar Mayer and Hershey's Syrup on lock, but they thought the combo was an inspired idea.

Underneath all of the odd symptoms, though, what troubled Jo most was a growing restlessness, a gnawing, tied-to-nothing, but totally imperative metronome of can't-keep-still.

Looking back on how she'd quit her job at the real estate company, she saw that that had been an expression of the impotent urgency. And maybe all the stuff with Bill and the vampires, too—

A sharp shooter went through her frontal lobe and made her gasp.

Cursing, she wobbled her way out of the loo and returned to her desk. Logging off her computer, she put her coat on, said goodbye to Tony, who was her next-door neighbor, and headed out the back to the dark parking lot. Her VW Golf was parked close to the exit because she tried to get to work early every day, and as she got in, she hoped she was going to be able to drive.

It was tough. Once she was on the road, the headlights of other cars were so bright, she had to put her sunglasses on and did not dare take the highway even though that cut about five minutes off her twenty-minute commute.

As she slowly progressed through the stop-and-go of the surface roads, she thought about Bill and that warehouse invite. The two of them had first bonded over a strange interest in vampires—

"Goddamn it," she muttered as the pain ramped up on her again.

Shaking her head to try to clear it, she refused to be derailed, as if the agony were an obstacle. So yes, she and Bill had bonded over the *vampire* thing, the two of them visiting spots around Caldwell where rituals or fights had taken place. She'd even started a blog about—

For a moment, her thoughts trailed off into the pain. But she forced them back on track, the terror that she was losing her mind giving her a preternatural focus.

Anyway, for a while, she had reposted stuff online about bizarre happenings and sightings in the city that other people had been talking about, but she'd had to abandon that. For one, it was a waste of time—

No, it wasn't, some part of her argued. *It was not a waste of time.*

"Whatever."

She had given all that up, though. And kind of deserted Bill, as well. Not that she didn't hang out with him and wasn't grateful for the push he'd given her for her job. It was just vampires . . . didn't hold much fascination for her anymore. Why should she worry about something that didn't exist—especially when she felt like crap, had started a new position, and was confronting the reality that, as much as she loved Dougie and his boys, she was going to have to move out of that apartment of theirs.

They were still living the college life.

Whereas she was trying to get where Bill and Lydia were. Eventually.

As Jo came up to yet another red light—why were they all red tonight?—she thought about her parents. Make that "parents." She was hard-pressed to imagine that she was going to be able to afford a place of her own on a salary like the one she had, but she would rather live around secondhand pot smoke for the rest of her life than go to Chance and Phillie Early for anything.

She had been adopted by them not as a child they'd wanted to raise, but more as if her mother had told her father she liked the little doggie in the window, and the pair had taken Jo home as they would have a new toy.

They'd have done better with something they could have put on a shelf in their mansion and pointed at when they'd wanted to show it off.

Real children didn't work that way.

But it was all good. She'd gotten her college education paid for by them, and then she'd gone her own way, leaving all the money, pretension, and loneliness behind.

Better to be on your own than in bad company. Besides, she had never felt like she fit in with them. Actually, she had never fit in anywhere.

When Jo finally got to the converted house her apartment was in, she had to drive around the block a couple of times to get a space. And then the walk to the front door was an exercise in mind over snow matter.

Hell, at least the near-zero-degree weather helped numb things.

After checking their cheap mailbox, she hit the stairs to the second floor and opened the way into a mess that made her want to cry. The living room was awash in pizza boxes, bongs, and Mountain Dew, and Dougie was asleep sitting up on the brown padded sofa that she had always thought belonged in a Febreze commercial—as the before-treatment example. God only knew where the others were.

She didn't leave the mail on the counter. That never went well. She took it to her bedroom with her, closed herself in, and went over to the bed. Her sit-down quickly became a fall-back, and then she stared at the ceiling.

As her head pounded and a sickly sweat broke out all over her body, Jo was more than scared. She was terrified.

Something was very, very wrong with her.

THIRTY-EIGHT

As Vishous materialized onto the lakeside porch of Rehvenge's Great Camp, he took a minute to look out over the frozen water. With the mountains rising on either side, and the randomly spaced islands in the far distance, the shit reminded him of a model train set, only life-sized: Somewhere in the picture-perfect landscape, there just had to be a lineup of old-fashioned cars, with a red caboose and an engine that let out little poofs of smoke, traveling on a rail that snaked in and out of various vintage-looking outposts that had been constructed of balsa wood and Elmer's glue.

He and Jane were going to come back here, he decided. The next time he was off rotation, and she was out of the clinic, they were going to spend a day and night together here and it was going to be fucking fantastic. They were going to eat too much, and then get under some homemade quilts, and he was going to fuck her twelve different ways to Sunday. And after they were done, they were going to fall asleep with her on his chest—and then he was going to wake up halfway through the day to find himself handcuffed to the headboard.

Whereupon they were going to do things that were still considered illegal in some Southern states—

The door creaked as it opened behind him, and Phury came out with a smile. "V, my brother. Glad to see you."

The pair of them clapped palms and slapped each other on the shoulder.

"You coming in? You want to eat?"

As Phury indicated the way inside, he was looking hopeful. Like he'd been worried about all that shit with Jane saving his life, and couldn't believe he'd been granted an opportunity to reassure himself on that front.

"Ah, yeah." V shrugged. "I'm not real hungry, but sure."

They went in together, and Phury shut things up tightly. The hearth in the main open space was roaring with a great fire, and on the far side, through the entryway into the kitchen, V caught sight of a roasted turkey just out of the oven.

His stomach grumbled so loudly, Phury laughed. "You sure you're not hungry."

"Yeah, I might be rethinking that hard line, my brother."

"Come on, I'll make you a plate."

The old house's floorboards groaned under their weight, and they had to file into the kitchen one after the other to fit through the jambs.

"Sit," Phury ordered.

So he did. "Where's Cormia?"

"She and the other Chosen are at the mansion tonight."

"Making the rounds, huh."

"There are some blood needs." The brother got two plates out and brought them over to the island. "Listen, V, about what happened in that alley—"

"I'm just glad you're okay." V sat on one of the stools. "And Jane, too."

Phury's yellow eyes locked on V. "I need you to know that I wouldn't have asked her to do that. I never would have—I'm responsible for myself out there. No one else is. She was unbelievably heroic, and I am incredibly grateful. But it would have been a horrible outcome for me to be alive at the end of that and your *shellan* not."

"I know." V almost reached out and squeezed his brother's shoulder. "And everything is good between you and me. No worries, true?"

"Thank you." Phury took a deep breath. "Now, what's on your mind?"

As Phury started working the turkey with a carving knife, peeling perfectly sliced pieces of meat off and transferring them to the plates, V wondered exactly how to put this. And then decided, fuck it.

"Who's up next," he demanded. "I know you know. You have to."

Phury paused in mid-slice transfer. "What are you talking about?"

"After my mother. You're the Primale. You have to know who she tapped for a successor. I won't tell anyone else, but I don't understand why it's such a goddamn secret."

Phury put the slice on the plate and looked up, those citrine eyes steady. "I have no clue. I've been wondering myself. I assumed you knew and were keeping it to yourself?"

Cursing, V patted his jacket and then paused. "You mind if I smoke?"

"Nope, not at all."

"Thank you, baby Jesus, to borrow a phrase from Butch."

As he lit up, he exhaled away from his brother. "This is just another of her bullshit games. We have a right to know. I don't like all the shady around this, especially if the war is supposedly ending."

"Have you asked Wrath?"

"No. Not yet."

As the brother put the carving knife aside, he said, "Stuffing?"

"Am I breathing?"

Phury shoved a spoon into the bird and piled high. "Mashed?"

"Do you have gravy?"

"Am *I* breathing?"

V cracked a smile. "Roger that. And affirmative on the gravy."

When a plate was put in front of him, he glanced up. "No veggies? Not that I'm looking a gift horse in the mouth."

"Vegetable matter is a waste of porcelain space." Phury pushed a knife and fork across the butcher block. "Ask yourself, would I sacrifice the surface area of mashed or stuffing for peas?"

"I love you."

After V put out his barely-smoked hand-rolled at the sink, the two of them ate side by side, Phury still on his feet, V parked on the stool. The kitchen was a nice mix of old and new, the appliances state of the art, the exposed shelves, beams overhead, and old, diamond-paned windows all about the been-there-forever.

"We got any prophecies I'm not aware of?" V asked.

"You know everything I do."

"You say the sweetest goddamn things."

After Vishous finished the last of everything on his plate, he lit up another cigarette. "I'll talk to Wrath, then."

"You know, I never had much dealing with your *mahmen*. She wasn't a big fan of mine—then again, I ruined everything."

"Ask the Chosen." V got up and took his plate to the sink. "I don't think they'll agree with that, true? You were their liberator."

As Phury made some kind of a sound that could have meant anything, V took the brother's empty and brought it over to the Kohler. "Where's your dishwasher?"

Phury seemed to shake himself. "Ah . . . sorry, we don't have one. I'll take care of it."

"Good. That sponge crap is above my pay grade." V lifted his curse over his shoulder. "Unless you want me to incinerate your basin—"

"Hey, Vishous?"

V pivoted away from the sink. Phury had shifted position so he was leaning back against the counter by the gas stove, his arms crossed over his chest, his long legs, both the one that was flesh and the other that was a prosthetic, crossed at the boots. His brows were down low, his multi-colored mane of hair flowing over his shoulders like some kind of sunrise.

"What do you need?" V demanded. "Whatever it is, I'm in."

"How about some forgiveness?" As V recoiled, Phury said in a low voice, "I feel like it's my fault."

"What is?"

"That your *mahmen* left the species." The brother tilted his head back and seemed to be staring up through the house to the heavens above. "I mean, maybe if I hadn't come along and fallen in love with Cormia and released all the Chosen . . . maybe the Scribe Virgin would have stuck around, you know?"

"Oh, hell no." V pegged the brother with hard eyes. "You don't own shit about any of it. Disappearing was *her* choice. Nobody put a gun to her head and made her peace out. The bottom line was, she wasn't getting her ass kissed enough so she decided to fuck off the race she created. That's her failure, not yours, mine, my sister's, or anybody else's."

Phury shook his head. "Apart from the loss to the species as a whole, I've been worried that I took your *mahmen* away from you and Payne. Like I'd betrayed you in some way. It's been killing me."

V marched over to the guy, grabbed on to those big shoulders, and gave Phury a good shake. "Snap out of it. Don't waste one more goddamn thought on it. She isn't worth your time—and the sooner you come over to my side of things, the happier you'll be. And forget the *mahmen* crap. Just because a female births something doesn't mean she's a *mahmen,* and when it came to the Scribe Virgin, that was true for the race, and me and my sister." He shrugged. "Ask yourself, if you and Cormia had a young, can you imagine—can you fathom even for a second—your mate deserting that kid for any reason, under any circumstance?"

"No." Phury shook his head. "Not at all."

"That's a *mahmen.* How 'bout your sister-in-law. You think Bella's leaving Nalla for anything?"

"God no. No way. Nope."

"Beth? Layla? Mary? I don't think so. So cut the guilt crap. The race had an overlord who barely functioned quit. That's an opportunity, not a tragedy for any of us to worry 'bout."

Phury took a deep, shuddering breath. "I guess you're right. Thanks, V."

"You're welcome. You're a softie, but I love you."

The guy laughed, as V had intended him to. But the truth was . . . Phury was one of the brothers that he worried about. Too big a heart, that one. Which was the good news and the bad news.

Vishous stepped back and had little interest in going to his next stop, but he wasn't going to quit until he got an answer from somebody. And at least he had a full roast on board.

"If I were you," he said as he went for the back door, "I'd be more worried that someone stole from you."

"Hmm?"

"Jane and I were just in the Treasury, you know, upstairs. That's where I found her after—well, anyway, there's something missing from one of your cases in there."

Phury frowned. "No one's been up to the sanctuary who shouldn't have been. Access is never granted beyond the original bunch of us who are allowed."

"Then it's somebody you know."

"What's missing?"

Vishous put his hand on the knob. "Looked like a book or something."

"A book?" Phury asked.

"I dunno. That was our guess. Maybe we're wrong—"

At that moment, V's phone went off and he took it out. "Shit, trouble downtown."

THIRTY-NINE

"You know, you don't have to do this."

As Marisol spoke up from behind the wheel of his Range Rover, Assail shook his head. "I rather think it is an imperative at this point. Your grandmother has cooked for us non-stop, and as much as we adore her food, all her one-sided effort is making us feel unchivalrous."

In the glow of the dash, the smile that hit his female's face was lovely, small and private, as if his thoughtfulness, and that of the other males in his househould, had touched her grandmother very deeply.

"I would have you look like this always," he murmured.

"Then all you have to do is be nice to my *vovó*."

"I intend to."

The bridge across the Hudson was lit from above, the illumination strung along its soaring suspension girders such that it appeared as though great wings were swooping over the river. Previously, he had always imagined them as that of a bird of prey. Now, he saw them as far more peaceable. A dove's. Or mayhap a seasonal cardinal coming in for a branch landing.

"I think it is amazing, the places life brings you." He glanced over at his female once more. "I would never have pictured myself here in Caldwell when I was in the Old Country."

"I know, right? It's all so random, and yet seems inevitable somehow?"

"Tell me of your family. Apart from your grandmother."

The change in Marisol was immediate, an abrupt tension stiffening her in her seat and furrowing her brow. "What do you want to know."

"You do not have to speak of them if you do not wish."

"It's fine."

"Perhaps another subject would be best?"

"Whatever you think."

Unsure of what to do, he went quiet. And the awkward silence in the vehicle lasted all the way through their getting on the Northway on the far side of the bridge and progressing several exits up to the first of the suburban areas where the Big Hannaford, as his cousins called it, was located.

"I think I've been to this store before," Marisol said as she guided them onto a descending ramp and to a stoplight at a four-lane road.

"Ehric tells me this is where we must go," Assail offered, "and I do not argue these things."

Although in truth, he didn't believe he'd been to a supermarket in . . . all right, so it had been a very, very long time. With little to no culinary skills of his own, he'd always been an eat-out kind of male, but Marisol was changing this. Just as she was changing everything.

When they arrived at the grocery, she found a space for them very close to the entrance, and he got out, buttoning up his fine black cashmere overcoat. Underneath, he was in one of his suits, which was a tad overdone for this sort of thing, sartorially speaking—but this was a bit of a date, was it not?

"May I give you my arm?" he offered.

It was a relief to have her accept the gesture, and as they walked to the garishly lit entrance, he told himself all was well. All was fine. He was going to leave the subject of family well enough alone, and when they returned home, he and his cousins would prepare a nice meal for Mrs. Carvalho—and hopefully thereafter, he and Marisol would discreetly retire upstairs for some private enjoyment.

And then what, a voice in the back of his head asked. *More of the same on the morrow? A housemale living out his hours—*

"I'm sorry, what?" Marisol asked as the automatic doors parted for them.

"Nothing, my love. Shall we get a cart?"

She went over and untangled one from the lineup, and then they were in the store proper, surrounded by a surplus of such magnitude, he was momentarily struck stupid. The fact that the interior of the grocery was lit up bright as the outer crust of the sun did not help. And then there was the ocular insult of aisle after aisle after aisle of colorful labels and logos and foodstuffs of incalculable variety.

"Don't tell me you've never been in a supermarket," Marisol said. "You look like you're facing Mount Everest."

"It is . . . a bit daunting."

"You want to do vegetables first?" As he just stood there, she laughed softly. "Maybe I should rephrase that. Let's do vegetables first. Come with me."

Assail followed her to the left, past a floral display where pre-made bouquets were wrapped in cellophane. He grabbed two bundles of white roses.

"She'll love those," Marisol murmured.

"One is for you."

He kissed her as he put them in the cart, and then they were penetrating a forest of fruit and vegetable displays.

As Marisol stopped them in the midst of the bins and bushels, and looked at him with expectation, he realized he was going to have to make the decisions—and tried to recall recipes from the Old Country.

Mayhap he should have thought this through a bit more.

But surely he could remember something. Surely . . . he could think of one dish, one soup, one meat.

As it turned out, Assail had to go way back in his memories. To the castle he had grown up in . . . it had had a kitchen separate from the main living area as a fire preventative, and he could remember being little and staying for hours and hours beneath the rough oak table, watching the *doggen* turning animal carcasses, and root vegetables, and grains, into proper meals.

"Turnips. Onions. Potatoes. Carrots," he announced.

Like a dam released, he connected with what he wished to prepare, and he was aware of a feeling of pride as he led the way now, picking and choosing and filling plastic bags . . . then taking his female and the cart to the meat counter and securing lamb.

After that, they were in the dairy section, and he had to pause to ponder how much cream he required—

"My father was a criminal," Marisol said in a low, tense voice.

Instantly, Assail grew quite still and then he swung his eyes to her.

"Have I shocked you?" she said tightly. "It's the truth. He died in jail under circumstances that I've never truly gotten to the bottom of. Could have been a fight. Or cancer. But I believe he was murdered, although I will never say that in front of my grandmother."

Assail blinked. "I am so sorry."

The way she shrugged and wrapped her arms around herself broke his heart. "That was how I got into . . . you know, my side of things. He taught me how to steal. How to break in to places. How to take things without being caught. And you know, all that would have been fine if it had been a case of him teaching the younger generation the family trade, so to speak. But that wasn't why he did it. He discovered that someone cute and disarming could be a great thief—and then he could have more things to sell for the drugs he wanted. It was all for him."

Abruptly, she looked at the egg section. "We're almost out of these. *Vovó* prefers the brown ones."

Marisol went over, picked out two cartons, and flipped open the lids to check for broken shells. As she did, she continued, "I actually got good at robbery because I wanted him to be proud of me. Pretty sick, huh? Become a better immoral deviant so Daddy will love me. I think that's why I fell in with Ricardo Benloise. He was older, powerful, and very disapproving. He was someone for me to try to please again."

As a vicious claw of jealousy went through Assail, he had to remind his bonded male that he had, in fact, murdered the man.

Funny how that could cheer a guy up.

"Ricardo was so like my father . . . except he was polished, not crude. And he was hella smart. It was a strange dynamic to be sure. They say that people find do-overs in their lives, folks who are like those who hurt us, so we can go through and do the relationship again. Get it right, or something. I don't know what I'm talking about."

On some level, the idea they were having this intimate conversation in the dairy and egg section, across the aisle from the ice-cream freezers, was utterly bizarre. But he certainly wasn't going to stop her from talking.

"What of your mother?" he asked.

Marisol shrugged and seemed to lose track of her shell-checking duty. But then she continued, both with the inspection and the talking. "She died when I was young. Thank God my grandmother stepped in when I was little and never left." She leaned over the lip of the cart and placed the eggs down with care. "That's why I will always take care of her. Plus, God, she's had a horrible life. She is a true survivor."

"So are you."

That smile, that one he loved so much, came back. "I guess I am."

Assail stepped in and embraced her against his chest. As he looked over the top of her head, he subconsciously tracked the movements of the human male and the human female down at the far end of the aisle by the precut-and-shredded-cheese displays. Both were in blue jeans and dark parkas and seemed to be arguing the merits of orange versus white cheddar strips.

As it occurred to him that that was a rather inane topic to pour so much energy into, that rippling sense of unease returned unto him.

"I think we're done shopping," he said as he eased back. "Shall we?"

"Let's blow this Popsicle stand."

"I beg your pardon?"

She laughed. "Just a saying."

To pay for their purchases, they went through self-checkout, and they split the duties, her picking things out of the cart, and him sweeping the foodstuffs across the red laser crosshairs of the reader. Every time a bar code was successfully recorded, the machine let out a *beep!* and a disembodied female voice announced the price and told him to place it in the bag.

Every. Single. Time.

By the end, he was seriously considering taking out his gun and killing the machine.

When they reemerged into the parking lot, his unsettled feeling returned. And as he helped transfer the groceries into the back of the SUV, he pictured an endless succession of nights such as this, to'ing and fro'ing from the supermarket.

There was no challenge here, nothing to conquer or surmount. No tally growing to justify his worth.

Just root vegetables, cream in a little box, eggs in two cartons.

Assail found himself wanting to return to the jubilant glow he'd felt as he had traveled home from the clinic, leaving the psychosis, the medical staff, the patient he had been behind. The world had seemed full of possibilities then. Now, he was left wondering where all that had gone.

Except nothing about the world had changed, really. And as he and Marisol traveled the stretch of bridge again, he tried to manufacture the optimism and failed.

"What about your family?" Marisol asked. "Are they still alive?"

"My *mahmen* and my father both died of old age."

"I am sorry to hear that."

"It is what it is. It does not bother me anymore as it was some time ago."

Which was the truth.

What did bother him was the fact that he had found the person he wanted to be with . . . but he did not know where his place in the world was anymore.

For a male who had always been self-directed, this was not a comfortable situation to be in.

"Dr. Manello is coming tonight, isn't he?" Marisol asked.

Assail looked away from the drop down to the icy cold waters of the Hudson. "I had forgotten. But yes."

And he was bringing Ghisele again.

God, that was another thing he didn't want to think about. Feeding reminded him of all that he was keeping to himself. Plus he hated the idea of being close to any female other than Marisol in any manner.

Biology trumped everything, though. Or maybe it was more like trampled.

It was rather like destiny, in that regard.

FORTY

After leaving the Great Camp in response to that text, Vishous re-formed downtown about two blocks away from a techno club that was pumping music so loud, you could hear the shit all the way down the street. Z was already on scene, and so were John Matthew and Qhuinn.

There was nothing to fight, however: No *lessers* were anywhere in sight. None of those shadow things, either.

No, this was about the aftermath.

His two brothers and John Matthew were kneeling around a figure on the ground, and as V came in for the close-up, he cursed. It was a male civilian dressed in good clothes that were getting ruined in the salted slush.

Death was coming, V thought as he got down on his haunches. And fast. The male's skin was chalky, his lips curled back from pain, his arms and legs flopping as if he were searching for positional relief that refused to come.

"What the fuck happened," V muttered as he leaned over and picked up a gun that was in the snow.

Checking the clip of the autoloader, he found three bullets left.

"Shot at it," the male was mumbling. "Shot . . . at it . . . but the bullets did nothing . . . they did nothing to it . . ."

Fucking lessers, V thought.

"Hold on," Qhuinn muttered as he took the male's hand. "Stay with us. We got help coming."

A scatter of talk came around the corner, and V stood up. Four humans—three men and a woman—stopped short.

"Oh, hell, he take that shit Johnny did?" one of them said.

"Yo, you need an ambulance? They can't arrest you if you're getting help for an OD—"

Vishous approached the group and didn't waste time or oxygen on them. He reached into their minds onetwothreefour and shut them all down. Wiping their memories clean, so that they would not recall seeing anything at all, he sent them on their drunken way by ringing hunger bells in their brains.

They were going to go on a mad search for Dunkin' Donuts. And would recall nothing else.

Where the fuck was the medical help? V thought as he refocused on the downed male.

Right on cue, the mobile surgical van arrived on scene, and his Jane was behind the wheel. With quick efficiency, she assessed the civilian, and then V helped her get the poor kid up on a stretcher and into the treatment space.

"I'll drive," Qhuinn said as he went forward into the cockpit and got behind the wheel. "John Matthew and Z are going to search the area."

"Let me assist you," V said to Jane.

"Can you have his chest cleared for me so I can monitor his heart?"

"Roger that."

As Jane turned away to get equipment out of locked cupboards, Qhuinn hit the gas and V worked to strip off the kind of clothes that Butch would have worn: everything was expensive and handmade. Too bad he had to treat the stuff like it was disposable. When he was down to the silk shirt, he didn't bother with the buttons, but jerked the two halves apart and—

"Oh . . . fuck," he muttered.

Jane wheeled around. "Do we have an open injury—*shit*."

Shit was right. The male's well-developed chest was lashed with welts, the skin swollen up in strips.

Just as V's had been when he'd two-stepped with that shadow.

V put his face into the civilian's. "What was it? What did it look like?"

The male struggled to focus. "Shot at it—"

"I know." V took one of those flailing hands in his own and squeezed, like maybe that would help the kid to focus. "Tell me what it was."

"A sh-sh-shadow . . . I could see through . . . it. Came out of no-where . . . the bullets did nothing . . . the bullets . . ."

Mother*fucker*. "Was there anyone else around? Did you see anybody else?"

"No. No . . . no . . . noooooooo—"

"He's arresting!" Jane said.

V spun around and grabbed for the portable defibrillator, unlatching the little table it was on and yanking the machine forward.

As the surgical unit lumbered on, bumping over the icy road, Jane leaned in and started chest compressions. She went hands-off long enough for Vishous to slap the electrodes on, and then they both stepped back.

"Clear," she said.

Vishous hit the button and sent the electricity in, the civilian's chest jerking up off the table, his arms flopping.

Jane went in and tested at the jugular. "Nothing. Again."

He is not coming back, V thought.

They did two more rounds after that. And when there was still no pulse, Jane continued chest compressions and ordered V to get the standard protocol of drugs. But even after they pumped that kid full of adrenaline and other things . . . there was still nothing.

Some ten minutes and God only knew how many miles of road later, Jane stood back and shook her head.

"We lost him." She cursed. "He's gone."

V looked toward the front of the van. "Yo, Q, take us to Havers's. We've got a body, not a patient, back here."

Throe watched it all happen from the rooftop of the club. He had taken care with himself this time, for he did not know what to expect and his previous arrogance—which had been grounded in what he'd assumed was the invincibility of his creation—had been replaced with a far more appropriate caution.

No more street clothes. He was dressed in all black, with a knit mask pulled down over his face so that nothing of him showed or could reflect light. He was also heavily armed, with sets of guns and rounds of ammunition strapped to his body. Finally, he had been sure to keep himself downwind of where the attack would take place—and he was not alone. This evening, he had brought with him two shadows, one to send down to street level, and a second to wait with him and be a protective backup if necessary.

Throe had a feeling that the Brothers were going to come quickly unto the scene, and assuming they did, it was critical that they not identify him in any fashion. He was not prepared to come forward. Yet.

And then there was too much waiting for his taste. The attack took far longer to transpire than he had anticipated, as the intended target was late, which was irritating.

But then all went according to plan. The male who had been summoned to meet finally arrived, and Throe sent down one of the shadows and observed keenly what transpired. This was a test on so many levels, including of his entities' ability to fight without conventional weapons. When he had ordered them to kill Naasha's ancient *hellren*, he had provided them with a knife. And he had done the same when he had sent them after those Brothers the other evening. But having witnessed that fight and seen what his creations were capable of with their bodies, he realized that weaponizing them may be a waste.

And he was right. His shadows were lightning fast with their forms, snapping out tendrils that caused pain without shredding clothes or seeming to break skin. Verily, that aristocrat proved no match for the ferocity of the attack, falling back from his feet, landing upon the ground—and as he fumbled to get out a gun, Throe nearly interceded.

But instead of the bullets stopping the shadow, they passed through the form and ricocheted off the buildings behind the entity.

Throe had waited for some kind of pain to register as it had done before. Except there had been nothing; the attack didn't even slow— and there had been the temptation to let the final course of the meal be served. Throe needed, however, for there to be a reporting of the incident. Thus, he had called off his dog, so to speak, the shadow returning to a heel, a balloon once again tethered unto him.

Down below, on the street, in the snow, there had been much gasping and rolling about, and then the male had done as was predicted. With a sloppy hand, he had gotten out a cell phone and texted something.

And like the saviors they preferred to think of themselves as, the Brothers had come unto the fallen, confirming what Throe had suspected: Yes, there was an emergency system in place, a method by which endangered citizens could ask for and receive aid from within the species. This was important information to have, and it was going to be managed with strategy.

As the heroic arrivals had clustered around the injured male, Throe had been sorely tempted to stay and continue to play witness.

But the risk was too great, especially as yet another Brother arrived.

With an unspoken order, Throe had called his shadows into travel, and return to home they had gone, arriving the now in the snowy yard behind the grand house.

Throe paused and considered his options in the cold. There was the prospect of doing another attack this evening, but no. He wanted to see how the natural course of this first one played out. How long it took for the story to percolate and be expressed on social media. How others in the race, especially other aristocrats, responded. What Wrath, the great Blind King, did.

When one was sowing the seeds of social dissension, one had to proceed with care, lest the bonfire thus started got out of bounds and spread in directions that did not support the larger goal.

Originally, he had assumed he needed an army of shadows to attack the Brotherhood and kill the King. But upon further reflection, he decided he did not need such a largesse. Instead, he could use what he had to create social unrest—and that was a far better avenue for him to realize his ambitions. If enough attacks like this occurred, in a short enough period of time, it would not take long before Wrath and the Brotherhood would be perceived as weak: Unable to protect their citizens, they would suffer a rightful fall from grace—and the race would be looking for a hero.

And vacuums needed to be filled, didn't they.

It was one of the laws of physics.

"Come," he ordered his balloons. "Let us get out of the cold. The dominoes have just started to fall, and it will be a while as of yet."

Naturally, his shadows did exactly what he told them to.

FORTY-ONE

Not long after Sola helped bring the groceries in, and Assail and his cousins started to cook, Dr. Manello came to check on the patient—which was fine, great, whatever, Sola thought.

It was just . . . well, that that other nurse in the long robes was with him. And hey, the woman was perfectly professional and solicitous, but Sola had to cop to feeling a spike of *that's-my-man*. Which was frickin' ridiculous.

In lieu of giving herself a time-out, she went downstairs and wasted ten minutes tidying her already neat guest room. And then she flipped through some TV. And then . . .

Unable to settle for some reason, she decided a shower was in order, and she was naked, and under the hot spray, when Assail came and found her: One moment she was alone and doing a quick wash of things . . . the next, a dark shape was just outside the shower stall.

Jerking the door open, she leaned out into the cold. "What did Dr. Manello say? Everything still okay?"

Assail didn't respond verbally. Instead, he took off his clothes, letting them fall to the damp tile floor.

His sex was totally erect, sticking out straight out from his hips.

"I need you," he said with a growl.

As she stepped back to make room for him, she was aware of a heady scent, some kind of delicious cologne that he had been wearing lately. Damn, the stuff went into her nose and through her body—

His hands were rough as he pulled her against him, and his mouth was the same, grinding, taking, demanding. And as she kissed him back, she was aware of a strange taste, as if he had been drinking wine? It was not unpleasant at all, it was just . . . a type of Cabernet she had never had before.

When he put one of her hands on his arousal, she started stroking him—and he climaxed immediately, coming on her belly, the ejaculations hot and powerful. In the back of her mind, she had a split second of disappointment that he had finished so soon, the session ending before it got started for her.

She couldn't have been more wrong.

Before she knew what was happening, he was lifting her up and she was grabbing on to the top of the stall's glass panels. Suspending herself at his hip height, he entered her core with a hard shove, the penetration slicing through her with an erotic sharpness. And as he began to move inside of her, an unusual tingling flowed throughout her body, as if her blood had turned to sparkles.

So hot. So heavy. So hard. And then his mouth was at her breasts, his dark head moving as wet suction locked on her nipples.

How great that his hair was already growing in, she thought in the back of her mind.

And then she didn't think about anything at all. Her orgasm was no ripple—it was a roar, a great fireball that incinerated her from the inside out, the sensations wiping everything out of her consciousness except the pleasure. Three thrusts later, and he came along with her, locking his hips into her pelvis, his sex filling her up.

But Assail didn't stop. He kept going, ravishing her, moving his mouth from her breasts to her neck, where he nipped and sucked at her. Gritting her teeth, she tried not to make any sound. This was not upstairs, where there was privacy. No, he had come to her down in the basement, as if he had been too impatient to wait.

At least his cousins and Markcus were upstairs cooking, her grandmother supervising them with frustration as the men tried to provide for her.

But that could change at any moment.

"I want more," Assail said in her ear. "I want . . . more from you."

Snaking a hand up the back of his neck, she pulled him closer. "Then take it. Take all of me—"

A lance of something so pleasurable it stung made her forget herself and she cried out as she lost her hold on the shower stall. With a squeak, her hand slipped down the glass, shifting her position, crashing them together, arms, legs, bodies tangling as slippery skin and awkward angles conspired to send her into a fall.

Assail scrambled to catch her as his arousal popped free, and then she was down on the floor by the drain.

She started to laugh. She couldn't help it.

"Okay, that was a traffic accident," she said as she looked up at him. "Good thing I—"

She stopped as she realized he wasn't laughing with her. And then his expression registered properly. Pain, dark and torturous, had drawn his face in tightly.

"What's wrong?" she asked.

That was when she noticed the faint red tinge to the water that was escaping through the drain. Shit. Her period.

"I'm not hurt," she chided. "It's a woman thing."

As he helped her to her feet, he seemed profoundly unsteady. "I am so sorry."

"What for? It happens once a month."

Assail just shook his head and gathered her close. "I am . . . so very sorry."

Sola rolled her eyes as she put her arms around him and gave him a squeeze. "I'm perfectly fine."

With gentle brushes, he nuzzled her neck, kissing her softly before hanging his head.

They stayed there for so long, the water began to lose its temperature, and even then, he didn't seem to want to leave.

"We have to get out," she told him. "They'll wonder what we're up to—and chances are, at least your cousins will get it right."

Making the decision for them, she cut the water off and stepped out. There were two towels hanging on the rod, and she took them both off, offering him one.

She could have sworn his hand shook as he accepted it.

"Did Dr. Manello have anything to say about your—"

"It all went fine," he replied roughly. "I'm fine."

Assail turned away to dry off and she watched his muscles shift under his smooth skin. Even though it had been just a few days, she could swear he was regaining some of his bulk already—but probably, as with her thinking that his hair was coming in, that was optimism over accuracy on her part.

"Assail, what's wrong?"

He stopped, his head dropping as if in defeat. "I am . . . I just am so sorry."

"I don't understand what for." She wrapped the towel around herself. "Everything is good. We're good. I'm good. You're good."

As she continued on in that vein, she wondered who she was trying to argue that to: him or her.

Exactly how the hell did he think this was all going to work, Assail wondered as he left the steamy bathroom and went back up to the first floor.

How did he think he was going to be with a human for the rest of their lives?

Opening the cellar door, he cleared his throat as all the eyes in the kitchen shifted to him.

"Marisol is coming directly. If you all will just excuse me? I'm afraid I slipped and fell in the bath—bathroom, I mean."

The lie sounded ridiculous to his own ears, and only Marisol's grandmother nodded as if that made perfect sense. Then again, she was incentivized to believe in the virtue of her granddaughter—and at least his cousins and Markcus stayed silent on the subject.

With his head in a tangle, Assail strode off for the stairs to his own room, and when he got to the second floor, he stripped everything off and went into his loo. Willing the lights on, he looked at himself in the mirror.

Under the illumination coming from the ceiling, he appeared downright evil, great shadows where his deep-set eyes sat within his skull, his body as yet unsated even by the intense session in Marisol's shower, the Chosen's vein he had just taken powering him up.

The loginess that came with feeding had yet to kick in and he prayed it would soon.

He was dangerous like this, a bonded male so close to his female and yet unable to have her fully.

And by that, he meant more than just her sex.

Putting his head into his hands, he ran his tongue over the sharp points of his descended fangs.

He hadn't meant to bite Marisol. Or rather . . . when he had told her he needed more and she had answered for him to have all of her, there had been no proper context for her consent. He had taken her vein with love, he had had her in the way he so desperately wanted, but in doing so he had . . .

Violated her.

Marisol had had no idea what he'd been asking for. And thus he had done the unforgivable.

After she had slipped and the contact at her throat had been broken, he had immediately realized what he'd done in his feeding-crazed state. Licking the wound closed in a clandestine manner, he had been too horrified with himself to tell her everything—and now, he was up here with a pit in his stomach and a pain in his heart.

Why in hell had he thought they could go on without her knowing? Fates . . . why had he assumed all would be well? For one, he was going to live centuries longer than her. How could he explain his not aging as she grew older? Indeed, he was going to look as though he were in his late twenties until about a decade before he died—and the same would be true of his cousins.

And then there was the feeding issue. He would have to take the vein of a female vampire on a regular basis—and now that he was healthy, he was liable to react like this.

He wanted Marisol, not anyone else. So he was bound to come at her as he had tonight, starved, demanding . . . and taking her vein.

Oh, and as for daylight? It was fine for him to play that bullshit night owl card up to a point. But how about when the seasons changed and there were over fourteen hours of daylight? Sixteen? What was he going to do when, on some nice summer afternoon, his female wanted to go for a picnic? How was he going to handle that?

Other than bursting into flames in front of her, that was.

"Assail?"

Closing his eyes, his entire body stooped at the sound of her voice. "Marisol . . . my love."

"I think you need to tell me what's going on here."

After the longest time, when he could see no other way about things, he said in a hoarse voice, "I agree. Unfortunately."

FORTY-TWO

As the mobile surgical unit rumbled through the streets of downtown, heading for the bridge to Caldwell's other side, Jane went into one of the overhead compartments and took out a clean sheet. Flipping the soft white fabric free of its folds, she laid it across the body and then pulled things up so that the civilian's face and head were covered. Then she took a seat next to Vishous.

When he reached over and clasped her hand, she looked at him. "I didn't know how to bring him back."

"His heart couldn't take it. There was nothing else you could have done."

"I know."

"Come here."

V pulled her into him and she leaned on his strength, his big body catching her. In her head, she reviewed everything in sequence, from her arriving and making the assessment to the transfer onto the table . . . to the chest compression . . . the defibrillator . . . the drug protocol.

"Did he have any identification on him?" she asked.

"Q?" V called out. "Did you find ID?"

"Yeah, I got it," Qhuinn said from behind the wheel. "No one I recognized so I texted it to Saxton."

Jane spoke up. "I want to talk to the family. When they're found, I want to be the one who's there for them."

"You got it," V said.

Qhuinn glanced over his shoulder. "ETA at Havers's is about twenty minutes."

"I texted them we were on the way," Jane muttered. "But should we call, too?"

V shook his head. "Let's just take a breather. They know we're coming."

"All right." She exhaled her sadness. "God, that's someone's son. Maybe mate. I just . . . I really hate to lose a patient."

"That's why you're such an amazing doctor."

As she stared at the body, she started to frame what she was going to tell the next of kin, trying out a couple of different approaches. Typically, family members needed to know two things: namely, that everything possible had been done, and that the suffering had been kept to a minimum—

V's fingertip under her chin brought her eyes to his.

"You know how tight I am with Butch, right?" he said. "How that cop is like . . ."

"You are brothers, the two of you." She smiled a little. "You couldn't be closer."

"When we were in that alley the other night, and Butch was injured"—V cleared his throat—"and I couldn't get to him? I was terrified that he was dying. And then you were there—and as I watched you take off to go treat him, I thought . . ."

There was a long pause, those diamond eyes searching her face. "I thought there was no one else in the world, and that included myself, who I would rather have taking care of him. I trust you that much. I believe in you *that* much."

Jane found herself blinking away tears. "You have the best ways of saying I love you."

"Nah." He stroked her face with his gloved hand. "I speak sixteen languages, true. And even with all those words, sometimes I don't know how to put what's in here"—he touched the center of his chest—"out to you right."

"I think you do just fine—"

Out of the corner of her eye, something moved and she glanced over to the treatment table.

Probably just a shift from the surgical unit hitting a bump.

She refocused on V. "When we arrive at Havers's, we need to go with the body to the morgue. I think it's important to just—I don't know, I want to see him there safely." On that note, she leaned around her mate. "Hey, Qhuinn? Has Saxton gotten back to you—"

The sound that percolated through the RV was like that of a pneumonia patient gasping for oxygen, the rattling a combination of loose fluid in the lungs and bronchial tubes that were clogged.

And then the dead body sat up with the sheet over its face.

"He's alive!" she barked as she jumped forward and went to pull the cloth away. "You're awake—"

Everything went into slow motion: her hand reaching out to the sheet and pulling it back, the cover dropping, the face . . . the gruesome, distorted face exposed.

And swiveling toward her like that of an owl, the neck vertebrae snapping one by one.

Jane screamed.

As the dead patient sat up and looked over at his mate, Vishous's brain, great and powerful though it was, took a second or two to catch the fuck up with reality:

1. That thing wasn't alive. Whatever it was, it was still dead.
2. This wasn't no *Weekend at Bernie's,* chillin'-with-the-stiff comedy sketch. What might have once been a stand-up

guy now had pupil-less white eyes and fangs that were
dropping down like it was ready to attack.

Annnnd 3. There were oxygen tanks in here and the engine
ran on diesel. So V couldn't use a gun, not unless he
wanted to run the risk of blowing them all sky high.

"Qhuinn! Stop!" V shouted.

But the brother was already stomping on the brakes because of
Jane's scream, everything jerking forward from momentum—and that
included the dead male.

As the corpse's torso slammed back down to the exam table, Vishous
put himself in front of Jane, shoving her away.

"Get out of here," V hissed. "I don't want to worry about you."

"You don't have to, remember?"

The patient had been tied down at the waist and the ankles for
transport, the chest band having been left free so they could work on
him. And this was a bene. That dead sonofabitch made like he was
going to come at V—only to find that he was stuck.

An unholy screech came out of that throat, and then the thing was
tearing at the binds that kept it in place.

Just as Qhuinn jumped into the back with his guns drawn.

"No bullets!" V yelled. "No fucking bullets! Oxygen!"

Before Vishous could marshal an attack, those heavy, nylon straps
got torn off and that corpse came at him like something out of *Evil
Dead,* head shaking back and forth a million times a second, the body
moving all wrong as if its joints were frozen.

As V got pile-driven toward the back doors, he wrenched around
and caught the latch, releasing the lever so that he and the patient fell
out of the surgical unit onto the snow together.

The thing landed on top of him, and talk about strong. The kid had
been built okay when he'd been alive, but whatever this shit was had
given him superhero powers: V couldn't hold off the attack long enough
to get his daggers out—or a gun, now that they were free of the van.

That snarling face was way too close for comfort, those jaws snapping, the teeth clapping together like in its head it was already tasting V's brains after it made an egg cup of his skull. And goddamn, a foul stench came out of its mouth, as if it were already rotting from the inside out, the digestive tract spoiling, the organs liquefying, the bones the only thing that stayed.

Enter Qhuinn the Magnificent.

All at once, V got a reprieve, and for a split second, he had no fucking clue why. But then he saw Qhuinn's arms around the chest, the brother's face grimacing as he hauled back with all of his strength.

The dead guy went crazy, letting out another of those howls, and he thrashed that head around, trying to bite at Qhuinn's face.

V instantly knew that was a bad idea. "Don't let him get you with his teeth!"

Qhuinn shifted his grip, slapping one of his palms on the patient's forehead and pulling back to expose the throat.

Fucking perfect.

Except as V went to unholster both his daggers, something entered his head and would not leave.

He bit off his lead-lined glove, unleashing his curse.

"Release!" he ordered Qhuinn.

When the brother didn't comply, V nearly slapped the guy. "Fucking let him go!"

Qhuinn caught the gist, and still hesitated, but then the thing nearly got him as it jerked its head and teeth forward to bite.

"On three!" Qhuinn hollered over the snarling and the screeching. "One, two—three!"

The brother went hands-free, jumping out of range.

And Vishous hit the chest of the patient with a nuclear defibrillator, his glowing palm going right on the sternum—

The shrill noise was so loud, V went deaf—and talk about your shakedowns. The body of the patient slapped, flapped, kicked, bucked—and took Vishous along for the ride; the energy exchange forming a lock between the body and V's palm.

Just when he thought his arm was going to be ripped out of its socket, there was a pop, like a balloon, and the patient was no more, a soft rain of particles falling on V. But that wasn't what he focused on. An entity seemed to escape into the night—and it was a shadow.

Or a part of one of those entities.

Something had transferred to the civilian during the earlier attack. And either it killed the kid, or was harbored within him to be released when the second "death" came.

In the silence that followed, there was nothing but his and Qhuinn's harsh breathing in the cold air.

"What the fuck was that?" Qhuinn asked.

As Jane appeared beside them, Vishous stripped off his leather jacket, his movements jerky and uncoordinated. The second his left sleeve was down, he wrenched his arm around, and his heart started to beat hard.

Looking at his skin, he measured the angry red stripe that the shadow he'd fought before had left in his flesh.

Had the wound faded? It seemed like it had faded. Did that mean he was safe?

Or had some of that gotten into him?

Jane knew exactly what was going through his mind, even if Qhuinn didn't. She leaned down and discreetly inspected things.

"It's definitely improved," she whispered. "I can tell. I remember exactly what it looked like."

A cell phone went off. Ringer, not a text.

With his brain jammed up, Vishous looked around in confusion—but then Qhuinn took out his own phone and answered it.

"Hey, Sax. You did—okay. His brother's with Havers at the clinic? Right, well, we're on the far side of the bridge." The brother's mismatched blue and green eyes swung around and locked on V's. "But we've had a little . . . there's been . . . let's call it a complication."

FORTY-THREE

"Did you use again?"

As Marisol asked the question, Assail's brain couldn't understand what she was asking, and as if she recognized this, she came a little farther into the bathroom and lowered her voice.

"Is that what you need to tell me?"

If only that was it, he thought.

I am not what you think I am. I am other from you. I look as though I am a human, and you have loved me as though I am, but I—

"Oy! Assail! Marisol!"

The urgent voice shouting up the stairs was not the kind of thing you ignored: It was Ehric, and there was fear behind that tone.

Instantly, Assail reached into the nearest cupboard and took out a loaded gun. "What?"

"Mrs. Carvalho! She fainted!"

Marisol bolted for the stairs, and Assail did likewise—until he was halfway down and realized he was naked. Doubling back, he took a robe and pulled it on—and out of habit, he kept his gun in his palm.

When he got down to the kitchen, the first thing he saw by the table were the plastic soles of Mrs. Carvalho's house slippers. The bottoms had a pattern of daisies to give grip, and they were scuffed and a little dirty.

She would not like for them to be showing, he thought stupidly, as he came around and got on his knees.

Marisol was already down beside her grandmother and speaking urgently to the woman. *"Vovó?"*

She switched in and out of Spanish, her words tripping and falling over each other, a terrified stampede escaping and trampling those who were weak in the pack.

"What happened?" Assail demanded.

Ehric shook his head. "We were cooking at the stove. She was sitting here. We heard her make a sound, and then she fell from the chair."

"Call Dr. Manello—"

Ehric ripped out his phone and backed away, and Assail touched Marisol on the shoulder. When she looked at him, he said softly, "We shall have the doctor come. Right away."

Marisol blinked back tears. "We can't take her to the hospital. Not a normal hospital. We can't . . . she's not here legally. I can't run the risk of her getting deported."

"Do not worry. I will take care of everything."

As Marisol refocused on her grandmother, Ehric approached and spoke into Assail's ear. "Dr. Manello is sending the nurse immediately. He is going to have to drive to the house as Doc Jane is evidently tied up—"

The knock on the back door was sharp, and a female voice called out, "It's Ehlena."

Evale and Markcus both lunged forward to let her in, and the nurse didn't waste time. She came around the far side of the table and put a duffel bag down.

"Hi, Marisol," she said. "What is your grandmother's name?"

"Mrs. Carvalho." Marisol patted the hand she was holding so tightly. "Right, *Vovó*, that is your name."

"Does she have any medical conditions I need to know about?" the nurse asked as she took out a blood-pressure cuff and a stethoscope.

"No, none," Marisol replied.

"Is she on any medication?" When Marisol shook her head, the nurse said, "Has she been sick lately?"

"No. She's very healthy . . ."

Assail stepped back and stood with his cousins and Markcus. The nurse worked efficiently, but she didn't give a lot away. Her face remained composed as she continued to ask questions, and Marisol had to sit back to give her room to work.

"You're saying she was recently in a car for a long time?" Ehlena said. "Does she have a history of blood clots . . . ?"

Sola was trying to stay present, and respond appropriately to the medical questions, and support her grandmother—but she kept slipping back to the past . . . to finding her mother drunk on various floors.

Some had been carpeted. Others had had tile. One had wood.

No, two had had wood.

She remembered them in a series of snapshots, and they came with smells, too—all of which were bad. Alcoholics did not generally smell good, whether it was vomit, body odor, or breath that reflected not only the last quart of tequila consumed, but also their body's decomposition and malfunctioning.

Her grandmother had never once been drunk. Had never not showed up when she'd said she would be somewhere. Had never raised a hand in anger or cursed a young girl for her mere existence. She had never tried to commit suicide only to have Sola knock pills from her hand. Had never disappeared for days at a time, leaving no money behind for food. Had never even overslept.

So seeing her grandmother down like this was stringing Sola between the two extremes she had grown up with, and it was hard not to
break down and pray through her tears.

On that note, she looked over the table at Evale—because his were
the first eyes she happened to meet. "Go to her bedroom. Her rosary is
on her Bible. Will you bring it up here?"

"What is a rosary?" the guy asked even as he started for the cellar
door.

"A necklace of beads with a cross. You'll see it there."

She refocused on her grandmother. The nurse was flashing a pen-
light into first the right then the left eye.

"What do you think is going on?" Sola asked. "Can you tell me
anything?"

"Dr. Manello is on his way. I'm just triaging at this point—her pulse
is weak, her pressure is low, and I think we're going to want to do some
blood work. He's better with humans than I am."

Sola shook her head at that last one. "So you don't know what's
caused this?"

"We need more information." Ehlena smiled at her patient. "But
you're awake, and that's a really good sign. Does anything hurt, Mrs.
Carvalho? Do you have a headache? Any pains in your calves?"

The shake of the head for "no" was slow in coming, but it was
firm.

"Can you squeeze my fingers?" the nurse said as she put two against
one palm. "You can? Good. How about on this side? Good. How many
fingers am I holding up. Three? Perfect. You're passing all my tests, Mrs.
Carvalho."

"Here is the rotisserie."

As Evale held out the chain with its well-worn beads, Sola didn't
bother to correct him. "Thank you. Thank you so much—"

An alarm sounded, shrill and painful to the ear, and everybody
jumped.

"The stove—damn it!" Assail ran across and turned off something that had started to burn on the cooktop. "Ehric—open the door. We have to get the heat and smoke out."

From the corner of her eye, Sola watched the men get dishtowels and wave them under the alarm, and the silence, when it came, was a relief, but not an improvement on the real situation.

That was only happening if her grandmother sat up, got herself to her feet, and started yelling at people for leaving those potatoes on way too long.

Ehlena got to her feet. "I'm just going to call Dr. Manello—he's coming as fast as he can. Will you excuse me?"

Sola nodded at the nurse, who went over in the corner, put a cell phone to her ear, and spoke quietly.

Leaning down to her grandmother, Sola put the rosary in her *vovó's* hand and spoke in Spanish. "*Do not leave me.*"

"*You marry that man,*" her *vovó* said in a weak voice. "*You marry him.*"

"*Okay, Vovó. I will.*"

"*Promise me?*"

"*You're not dying.*"

"*That is God's will, not mine. I am happy to go home to Him now that I know you have someone to love you.*"

Sola swiped her eyes. "*You're not going anywhere, Grandmother.*"

"*You are safe with him. He stares at you . . . like you are his whole world. This makes me happy—I can die now happy.*"

"*Stop talking like that. Right now.*"

"*Child . . .*" Her grandmother seemed to struggle to focus. But then she reached up and touched Sola's face. "*I am old. It is my time—I can't live forever. But now . . . I don't have to worry. He will take care of you. I am . . . at peace as long as you swear to me now . . . you will marry him.*"

Sola had to wipe her eyes again. This wasn't happening, she told herself. This couldn't possibly be happening. She did not bring her grandmother all this way back north just to have her die.

Oh, God, I've killed her, she thought.

"Marisol, swear to me." The voice was weak; the demand was not. *"Or I cannot be at peace."*

"I swear to you . . . I will marry him."

FORTY-FOUR

The hardest part of any doctor's job was talking to the families of patients who had died. To look a grieving spouse, child, father, mother, brother, sister, in the eye and have to tell them that, in spite of everything you had learned and all that was at your disposal, you had not been able to keep their loved one alive . . . was a nightmare.

But what the hell did you say about something like this? Jane thought as she stared at the mobile surgical unit's empty exam table.

As the RV slowed and made a fat turn, she sat back down beside Vishous and tried to put the series of events into perspective. Into a rational framework. Into something that could be explained without the use of the word "zombie."

God in heaven above, she thought. Not for the first time.

They didn't even have a body anymore.

"Almost there," Qhuinn said from up front.

Leaning around V, Jane looked down the surgical unit's interior and through the front windshield. She couldn't see much but evergreens and skeleton trees all covered in snow—no, wait, there was the farm-house.

Havers's underground medical facility was located on the far side of the Hudson, deep in a forest, and it was accessible through various entry points, all separated by plenty of distance. The one they were going to use was the faker homestead with the barn out back, the one that appeared to be where peaceable humans resided, the ruse to hide the rest.

This was where deliveries came in, and also, when sadly applicable, bodies.

After Qhuinn turned them around in the drive and parked them butt-in to the barn, Jane got out of the RV and took a series of deep breaths. She still had no idea what she was going to say to the civilian's next of kin. Cause of death: cardiac failure due to traumatic injury. Cause of reanimation: no clue. Secondary cause of death: incineration by my mate's hand.

"Come on," V said as he put an arm around her shoulders.

She hadn't been aware of just standing there in the cold, but Qhuinn had already opened the side door of the barn and was waiting. Getting with the program, she was all in her head as they checked in with the security monitor, were granted access to the elevator, and descended down to the clinic. As they got off, it was into a warm, well-lit, utterly undecorated corridor that looked exactly like all the ones in human hospitals.

"Damn it, I always forget which way to go," she muttered.

Yup, just like St. Francis. Lost and there was no signage.

"This way," V said.

After a bunch of turns that she didn't track, they came around a corner and found what looked like almost all of the Brotherhood standing in a clutch. Havers, the race's physician and Marissa's estranged brother, was by them, all college-professor-like with his tortoiseshell glasses and his bow tie.

Everyone got good and quiet as Jane and her two escorts approached, and she hung back as V and Qhuinn answered a lot of very difficult questions. And answered some more. And . . .

"Excuse me," she cut in. "But where is the next of kin? I want to go see him now."

Havers cleared his throat. "What are you going to tell him?"

"What I know to be true."

"Are you certain that is wise?"

Jane frowned—and before she knew what she was doing, she stepped in tight to the healer. Even though he was taller than she was, she glared right up into those glasses.

"I'm not going to lie to him, if that's what you're suggesting," she snapped. "He has a right to know everything we do, and if I can't explain something, I'm going to let him know that."

"There could be larger consequences," Havers hedged. "This could be a threat to the species at large, and one wouldn't want to cause a panic."

As the healer looked around, seeking backup from the Brothers, she was done. "Not my problem. I'm a physician first, the rest of you can worry about politics. Now where is my dead patient's brother."

The fact that everyone just stared at Vishous pissed her off. Like she was a problem to be managed by him?

"She's one hundred percent correct," Vishous said. "She should tell him what she knows and what she doesn't. It's up to us to put it in context. But there will be no lying or subterfuge—and I'm going to make sure no one interferes with what she has to say. Anyone have a problem with that."

That last one was not phrased like a question and he was pegging Havers with hard eyes as he laid it out there.

The healer looked to the floor and nodded. "But of course. Right this way."

Havers led them down the hall even farther and then into a waiting area that was half full with lots of chairs. As they passed through, Jane noted the patients and families who were milling around, or sitting watching the TV, or standing in line at the reception desk. Many of

them waved to the healer, smiled at him, greeted him with respect—
and he was gracious in return.

It was a reminder of Havers's complicated nature. He was good to
the people who came to him for help, he truly was. It was just outside
of that sphere that made you want to smack him sometimes.

Now there was signage, the overhead plaques with arrows directing
people this way and that to things like RADIOLOGY, OUTPATIENT SUR-
GERY, OBSTETRICS, WELLNESS CARE. Eventually, Havers took them
down a short hall that had four closed doors, two on each side. Beside
them, discreet labels read FAMILY COUNSELING.

"He is in here," Havers announced as he went to knock on one of
the panels. "He is Aarone, son of Stanalas."

V caught the healer's arm. "She goes in alone. You and I are waiting
out here."

"Actually, Vishous, why don't you and I go in together?" Jane pivoted toward him. "You were there. You might offer some insight I cannot."

"You got it."

Jane was the one who knocked, and when there was a quiet "Come
in," she opened things up. A very well-dressed young male with blond
hair and pale eyes was sitting in one of six chairs. He was obviously
nervous, his palms stroking up and down his thighs, his shoulders
braced.

"Hello, Aarone," Jane said as she entered. "I'm Dr. Jane Whitcomb,
and this is my mate, Vishous, who has medical training. I'm here to
speak with you about your brother—"

"Half-brother." The male looked at Vishous. Looked back. "He's my
half-brother, but we're very close. What's going on? I got this phone call
and I came here, but no one's telling me—is Whinnig okay?"

The words came out in a rush, his anxiety clearly overcoming
him.

"May I have your permission to speak with Vishous present?" When the male nodded, she approached him. "Is it all right for me to sit down next to you?"

"Yes, of course." Aarone got to his feet and offered his palm for a shake. "Forgive my manners."

Jane took a seat and waited until he'd resettled and those pale eyes came back to her. And then she spoke. "I'm so sorry, your brother has gone unto the Fade."

She used the traditional vampire way of communicating death, out of respect, and the reaction was immediate. The male began to tremble, his eyes glassing over with tears.

"What—how? He was perfectly healthy. I just had First Meal with him a couple of hours ago. How did this happen?"

Jane handled the sad business like a total professional, and as Vishous stood with his back against the door—in case Havers got any bright ideas—he could only respect his mate even more. She told the male what happened event by event, with a calm, firm voice. And as for the parts that couldn't be explained, she owned up to them and fielded the questions as best she could.

And then the male looked across at V. "You don't know what it was that attacked him? I don't understand?"

Vishous cleared his throat. "The only conclusion we can draw at this time is that the Omega is changing its strategy and sending something new out into the field." Even though those entities had not read as part of the evil one, what else could be behind them? "We will get to the bottom of this, though—I promise you."

The young male burst up and paced around in the tight quarters. "And meanwhile, I have no body to bury. Just a nightmare story and a whole lot of I-don't-knows."

"I'm sorry," Vishous said remotely.

Jane handled the anger better than he did. "I realize this is very hard.

I lost a sibling myself, and frankly, I'm still not over it. I really wish we had more for you, I truly do."

The male stopped and faced her. "How do I know that Whinnig made it unto the Fade?"

"Was he a kind male? A just and kind male?"

Those tears, the ones that had come before the anger, reemerged. "Whinnig was the best. He was my closest friend. We went everywhere together. We have always been inseparable—especially after all of our parents were . . . they didn't make it through the raids."

V closed his eyes in commiseration. So much fucking loss. He fucking hated the Omega, he really did—

Vishous flipped his lids back open. "Tell me something, did your brother mention where he was going tonight?"

If they were inseparable, where had Aarone been?

"He was meeting someone. I don't know who, though." The male looked over. "He never had anything to do with the Lessening Society, if that's where you're going with this."

"Not at all. I was just wondering."

At least they had the cell phone that had been used to call for help. V was going to go through that as soon as he could. Look for numbers. Contacts. Although come on, like the Omega was going to reach out and touch people through a goddamn phone call?

"And it's such bad luck, what with that will," Aarone said.

"What will?" V asked.

The young male dragged a hand through his hair. "We had different *mahmen*, Whinnig and I. He was born first and his *mahmen* died on the birthing bed. We found out, like a week ago, that his uncle on that side of his family had recently died and left him this huge estate? My brother and I are . . . we are well off, it is true. But he invited me to go to celebrate this windfall with him. We were going to travel, get out of Caldwell during this winter weather . . . but that is not going to happen anymore."

V measured the male again. The clothes were fine, that cashmere coat and those fancy loafers the kind of thing that required cash and taste to afford. And the accent was straight-up *glymera,* all the way.

"Who was the uncle?" V said.

The name given didn't ring any bells. But then the aristocracy's shit was not something he had ever much bothered with.

Jane spoke up. "I'd like to suggest you speak with a counselor, Aarone. The clinic here has a number of them on staff. They can really help with grief."

"I don't want to talk to anyone."

"Just keep it in mind. And if you have any questions, or you want to speak with me again, all you have to do is ask and I'll be here." There was an awkward pause. "Do you have someone who can pick you up? Help you get home?"

More with the hair dragging. "My girlfriend is at my house. It's our two-year anniversary. She's supposed to be getting something ready for us, and that's the only reason I didn't go out with Whinnig tonight. Bad timing, huh."

"How about we call her and ask her to come get you?" Jane offered.

"I'm fine."

Jane got to her feet and put her hand on the male's shoulder. "I think it would be best for you not to be alone right now. This is a bad shock made so much worse with everything we don't know."

After a moment, the male stared up at Jane. "Was it a brother or a sister? The one you lost?"

"It was my little sister, Hannah. She died when she was young, but I remember everything."

"And you're not over it."

Jane shook her head. "No. But that doesn't mean I'm not living my life, either. We take our dead with us through our lives, and that's the way it should be. And again, if you believe the good and the just go to the Fade, then your brother is there. Believe in that. How he died doesn't change who he was, do you understand? No matter what happened, it was *not* his fault and it will not change his afterlife."

There was another pause, and then the male got to his feet and threw his arms around Jane. As the pair of them stood together, V looked down at the floor out of respect.

And thought of his *mahmen* for no good reason.

FORTY-FIVE

s Sola stood outside her grandmother's patient room—
which was just two doors down from where Assail had been,
she decided she never, ever wanted to see the inside of this
facility again. Between her experience after the abduction, coming here
for Assail . . . and now this?

She was beyond done—and praying that the three-strikes-and-
you're-out rule applied.

"He's been in there for so long." She looked over at Assail, who was
beside her. "I mean, what are they doing to her?"

Dr. Manello had been amazing, getting them here in record time,
running more tests, checking everything. But it had been hell. Sola
hated limbos when they didn't matter. When it was something like this?
Having no firm footing was flat-out unbearable.

As she stared at the closed door, she tried to see through the panel.
When the whole X-ray vision thing didn't work, she gave mind reading
a shot—and also got nowhere. Finally, in desperation, she attempted to
see into the future.

Total no-go. So much for superpowers.

"No matter what it is," Assail said softly, "we will deal with it. You are not alone."

She refocused on him. He was staring at the ground, his face grim, his eyes unblinking. His profile was, as always, so striking, the angles of his cheekbones and his jaw so perfect, his jet-black hair a striking contrast to his skin, his brows an elegant slash.

Standing shoulder to shoulder with him, she realized that up until now she had always felt alone. Her grandmother was someone to take care of, someone to watch over, not a partner. And Sola's biggest fear, when she had been on the wrong side of the law, had always been what would happen to her *vovó* if something happened to her. She was all the woman had.

Sola's own health and safety had been a burden for that reason.

But now, in the midst of whatever crisis this was, she found that she had backup—and not in the gunfight kind of way. No, she had someone at her six to process decision-making with. To share grief with. To collapse against when she needed a fall-apart before she could keep going.

She reached over and took his hand. "I'm so glad you're here."

His eyes, as sad as her own, lifted. "I will not desert you in this."

If that was not a vow, she didn't know what was.

Leaning in, she put her hand on the side of his face and brushed his lips with her own. "Thank you—"

As the door to the patient room opened, she stiffened and tried to read the features of the doctor. "What," she demanded.

But Dr. Manello didn't seem offended by the rudeness. "We're looking good. We're looking reaaaaaaal good."

"Wait—what?" She shook her head. "What are you—wait, *what?*"

He smiled. "Her heart's good. Her blood work's fine. There's no evidence of a blood clot or stroke. Her pressure's still a little on the low side, but she hasn't been eating or drinking much so she's dehydrated and she needs to get some rest—"

"No more cooking!" Sola stamped her foot. "She's been at that god-damn stove since we got out of the car—I've told her to sit down and let us wait on her. She's so stubborn!"

In spite of its quick onset, her burst of anger burned out quick, and in its wake came a shaky relief that made Sola sag against Assail.

Dr. Manello nodded his head. "She is a little set in her ways from what I've seen. And listen, going forward, use me. Tell her that she has to behave better or you're calling her doctor in to read the riot act to her."

Sola put her hand over her pounding heart. "She scared the crap out of us."

"I think she scared herself. And I want to keep her here for a day or two, just to make sure we're not missing anything."

"That's a great idea. Keep her as long as you like."

"Just so you know, she is not happy with this plan."

"I don't think she would be," Sola muttered. "But it's not her call."

Dr. Manello gave her shoulder a squeeze. "Go on in there. You guys are welcome to visit anytime, and call me if you have questions. Don't be alarmed at the IV. We're just running fluids into her and some electrolytes. And the monitors are simply there to keep track of things. I'm going to repeat some tests tomorrow at nightfall and we'll see where we're at. But again, a couple of days of observation here would be great for me."

"Then that is what we're going to do. Thanks, Doc."

"You are so welcome."

Sola glanced at Assail. "I'd like to have a moment alone with her? So I can yell at her?"

He bowed low. "But of course. I shall wait here."

After she kissed him again, she went for the door like an avenger, opening it wide with every intent to yell—but then she had a sudden wobble as she saw her grandmother so small in the big bed. And she was really glad the doctor had given her a heads-up on the IV and the equipment. If she hadn't known better, she would have been alarmed.

"*Vovó, you're staying here,*" Sola said before the woman opened her mouth. "*Stop with that right now. It's doctor's orders and we are going to do what they say.*"

Talk about a glower. Her grandmother's eyebrows dropped so low, she looked like she was peering through venetian blinds.

But there was no argument. Which told Sola she wasn't the only one spooked by what had happened.

Sola went in and pulled a chair over to the bedside. Taking her *vovó's* hand, she smiled a little. "*I'm really glad you're okay.*"

There was a grunt. But then her grandmother sighed. "*I am older than I think I am.*"

"*I pushed you pretty hard with that car ride. In this, I am sorry.*"

"*I am glad we are here. It was all worth it.*"

They sat in silence for a little while. And then her grandmother closed her eyes.

"*If you don't marry him, I'm going to die—*"

"*Vovó! What are you saying!*"

Her grandmother opened one lid. "*That if you do not marry him, it will kill me and my death will be on your conscience for the rest of your life. That is what I'm saying.*"

Just as Sola was about to absolutely-not-fair that one, her grandmother winked at her. "*Gotcha.*"

"*That is* not *okay, Vovó. And you know it.*"

"*I will use anything I can.*"

"*Listen, your message has been received. Okay? There's no need to press anymore. Your job, if you want to look at it like that, is to live long enough to see the ceremony. How's that sound?*"

"*But then you will never go down the aisle. Just to keep me here.*"

"*We'll see about that.*"

"*Where is he?*"

"*Waiting outside.*"

"*Bring him in. I want to see my grandson-in-law.*"

"We aren't married yet, Vovó," Sola said dryly.
"Not my fault, is it."

Assail stayed outside of that patient room, mired in a skittish, annoying energy that made him want to run laps up and down the training center.

Indeed, this whole growing-a-conscience thing for him was full of angst. After a lifetime of not caring about anyone over himself, to be this concerned with Mrs. Carvalho was a change—on top of the guilt he was now carrying about—

When Marisol opened the door abruptly, he stiffened. "Is she okay? Shall I summon the healer?"

Marisol shook her head and smiled. "She wants to see you."

Assail straightened the loose cashmere sweater he had pulled on before leaving the house—and found himself wishing that instead of casual slacks, he were in a tuxedo.

As if formality would somehow increase the older woman's chances of survival.

Entering the patient room, he had a brief hiccup of dissociation as his brain connected the dots . . . and came to the realization that Marisol's grandmother was in an identical room to the one he had spent all that time in. But before memories could tackle him and render him useless, he snapped out of it and told himself to smile.

"Mrs. Carvalho," he said as he approached the bed. "You are looking very well indeed—"

The elderly lady interrupted him with a weak voice. "If you do no marry my granddaughter, I will die—"

"Vovó!" Marisol snapped. "Are you even serious right now!"

The woman put her arm over her forehead. "I am feeling faint. I feel no good—"

Alarmed, Assail all but lunged for the door. "Madam! I must summon—"

"Baloney," Marisol said as she put her hands on her hips. "Why aren't any of those machines going off?"

Mrs. Carvalho dropped her arm and appeared irked by the logic. "They no work. Pieces of junk."

"You need to stop this right now—"

Marisol's grandmother looked at Assail. "I must have my granddaughter taken care of and I choose you—"

"Okay, that's it." Marisol threw her hands up. "We're leaving—"

Assail approached the bedside and took the old woman's hand. Staring deeply into her eyes, he lowered his voice. "I do not deserve her. You must realize this."

Mrs. Carvalho smiled so deeply, she glowed with the beauty she must have had when she was young. "And that is why I choose you. You recognize she is best."

"She is everything. She is the whole world."

"You make me happy. I sleep now. You a good man."

As those eyes began to close, Assail rubbed his thumb back and forth on that gnarled hand. The bones were too close to the surface for his comfort, a reminder that this fixture in Marisol's life—and now his own—indeed did not have an eternity in front of her.

"I am not a good man," he found himself whispering. "Not even close."

"God sees what man does not," Mrs. Carvalho murmured.

As the woman reached out her free hand, a clear beckoning to Marisol, it was a little while before the granddaughter answered the call of her elder. But then Marisol too was holding on, the pair of them united by the frail, fierce spirit on the bed.

In the thick silence that followed, Assail looked across at Marisol with dread. She was staring at her grandmother, her face sad and serious.

What the hell am I going to do now, he thought.

FORTY-SIX

Qhuinn barely got them all back to the Brotherhood's mansion before dawn's early, ass-kicking light rained down out of the sky. The second the brother hit the brakes on the mobile surgical unit, Vishous opened the side door and hopped out, reaching up to help his Jane. As she accepted his hand, even though she didn't need it, it felt so good to aid her in some small way.

Shutting things, the three of them jogged over to the entrance and went into the vestibule. As soon as he put his face in the camera, the inner door opened, and Beth let them in.

"You guys just made it," the Queen said. "We were worried. Come on in and eat."

The other brothers who had been out at the clinic had dematerialized home, but V had wanted to be on backup for Qhuinn on the drive back. And he hadn't minded the decompression time.

Some nights were longer than others.

And some were outright hell.

As Beth and Qhuinn headed off for the crowded dining room, V hung back. "You want to eat something?"

Jane looked through the elegant archway to the packed, fancy table and squared her shoulders. "Sure."

When she started in that direction, he caught her hand and stared into her forest green eyes.

"Tell me what you really want to do. Be honest."

"I'm exhausted." She sagged. "But I'm afraid to tell you that because . . . well, I just don't want you to think it's going back to the way it was—"

Vishous swooped down and picked her up. "I'm taking you to the Pit. And I'm going to feed you soy packets and ketchup. And it's going to be the best meal you've never had."

She laughed. "You know, my MSG levels are running a little low."

"Actually, I lied about the soy sauce. I'm going to call Fritz and have them walk some food over, 'kay?"

Jane relaxed in his arms, and he loved the loose feel of her body. "That sounds perfect. I love everybody, but I'm just . . . I can't chitchat right now and I don't want to be rude."

"I gotchu, true?"

Feeling strong as a mountain with his female in his arms, V strode off through the majestic, multi-colored foyer to the hidden door underneath the grand staircase. As he took them down into the underground tunnel, his bonded male was front and fucking center—and that protective instinct and purpose was a grounding he hadn't had for a very long time. His shitkickers literally landed differently on the concrete beneath his feet, and his brain was sharp in a way that made him feel like a laser.

I love this, he thought. *So much it scares me.*

But he could trust Jane. He knew that in his soul. She would never abuse this power she had over him—hell, she probably wasn't even aware she had it.

"Why are you smiling?" she said softly.

He stopped as they arrived at the door to the Pit. "Do you know what is even more important to me than love?"

"What's that?"

V shifted her around so he could look her in the face. "Trust is more important to me. And I realize . . . that you got my back."

Jane reached up and stroked his face. Then she ran her fingertips over the symbols that had been tattoo'd into his temple.

"Trust," she said, "is just another word for love."

Her smile was so radiant that he had to kiss her. And at first, it was a communion kind of thing, a brush of mouths that was reverent and nonsexual.

That did not last. Before he knew what was happening, he was licking his way into her, dropping her to her feet, holding her against his hardening body.

His hands smoothed down her shoulders to her waist, her hips, her ass. And as he curled his greater height around her, his head started to spin.

"Jane . . ."

"Yes," she whispered.

He was tempted to do it right where the hell they were, but he was worried that Fritz might come and check on them to get a food order. That poor *doggen* had seen a lot in his centuries of service, but a brother banging his mate in the brightly lit tunnel was pushing the bounds.

"Come on, let's hurry," V said. "I need to be inside you."

They scrambled their way up the shallow steps, burst into the little hall, and started taking their clothes off before they hit their bedroom. With a sloppy kick, V shut the door behind them and then they were doing a whole lot of strip-kissing.

"I love you naked," he gritted out against his mate's mouth as they finally stood against each other with no barriers.

The whole vertical shit did not last. Next thing he knew—thank fuck—he was on top of Jane on the bed, and even though there were so many other things he wanted to do, so many places he wanted his mouth, his tongue, his hands, he really needed to be inside of her.

For a male who existed separately from everyone, even his brothers, he had to have this unity with his female, with Jane. She and she alone was the one who he could be both strong and vulnerable with, his brilliant, beautiful, full-of-compassion female.

She was right.

At the end of the day, absolute trust was the working definition of true love.

As Jane looked up at Vishous, she tilted her pelvis so he could go in deep and she braced herself for a wild onslaught of passion. Not this time. Instead of pounding into her—which she would have been totally fine with—V moved in a slow wave, his erection sliding in and out, the passion more like lighting a lovely candle instead of burning the house down.

And he stared at her the entire time, those diamond eyes, those wonderful, cynical, often chilly but never cruel, diamond eyes with their navy blue rims boring into her own.

For some reason, just before she began to climax, she found herself reaching up to his face once again.

"You're going to be okay," she heard herself say. "That shadow is not in you. You're not that civilian, I promise you. That is not going to happen to you."

Vishous froze, his eyes growing wide. "What?"

"It's all right. Look at your arm. Go on."

He blinked quick a number of times. And then instead of checking the wound, he said in a voice that cracked, "How did you know."

"Why wouldn't you wonder?" She shrugged. "How could you not? If I were you, that's what would go through my mind. You were wounded in the same way that civilian was, just to a much lesser extent. I would be worried it might spread or something might be harbored inside of me, but that is not what's going on."

As he shifted and looked at his arm muscle, his stare narrowed. "It is getting better."

"I agree. And even though we don't know for sure, it is logical to assume that is a favorable sign. Also, you have been acting no different, and honestly, that civilian's wounds were over half his body—more than half."

V refocused on her eyes. "I want it gone. I don't want that shit in my skin anymore."

"Those shadows are so much more dangerous than we thought."

"The fucking Omega has to go."

"I agree."

After a moment, he dropped his head and started to kiss her again, and she kissed him right back, giving him everything she had, trying to reassure him not just about his own injury, but the very future of the race. Which was maybe nuts. But sometimes that was all you could do—just pour your hope and love into your partner because they needed the support, even though it arguably wasn't going to change or improve what was really going on.

With a luscious sigh, Jane arched into her release, the tide cresting in a quiet, profound way, the warmth, the tightening around his arousal, the sweet, sweet relief cleansing her, wiping out, at least for the time being, all the ugliness that she had seen tonight.

"Oh, God, Jane . . ." V groaned as he, too, found his orgasm.

The pleasure seemed to last forever, and then they were spooning in a warm cocoon, the duvet yanked over their bodies, his head on his pillow, hers on the inside of his arm.

As they lay there in the dark, Jane closed her eyes.

"What about food," she mumbled as she started to fall asleep.

"This is all I need," V replied.

"Me, too . . ."

Her last thought before she drifted off was that no, in fact this was not like it had been previously when she'd come back exhausted from work. She was tired, it was true, and it was from her job. But instead of being in here alone, she was very much in this together.

With the one she loved.

FORTY-SEVEN

"Detective de la Cruz, how nice to see you again."

As Vitoria came forward across the gallery space, she offered the man her hand. "I didn't expect you so soon. It's not even ten in the morning."

"Traffic was light."

He was dressed in a version of what he'd had been in the day before, the blazer dark brown this time, the pants black, the shoes slush-worthy and streaked with dried salt stains. He had something in his hand, but not a notebook. A clipboard? No, it was a thin laptop.

"Would you like to go somewhere to talk?" he said.

"But of course. This way."

As she led him over to the stairs to Ricardo's office, she was aware of a curling anxiety. She hid it by reminding herself that if she couldn't handle this kind of heat, she had no business thinking that she could run her brothers' illegal empire.

And no, she was not going down to the station to meet de la Cruz. He had given her a choice of that or him coming to her. Not a tough decision.

When they were in her brother's expansive bowling alley of an office, she walked forward to the desk—but stopped halfway there and turned on her heel.

"Here I am again, being rude. I've forgotten to offer you something to drink once more."

"I'm good. Thanks."

"As you do."

She went the rest of the way, noting that she'd left that chair she'd sat in the previous day still out of place and turned around. Ricardo would not have approved, and she had to resettle it back where it belonged.

Smoothing her pink and black Chanel suit, she faced him. "So tell me, Detective, have you found something on the security tapes?"

"Yes. I have."

As she stared at him, she trained her face to slowly disintegrate into an expression that approximated fear and worry. "Are my brothers okay?"

"Do you mind if I bring that other chair around so we can sit together?"

"No. Not at all."

Feigning like she had to take a seat or she would fall down, she swept her hair over her shoulder, lowered herself into the chair she'd rearranged, and crossed her legs.

Beneath that show of femininity, she was all calculation.

De la Cruz joined her on the right side and put the laptop on his knees. "So we were able to gain access to the security footage thanks to the laptop you allowed us to take from that security room. We were very surprised how far back the recordings went."

"How far did they?"

"Over a year."

"A year?"

She made a show of tracing his face with her eyes, as if she were attempting to read his features. "So what did you find?" she asked in a weak voice.

"We thought that isolating the relevant footage would be a challenge, but your brother was very regimented. Every morning—right
about this time, actually—he walked the gallery space below. We discovered this when we started watching the footage, and because of this
habit, we were able to zero in on the night in question with some efficiency."

"What happened to him," she asked in a flat voice.

His brown eyes became grave. "These images are going to be difficult for you to watch. But I have to ask you if you recognize anyone in
them."

Bracing her palms on her knees, she pulled her skirt down a number
of times and made a show of swallowing hard—which was in truth not
an act. She was suddenly quite emotional. "I find I am nervous."

"I'm sorry. I really am. But if we're going to catch your brothers'
killers, we need to pursue every avenue we have. And you are one of
them."

"I don't know anything about their business, though."

"I understand that. But sometimes things get jogged." The detective
touched himself on the head. "The mind can recall things that we're not
aware of knowing."

"Show me."

He flipped open the cover of the laptop. After typing some commands, he swiveled the thing around so it faced her.

"The relevant images have been copied and merged from the various
cameras. You'll see the time counter and feed number change in the
lower right-hand corner as a result of this. But just concentrate on
what's happening, okay?"

Vitoria leaned in. There was a video box in the center of the screen,
showing a black-and-white depiction of the outside stoop of the back
entrance of the gallery. Just as de la Cruz had said, there was a time
counter in white with a roman numeral "I" next to it off to the side.

"You ready?"

"Yes."

He hit something, and the counter started to move. "You'll note that—"

"Shh," she said as two figures came into view.

Men. Tall and big, with one of them dressed nicely in a fine overcoat. The other was wearing a leather jacket of sorts. It was difficult to see their faces as both were looking downward, and they stood before the closed door for just a moment before it was opened for them. They paused, evidently to converse with someone, and then they were inside—and the camera view changed, switching to out in the gallery space proper.

A man without any outerwear on walked them into where the art was and must have told them to stop where they were, as he went alone to the door to Ricardo's office. There were two guards on either side, and after a momentary discussion, the first guard disappeared, clearly to take a message upstairs.

Thereafter, the man in the high-quality overcoat spoke to the pair of sentries as his associate in the leather jacket went on a stroll around the pieces that had been installed. And then the first man took something out of his coat—a cigar. He motioned to it and spoke as though he were asking the guards' permission to smoke.

The guard on the left pointed to a sign and shook his head. The overcoat man asked something else. After a second, the guard on the right shrugged . . . opened the door to the staircase—

The attack was so swift, Vitoria's eyes couldn't track it. The overcoat man was suddenly on the other guard and snapping his neck—while the one in leather came over and stabbed the other one. Twice.

"*Oh, God,*" she said in Spanish. It was not hard to figure out where this was heading.

There was some quick conversation between the two men. And then overcoat's henchman dragged the guard who had been stabbed behind one of the exhibits and they both disappeared into the stairwell to Ricardo's office.

"There are no cameras in your brother's office—or its staircase," the detective said quietly. "So we don't know what transpired exactly."

The end result was obvious, however. Within minutes, the two men emerged and the henchman had someone over his shoulder.

"We believe that is your brother," the detective said. "Ricardo."

Yes, she thought as tears came to her eyes. She could recognize the suit, the shoes, the back of the head.

There was a pause as the men looked around, as if to ascertain whether their presence had been noted or an alarm was sounding. And then they were moving fast, entering the staff area.

"There are no cameras in that back area." The detective cleared his throat. "But you'll see them come out . . ."

And there they were. Emerging from the rear door . . . and disappearing out of camera range.

Vitoria sat back and did not have to pretend the upset. Putting her hand over her mouth, she closed her eyes. When she had gone to that bolt-hole up on Iroquois Mountain, and found her brother's remains in that basement, she had had the end of the story. The detective had just provided her the beginning.

When she could speak, she said in a rough way, "What of Eduardo? Have you found anything of him?"

"No. We have not."

"Why would anyone hurt them?" she asked, partially to have it look good, but also as an expression of her true sorrow.

They had been children once. They had all been children . . . once. How had it come to this? Then again, given how hard and horrible their youngest years had been, and the means by which Ricardo had lifted them out of that poverty, how else could it have ended?

"Why . . ." she breathed.

"Ms. Benloise, do you really want me to answer that?"

She pulled herself out of the past. "Yes."

"If you notice the time stamp, you'll see that it's well after business hours. And yet there are three guards on the premises as your brother works late—and the security cameras watch only the back door and gallery space, not either of your brothers' offices or the entire rear portion of this building. And the reality is, when we continued to view the footage, there were a number of other people who came and went, all after hours, all to see your brother upstairs. You've got to ask yourself, what kind of legitimate business could he possibly be doing?"

"I . . . I don't know." She looked into the man's kind brown eyes. "What of the bodies, though? There were dead guards when they left?"

"One of the men came back. It was just before dawn. He worked fast and took them out. They must have gotten access to the security code or a key somehow. By the time the staff returned in at nine a.m., everything was cleaned up."

Vitoria sat back and stared straight ahead.

"My question to you is," the detective said, "do you recognize either of those men who took your brother?"

"Let me watch again."

She reviewed the footage two more times, leaning in as close as she could get to the screen. When she sat back again, she did not have to lie.

"No, I do not. I've never seen them before."

But she would recognize them in the future, for sure. That was why she had watched again and then one more time.

De la Cruz cleared his throat. "This should not surprise you, but that was not the first time that man in the overcoat came to see your brother."

"No?"

"He had been there before that night. We have the footage a good month or so prior to that attack—and he had been to the gallery a number of times."

Vitoria made a noncommittal noise and stared ahead, summoning in her mind the features she had seen on both of those killers.

"Ms. Benloise, you told me that you were staying in your brother's West Point house."

"Yes," she heard herself say. "I am."

"Would you mind if we searched those premises and got access to any video monitoring equipment there is on that property?"

Vitoria tried to marshal her thoughts—and after a moment, she nodded. "Certainly. Help yourself."

It was naive of her to think that no other people would have shown up on the footage—people who might be arrested in conjunction with illegal activity thanks to what she had allowed the police to see.

Was she doing herself and her ambitions harm in granting further access? What if the business she had come to take over got decimated by all this evidence? Then again, the police undoubtedly knew far more than they were letting on.

And if she had to start everything from scratch, then she would.

The detective started to talk again, but she wasn't paying him any attention. She was too busy trying to chess-move this evolving situation. And in the end, she knew she didn't really have a choice with regard to the West Point house. If she didn't give them permission, it would be as it had been here at the gallery—they would very certainly get a court to clear any obstacles she might put up.

Besides, it was critical that those two attackers be stopped, whether she did it behind the scenes or the police did it in front: If she wanted to be in business, she might well be a target as Ricardo and Eduardo's sister—kill or be killed had never been more applicable.

Although that was assuming those men were still alive. Perhaps their fates had already been served by someone else?

"I want to help you in any way I can," she intoned, whether or not that was appropriate to whatever he was saying.

"We appreciate that." There was a pause. "I just have one more question for you. What were you doing here the night you came after hours?"

Vitoria shook herself. "I'm sorry?"

"The security footage from three nights ago shows you arriving at the rear door and being let into the gallery by a man. Can you please explain what you were doing?"

She cleared her throat and projected upset. "As I hadn't heard from my brothers, I called a number they had given me long before all this. A man answered. He told me to come to the gallery as soon as it was convenient and so I did."

"Does that man work for the gallery?"

"I believe he does security. He made me feel . . . very uncomfortable. He threatened me—I was scared so I departed as soon as I could. And you know, it was odd. Margot and I—when she came to see me before she left the night she was killed . . . you know, I never put this together . . ." She looked up in alarm at the detective. "But she brought him up. She told me . . . she said he had made a pass at her, but she had turned him down and . . . I mean, she seemed scared."

"What is the man's name?"

"Streeter. His name is Streeter. I didn't mention this before because where I am from, we do not speak of such things. But it is all different now. Everything . . . is different now."

"Would you be willing to come down to headquarters and give a statement?"

"Is there any way I could do it tomorrow? I really . . . I want to go lie down. I'm not feeling well . . ."

"Absolutely."

She stared into his eyes. "I want you to catch those evil men, Detective de la Cruz. They need to be in jail for the rest of their lives for what they did to Ricardo—and what they must have done to my other brother."

De la Cruz nodded. "That's my job, Ms. Benloise. And I'm very good at it."

FORTY-EIGHT

As night fell, and Jane continued to sleep in their bed, Vishous went out naked to his computers and sat in his Captain Kirk chair. He had taken his leather jacket with him as he'd left their room, and after he lit up a hand-rolled, he went fishing in its pockets.

The civilian Whinnig's gun was your garden-variety poodle shooter, a nothing-special Smith & Wesson nine millimeter, and as he kicked out the clip, he checked the bullets. There were three left, and he freed them of their confines, rolling them around in his palm.

Why hadn't they worked against that entity? V had shot the shit out of the shadow that had gone after him and had wounded it. But Whinnig had said that his bullets had gone right through without effect—and his injuries had certainly been consistent with an undeterred attack from a strong enemy.

Maybe the report was false. After all, the kid who had died—and come back, hello—hadn't been combat trained. But, Jesus, how trained did you have to be to notice whether or not you were wounding the thing trying to kill you?

Sitting forward, he lined up the three bullets in a little row, their flat bottoms and copper-colored hats exactly what you'd expect to see from the kind of civilian ammo you could get in a Dick's Sporting Goods store.

The thing V worried about was whether the Omega was improving on a prototype. Shoring up weaknesses in a creation to make it a more effective weapon. The vampire race's enemy was soulless, evil, and a scourge on the fucking planet—but it was far from stupid. And a weapon that couldn't withstand getting shot at was less effective than one that could.

V sat back and smoked for a while, his brain cranking along on the variables.

When his mental calculator kept showing him zeroes, he got frustrated and decided to check in with some of the Facebook groups to see if anything was out in the species yet about the attack. The brother, Aarone, had gone home and was undoubtedly talking to people in the *glymera*.

Nope. Nothing yet.

Then again, the aristocracy did consider themselves above social media—

As his cell phone went off with a text, he threw out a hand and grabbed the thing. When he saw who it was from and what it was about, he cursed and got to his feet.

Heading back to the bedroom, he snuck in, not wanting to disturb Jane—or Butch and Marissa, who were sleeping next door. And he was doing okay on the whole getting-dressed thing until he slammed his bare foot into the corner of the dresser.

Sure, he managed to keep the HOLY FUCKING WHAT THE FUCKBITCHASSFUCKINGPIECEOFSHIT WAS THAT to himself, but the thunderous toe-to-wood contact sound was nothing he could control.

"V?" Jane said in a sleepy way.

"Hey." MOTHERFUCKINGOWFUCKOW—he rubbed his foot. "Sorry. Didn't want to wake you."

Of course, now that you're up, honey, can you amputate my lower leg on this side? That'd be great. Thanks.

"You okay?"

"Perfect." Fishing through the dresser, he grabbed and yanked on the first pair of pant-like anything he came to. Then he pulled on a T-shirt. "I gotta leave for a second before the Brotherhood meeting."

"Mmm, love you. I'm going to go down to the clinic—what time is it?"

"Six p.m. You have another twenty minutes. Love you, too."

Closing his eyes, he concentrated . . .

. . . and after a Tilt-A-Whirl, came out on the Other Side, in the Sanctuary. Without missing a beat, he strode across the cropped Astroturf-but-it-was-"real" lawn toward the Treasury.

As he closed in on the building, Phury stepped out of its entryway and lifted a hand. "Hey, my brother," he called over. "Thanks for coming."

"No problem." V slowed as the guy gave him a strange look. "What. Why are you staring at me like that?"

"Interesting pants."

"Huh—oh, *fuck.*"

As V checked out his lower half, his only thought was thank God it was Phury and not anyone else: He had on Jane's pink flannel PJ bottoms. The ones that had My Little Cocksucking Pony all over them. The ones that had been given to all the females in the house by Lassiter—not because he liked My Little Motherfucking Pony, but because the fallen angel knew when the ladies wore them, their *hellrens* were going to have to see Apple Jack and Rainbow Dash in their nightmares.

And now V was sporting a set like he was a fan.

Oh, and P.S., they were high-waters because he was ten inches taller than his *shellan.*

"That is the last time I get dressed in the dark, true," he muttered.

"Hey, it could be worse."

"Yeah? How."

"You could have put the top on, too."

"Will you be offended if I just take them off?"

"Do you have boxer shorts on?"

"Fuck no."

"Then let's keep those puppies where they are, shall we?" Phury gave him a condescending smile. "Just in case any of the Chosen are up here. Modesty, you know."

"Personally, I'd pick my one-balled wonder routine over this, but yeah, sure. Whatever you want." V nodded toward the Treasury's interior. "So what we got, Primale?"

"It's bad." Phury's glowing yellow eyes narrowed. "Epic bad, actually."

The two of them went inside, the bins of sparkling gems like fires banked, the wealth at once extraordinary and an as-you-do.

The brother went over to the display case with the burn mark. "So guess what was in here."

"Fritz's cookbook and he finally got it back." V patted around for a hand-rolled and realized he hadn't brought any with him. "Damn it."

"I wouldn't let you smoke in here anyway." Phury opened the case's glass lid. "And this was a cookbook, actually. But it's the kind you don't want in anyone's hands—which was why it was here."

"I'd like to remind you we can't get lung cancer," V muttered. "And everything is perfect up here, remember. I'll bet if I exhaled, rose petals would come out of my mouth—but I digress. Cookbook? What are you talking about?"

"It's a book of conjuring spells. Whoever has it can bring bad things to life."

V ditched the levity quick. "The shadow entities."

"That's what I'm thinking. Those things just started showing up, didn't they."

"But why would the Omega need a book? If he knows how to—"

"You were right that first night. I don't think it's the Omega. Which is only one of a whole host of problems we've got." The brother passed his hand over the burned spot. "Because check this out, the other reason the book was stored here was because it can't be destroyed—if you burn it or try to rip up the pages, you release all of the spells at once. So this was deemed the only safe place. No one was supposed to get to it."

"Where the fuck did it come from?"

"I don't know about its origins. I'm just passing on what Amalya, the Directrix, told me. She's really upset—not just because of the book being gone, but because we're both wondering who got access to the Sanctuary when they weren't supposed to be here? Let me ask you, when were you and Jane up here that you noticed it was gone?"

"I told you the night after. When I saw you at the Great Camp. Jane and I were just—well, she ended up here after she was shot." He thought about Lassiter. "And I came to her. She pointed it out to me."

Phury cursed. "I'm going to have to talk to Wrath about this."

V stared at the doors that were open. And decided that if there were ever a moment in his life to be diplomatic, now was it.

"Listen, my man, I don't know how to say this nicely." He tried to pick his words carefully. "But is there any chance one of your Chosen might be doing an end run on this thing?"

Oooooor he could just put the shit out there.

"Absolutely not." Phury glared at him. "Those females are—"

"Out in the world. Making connections. Forging relationships with people they meet at the Audience House, online, while they work. How do you know that one of them didn't take it, either for their own use, or someone else's."

Phury crossed his thick arms over his chest—and V was pretty damn sure that if the brother wasn't a gentlemale, he'd have been throwing the kind of punches that knocked out teeth.

"My Chosen would never do anything to endanger the race."

"But think this through." V put his palms up, all let's-chill. "No one else is allowed here without permission. So either one of two things happened. Someone who does have access took the book, or someone who has access took the book for somebody else. There are no other logical explanations."

At eight o'clock that night, Vitoria pulled her brother's Bentley into a parking space about seven blocks down from the gallery. It was a legal space, although there was no reason to put anything in the meter because it was after six p.m.

The snow that had been forecasted had arrived, and before she opened the driver's side door, she pulled the hood of her black sweatshirt into place and zipped up the parka she had used to keep warm while climbing the mountain. After a pause to check her phone, she got out and kept her head down as the wind blew flakes into her face.

As she walked away from the Bentley, she left that door open and the key fob on the center console.

Pity that she did not have someone to bet with concerning how long it would take for somebody to steal the Flying Spur. The weather was bad, it was true, and that could decrease foot traffic and therefore the number of thieves. But it was a $250,000 sedan. Some junkie or another would take advantage of good fortune. It was the way of the human race.

Vitoria kept up a brisk pace as she went along, hands in the pockets of that parka that added to her bulk, head still down, her face obscured by the hood.

She went deeper and deeper into downtown . . . until, some number of blocks later, she got to the bridge that spanned the river.

Courtesy of the many on- and off-ramps that fed the four lanes across the waterway, there was a vast, dark netherworld underneath the great elevated stretches of pavement—and she kept her pace as she proceeded into the sheltered area. Here, the wind gusts lessened and the snow was blocked from falling to the rock-hard, frozen dirt. Cocoons of homeless people dotted the barren landscape, their bodies curled up in filthy blankets such that they became boulders on the face of poverty's moon. And all around, loose newspapers danced about countless abandoned bottles empty of booze, like children showing inappropriate levity.

Overhead, traffic was a steady stream of ambient noise, the heavy weights of cars and trucks bumping along, coughing out the occasional horn or siren.

Vitoria walked all the way to the far side, to the place where the highway began its elevation from the earth, the parting of two planes creating an especially private area.

And there he was.

Streeter was precisely where they had agreed to meet, his tall body likewise in the same clothes he had been wearing during their arctic trip. As she approached, he flicked his cigarette away and exhaled.

"Hey, what's going on—"

She shot him twice. Both times in the chest.

The suppressor did its job beautifully: The loudest sound was of him falling to the ground and landing faceup in a flop.

Two steps forward brought her to him. As he gasped, he lifted one hand up as if to ward her off while the other grabbed on to his chest.

She put a bullet into his forehead and a final one through the front of his throat.

Then Vitoria re-tucked the weapon into the waistband of her snow pants and walked away, head down, hands in pockets.

As she went, she noted the warmth of the barrel as it rested against her body, and thought, oddly, about the last time she had had sex. It had been a while since she had had something hot, round, and hard against her lower belly. Too long—although part of that was because it was difficult to be discreet back home. She would not have that problem here.

But that was a concern for another time. Now, she had to continue with her plan for the evening.

She would much have preferred to catch a bus or a subway back to the gallery. A taxi would be even better. But she couldn't risk anyone seeing her or interacting with her. So she walked out from under the bridge and hooked up with a city street.

Now the snowflakes fell upon her once more, and her breath came out in puffs, like smoke from a locomotive's engine.

It was nearly forty-five minutes of trudging before the gallery came into view, and she avoided entirely the rear entrance. Instead, she went in through the front, just as though she were a legitimate customer. Thanks to de la Cruz, she knew that, for some reason, her brother had no monitoring cameras on what was the primary entry. Then again, his illegal associates had come and gone through the back one—and Ricardo certainly had never had any intention of turning security footage over to the police.

No, upon further reflection, Vitoria was willing to bet that he had kept it for his own records, as an insurance policy in case anyone got any bright ideas.

She'd left through the front, too. And had not engaged the security alarm.

That way, there would be no record of her having left the premises and returned. And to that end, she was careful to circumvent the camera field that monitored the gallery space and the doorway up to Ricardo's office.

One other advantage to her having watched the footage de la Cruz had showed her so many times was that she had figured out where the blind spots were.

Accordingly, she went into a dark corner that had no security coverage and changed back into the office clothes she'd left there. Then she stashed the parka, snow pants, hoodie, and gun in the hollow three-dimensional representation of a toadstool. After that, she took a circuitous route around so that she could go into the staff area unseen. . . . only to make a show of striding out of there with her coat and bag.

Certain she was being watched and recorded by the cameras, she walked through the gallery space and checked the front door even though she was out of frame for that . . . then she reentered the camera's eye and walked to the rear exit.

After engaging the alarm, she stepped out and locked up.

Then she looked left. Looked right.

Frowned.

Walking out of frame, she waited for as long as she guessed it would take for her check around and see where the Bentley should have been.

With hands that deliberately fumbled the keys, she let herself back in and disengaged the alarm, making sure to relock the door. Then she got out her phone. Dropped it. Picked it up and pushed her hair out of the way.

With hands that she made shake, she dialed a number and put the cell up to her ear. When the call was answered on the third ring, she made sure her voice was panicky.

"Detective de la Cruz? I'm so sorry to bother you, but you told me to call you if anything strange happened? Well, my car appears to have been stolen."

FORTY-NINE

On the heels of a nightmare about being chased, Assail woke up with a jerk that flopped all his four limbs. For a split second, he had no idea where he was—was he still in an alley with slayers behind him? Was Marisol screaming for him to help her—except he knew if he went to her, he was bringing death along with him . . . ?

But then he looked around the training center's break room and reality's most recent sequence came back to him: he and Marisol bringing her grandmother into the Brotherhood's clinic; them receiving the good news that everything was essentially fine; the two of them coming to the decision that he and Marisol would stay through the day in case they were needed.

And then him sitting in this chair, and clearly passing out.

"Are you okay?"

He looked across the room. Over at the counter where the food was served, Marisol was putting things on a tray: two mugs that steamed, eggs, hash browns.

"Yes, yes of course." He sat up and rubbed his eyes. "I didn't mean to fall asleep."

"We're both exhausted." She came over and pulled another chair close. "So I guess they like breakfast for dinner here—and that works for me. I got enough for two."

He wasn't hungry, although that was not because he'd eaten anytime soon.

"Here." She sat down and put the tray on her knees. "Drink this."

He took the mug she offered so he wasn't rude, but a couple of sips in, he decided it wasn't a good idea. He was jumpy enough.

"Eggs?" she offered.

"Not at the moment. Thank you, though."

"Like I said, I got plenty for both of us."

"Thank you." He sat back and concentrated on the warmth that was transferred through the mug to his palms. "You are very kind."

As Marisol proceeded to eat, he wasn't aware of there being any strained silence, but then she exhaled and stopped chewing.

"Look, I'm so sorry," she said. "But you know she doesn't mean it, right?"

Assail frowned. "Forgive me, what?"

Marisol put her fork down and wiped her mouth with a paper napkin. "That stuff my grandmother was telling you about marrying me or she'll die? That's all a bunch of bullcrap—she's just playing with us. Not that that is an excuse."

"She has done nothing to make me feel uncomfortable."

"You sure about that? Because ever since she laid that on you, I've sensed the distance and strain, and I don't blame you. Nobody needs pressure like that. I just want you to know that I do not expect anything. I'm happy to—you know, however we are is okay with me."

Assail closed his eyes. Tried to speak. Failed.

"Wow," she said dryly. "That bad, huh."

He lifted his lids. "I am sorry—what?"

"Whatever you were trying to tell me back at your house. You know, before she collapsed."

As she got to her feet, he sat forward. "Marisol . . ."

When he couldn't finish things, she walked over to the refrigerator unit, where the Gatorades and the Cokes were. Staring into the display, without taking anything out of it, she murmured, "It's all right if you've changed your mind. About us, I mean."

"I haven't."

Marisol turned back around to him. "Yes, you have. I can see it in your eyes. It's in your voice. It's all around you. Something has changed, so which is it—whether you want me or whether you want out of the life?"

As he stayed silent, she shook her head. "Just so you know, either way I'm going to be okay. I will be perfectly fine without you—not because I'm not in love with you, but because I'll be goddamned if I let anything other than a bullet take me down."

While she was speaking, Assail focused on the side of her neck . . . the place where he'd bitten her.

"Will you please look me in the eye," she muttered as she put her hand to her throat. "What the hell are you staring at?"

Assail wanted there to be another way. Prayed, once again, for some solution to come to him. Begged fate for a different path.

In the end, however, there was not one—and he simply could not keep going with the lie. No matter that it would cost him his female, or that there had to be a better time, she had a right to know.

"What," she snapped. "Just say it."

As Assail put his coffee mug down on the floor, he was very aware that it was going to be the last thing she ever gave him.

Shifting his weight, he rose from the chair and began to undo the buttons of his fine silk shirt, one by one.

"What are you doing?" she demanded. "I am not interested in sex right now, FYI."

Pulling the shirttails free, he went all the way to the bottom and then removed his cuff links, putting them in the pocket of his slacks. Opening the two halves of the shirt, he let it fall from his shoulders to the ground.

"Tell me what you see, Marisol," he commanded.

"What?" Impatience had her shaking her head. "What the hell is this about?"

"Look at me. Look at me closely. What do you see."

Her eyes made a cursory pass over his chest and his stomach. "I see a man. I see you. I mean, what?"

"Do you remember what I looked like the first night you came unto me here?" Her wince told him she did. "Remember what my body looked like?"

"You were sick."

"Enough so that you thought I was dying, yes?"

"It's why I made the damn trip."

"And what do I look like now. How have I changed."

That last one was not a question. It was a challenge.

She shrugged. "You're a lot . . . healthier. Stronger. More yourself."

"How many days has it been, Marisol."

Now she frowned. "I don't know. Three. Four?"

"What about my hair?" He pulled at the lengths that were easily two or three times as long as they had been. "How is it different?"

As he continued to push her, the change in her was minute, but powerful. Instead of being animated by anger, she stilled and seemed to barely breathe.

"Think about where I was compared to what I am as I stand before you now," he said roughly. "And admit to yourself that you've noticed these things over the past couple of days and questioned how it was possible. You've seen how much weight I'm putting on so quickly, how fast I've rebounded. I know you've seen the difference, but you've put it to the back of your mind, haven't you. You've wondered—but then been so grateful I was okay that you just . . ." He made a poofing motion next to his head. "Didn't dwell on it."

Marisol crossed her arms around her torso. "So. You're better."

"Ask yourself how. Ask yourself . . . why. And the answer will not add up. It's too much improvement too quickly, and you know I've hidden nothing because you've seen me without my clothes. You know something doesn't seem right about me. You've sensed it for a very long time—since the first moment I confronted you when you were tracking me. It's always been there in the background, but there were too many reasons not to look too closely into it."

The fact that she took a step back from him broke his heart. But he reminded himself that this was the inevitable end—and he would bear the burden, not her.

He would tell her the truth and then, given that her grandmother would soon be free to leave the clinic, he would strike both their memories. Yes, he could have just done the latter without revealing himself, but his love for Marisol meant that he had to come clean and feel her disgust and anger—because he deserved both. And there was another reason to do it. He was soon to feed from Ghisele again, and at least this way, he would not run the risk of a sexual liaison with Marisol where she could be hurt. Or have something taken from her without her knowing what was happening.

As a bonded male, he was just too dangerous.

"Isn't that right, Marisol? You have wondered about things, things you can't understand and can't explain."

"Yes," she whispered, her brown eyes wide.

"Your hand is on your neck."

"Is it."

"Yes. When you looked in the mirror in the bathroom, and you saw the bruises there, what did you tell yourself?"

Her voice became very quiet. "Nothing."

"Did you get your period? When you were in the shower, there was blood in the drain—did you get your period."

Marisol's eyes shifted away. "Ah, no. No, I didn't."

He had to wait for that stare to return to him. "I am not like you, Marisol. I am . . . so sorry. But I am not one of you."

Abruptly, he saw her chest begin to pump up and down, faster and faster. "You're scaring me."

"I'm sorry. I am more sorry than you will ever know."

With that, he curled his upper lip from his fangs and descended his canines, releasing a growl.

Sola could hear nothing but the thunderous beat of her heart as the man she had thought she'd known stood before her, revealing . . . fangs. Fangs that she would have argued were cosmetic—except for the fact that they moved.

They grew longer in front of her very eyes.

"I am so sorry, Marisol."

Or at least that was what Assail must have said. She couldn't hear a goddamn thing.

Her eyes traveled over his face, his neck . . . his pecs . . . those abs. And she saw clearly what she had, in fact, wondered about without acknowledging: In the last forty-eight hours especially, he had appeared to put on fifty pounds of muscle, his skin no longer loose, his body beginning to return to its previous condition.

In quick succession, other things filtered through her mind: She had never seen him out in the daylight. His glass house was shrouded in strange drapes she had assumed were for privacy, but now? Then there were the lights that went on and off. The people that—

Dizziness swept through her. His cousins. Everyone here in this facility.

Doc Jane coming and going from his house even though, now that she thought about it, there hadn't been any cars on the drive to drop her off or pick her up. The same had been true of Rhage. Ehric and Evale . . .

Then Sola remembered the blood around the drain in the shower . . . and the bruises at her throat. Over her . . . jugular. "Oh . . . *God.*"

Without conscious thought, she turned and bolted out of the room, running as fast and as hard as she could, pounding down that corridor with no destination in mind—just high-octane panic energizing her body.

Except then a bright glow became her goal, as if it were the horizon, as if it were freedom, and as she closed in on it, she tore open a glass door and shot through into—

It was a pool. An Olympic-sized pool—

Just as everything registered, Assail appeared directly in front of her. Out of thin air, he was suddenly *there*.

Sola screamed, the sound echoing around the vast domed area of tile, and she tripped as she tried to turn and run once again. Landing with a hard slap, she whipped around onto her back and crab-walked away from him, horror and her mind's inability to process what he was showing, telling her, turning this into a nightmare.

This could not possibly be real—

Assail stayed right where he was. And eventually, the fact that he wasn't crowding her or being aggressive in any way broke through her terror.

Sola stopped paddling with her hands and feet and lowered her butt to the tile. Her breath was still exploding from her lungs, her fear a roar in her chest . . . and yet he was . . .

Heartbroken.

As Assail stood there, shirtless and shaken, there was such a depth of pain in his eyes that, under any other circumstances, she would have wept for him—

"Hey, we good in here, folks? Need anything?"

Sola spun her body toward the male voice. That big blond man, Rhage, had poked his head in and was looking like he was prepared to intervene if necessary.

He is not a man, she thought.

He is a vampire—

She was *surrounded* by them. Dear God, her grandmother was in a hospital bed, and—

As Sola started to throw up, she caught sight of a stack of towels and crawled over to them, her palms and shoes squeaking on the damp tile, her stomach evacuating those eggs just as she grabbed something to catch them in.

From out of the corner of her eye, she saw the two men—*vampires*—talking. Rhage was shaking his head like he didn't approve, but Assail had put his body in between her and the other man, as if he weren't going to stand for any interference.

That cologne of Assail's, that heady, dark spice, abruptly canceled out the chlorine in the air.

"You fix this," Rhage said. "You need to fix this, my man. Or I will."

Assail replied something and the man—vampire, fucking *vampire*—left.

"Are you going to kill me," she croaked out.

"No. No harm will befall either of you here." Assail nodded toward the exit. "And as soon as your grandmother is medically cleared, you can both go. You never have to . . . you do not ever have to see me or any of us again. You will not even remember—"

"I will remember *everything*," she bit out. "I will—"

"No, you will not."

That dizziness came back as she extrapolated what that meant. "What are you going to do to me?"

"I will make it so that you will not recall any of this. It will all be gone, this moment here and all that came before it as it pertains to me will not exist for you. You will be free of this as you return to your life."

"I don't believe you."

"It's true—"

"You've lied to me how many times now?"

"Marisol . . ." As his voice cracked, he cleared his throat. "Marisol, you have never been hurt around me and I will not permit anything to give you worry or pain."

"That's not true," she said roughly. "You have betrayed me. I am in pain now."

He closed his eyes and lowered his head. "I am so sorry—"

"Get away from me," she demanded, "and I don't want you any-where near my grandmother. And know this. If any one of you does anything to her, I will fucking kill all of you. I don't care what you are—and I want her off those drugs or whatever the hell you're pumping into her this goddamn minute. She and I are leaving right fucking now. We are getting the *fuck* out of here."

FIFTY

hury left the Sanctuary first, and V had every intention of following in the brother's shitkicker steps. Not surprisingly, however, the guy didn't really want him around, considering the shade he'd just thrown on all the Chosen. So after they closed up the Treasury, V found himself giving the brother some space by going on a wonder.

Wander, he meant.

Although the former was probably more what this was, he thought as he closed in on the Scribe Virgin's private quarters. With every step he took, he intended to stop and ghost out so he could make it to the Brotherhood meeting. With each increment of forward motion, he truly meant to reroute. With all the one step, two step, three step, four . . . he had another destination in mind.

Instead of going the peace-out route, though, he ended up entering his mother's quarters through the retracting panel and standing in that courtyard. The songbirds silenced as his presence registered on them, and the longer he stayed there, the more those brightly colored wings fluttered and the little-grip feet shifted the wee things up and down on their branches—the aviary equivalent of nervous pacing, he decided.

V kept thinking about what Jane had said about her little sister. How the loss never went away.

Put in that kind of context, he felt like his *mahmen* had died at his birth. If he were honest with himself—and he hated to be when it came to shit like this—he had been missing what-had-never-been as if it were more like a something-that-was. And now that the Scribe Virgin was actually gone, he somehow had the space to realize he was mourning that which he'd never had.

And FFS, this struck him as a colossal waste of introspection: As much as he respected Mary and her whole talk-it-out deal, he'd never found any relief in dropping the proverbial trou on his weaknesses—whether it was in private or in front of somebody with anime eyes and a master's in social work.

Way too many people cloaked themselves in the mantle of victimhood, creating a vacuum of identity that they expected the world to rush in and fill with compassion that was undeserved.

Although that being said, maybe he was just a defensive, judgmental piece of shit.

Probably. God, he didn't know what the fuck to do with himself anymore. He'd been really all over the place lately.

As he crossed over the white marble, he stopped in front of the water fountain. Then sat on its hard stone outer rim. The water came out of its spigot and fell in crystal droplets that were always in exactly the same place, the spray like a pattern in cloth, fixed within its arching descent and utterly symmetrical—as opposed to how it would have been down below, all random twinkles and somehow more beautiful because of that.

He thought of the Scribe Virgin's regimentation of the race: her mandates that covered the way her Chosen had to live and worship . . . her breeding program . . . the rules and regulations of the classes.

She had even forbidden questions being asked of her. Like, literally, no one, not even Wrath, had been allowed to ask her anything.

Okay, fine, she had kind of let Butch get away with it. But that was it.

As memories of her tangled him up, he reached down to the water for no particular reason, trailing the fingertips of his curse in the depths—

A strange flushing warmth hit his upper arm and he looked down.

The wound that the shadow had made in his flesh shriveled and disappeared, as if chased away, no remnant of its red flush remaining.

"What the fuck," V breathed.

And then it dawned on him.

"My bullets," he announced to the songbirds. "That's why my fucking bullets worked."

Back down at the Brotherhood's training center, Sola burst into her grandmother's hospital room.

"We have to go," she said as she went to the shallow closet. "We need to go. We're leaving right now—"

Her *vovó* sat up in the bed. "What you speaking of?"

"We're leaving." She got her grandmother's clothes and wheeled around. "We need to get you dressed. I'll help you—"

"I am not leaving—"

"Yes, you are." Sola pulled the covers back. "We're—"

"Marisol! What is wrong!"

The sharp tone was exactly what had always worked on her as a child, and her inner ten-year-old overrode her adult impulses, freezing her in place.

But she was not about to vampire the poor old woman. For godsakes.

"They are bad people," Sola choked out. "They are . . . not good people, *Vovó*. We need to escape—"

"What do you say." Her grandmother made a dismissive sound in the back of her throat. "They treat us good. They treat us—"

"I'm not arguing with you about this."

"Good. Then we are no going!"

Sola closed her eyes. "Yes, we are. You have always trusted me when it comes to our safety. Always. That is the way it works with us. And I'm telling you right now, we have to get out of here."

Her grandmother crossed her arms over her bosom and glared. "Not good people? The night of your abduction, who freed you?"

"I freed myself."

"Who got you back to Caldwell. Who took care of you when you injured."

"We're not going to talk about this—"

"When I was sick last night, who came for me? Who stayed with you? Who care for me now!"

Sola looked in a panic at the IV line. "We don't know what they're giving you!"

"You lost your mind. I feel better. I not going. You leave you want. I stay."

"You are coming with me—"

As Sola reached out a hand, her grandmother slapped it away. "You no boss of me. You want to be idiot, go—leave. But I stay here and you no make me do anything." Those eyes were fierce as a tiger's. "I know bad men, I know bad people—I lived through more than you. I seen cruelty, it has been done to me. These people are no bad. They protect us. They help us. They heal us—and that man? He love you. He love you all his heart and you are stupid girl. *Stupid!*"

The English train ran out at that point. What came out next was a fury of Spanish that nearly blew Sola off her boots.

When her grandmother finally took a breath, Sola cut in. "You don't know what you're dealing with."

"And neither do you if you think they bad." Her grandmother made hand motions toward the door. "Go. I no want to talk to you. Go! I kick you out! You no good—"

All at once, alarms started to go off, the shrill alerts adding another layer of panic onto Sola's already stratospheric base.

"*Vovó?*" she said as her grandmother stopped talking and seemed to struggle for breath. "*Vovó!*"

FIFTY-ONE

V beelined his shit out of the Sanctuary, re-forming in the mansion's foyer. Taking the grand staircase two at a time, he all but flew up to the second story and burst into Wrath's pale blue study. The Brotherhood had already started to gather for the meeting, everybody talking over everyone, all those male voices like a wall he had to break through.

Fortunately, they all went silent as he crashed into the room.

"I figured it out," he panted. "I got it!"

There was some generalized throat clearing, and then someone muttered, "You're ready to come out as a My Little Pony fan?"

"What?" V said.

"No offense," somebody else chimed in, "but you have seriously Rainbow'd that Dash of yours."

Rhage put his palms up. "Which is cool—"

"Hey, whatever you like—"

"My best friend is an Apple Jack—"

"See what I have to live with?" Butch said mournfully. "I don't care about the color, it's the cut that kills me. Showing that much ankle. In winter?"

V looked down at himself for the second time—and the view hadn't improved in the slightest. Still high-waters. Still pink. Still flannel.

Still Fuck Me Pony.

Wrath spoke up from behind his father's grand desk. "Can someone tell me what the hell he's wearing?"

Vishous ripped those fucking pj bottoms off so fast, he nearly split the seams—and he would have thrown them in the fire, but for all he knew, Jane liked them.

"We done?" he asked his brothers as he met 'em in the eye one by one. "We fucking done now? So we can talk about what's killing civilians? Or do you bunch of ass eaters want to waste more time. While people are dying."

From over in the corner by the fire, someone said, "Okaaaay, let's not humor shame."

Annnnd that started the deluge. "I'm feeling very shamed right now—"

"Completely shamed, and I was just expressing myself—"

"Can someone bubble-wrap me and give me a puppy to hold? 'Cuz my work/life balance has seriously suffered—"

"What happened to your other nut? Was one of those ponies hungry?"

That last one came out of Lassiter's mouth, and V seriously thought about marching over and punching that angel in the junk.

But for all V knew, the fidiot was wearing a solid gold jockstrap.

Behind his desk, the King was smiling. "You know, normally I don't miss my sight. This is not one of those fucking times."

"He's nakey," Rhage supplied helpfully. "Well, half-nakey, and it's the business half that's out in the breeze if you get my drift. And can I just say, it's so good not to be on the receiving end of—"

"My little mermaid!"

"How's your water hose—"

"Harpoon—are you, Hollywood?"

"Okay, what does that even mean," Rhage muttered. "And all of you are motherfuckers—every single one—"

"All right," Wrath said. "Enough. V, what you got?"

"One meat, one veg, and a side of pissed off," someone cracked. "And a knitting addiction he refuses to come clean about."

The King put an end to it by throwing his fist into his desk—but he was still smiling. "V. What."

Before V launched into the report, he thought about telling them all to kiss his ass. But considering he had both his buck and that ass exposed, he was worried someone might take him up on the offer—and then he'd have to kill them. Which would get messy. After all, he was willing to do Fritz a solid, but there were more effective ways to create work for that *doggen* and his staff.

Besides, George, the King's golden retriever, got worried when people yelled too much and got rowdy. The dog was already leaning into his master's leg. Real violence broke out around him and they were liable to have to send him to counseling.

V got serious. "The civilian who was attacked last night stated that when he shot at the shadow, his bullets were ineffective. That was not my experience. When I shot at the one that came at me, my bullets caused damage. I couldn't reconcile this—until I was up at the Sanctuary just now. I put my hand into the water, and the remnants of my wound healed like that." He snapped his fingers. "And that's when it dawned on me. Our bullets have water from the Sanctuary in them. Those hollow tips that I fill for all of you, that's the difference. And it's a material one, evidently. Because without that little booster shot of the holy-holy, those fucking entities can't be slowed down—and if they get you? You're Norman Reedus with the bad things in the afterlife."

The Brotherhood had always treated their bullets in such a way, going back for a hundred years. It had helped against the slayers—and clearly it did the same with the shadows.

"I'm going to see about increasing our ammo supply," he said. "I want all of us to be prepared. The aftermath of those attacks—I don't want any of you like that. I don't want *me* like that."

There was a grumbling of agreement, and then Wrath spoke up. "Where can we buy hollow tips in bulk without the humans getting up in our asses?"

"I got this," V concluded. "Don't worry, my Lord. I'll take care of everything."

"Good. And, Phury, let's talk about that little book problem." The King looked around. "I think we know now where the shadows came from. But we don't know who the fuck was up there when they shouldn't have been."

Down in the training center, Jane was just coming out of the office's glass doors, when she heard a patient alarm start going off. Falling into a jog, she burst into one of the inpatient rooms—and was surprised to see Sola standing next to her grandmother, who was in the bed.

"Well, hello," Jane said as she went around and checked the monitors while silencing them. "How are we doing?"

Mrs. Carvalho, Jane thought. Manny had texted her about the admit.

Jane smiled at Sola and then refocused on the patient. "Looks like you've had an episode of elevated heart rate. How are you feeling? Dizzy? Nauseated?"

Mrs. Carvalho lifted her chin. "Tell her out. I no—what is word—no consent to her here. Tell her go. Right now."

Jane looked back and forth between the two women. Sola was every bit as stone-faced as her grandmother, the younger woman's eyes locked on the floor, her arms crossed over her chest.

When nothing but a boatload of awkward silence followed, Jane cleared her throat. "Even though I may have intruded on something personal here, I'd like to examine you, Mrs. Carvalho. You're due for—"

"That is fine. She leaves, though. Go. Go! Stupid girl."

There was a further commentary in Spanish, and Jane was glad she couldn't translate it. She was pretty sure there were some very private things in there—things that had nothing to do with medical situations, and therefore had nothing to do with her.

"Listen," Jane hedged. "I'm just going to go get my stethoscope and give you two a brief moment. When I get back, though, if this is not resolved"—she glanced at Sola—"I'm going to have to ask you to leave, unfortunately."

"Do it now," the grandmother ordered.

"I'll be right back," Jane murmured.

As she stepped out of the room, she jumped. Assail was coming out of the break room and buttoning his shirt up at the same time.

"Is she okay?" he asked frantically. "Marisol's grandmother?"

Hmm, Jane thought. Maybe the couple had been caught in flagrante?

"I think so. I just need to check her out."

After he finished tucking in his shirttails, he seemed at a loss. "I hope . . . well, I hope all is okay."

"Why don't you go in there?" Jane smiled. "I think there might have been a family argument or something. Maybe you can help smooth it over."

"I doubt that," the male said with sadness. "I seriously doubt that."

Jane frowned. "Hey, after I'm finished in there—assuming nothing is going south—how about I do our exam? And Ghisele is coming down to feed Luchas. I'm sure she'll oblige for you—"

"I'm fine. But thank you—"

"That wasn't really an offer," she said gently. "More like a plan we're going to work on together. You're still my patient, even if you're doing great."

When he just shook his head and disappeared back through the break room door, Jane decided that it was a full moon even if the calendar didn't know it. People be cray tonight.

As she went to reenter Mrs. Carvalho's room with her stethoscope, somehow she was not surprised that Sola was marching out like she had lost an argument. And the woman was so upset, she didn't seem to be aware of what was in front of her—so they ran into each other.

"Oops, sorry," Jane said as she reached out to steady Sola. "My fault."

The other woman jumped back so fast and so far, she nearly put herself through the concrete wall across the corridor.

In fact, she shrank back in fear, her eyes panicked, her face pasty as hell, her body shaking.

Okay, Jane thought. Sola's grandmother was elderly and had had a fainting spell of some kind, but she had no acute issues that Manny had been able to isolate—so this high emotion was completely out of place. And considering what Sola had already been through coming here and standing by Assail when he'd been so compromised . . . there was really only one explanation, wasn't there.

"He told you," Jane murmured. "About what he is. Didn't he."

One of Sola's hands dove into the open collar of her fleece, and she outed a small gold cross. "Stay away from me. Just stay away—"

"That doesn't work, FYI." Jane gave the woman a sad smile. "Makes for great scenes in movies and books, though. They're not soulless, god-less, or immortal. Trust me, I've seen more love here in this world, more devotion—and tragically, more death—than I ever did on the human side."

Sola blinked. "Wait . . . what?"

"I'm not a vampire." Jane flashed her flat canines. "See? No points. Never had 'em, never will."

Of course, it was best to keep quiet about the whole ghost thing. That was not going to be helpful information to share at this moment.

"What—how . . . why are you here?"

Jane shrugged. "I fell in love with one. And he fell in love with me." *And then I died and his mother brought me back to life—it's great to have demigods as in-laws.* "I live here now."

Sola put her hands to her face, as if she were trying to reassure herself that she hadn't lost her mind. "I don't understand any of this. I don't understand how . . ."

"It's a hard transition, I'm not going to lie. It was hard on me. But I'm not the only human here—Manny's one."

"Dr. Manello?"

"Mmm-hmm. He's my brother-in-law, actually. Mated to Vishous's sister, Payne. Manny's just as human as you and I. And then Rhage's mate, Mary—"

"Rhage. The big blond man."

"Male. They go by the word 'male,' not man." Jane glanced at the closed door they were in front of. "Look, let me make sure your grandmother is stable. And then how would you like to go for a little stroll with me. We can just talk." She put her hands up. "You can trust me. I took the Hippocratic oath—I am sworn to do no harm, okay?"

It was a long, long while before Sola answered. And when the woman did, it was with a short nod of the head.

"Stay right here." Jane took her phone out of her white coat pocket. "I'm going to text Manny and tell him we'll be back in a bit—assuming your grandmother is all right. Then I'm going to break protocol and try to tell you what's going on down here."

FIFTY-TWO

"No," Phury was saying up in Wrath's study, "I don't know the book's origins. I've spoken to Amalya and she told me she would look into it further. Now, what is clear is that . . ."

As Phury continued to talk about the missing tome, Vishous went to get a hand-rolled and cursed as he patted his muscle shirt. And then the heating came on and he caught a cold draft on his ass cheeks that turned him into a grower, not a shower. Just as he was eyeing the exit, and wondering if he maybe could go grab a throw rug from the hall and use it as a kilt, Butch sidled over and took off his fleece.

"Here, my man. Use this."

"Thanks, true."

The cop nodded and leaned back against the pale blue wall. "Welcome."

V tied it around his waist, using the body to cover his cheeks, and the long sleeves to hang in front of his hey-nannies.

"So we find the book," Wrath announced. Like that was going to be as easy as locating a can of franks and beans in a supermarket's Shit-

Through-a-Goose aisle. "If it tells you how to manifest these things, it probably has a way to get rid of them, right."

Not a question. More as if the King had decided how this was going to go. And Vishous liked that in a leader. He just had a feeling they weren't going to get lucky on this one.

Then again, he was the only asshole without pants on in the room, so . . .

"Last item," Wrath announced. "Turns out there was a complication with that civilian who was killed last night."

"Other than the fact that he woke the fuck up after he died and tried to eat Vishous?" someone piped in.

"Is that where your bottoms went—"

"Not the complication I'm talking about," Wrath said sharply. "Saxton, how about you tell the group what's doing."

The King's solicitor stepped out of the crowd. Saxton was dressed not in the garb of the sword, but that of the pen, the male's trim figure sporting a tweed suit the color of the Highland moors, a cravat at his throat.

Given that everyone else, except for V, was in black leather and weapons, he was like a *GQ* model walking into an MMA fight.

"Thank you, my Lord." Saxton bowed to the assembled, his blond head dropping low. "The civilian who died last evening was named Whinnig, son of Stanalas. He and his bloodlines, on both sides, are members of the *glymera*, his *mahmen* having passed at his birth, may she rest unto the Fade. Although the attack was clearly random, it has created a trusts-and-estates issue. Whinnig had been recently named the sole heir of Groshe, his *mahmen*'s brother. I was in the process of settling things, having run into conflict with Groshe's second mate, Naasha."

"The one who had the blood slave," Wrath interjected. "Who died."

Saxton cleared his throat. "The house, as you recall, was burned down that evening."

As the solicitor quieted so that the others could fill in the blanks— namely that Assail and Zsadist had gone in there and not just lit the fire, but settled the score with that female for what she had done to Markcus, the poor kid—V wondered why the hell this mattered.

They were talking about the war here, not domestic issues among the upper classes.

"The estate is very sizable," Saxton continued. "And again, Groshe had provided for Whinnig in favor of his mate, Naasha. She had been prepared to contest the will given her long association with the deceased."

V cracked his neck and decided if the damn attorney didn't get to the point, he was going to have to sneak out for a cig. And pants.

"She was aided in this endeavor by her paramour at the time, Throe." Muttered curses paused the solicitor. "Her own death, however, superseded these ambitions—"

"Where did that piece of shit Throe end up," Vishous asked. "Other than coincidentally in that alley next to the first shadow attack?"

Saxton cleared his throat. "We believe he is residing as the paramour of another member of the *glymera*. It is not a dissimilar arrangement to that which he had with Groshe and Naasha—namely, an elderly *hellren* with a younger *shellan* who is not getting . . . adequate attention . . . shall we say, in some regards."

Saxton did not need to mince words in this crowd, V thought. The guy should just lay it out that Throe was a banger of trophy wives, true.

"So he moved on when that funding stream dried up," somebody muttered.

"Or, put another way," another chimed in, "whatever his faults, at least he's not into necrophilia."

"Anyway," Saxton gently re-steered, "with the death of Whinnig, Groshe's estate will go to his secondary heir."

A strange ripple went through V, his tuning fork struck, and he braced himself for a portent—

All at once, a vision of a gracious Southern mansion, the kind with plenty of porches and live oaks with Spanish moss hanging off of them, barged into V's mind.

"Who's his next heir," he heard himself demand.

Saxton cleared his throat again. "It is Murhder, formerly of the Black Dagger Brotherhood."

Absolute. Fucking. Silence.

For once, no one made any cracks. But there were also no curses. No one even moved or breathed.

Finally, Vishous closed his eyes and shook his head. "Sonofabitch."

Saxton took the comment as the cue to drop the other shoe. "Legally, I am required to give Murhder notice of his inheritance, and as I have no phone numbers or email addresses for him, it appears as though I will have to go down and see him in person."

"You do not want to have contact with him," Rhage said grimly. "That's a bad idea. I love the brother, but he's completely insane."

There was no levity in Hollywood's voice—and nor should there be. In the history of the Black Dagger Brotherhood, only one male had ever been removed from the roster for losing his mind, and Murhder held that illustrious distinction.

V shifted his stare to another side of the study. John Matthew was listening intently, but it seemed to be out of professional duty.

Did the guy have any idea that they were talking about Xhex's ex?

Shit. Things were so about to get complicated.

"You don't go alone," V said. "Some of us will go with you."

"No." Wrath shook his head. "If any brothers show up down there, he'll think we're hunting him and he could attack. Saxton and Ruhn will go and speak to him. Send a letter to the addy first, and then go— so he's got some warning. Besides, it's good fucking news. Who doesn't want to be rich."

"Someone who's clinically goddamn insane." V headed for the door. "'Scuse me, but if I don't go have a smoke, my head is going to explode."

"Put some pants on," somebody called out.

Vishous flipped whoever it was the bird as he marched the fuck out of that study and dematerialized down to the foyer. Stepping through the vestibule, he walked right out into the snow, with only Butch's fleece and a muscle shirt on.

He didn't even feel the cold. Which was what too many pieces of WTF news did to a guy.

Passing by the winterized fountain, and then the lineup of cars, he went to the Pit's front entrance and let himself in. Before the heavy weight even closed, he was at his desk, lighting a hand-rolled, and then he was leather'd up, shitkicker'd, and gun-gathered. He was almost back out the door, with plenty of cigs in his pockets, when his phone went off with a text.

As he saw what it was about, he muttered, "Mother*fucker*."

As Sola stood in that concrete corridor, she wasn't sure she wanted to go anywhere with the doctor. All she knew was that she couldn't stand being where she was, her grandmother wouldn't let her in that room, and she couldn't leave the facility without the older woman.

Screw thinking this facility was the government's. These people weren't just outside of the law, the law didn't even apply to them.

Vampires?

As the word ricocheted around her head, Doc Jane came out. "Everything looks good right now. But that spike means we want to watch her a little longer. We need to make sure she's stable before we release her."

Sola stared at the woman's face, tracing everything from her hairline to her nose, her eyelashes to her chin. She wasn't sure what she was looking for, but she knew one of the problems she now had was why the hell she'd hadn't known that Assail was a—

"Come on," Jane said quietly. "Let's take a walk. You need to get out of here for a minute. I know exactly where your head is at, and it is a really tough place."

It was the understanding and the compassion being offered that set Sola's feet into motion. She was so confused right now, and the idea that someone, anyone, had walked this absolutely fucking bizarre path her life had veered off onto was . . . well, not a relief, exactly. Because her situation was still the same. But at least she wasn't totally alone.

Jane took them down into an office that looked—well, perfectly normal. Like the kind you'd see in a school. A business. A home when the person worked out of their house.

There was a chair. A desk. Cabinets. A phone and a lamp. An overhead fixture with fluorescent lights in it.

As Jane opened the door to what appeared to be a supply closet, Sola shook her head at all the essentially average—and decided it was just like Assail. On the surface, nothing seemed different or unusual. But the underlying purpose, the truth beneath the appearance of "usual," was a wormhole from which there was no escape.

Vampires. In Caldwell—

Shit, they had to be other places, too. All over the world—

"Through here, Sola," Jane prompted.

Sola followed the command on autopilot, her higher reasoning too engaged on the extent and implications of everything to concern itself with why she was walking into a shallow space of shelves full of pads, pens, and printer cartridges. But then the back wall, which certainly looked to be solid, opened to reveal a dark space.

"Nothing will hurt you," Jane said. "Come on."

Sola stepped through . . . and found herself in a tunnel. A . . . tremendous tunnel that was big enough to drive two SUVs side by side through, and long enough so she had absolutely no sense of where it ended in either direction.

"I'm not supposed to do this, but I don't care." Jane started walking off to the left. "It's not going to hurt anyone."

Sola fell into stride with the woman and put her hands in her fleece's pockets. She looked around incessantly even though the walls were smooth and unadorned, the floor was concrete and nothing else, and the rows upon rows of ceiling lights were just the identical boxes of fluorescents over and over again.

"The species has existed for as long as humans have been on the planet," Jane said. "They're an evolutionary offshoot of us—or, depending on who you ask, they were created by the Scribe Virgin as a superior species. For me, as a scientist, I reconcile the two creation theories by believing that the mother of the race probably interjected a little of herself at a certain time in human history, introducing a variation to our double helix that took things in her direction."

"The Scribe Virgin?" Sola asked weakly.

"My mate's mother, actually. But that's a story for another time."

They came up to a shallow set of stairs that led to a steel door with a pass-code pad next to it—but Jane just kept going.

"The thing is," the woman continued, "you've got to ask yourself why all the vampire myths? Everything has a basis in truth—and the two species have been coexisting and interacting for eons. Vampires, however, don't want to be known. They have no interest in courting notice—they have enough to worry about with the Lessening Society."

Sola glanced over at the woman. "Lessening . . . ?"

"It's the enemy. The Omega has been trying to eliminate the vampire race for centuries. It's a family thing—again, long story." Jane shrugged. "I found it all hard to believe, too, trust me. It's also very scary to learn that something you thought was only a Halloween joke is in fact just like you and me. Except with fangs, of course."

As they came up to a second set of shallow steps, Jane paused. "The thing you have to remember is that they only want to live their lives in peace. They're like all of us in that regard. They want to grow up, and fall in love, and settle down—have a family. Deal with the ups and downs of life. They keep themselves separate because, let's face it, as much as the human race tries to pretend otherwise, at its core, we are self-interested, dangerous, and unreliable. We can't even treat each other with respect and tolerance—and vampires are a micro-minority."

Jane turned away, did something, and a bolt shifted free with a clunk. Then they were leaving the tunnel for a small stairwell that opened up into a . . .

Sola recoiled.

It was a wood-paneled hallway . . . that was full of clothes. No, really, she thought. She was looking at racks of what seemed to be— yes, they were men's clothes—and the suits and slacks, shirts and jack- ets, were hanging on a series of metal department-store racks that ran the distance of the tall, thin space.

"Don't mind Butch's wardrobe. He tries to keep it in his and Ma- rissa's room, but it's just gotten to be too big. We've learned to live with his shopping addiction."

Jane went to the left again and Sola hurried to catch up, although it wasn't like there was far to go.

It also wasn't as if she were walking into a Vincent Price–worthy Gothic mansion or anything. Nope, this was just a simple house. A perfectly normal single-story kind-of-cabin-ish place, with an open space and a galley kitchen in the front, and what was clearly a couple of bedrooms in the back—

"A foosball table?" Sola murmured.

"Butch, V, and Rhage love to play." Jane went into the little cooking area. "How'd you like some non-caffeinated herbal tea? I think you've had enough jolts for this evening, don't you agree?"

Sola didn't answer, but went over to check out a desk full of com- puters . . . and then the black leather sofa . . . the rug . . . the lamps . . . the coffee table with copies of *The New England Journal of Medicine, Sports Illustrated,* and the Sharper Image catalog on it . . .

"I'll take that as a yes," the woman said as she started filling up a kettle.

"May I sit down?"

"I think that would be a wise idea, my friend."

Sola was careful as she put her weight down on the sofa—but as it felt like a normal couch under her butt, she realized she was being weird.

So normal, she thought. It was all so . . . just average and everyday.

She must have sat there for a while, because suddenly a steaming mug of something that smelled divine was in front of her.

"Try this. Lavender and rose hips and wonderful things." As she glanced over, Jane sat down and took a sip from her own mug. "It's very calming."

Sola took the thing and drank from it, and as the warmth hit her belly, she worried for a second she was ingesting some kind of brew. But when, ten minutes later, she was perfectly fine, she felt foolish.

Sola turned and faced the doctor. "The ghost peppers. God—now it makes sense."

"I'm sorry?"

Sola stared into her tea. "Ehric and Evale . . . they, ah, they were able to eat ghost peppers like they were just potato chips. You remember? I couldn't understand why they didn't end up doubled over and drooling from the pain."

"They are anatomically very different from us. They have six-chambered hearts, for example. Their pregnancies last eighteen months. They need to feed—"

"Feed?" Sola said.

"A vampire has to take the blood of the opposite sex on a regular basis to stay strong. So yeah, they do have fangs for a reason, but not because they are trying to kill innocent virgins or 'convert' people. You can't get 'turned' into one. You either are a vampire or you aren't—well, that's not entirely true. Half-breeds do happen, but they are rare and the rules are even stranger for them. They tend to have a hodgepodge of characteristics from both species."

Sola reached up and touched the side of her throat. "Is that why Assail . . ."

"Did he try and take your vein?" When she nodded, Jane said, "It's an instinct in the bonded male. He must be horrified, but he no doubt couldn't help it—especially if he was aroused at the time."

"Wait . . . bonded?"

"When a male finds his mate, he bonds. It's very different than the whole fall-in-love thing humans do. Vampire males kind of click into place with a particular female, and when that happens, they're like that for life. They emit a bonding scent—which fortunately smells faaaantastic—and they want to take your vein. It's their instinct. Oh, and God help anyone who screws with their female. They will kill without hesitation and with very little provocation. They can be dangerous."

Abruptly, Sola thought back to her getting free from Benloise's kidnapping. Assail had stayed behind . . . and then somehow magically met them all at that rest stop on the highway later. And yes, when he had gotten in the car, there had been blood dripping from his chin.

He had killed to protect her, she thought. To protect . . . what he thought was his.

"I'm not going to lie to you and tell you that living on this side is easy," Jane said. "I mean, it's a violent, war-filled life, what between the Lessening Society and now . . . well, there's a new threat, we think. And even if you can get past all of that, you still have to handle the normal stuff in a marriage." The woman laughed softly. "Trust me, there are all kinds of things that people have to work out and love each other through, and that's true whether you're human or vampire. But I can tell you, I'm happier now than I've ever been. And I'm with the right male. V's not perfect, and neither am I, but we love each other—and at the end of the day, the soul's need to connect is what it is."

"I can't believe I didn't know." Sola sat back. "I mean, now that I think about it . . . there were so many clues."

"The brain has a way of confirming its own hypotheses. It's how we function in our world. That which fits within our definition and perspective of our existence is retained, if not amplified. That which does not is either rationalized or cast aside until an event so great or profound occurs that we must rethink everything."

Like your boyfriend coming out as Dracula, Sola thought.

And then she frowned. "Wait, so that other nurse . . . Ghisele?"

"Assail has taken her vein as he's recovered, yes. She's a Chosen, so her blood is especially pure and powerful. It's why he was able to re-bound so fast."

"Oh, great," Sola muttered. "So he cheated on me as well—"

"He didn't have sex with her. Absolutely not. Feeding in those con-texts is just like a blood transfusion. It's a medical event, not an inti-mate one. Vishous has to do it with someone of his own species. Rhage, too. Payne—because she can't get the strength she needs from Manny. It's necessary, but unpleasant for them, because they would always rather be with their mate. With us."

There is no "us" for me, Sola thought.

She sat forward and put her mug on the coffee table. "Well, it doesn't matter."

"Are you sure about that?"

Sola stared straight ahead without seeing anything. "Assail's going to wipe my memories, he said. Make it so all this"—she motioned around the room—"doesn't exist. Assuming that is possible."

"It is."

At the sad tone in the woman's voice, Sola refocused on the doctor. "How do you know?"

"Vishous did that to me. He took . . . my memories from me. But fate had other plans for the two of us, thank God." The other woman frowned. "The amnesia thing is the standard procedure if a human gets too close. It's the reason vampires have been able to lay low as success-fully as they have. But it doesn't have to be like that."

"When it comes to me, it does." Sola shook her head. "I'm out of here. In fact, I would leave now if my grandmother would let us. I can take care of myself and my own. I don't need this—and I don't need him."

As she laid that out there, she meant each and every word. This whole thing was so far and away more than she could handle, it was on a whole different planet.

She was going to get gone the second she was able, and she was never going to look back. And hey, if Assail did what he said he was going to, she wouldn't remember any of it. So she wasn't going to have to worry about all this confusion, panic, and scrambling sense that reality was not nearly as concrete and settled as she had always thought it was.

She also didn't have to worry about missing him.

Not that she would have anyway.

Nope. Not at all.

FIFTY-THREE

As Vishous materialized downtown with Rhage, he knew what he was riding up on before he was even fully present.

Yup, there was a civilian down in the dirty snow, writhing in pain, with no visible marks or tears on his clothes and no scent of blood in the air. The new twist was there was another male with him—who looked as though he had seen a ghost. Natch.

"We-we-we were just walking along, heading for the club," the guy who was on his feet said. "It came from out of nowhere. It was like a shadow—it was . . . and then it was just gone. After it attacked him, it just disappeared . . ."

V knelt by the injured male and captured the pinwheeling arm. "We're going to help you, buddy. We've got help coming."

He looked around as Rhage stepped in close to the witness and tried to calm things down. The alley was not off the beaten path at all. It was a pass-through between clubs, and there were pedestrians of the human and nosy variety walking by just out there on the four-lane street proper.

"Please . . . I'm dying . . ."

V refocused on the civilian who had been attacked. "I gotchu. You're going to be fine."

That last one was a lie, he feared.

"I'm dying . . . I can't see anymore . . ."

Fuck. If this kid turned out like the last one did, how in the hell were they going to isolate that?

A scattering of laughter had V glancing over his shoulder. Four human women came around the alley's corner, the drunken bunch walking in an intertwined lineup, as if they were functioning as their own crutches. As their sloppy feet tripped and slid in the snow, their giggles were the kind of thing that made V want to outlaw drinking for the human race.

"Oh! Someone had too much!" one of them said, pointing to the civilian.

"Tipsy, tipsy!"

Giggling. More giggling and pointing. More stupid fucking comments from the Instagramming set about someone who just happened to be dying.

Vishous nearly got up and yelled, *Hashtag that, you bitches.*

What kept him quiet was the fact that, for once in their Snapchat lives, they didn't get a phone out to document the scene. They were just too drunk and high, and as much as he really wanted to tell them off, he wasn't about to waste his time on non-criticals—although at sunrise, when he lay his little fucking head to sleep, he was going to put some curses on them: five-pound unexplained weight gain—in the left butt cheek only; accidentally deleted social media accounts; spray tans that turned into raging cases of dermatitis.

He'd wish them all an STD, but they were probably going to have that covered by the end of the night on their own nickel.

V turned back to the patient and prayed like hell Manny's driving skills held up. "Just hang with me—"

"I can't breathe . . . I'm . . . not . . . breathing . . ."

The civilian's chest began to pump up and down, the inhales and exhales so congested that they were like whistles.

"Rhage," V hissed. When his brother looked down, V nodded his head toward the civilian. "Give us some space. *Now.*"

"What's happening?" the male asked. "Is he—is he dying? What's going on?"

Thank fuck Hollywood took the direction and ran with it. With quiet reassurances, he drew the friend out of the alley and around the corner—which was going to spare the male what happened next.

Or what V worried was coming.

"I don't . . . feel . . . right," the injured guy was saying. "Something . . . happening . . ."

V released the hand he'd been holding and discreetly unholstered his gun. With efficiency, and without having to look because he'd done it so many times, he took a suppressor off his belt and fit it on to the muzzle.

He did not take his eyes off the male as the last breath was exhaled.

"You're okay, buddy," he said roughly. "You're going to be just fine . . ."

Even though death had come, he wanted to reassure the poor sonofabitch.

And as he promised, Vishous was ready with the gun when, some ten minutes later, the body jerked once . . . twice . . . and woke the fuck up as a demon.

Before the undead could get its groove on, V put the gun to its temple and squeezed off three rounds right into the brain. There was no noise, other than the flopping of the arms, and only he, with his vampire sense of smell, caught the whiff of the gunpowder and fresh blood in the cold, cold wind.

Praying for stillness was not what you usually went for with a corpse. But as V waited to see what happened next, he was hoping like fuck that nothing moved. That there were no twitches. No jerks. No jiggles.

When two good solid minutes of statue passed, he put his weapon away with the suppressor still in place, and then snagged a knit cap that he kept on him.

He put the thing on the kid's head to hide the bullet wounds and then whistled. Just as Rhage and the friend came back into the alley,

Manny pulled the mobile surgical unit around at the far end and trundled down.

"Is he dead?" the civilian asked. "Oh . . . God . . . is he dead?"

Five stories directly above the scene, Throe stepped away from the lip of the roof and addressed his shadow. "You did very well. Now off you go."

As he made a waving motion, the entity disappeared into thin air, leaving nothing in its wake—and Throe once again peered over the edge of the building to the alley down below. A large RV had shown up, and Vishous—yes, the Brother with the goatee was named Vishous, if he recalled—gathered up the body and carried it quickly into the belly of the vehicle.

Rhage, the blond Brother, put his arm around the shoulders of the weeping civilian. And then the pair of them dematerialized.

Throe stayed where he was as the Brotherhood's presence rumbled off.

They had to be on to his plan, he thought. Why else would Vishous have killed the injured civilian? The Brother had drilled three bullets into that head, and then Rhage had left with the other one, as if he were going to strangle, stab, or shoot the male.

They were controlling the situation through elimination. Making sure no one could talk about the attacks. Hindering Throe's progress toward social disruption.

"Damn it," he muttered.

And what if they know of his identity?

Filled with frustration, he paced around the ductwork and mechanicals, trying to think if he'd done anything to give himself away—then again, if the Brotherhood knew or suspected it was him, they would come and find him. It wasn't as if he were hiding himself at that mansion he'd taken over.

Of course, that could create a problem considering he'd murdered the owner and his too-young *shellan*. Sooner or later, he was going to have to account for their whereabouts—but he had a plan in place for that.

Tropical vacations, you know. Especially given that the couple had a geriatric half whose bones ached in the cold. Not a foolproof explanation, but it would buy Throe enough time to create sufficient chaos in the race that the last thing anyone would be worried about was the whereabouts of the mismatched pair.

Assuming the Brotherhood didn't continue to contain that chaos.

Anger rose in the back of his throat, tightening his airway such that he wanted to scream it free. But then he calmed himself and refocused on the positives. The Brothers would not be able to make this all go away—if they killed enough members of the aristocracy, sooner or later they would be discovered and that would work well in Throe's plans. Further, he had made an important refinement in this attack, one that had been an inspired tweak if he did say so himself.

It was better to target one of a pair. That way, there was a witness uncompromised by injury, with a clear recollection of events and a voice that was going to require expression.

Unless the Brotherhood eliminated them.

Then again . . . maybe they would not. Wrath seemed to have standards for behavior now.

Well, Throe would find out, either way. And perhaps it would be to his advantage. After the previous night's exercise, he had waited for testimony of the attack to appear—but the only thing that had come was a statement of the death from a half-brother he had been unaware of Whinnig possessing. All he had known about the son of Stanalas was that he had managed to walk off with Groshe's money—which should have been Throe's for all he had done to service Naasha's endless demands.

Yet there had been no details about the shadows shared. Just a listing on one of the race's Facebook pages that the family was *requesting privacy during this time of grief.*

Stupid fucking discretion.

Well, he'd fixed that—or tried to. No *glymera*, this time. Just two regular civilians that he'd had to wait to go by, sure as a deer hunter in a stand had to be patient. And then they had arrived—and he had sent his shadow down to do what it did.

At least his entities were functioning well. They had no sense of self or purpose other than the commands he gave to them—so there was no disgruntlement or disagreement as Throe sent his shadow to kill the male on the right, but not the left. And when he'd been comfortable with how much injury had been meted out, he called the thing back with every confidence the order would be followed at the instant the mental thought was sent in its direction.

And it had been.

If only the rest were going so obligingly.

As he felt his impatience ramping up, he knew he had to gather himself. This was no good, this agitation. Besides, these one-on-one attacks, although important, were not the bigger step he was going to take. No, that would come soon.

Closing his eyes, he pictured his Book and was instantly calmed, sure as a young to its comfort blanket. All would be well, he told himself—and it wasn't going to take *that* long. He was setting in motion a civil war, and in this era of viral social media and polarized, extreme emotion, he had the wind at his back.

Wrath and the Brotherhood did not stand a chance against him, and they were soon going to find that out. He just needed a couple more of these "random" attacks, and then he was going to stage his finale.

It was so perfect, he impressed even himself, he thought as he disappeared into the night.

FIFTY-FOUR

As Assail sat in the training center's break room, he contemplated all of the evil things he had ever done or thought. He started from the very beginning when he'd stolen from his cousins the sweets made for them by his parents' staff . . . and continued all the way up until he had murdered that female Naasha, who had kept Markcus chained in her basement—as a blood slave.

Oh, wait, he had burned down that house, too. With Zsadist's help.

That Brother, as a former blood slave, had had an abiding reason to participate in the destruction, although Assail had been the one to kill the female as she had sat in her beauty chair, prepared to be pampered.

After which the flames had been ignited, and Assail had resolved to stay in the midst of the blaze. At that time, with Marisol gone from his life, incineration had seemed a very reasonable end to the pain of missing her. The Brother had been determined upon another course, however—and had dragged him out of there.

And so he was here again, he thought as he stared across at the Coke machine. Missing Marisol as if she had died even though she was well enough and very much breathing.

Sitting forward in his chair, he put his head in his hands. Two hours had passed since he had told her, since she had run from him, since the truth he had not wished to share had shattered them as glass beneath the head of a hammer—

As the door opened, he sat up to attention and felt a bolt of something like hope light the cold meat locker behind his sternum.

"Oh, 'tis you, Vishous," he muttered as he sank back in the chair.

"You're about as cheerful as I am." The Brother took out a hand-rolled, lit it, and grabbed an ashtray off a table. "Listen, Jane told me what's going on with you and your girl."

"I don't want to talk about it."

"Good, because that's not why I'm here."

As V settled into the chair next door and crossed his legs ankle to knee, Assail realized there had been a further reason why he'd come clean instead of just wiping away Marisol's memories of him. There had been a treacherous optimism, deep down inside of him, rooted in the place where his love for her had grown from, that she would somehow understand and accept him. That she would rise above the surprise, fear, and disgust, and see him not for his species, but as one who loved her to his very soul.

He should have known better.

"So we've got a problem," the Brother said as he put his ashtray on his knee and tapped his hand-rolled.

Don't talk to me about problems, you sonofabitch, I'm bleeding out over here, Assail thought.

"Yes?" he intoned.

"The species is facing a new threat and I need hollow-tip bullets."

"I believe they are sold at all gun outlets—"

"I need a quarter of a million dollars' worth of them."

Assail blinked. "I beg your pardon?"

"You heard me." V exhaled. "A bulk sale of that size? No way the human authorities won't get their panties in a wad. So I want you to make it happen, just like you did for those guns you—"

"I'm out of that business, I'm afraid." Assail waved a dismissive hand. "I am retired."

"So un-retire."

Assail sat forward again and rubbed the back of his neck as it began to ache. "Forgive me, but as much as I respect the Black Dagger Brotherhood, I am fairly certain I have not been conscripted into your ranks. Neither you nor Wrath may order me to do aught—"

"I just put three bullets into the skull of an innocent kid to keep him from turning into a monster after he died. So you can get off your sanctimonious high horse and help us out, true."

Assail frowned. "Has the Omega endeavored to wield a new weapon?"

"As far as we can tell, that's what's up."

"And hollow tips stop them?"

"If they're dipped in the fountain of my *mahmen*'s private quarters and sealed up they do. Or at least they do a better job than conventional bullets. I want to offer them to the civilian population. Phury and the Chosen have agreed to help me—and even though I hate the idea of those females touching anything that's part of this war, if it'll help people stay alive, I'ma do that shit."

Assail thought of the phone call he'd received on the burner he'd previously used to conduct business with, that female who had inquired as to whether he was satisfied with his shipment. He hadn't thought much of it at the time, but clearly after Benloise's demise, a new supplier had found a way to get into contact.

"All right," Assail said. "But I'd prefer, if you don't mind, to put you in touch with the distributor directly. That way you can get what you want and I can stay out of it."

V took a drag and spoke through the exhale. "Kind of a change for you and your capitalistic mores."

"Money means little to me now."

Vishous frowned, his dark brows sinking low over his bright white eyes, those tattoos at his temple shifting shape. "Yeah. I know that feeling. It sucks when you lose your female."

"I told you, I'm not talking about it."

The Brother got to his feet. "I need you to do what you have to in order to set things up for me and your supplier, but move quick. These attacks are happening regularly."

"Aye. I shall have to get home to arrange things, however. The phone that I use is there."

"I'll have someone drive you out—"

"Actually, just send someone to the house, will you? Tell my cousins that the burner is in the left top drawer of my desk."

"Roger that. Thanks."

As Vishous strode to the door, his heavy boots marking the path with hard strikes, Assail envied the Brother his purpose . . . but it was rather in the way one might view an artifact from an ancient civilization, a leftover from a period in history long, long ago.

An anachronism that was naught but a curiosity without current relevance.

Before Vishous opened the way out, the Brother looked across the break room. "You know, you don't have to strike her memories. You can keep her, if you want. Wrath's a lot more lenient about that shit—and he should be, considering his Queen is a half-breed."

Assail thought about brushing the conversation point off, but instead he shrugged. "A fine piece of advice, and much appreciated. However, my female is summarily horrified by me, so I'm afraid that will not be a course of action which will be available to me now or in the future."

"That sucks."

"You know, I find you have put together two most salient words on the subject."

When Vishous left without any expression of heartfelt emotion or deep, male-tinted commiseration, Assail began to truly like and appreciate the Brother. And as for this new threat to the species? There was a time when it would have at least moderately intrigued him—insofar as it might possibly have affected his ability to garner income. Now, he was providing an introduction only out of a lukewarm obligation to . . .

Hell, he didn't know why he was bothering at all. The idea some innocent had been killed by the Omega was not a newsflash, and he certainly wasn't scared of the Brotherhood retaliating against him if he chose not to honor his word. That fear, after all, would have required some interest in staying alive, and he had none—

As the door opened again, he didn't bother to look up. "More advice? Or another demand."

"Neither," Marisol said.

Assail whipped his head up. "Marisol . . ."

She frowned at that, and he guessed she didn't want her name rolling off his lips ever again. But instead of setting that boundary, she cleared her throat.

"I need to go to your house at some point. I want to get my things and the car. There's no hurry, though. At least not until my grandmother is released."

She was so beautiful as she stood there in her casual clothes of winter, the black fleece bringing out that blond hair she'd given herself, her blue jeans loose and comfortable, her shoes practical for the season.

To him, she might as well have been in a ball gown and draped in jewels—

Abruptly, her weight went back and forth, and she crossed her arms around herself as if the way he were looking at her made her uncomfortable.

"As you wish," he said, lowering his eyes. "Whenever you want to go, just let me know—and if you don't feel comfortable with me coming along, then you may of course go with whomever you wish."

"Except during the day," she said bitterly. "Isn't that right."

After a moment, he replied, "That is correct."

You know, Sola thought, it would be so much easier to be angry if the guy didn't look so hollowed out and defeated.

Across the break room, Assail sat in a chair that, under different circumstances, she would have said was far beneath his standards: For all the time she had known him, he had had the air of a wealthy man. No, it was more than just wealthy. It was rich-for-all-of-his-life, the arrogance and intelligence he had worn along with his handmade clothes the kind of thing that she suspected came only when generation after generation of a family had had tremendous assets.

The kind of thing, for example, that Ricardo Benloise had tried to approximate, but had never quite gotten right.

"I should go," she muttered.

Yet for some reason, she just stood there. As opposed to retreating out into the corridor and . . . well, just standing out there.

She and Jane had talked for only a little bit longer after she had laid down the law about leaving—and then, whether it was that tea or just exhaustion, Sola had leaned back and crashed for a good hour and a half. When she'd woken up, Jane had been texting on her phone and looking worried—and the woman had seemed relieved to be able to come back to the clinic and return to work. Or maybe it was something else.

Who knew, and Sola most certainly hadn't asked. She already had too much banging around in her brain.

"Is there anything else you require?" Assail said without lifting his head.

Yeah, actually, can we go back to when you were just a recovering cocaine addict who had given up a life of crime and the two of us were going to off-into-the-horizon together to live happily ever after with my grandmother?

"I can't decide whether I wish you had told me sooner or not at all," she heard herself say.

"I can answer that." He moved his head back and forth as if his neck were sore. "Not at all would have been better."

"So you like being a liar."

"When it comes to you"—his moonlight-colored eyes looked up at her—"I do not. Which was how you and I have come unto this estrangement. No, I say that rather because you looking at me as if I am a dangerous stranger is a far, far worse reality than even my deepest stretch of paranoia."

"Don't guilt-trip me."

"'Tis a statement of fact. And besides, there is no guilting you about anything. I know you far too well for that—"

"You don't know me at all."

"Indeed? That is an incorrect statement. I believe the correct one is that you *wish* I didn't know you."

His eyes shifted away and yet did not seem to light on any concrete object.

"I want to throw things at you," she blurted. "I want to curse you and punch you, and if I had a gun, I would shoot you."

"I can get you a weapon, and there is a gun range down here."

"Do not mock me."

"I am not. Trust me, death is preferable to this state I am currently in."

As he rubbed his palms together, she couldn't tell whether he was trying to warm that which was cold or was regarding with glee the prospect of a grave.

"Do you have any idea how hard this is?" she said abruptly, tears forming in her eyes. "To be here, once again."

Assail looked up in alarm, and she spoke before he could ask anything. "My father . . ." She brushed her cheeks impatiently. "My father was everything to me when I was young. He was my hero, he was my protector, he was . . . my world. He worked outside of the home my grandmother and I lived in, and I didn't see him very often—but when he came to stay with us from time to time and brought us money for food and blankets and clothes, I idolized him."

Well, shit, she thought as her eyes refused to get with the program and dry the fuck up.

"I was twelve years old when I found out what he was doing—what his work was, what he was. He was a thief. He stole things from people and for people—and worse that than, he was a druggie. The shit he gave us? He didn't buy any of it. I found out later it was always handouts he got from shelters or churches. He never took care of us—he just wanted it to seem like that was the case."

Her tears were coming so hard now, she stopped bothering to try to mop them up. "When he got arrested and was put in jail the first time, he sent word to my grandmother in the village we stayed in. He had a stash of money he kept in the walls of our shitty house, and she got it out and gave it to me. She told me to take it to the jail and bribe the officials to let him out."

Sola sniffled hard and then marched off to a napkin dispenser, snapping a bunch free and cleaning herself up.

When she felt like she could continue, she turned back around. "I was twelve years old, walking twenty-five miles on my own with more money than I had ever seen in my life. My grandmother regularly went hungry to make sure I had food—and yet there was all that cash in the fucking walls of that fucking house! And it was for him!" She blew her nose again. "I made the trip. I gave the money over. My father got out—and as we were leaving the jail, I remember him stopping and staring at me."

Sola closed her eyes. "I can still see us, clear as day, standing there together, in the hot sun. I was thinking he was going to break down in front of me and apologize for being what he was. And stupid me, I was ready to forgive him. I was ready to tell him, *Papa, I love you. I don't care what you are. You are my papa.*"

The scene played out in her mind. And all she could do was shake her head. "You know what he said?"

"Tell me," came Assail's rough reply.

"He said he could use me if I wanted to earn some money. You know, to take care of my grandmother." Sola popped open her lids, got another napkin or two, and pressed them into her eyes so hard, her sockets hurt. "Like that wasn't his job. Like that woman who had stood by him all her life was my problem if I wanted her to be. And if I didn't man up, and she starved or got ill as she aged? Then that was an oh-well."

"I am so sorry," Assail said softly. "I am . . . so sorry."

Eventually, she let her arms fall to her sides and pivoted to face him. "I decided to become the very best thief I could be. 'Cuz that's what twelve-year-olds who are scared and alone and need someone, anyone, to help them in the world do. I learned how to steal and break and enter. How to lie and cajole. How to evade the authorities and get jobs done. It was a hell of an education—and I guess I should be grateful that he never tried to sell me as a prostitute—"

The growl that percolated up out of Assail's chest was such a sound of warning, it pulled her out of her emotions for a moment.

"Forgive me," he said as he lowered his head once more. "I cannot help but be protective. It is my nature."

She stared across at him for the longest time. "And that's why I want to hurt you. You were . . . another everything to me. You were my world, up and walking around on two feet. But it was a lie. It was all . . . a lie. So here I am again, reeling from a truth that is too ugly to understand or accept. The only difference is that I'm not twelve, and I'm done with trying to contort myself into someone else's reality. I refuse to do that ever again."

"I understand." Assail nodded his head. "I accept all responsibility, and I will not implore you for a forgiveness you should never have to give."

As a profound silence ushered out all sound in the room, she wished he would fight with her. Argue with her. Give her something to rail against.

This stoic sadness of his was so much harder to handle.

Because it suggested, as much as she wanted to feel to the contrary . . . that this man—no, vampire—might actually truly, deeply . . .

. . . love her.

FIFTY-FIVE

The following morning, Vitoria was sitting across from Detective de la Cruz down at Caldwell police headquarters when her burner phone went off in her purse.

"Would you like to answer that?" he asked her.

"Oh, no, Detective. This is all so much more important. It's probably just gallery business."

He nodded and put a folder on the table between them. "So you understand that you are not a suspect in any of this. You are not even a person of interest."

"That is correct. That is what you've told me."

The man pointed up to the corner of the shallow, utterly unadorned room. "And this is all being videotaped."

She made a show of looking up to the camera and then nodded. "Yes, that's what you told me was going to happen."

"And you have declined to have a lawyer present."

"Why would I need one? My car was stolen. I am a victim."

Detective de la Cruz opened the folder, which turned out to only have a pad of white lined paper in it. "So I'd like to go over a couple of things again, if you don't mind."

As he paused to collect his thoughts—or perhaps to pretend he was—she glanced around the room. It was in dismal shape, the egg-carton soundproofing worn away where the back of his chair hit the wall, the brown carpet pitted and stained, the ceiling tiles yellowed with age. Even the wood top of the table was fake, the grain pattern repeating over and over across its surface.

It was vaguely insulting to think that people who worked in this environment were armed with laws that could send her to jail. If she were going to be threatened like that, it would have been more apt for the police to be housed in a military installation with bulletproof windows, tactical vests, and flamethrowers.

But no, these folks were more like data processors in a company that was about to go under.

"Have you found my car?" she prompted.

"The Bentley was your brother's, wasn't it?" He looked up. "Correct?"

In her head, she cursed the man in Spanish. And then said calmly, "Yes, of course. It was Ricardo's. Forgive me."

"I totally understand." The detective smiled. "So last evening, around what time did you come out and discover that the Bentley was gone?"

"It was right when I called you. Nine o'clock, perhaps? Ten?"

"And you stated the key was in the vehicle."

"I'm afraid I'm a little forgetful. Women drivers. You know."

"Actually, my wife is a better driver than I am. So is my daughter. But that's neither here nor there." He lifted up the pad. "So we did locate the vehicle. Unfortunately, it was involved in a hit-and-run down on Twentieth Street. A police cruiser found it and towed it in."

He took out two color photos, both of which provided different angles of the beautiful car smashed grille-first into a concrete median that went around some sort of road repair work.

"Oh . . . dear," she murmured.

"At this time, we have no suspects in the theft."

"No?"

"But we're concerned the vehicle might have been used in the commission of a crime."

Vitoria made a point of lifting her eyebrows in alarm. "What kind of crime?"

"Do you recall mentioning a man by the name of Michael Streeter?"

She nodded. "Of course. You and I spoke of him. He was the security guard I met after I arrived here in Caldwell."

"He was found dead at dawn."

At this point, Vitoria slowed everything down and made sure she chose her response and words well. The detective, she noted, was giving away no details in an attempt to trip her up.

"Where? What happened to him?" She leaned in. "Do you think he might have taken my brother's car?"

"Why would he do that?"

Vitoria shrugged. "I don't know. He just seemed . . . well, as I told you, he made me very uncomfortable and I wasn't the only one. Margot Fortescue also found him worrisome."

"Well, the car is being carefully dusted for prints. The CSI team is going over it with a fine-tooth comb."

"CSI. Like the old TV show."

"Exactly." The detective sat back. "I imagine we'll find lots of prints of yours."

"Yes, you will." She fanned her hands out. "I drove it for an entire day. Perhaps two."

"I don't blame you. It's a work of art on wheels—or was." There was a long pause. "Do you have any reason to think somebody would want Streeter dead?"

"I am not familiar with him at all. So I can't really say."

"We spoke to his girlfriend. She told us that he dabbled in drug dealing."

"Well, there you go."

"Mmm." The detective sat forward. "You know, I've been either a policeman or a homicide detective for a lot of years. I mean, we're talking decades. And I've developed a sense about things."

"I imagine you would."

"I guess I just think it's a little curious."

"What is?"

He shrugged and pulled the lapels of his sport coat in closer. The jacket was dark gray this time and didn't really go well with his coloring, in her opinion. "Well, your two brothers disappear. And you show up in Caldwell. And suddenly, I've got bodies in different places. Two deaths in the same gallery in how many days? With the only real change that I can see being your arrival."

Vitoria put her hands up to her heart. "I am a woman, Detective de la Cruz. Where I come from, we are not capable of any such things— how can you insinuate I could possibly kill anyone? Much less a security guard who was so much bigger than I am."

"He was shot multiple times at point-blank range. Execution style. Guns are a great equalizer for height and weight discrepancies." He made a steeple out of his fingertips. "And here in the States, women are equals—or at least I treat them as such. So it means they can drive well, and they can stand up for themselves, and they live their own lives. They can also decide to take over a drug ring for themselves, kill off family members, and make people who ask too many questions or get in their way wake up dead. How about that."

Which card to play, she thought. There were a couple of choices.

After a moment, she lifted her chin. "Detective, I have been nothing but accommodating. Your officers are at the West Point house now, as we speak, getting security footage—"

"Well, see, there's a rub on that one. You did let them in, it's true, and we thank you for that. But it turns out the cameras were off, and have been for quite some time. So if you're using that as an example of accommodation, it would go further if there was anything for us to use."

She already knew all this, of course. It was the first thing she had checked when she had gotten back there last night.

"When were they turned off?" she asked.

"We're looking into that."

"I'm sure you'll let me know what you find."

"You can bet your life on it."

Vitoria drew her long hair back and clasped her hands primly in front of herself. "Is there anything else for me?"

"Not right now, no. But something tells me there will be more. And I'm never wrong about these things."

"There's a first time for everything, Detective." She got to her feet. "I also want you to know that I realize you are just doing your job here. I shouldn't take things personally and I won't. You don't have any suspects for either of those deaths, no solid ones, at any rate—or you wouldn't be throwing baseless accusations at me. My conscience is clear. I do not need a lawyer. And you may feel free to call me back down here anytime you like."

"So you think you're leaving, huh."

"Are you making me a suspect? Or . . . how did you say it, a person of interest?" When there was a pause, she smiled at him. "Then I'm free to go, aren't I."

"Do you mind if we fingerprint you before you take off on us?"

It took everything in her not to narrow her eyes and glare at him. "Of course not, Detective. Provided you give me something to wash my hands off with afterward."

FIFTY-SIX

*V*ishous had a plan and not a lot of time. As he sent himself up to the Scribe Virgin's private quarters, he was fully armed, and sporting two empty two-liter plastic bottles of what had been Mountain Dew.

Evidently, there had been a *Saved by the Bell* marathon on during the day and Lassiter had had to keep himself awake for it.

As V penetrated the marble walls, he went right over to the fountain. Yes, he could have used a pair of sterling-silver water pitchers from the dining room. Or crystal flower vases from the second-story sitting area. Or gold urns from the foyer.

But hey, he had rinsed these bitches out in the billiards room before he'd made the trip, and what he needed were containers that held water. There was no reason to turn this into a ceremonial thing.

Getting on his knees, he unscrewed one of the green lids and pushed the open bottle under the surface of the water. The fill-up went well, air bubbles coughing out as the level rose inside the Dew. When things were done, he outed it, capped, and put the thing aside.

Repeat.

The plan was to take this water back to the Brotherhood mansion and get an assembly line going down in the cellar, in the room where he made his daggers. The Chosen who were willing to eyedropper hollow-tipped bullets for him so he could seal them with lead caps would undoubtedly be more physically comfortable up here, but he didn't like the idea of the war invading this sacred space—

The hairs on the back of his neck prickled, sure as if a hand brushed his nape.

Stiffening, he sent his instincts out—and knew that there was someone right behind him.

Knew instantly who it was, too.

Closing his eyes, he shook his head and sagged with defeat. "It's you. Isn't it. She picked you."

As the second bottle finished filling up, he took the thing out of the fountain and slowly turned around.

Lassiter, the fallen angel, stood with his feet planted on the white marble floor. His entire body was lit from within, and stretching out on either side of his torso was a magnificent pair of iridescent wings.

Glowing as he was, he was one of the most beautiful sights Vishous had ever seen, as awe-inspiring as a mountain range, as arresting as a perfect sunset, as broad as the ocean, as high as the heavens.

He was too much to be contained in any kind of form, and V blinked, not because things were necessarily that bright, but because the signals that his optic nerves were sending to his brain were too strong, too many, too resonant.

Lassiter's voice echoed throughout the Sanctuary even though he did not speak out loud. *I bring greetings from your* mahmen. *Rise, and know that you are blessed in this life as you are her son and you are worthy.*

V got to his feet with a mind of shutting those blessings down, fuck him very much. But then he thought of Jane and canned the anger.

Still, he felt compelled to say "I don't believe in my mother."

Belief is not required.

For some reason, that unsettled him. Maybe because it meant some-one else was driving destiny's bus—but like he hadn't already figured that out?

"She doesn't exist anymore. She's out."

That which is not alive cannot die. It is as time, extant and all around whether acknowledged or not.

Abruptly, and against his will, the shit came out, the fucking shit that he didn't want to admit, even to himself . . . the cocksucking shit that had been bothering him ever since he had come up here and found that dumb-ass, emo missive she'd left for him and him alone:

"Why wasn't it me?" he heard himself ask. "If I am her son, why didn't she pick me to succeed her?"

It was the height of narcissism to even wonder such a goddamn thing in passing. To admit it to anyone, much less Lassiter, FFS, made V feel like a candidate for a bitch slap across the crybaby.

Lassiter reached out a hand, but he didn't touch V. He stopped about two inches in front of Vishous's chest.

Even though there was no direct contact between them, a warm feeling lit off inside V's chest and grew in intensity until it suffused his entire being—and him, being him, he thought . . . man, it was going to suck to come down from this high.

Except then . . . he realized that the warmth had a pitch, like a song would, a hum that was specific to one and only one entity he had ever been around.

This was his *mahmen,* he realized. This sense of love enveloping him was . . . her.

She has not disappeared. She is still with us and with you. Lassiter lowered his hand. *And she did not pick you not because she didn't love you, but because she did.*

Even though Lassiter wasn't rocking the glow-motional connection anymore, Vishous could still feel the sensation deep in his bones. And as he pictured the Scribe Virgin's diminutive figure in her black robes, with that white light shining out from under her hem, the warmth re-intensified.

She is in all of us. She missed her creation up here, and when she freed herself, she was able to reenter us. She is not gone—she is back where she started and happiest for it.

At that moment, a movement out of the corner of V's eyes drew his attention to the colonnade in front of his mother's bedroom suite—and when he saw what it was, he was both utterly astonished . . . and completely unsurprised.

It was a black cat. But not just any black cat.

It was Beth, the Queen's black cat. The one she had brought with her to the mansion all those years ago.

As V's stare met its glowing green one, a sacred aura surrounded the feline, and he realized She had been with them all along. From the very beginning, She had been with them . . . right in their midst without them even knowing it.

With a feeling of inevitability and peace, the last of V's puzzle pieces fell into place, the hole that had been vacant filled with an answer to a question he hadn't been aware of asking for all these years.

Yes, Lassiter said, *in spite of her faults, she always loved you and your sister, and now she can show you. And she always loved her creation, too—and now she can show that as well. Therefore, close your eyes and see what is to come as only you can. You must guide the end, do you understand? You shall guide the end—*

"—Vishous? V, wake up, sweetheart—"

V bolted upright in the dark, sweat pouring off his face, chest screaming in suffocation, heart pounding.

Only Jane's voice and scent were able to reach him through his panic, and even then, he wasn't sure what in the hell was going on.

Throwing out a hand, he grabbed on to her and held her close—and as he felt her arms tighten on him, he started to shake. But it was only

a dream, he told himself. What he'd just seen was only a dream—
a weird, fucked-up contortion of him having had a late day, and
Lassiter-binge-watching TV in the billiards room, and finally the car-
bonara served at Last Meal.

"I'm okay," he said into Jane's soft, fragrant neck. "I'm all right . . ."

"You're just fine. Shhh . . ."

She stroked his hair and his shoulders, soothing him until he released the tension in his body. When he finally went limp, he collapsed
back onto the pillows and urged her on top of him.

"What were you dreaming about?" she asked.

The images that came to him were too disturbing, so he shook his
head. "I don't know. I don't . . . I can't think about it."

"Okay. That's all right."

"What time is it?"

There was the sound of covers rustling as she twisted around to see
the clock by her side of the bed. "Almost six p.m. We'll both be late if
we don't get up soon."

"Can we just lie here for a little bit?"

"Absolutely."

V tried to close his eyes, but that was not a good idea as it just
brought the strangeness back. Then again, open and in the pitch-black
didn't work, either.

Willing the lights in their bedroom on, he was instantly calmed
further. Everything was just so prosaic and as-it-should-be that context
came easily—and in the right direction. All was well and normal.

Just a dream.

He looked at Jane. "I love your face."

"I love yours, too." She smiled. "And you're most handsome when
you just wake up."

V leaned and kissed her, and the next thing he knew he was mount-
ing her and penetrating her sex with his own. Which was even better
than the lights coming on, he decided as he began to pump, the pleasure wiping away the dregs of whatever that weirdness had been.

As he started to orgasm, and his female came along with him, he turned his head—

Through the open doorway into the bathroom, he saw that there were two Mountain Dew bottles sitting by the sinks, both filled to the very top, their labels facing out toward him.

"Damn it," he muttered as he squeezed his eyes shut.

Sure, that shit about his mom was fine. But Lassiter, it appeared, was the race's new boss.

Great. Nothing like putting a five-year-old behind the wheel of a car and giving the little shit the car keys.

Big ol' angel wingspans aside, the ride, which had already not been all that smooth, was about to get bumpier than a motherfucker.

FIFTY-SEVEN

ola woke up in total confusion. She couldn't remember where she was, and the remnants of a dream about vampires lingered—

Oh, wait.

That wasn't a nightmare. And yup, she was still in their underground facility, out in the corridor, sitting on the hard floor next to the door to her grandmother's room. Her butt was flat as a pancake, somehow managing to be both numb and painful as a result of cushioning her weight for—what time was it? How long had she been asleep—

All at once, her thoughts slowed to a halt and she looked across the way. Assail was seated in a mirrored pose, his legs stretched out, his head down chin on chest, as if he were asleep, too.

She hadn't heard him come out to sit with her.

Looking around, she found that they were alone together, no medical staff walking about, none of the other people she'd met during her time here in sight, either.

Down at the far end of the corridor, she could just barely see the exit that she'd come and gone out of how many times now?

She thought back to when Assail had brought her here as a patient.

She had been in such rough shape—head injury, shot in the leg, traumatized to all hell and gone. Doc Jane in particular had been so kind to her. Hell, the woman had been kind to her all along—

From above, there was a rhythmic sound, like a machine turning over, and then she felt a warm fall of air hit the top of her head. Glancing up, she measured the vent that was some ten feet overhead. When she lowered her chin, she jumped.

Assail had woken up and was looking at her with those sad eyes of his. When he didn't speak, she cleared her throat.

"I've wanted to ask you something," she said in a quiet voice. "Why don't you just scrub my memories now? I mean, if you can do it, why not simply make all this go away? That way you won't feel as bad."

Why was she worried about where he was at? she wondered.

"I will always feel badly and it would hurt you." He motioned to his head. "If someone has had their memories stripped, but they're around the very thing that has been taken from them, it is very painful."

"Oh."

At that moment, there was a ringing sound and he took out a cheap-looking cell phone. "Pardon me." After she shrugged, he accepted the call. "Hello? Yes. How kind of you. Yes. In person? Where? When?" There was a pause. "How accommodating of you. Fine. I will be there, yes."

He hung up and stared at the phone. "I am going to be putting the Brotherhood in touch with a distributor for arms. I must go and meet with her in person. You mentioned you would like to collect your things. Perhaps we can depart soon and get you ready to go? I do not believe the Brotherhood will allow you to bring your car onto the premises. However, we can drive it out from my house, and pack it somewhere safe, such that you will not have to return to my property ever again."

Assail looked over at her. "You will be free to go as soon as your grandmother is released. Just as you wish. And I promise not to interfere with any of your . . . I will not get in your way."

"Will you be coming back here with me?"

His chest—which was even larger now, it seemed—expanded as he inhaled. "I should be the one to rid you of your memories. I will do the most thorough job because I have been there for so many of your experiences."

"Oh. Okay."

"So would you like to leave with me the now?"

"I should speak to my grandmother first." Assuming the old woman would grant her an audience without trying to hit her with a bedpan. "But yes. Thank you."

"I shall arrange for transport. Excuse me."

As he got to his feet, there were several cracks as if his spine were realigning itself, and then he walked slowly and stiffly toward the office she had gone through with Doc Jane.

Sola watched him go. And was surprised to find that, like him, she was very sad.

Trying not to dwell on that, she dragged herself off the floor and stretched until things resettled into a more functional order. And then she knocked politely on the closed door she had been sitting vigil next to.

"*Vovó,*" she said softly. "May I please come in?"

As Assail emerged from the office, he was grateful for Vishous being so accommodating. The Brother had just woken up, and yet he was willing to skip First Meal and come down immediately to get Marisol to the glass house for her things. Assail had also contacted Ehric and explained what had happened and why Marisol needed some privacy on the property. Thus his cousins were going to take Markcus out for the evening.

Assail didn't want her to have to see all of those males. She'd been through enough.

Although now his cousins were heartbroken, too. It was funny how those two females turned that mansion into a home. Without them, it was just glass walls and a view that mostly couldn't be seen because of the drapes he kept down all the time.

In the end, Assail had decided not to mention the meet-up with the arms dealer to his cousins or to Vishous—because he wasn't sure exactly who he was communicating with. He didn't want to waste Vishous's time if this was an underling—or worse, members of the human-law enforcement agencies on a fishing expedition. And his cousins were frustrated and trigger-happy on a good night. Finding out that they were going to lose what felt like members of the family was not going to help that.

Further, the woman on the other end of the call had requested that he come alone.

So fine, he would go meet her after Marisol was taken care of. And he would return to the training center only when his female was ready to leave.

It wasn't good for her to be stuck seeing him all the time.

And she wasn't his female anymore, anyway.

Just as he was coming up to Mrs. Carvalho's room, Marisol stepped out and rubbed her eyes. He wanted to ask her if everything was all right, but he didn't think she would tell him—and besides, he knew that answer already.

He cleared his throat so she would realize he was there. "We're just waiting for—"

"I'm here," Vishous announced as the Brother came out of the office. "Let's do this. The Mercedes is down here for a wash. We'll take that car."

Vishous nodded at the two of them and then strode by, heading for the exit.

Assail indicated the way forward for Marisol. "After you."

"Thank you."

As the three of them walked along, Assail guessed the formality between Marisol and him was better than anger or sorrow. Fates, when she had cried in front of him, and told him the story of her father, he had never felt so small in his life. To have taken her back to that terrible moment—because he had done something similar—was to put a curse upon her.

When their trio came to the heavy steel door at the end of the corridor, Vishous held things open, and then they proceeded across the parking area to a black S600 that sparkled in the fluorescent lights.

"You're both in the back," V informed them.

Assail opened one of the rear doors for Marisol, and then he went around and got in himself. The sedan was so long, it felt as though the Brother was in a different zip code, and the heat came on quickly, which was a benefit as no one was wearing a coat.

It was quite an ascent until they got up to ground level, and Marisol stared out of the tinted windows even though there was nothing to see.

"So no one knows where you are here?" she murmured. "No one can find you?"

"That's the idea," V said from in front.

"Humans leave you all alone, then."

"Or we make them."

Assail cursed and wanted to tell the Brother to ease up on the aggression. Then again, good luck with that. It would be like trying to get a German shepherd to greet hat-wearing strangers with a rollover-rub-my-belly.

"We'd just be hunted," V tacked on. "So it's a case of survival for the likes of us."

"You don't think you'd be accepted?" Marisol asked.

"How's that immigration policy of yours working out?" When she didn't reply, the Brother muttered, "Exactly."

"Perhaps we should speak of something else," Assail offered.

Like the weather. Sports.

Anyone read any good books lately? he thought to himself.

"So," Marisol said as she turned to him. "Are you two going to that meeting alone?"

"What meeting?" Vishous asked as he looked into the rearview.

"It's nothing," Assail informed the Brother.

Marisol spoke up. "He's meeting with an arms dealer—I thought to put you in touch directly with the supplier?" Her eyes narrowed. "Unless that isn't the case—"

"That's what he's supposed to be doing," V cut in. "I just didn't know it was happening tonight. Or that he was going on his own. Do you trust these people?"

No. "But of course," Assail muttered.

The Mercedes slowed and then stopped. After the Brother put the sedan in park, he twisted around. "You're going to get yourself killed."

"I most certainly will not."

"Who are these people?" Marisol asked. "Wait, did you meet them through Benloise?"

Assail put both his palms up. "I would like to table these discussions for a more appropriate time—"

"I'm going with you," V announced. "I don't give a fuck whether you live or die. What I can't do is lose that connection. You get popped, and I won't get my ammo."

"Are you armed?" Marisol demanded. "Do you even have a knife on you?"

Assail rolled his eyes. "I will get something at the house."

"You sure about that?" she countered.

"Yes."

There was a very long, disapproving silence. And then she blurted, "I'm going, too. I'm going with both of you."

Assail glared in her direction. "Absolutely not. I'm not putting you in any kind of harm's way—"

"But you're more than willing to go to a meeting like that unarmed, guarded by someone who doesn't give a shit about you? Are you insane?"

"I was until you showed up, remember," he said dryly. "And then things got worse after I returned to mental health."

She looked at Vishous. "Do you have any extra guns I can borrow?"

The Brother started to smile. "You know, I like you. But can you shoot?"

"Only to kill," she said grimly. "No, I take that back. If someone doesn't respect me properly, I can get pretty goddamn trigger-happy, and I like places that take a while to heal."

The Brother smiled, flashing his fangs. "Fair enough. You want to assume the risk on his behalf, that's on you. Plus frankly, my other brothers are all out in the field. With those attacks happening every night, it's all hands on deck. If I don't have to pull one of them in on this, that would be great."

The pair of them nodded at each other—and then stared at Assail.

Assail was tempted to point out to Marisol that she didn't want to have anything to do with him. Except yes, he was pathetic enough to beg for a little more time in her company, even if it was in this context. And no, he knew better than to try to dissuade her from the danger.

No one was going to do that, even though the idea of her getting shot at made him considering the merits of insanity with an open mind.

There was just one rub. "The woman won't meet with me if I don't come alone. So this is all a moot point."

"It's a female?" Marisol said.

"Aye." He shrugged. "And now that I think about it, that means both of you will be waiting safely in this car, which I believe is bullet-proof, is it not? Funny, now I'm not as worried about this brilliant idea."

Marisol sat forward in her seat. "Where is this meeting supposed to take place?"

"A warehouse down on Thirtieth Street."

"Benloise had one there. What's the address?"

"Four-four-oh-nine."

"That's it. That's the one he owned."

"You're not going inside, Marisol." Assail looked away to the blacked-out window and measured the dim reflection of her in it. "And I'll be fine."

Actually, he didn't care one way or the other what happened to him. But at least Vishous would keep her safe. That was the important thing.

That was all Assail cared about.

"Let us proceed to my house," he said, "so that we may collect her things. And then let's go to the warehouse and get this over with."

FIFTY-EIGHT

As Sola came up from the basement with her grandmother's suitcase in one hand and her own duffel over her shoulder, she took a last look around Assail's kitchen. There was a stainless-steel saucepan that her *vovó* had used sitting on the stove. The thing was perfectly clean, and the lone standout in the otherwise tidy, put-it-all-away neatness.

Almost as if the thing had been left out as a shrine, and not just to the food.

Ehric and Evale, and that young man—male—were nowhere to be found, and she had a feeling that Assail had told them to go.

She missed them. She wanted . . . to say goodbye to them.

In such a short time, the six of them had formed a little family unit, a ragtag bunch of unrelateds who had bonded in quick order. And as she thought about them living here together under this roof, the strangest sensation hit her in the chest. She didn't want to acknowledge what it was. She really didn't.

But this felt like . . . home.

"May I help you with your things?" Assail asked politely.

"No." She looked back at him. "Thank you. I've got them."

"As you wish." He bowed solemnly. "We will leave your car at a secure place downtown so that you may retrieve it. And worry not. Our staff can go out during the day even though we cannot. So you may depart at dawn, should you wish to."

"All right." Unease rippled through her, but she hiked her duffel higher on her shoulder and shoved the anxiety away. "I guess we go?"

"Yes."

At that moment, Vishous came in from the front of the house. "I gotta give you credit, Assail. You got good toys, true?" Without warning, he tossed something at her. "I think the lady'll like this one."

She caught the gun by the grip and brought it up for a look-see. It was a very nice S&W, actually. Nine millimeter.

"If you want a holster—"

She interrupted Vishous. "I have one in my bag."

"Good deal."

As Assail took no weapons and was given nothing, she assumed he had armed himself. And yet she hesitated. She wanted him to have a rocket launcher on his back. Bulletproof everything. A crash helmet.

"We gonna do this or what?" Vishous said sharply.

"Let's go." Sola headed for the door. "I'll follow you in my car."

The men—males—fell in behind her, and she heard Vishous ask if Assail was going to ride with her.

Before she could answer, he replied, "I believe she would rather be alone. Thank you."

Getting into her cold car, she wasn't so sure of that. Which was a surprise. But it was so emotional, this idea that she really was leaving here. Leaving him. Leaving this whole strange episode in her life—

Okay, she totally needed to let all that go.

The engine was slow to crank over, and the heater started blowing an arctic blast at her feet, so she cut the fan off quick. As she plugged in her seatbelt, she looked over her shoulder at the glass house and remembered coming here for the first time on her skis. She had hidden in and among the trees and tried to get a bead on what was doing inside. And that was when she had noticed the illusion drapes—the furnace coming on inside had ruffled them ever so slightly, causing a disturbance in that which should have been static.

Little could she have guessed what pulling them back would reveal.

Snapping herself to attention, she put the engine in gear and fell in line behind the Mercedes, leaving the house and the peninsula in her wake.

As she took a left to get onto the bridge, she told herself to take a good look at the glowing cityscape up ahead. She had always loved this view at night, the skyscrapers so majestic, their random lights like stars in a fallen sky—and then down below, the river's dark and slow mystery.

She was never coming back to Caldwell.

And God, even though it made no sense, she wanted to cry.

Refocusing once again, she stuck on the Mercedes's tail. They had agreed to leave her car in an open-air lot that Vishous had a pass card to, and as they came up on it, something started to ring in her mind. A warning. A . . .

Shaking her head, she pulled up to the gate and realized she hadn't gotten the card. Before she could put her window down, Assail was on it, coming over and swiping things so that the arm lifted up.

It was as she took a spot right in front that the math added up, and she all but leapt out from behind the wheel without putting things in park.

"Benloise has a sister," she said urgently. "Vitoria."

Assail shrugged. "I did not know that."

"You can't go into that meeting alone. She could be coming for you."

"I don't know if she's who I'm meeting. And besides, why would it matter—"

"You killed Ricardo." Sola stared him straight in the eye. "I know you did. I never asked you, but I know you did. And Eduardo, too. Didn't you. *Didn't you.*"

Assail really wanted to get Marisol back into the Mercedes. He didn't like how exposed they were, and he also wanted to cut off this conversation. But clearly, his female was not budging until they were finished with this subject.

Not that she was his female.

"Marisol"—he indicated the nice, warm, fucking bulletproof Mercedes—"perhaps we may continue this discussion in a more suitable environment?"

"What if she knows. What if she's calling to set you up?"

"Then I will defend myself. Let us get in the car—"

"There are security cameras at the gallery. At the West Point house—"

"We were careful with the latter," he muttered.

"So that's where you killed him? Or was it at the gallery."

"It doesn't matter—"

"I told you, the address you're going to is Benloise's warehouse. I worked for him. I know what he owns. Why are you meeting the supplier on his property if the man is dead?"

"Because that is what I've been instructed to do—"

"You can't go in there—"

"Enough," he cut in sharply. "This is *not* your concern, Marisol. Now get in the goddamn car before we're spotted by *lessers.* You may be human and of no interest to them, but they will sense me and I do not want you to get hurt."

"I'm not going to let you get yourself killed."

But at least she was moving as she muttered this, getting her things out from the back of her car and walking them over to the popped trunk of the Mercedes. And as she put the suitcase and the duffel in, she was speaking in a barrage of Spanish—but he didn't care if she was cursing every bone in his body as long as she *gotinthefuckingsedan.*

When they were finally back in the back, so to speak, she didn't turn to him. She pulled herself forward using one of the headrests in front.

"He's going to die," she announced to Vishous. "She's going to kill him."

"Your grandmother?" the Brother said. "I've heard about her—and yeah, I can feel that. Even if she's in a hospital bed—"

"This is a setup—"

"Marisol," Assail interrupted, "there is no way, even if this is Benloise's sister, that she will know it is me. No way. This is a business interaction through proper channels—and besides, even if it is his sister, she will not be of his nature. She's a female, after all—"

The glare that swung around to him was enough to make him consider cupping his sex in protection.

"Do I look weak to you." It was not a question. "Do I look like I can't handle my shit to you."

Okaaaay, Assail thought. He was probably going to have to recast his rather old-school opinion of the "weaker" sex, wasn't he. His Marisol was certainly not, and never had been, a fainting flower to be insulated from the most minute of inconveniences.

And P.S., he was getting seriously aroused right now, even though that wasn't fair to her.

"Well?" she demanded.

"No, you are not weak." As his voice deepened, he cleared his throat. "You are the most magnificent, powerful force I have ever seen. You can bring me to my knees as no one ever could or ever will again."

She blinked. Then looked away.

In the awkward silence, he studied her profile and wished there was another way for them. Then he dragged himself out of that black hole of disappointment.

"And as I was saying, even if it is his sister, I doubt she will know what transpired. Benloise's remains are well disposed of, and Eduardo's? They were consumed by coyotes, given where we left him. So all is well."

"I hope you're right," she said tightly.

He wanted to tell her that was kind of her, but he kept that to himself. Instead, he switched to the Old Language so she would not understand what he was saying as he spoke to Vishous.

"Pray, if I fall and cannot be revived in this, I ask that you see her safely unto her grandmother and then back out into her world. Strike her memories with care and send her off with a pleasant recollection of all this, something that shall not cause her to suffer any pain. I request this with the utmost respect unto you, and as her bonded male."

Behind the wheel, the Brother looked up into the rearview mirror. With a single nod, he replied, *"It shall be done."*

Appeased, Assail eased back into the seat. The windows were tinted so darkly, he could barely see out, although the streetlamps were light enough to glow as if through fog.

At least he knew she would be okay—

"Vitoria looks like Ricardo," Marisol said tightly. "You'll see it in the eyes and the shape of the face. I never met her in person, but there were pictures of her at his house—the two of them were very close. Do us all a favor, if it's her, just get out of there. Don't assume she won't recognize you. You just . . . you never know."

Assail turned and stared at the woman—and told himself not to feel any hope given that Marisol seemed so worried about him. "All right. I will."

FIFTY-NINE

itoria went to her brother's warehouse in as circuitous a route as she could. She was generally no fan of inefficiency, but she had to make sure that none of Detective de la Cruz's ilk were following her, and it took some time to reassure herself that they were not. When she finally pulled Ricardo's Rolls-Royce into the facility's vacant parking lot, however, she was satisfied she was on her own.

That was the only thing she was satisfied by, though—and not just because that detective was proving to be a Latino version of Columbo.

Looking at the passenger seat beside her, she frowned at Eduardo's journal. Of all the numbers she had called, the man she was meeting was the only one to respond. This was worrisome. She had expected there to be a great hunger for what her brothers had put out on the streets, but she feared that, in the intervening year, the ecosystem had rerouted itself, found other suppliers, and moved on.

Regaining lost business was so much harder than simply stepping into the shoes of a functioning concern.

But she was ready to fight to get back to where things had been.

As she got out of the Ghost, she approved of this location. She had discovered its existence in paperwork on Eduardo's desk, and she could see why it would be a good place to exchange goods for cash. The building's floor plan took a sharp corner, one whole wing extending out from a base, and that formation, coupled with an adjacent structure that appeared to be garage space or storage units that angled in, meant that a private courtyard was formed.

And clearly, that had been cultivated. The privacy, at any rate: The security lighting was all trained elsewhere, a dark pit of anonymity enveloping the center area.

No one could see from the street who was parking. Who was getting out. Who was carrying what. Who was going inside or emerging from the interior.

Quite smart.

Proceeding to the door that had a pass code, she entered her mother's birthday and stepped into the dim, damp interior. No light fixtures came on, but as she turned on the flashlight on her cell phone, she located a switch and flicked it.

Very smart.

All of the windows had been painted black. So there was no way to know anyone was inside.

Vitoria left the door open, using a stopper that was left by the jamb. As was typical of her brother, the interior was neat as a pin and largely empty, although not completely so. Interspersed within the cavernous space, there were large crates, some big as sofas, others the size of cars, even houses. A forklift sat, with the keys in it, off to the side, and she noted, as she walked around, that there was a garage bay at the end for such ungainly deliveries.

So she had been wrong, she thought as she inspected one of the crates and read the address plate. Art for the gallery was actually stored here. This wasn't a place solely for the illegitimate side of things. Then again, her brother had carried on both businesses from the gallery.

And speaking of business, with any luck, this would result in an order—

The sound of a car pulling up spun her around. She was dressed in her parka and black pants, and she had her gun and her suppressor with her, all of it retrieved earlier in the day from the base of that artwork she'd stashed it in.

There was no way she was attending this unarmed. Even though this client was one Eduardo had marked with a star—indicating, per his system, that whoever it was paid on time, caused no trouble, and regularly ordered—she could trust no one.

Hopefully, however, he was a businessperson, just as she was, and there would be no difficulty.

As a single car door shut solidly, and footsteps came up the concrete steps, she put her hand into her pocket and gripped her gun, flipping the safety off.

She was going to have to find some more help, she thought as the door creaked while it was opened. She was a bit more exposed than she liked—

Vitoria recognized the fine coat first. . . . the fine overcoat that was cut to perfection and hanging off a large pair of shoulders.

And then she saw the face. That . . . fucking . . . face . . .

Of the man who had kidnapped her brother.

It was him. From the security footage. She was absolutely positive—and in a quick slideshow, she saw Ricardo's body hanging on the wall, battered, bruised, that throat torn open.

Before she had a conscious thought, her rage brought out her gun—and she began to shoot.

Assail saw the family resemblance at the very instant that the woman's eyes peeled wide—as if, somehow, she recognized who he was. There was no time to think further, however, as she took out a gun and started discharging bullets as if she knew he was going to dematerialize out of there at any moment.

But he didn't care about himself, as he dropped down and rolled out of shooting range; all that mattered was whether Vishous had hit the gas—and from the flare of headlights that pierced the partially open door Assail had come through, he was willing to bet his life protocol was being followed.

He just prayed the Brother had the sense to lock Marisol in. Or she was liable to come bursting in with her own gun drawn.

"I know you!" the woman screamed as she continued to shoot. "I know what you did!"

Pop! Pop! Pop!

Except it was more than just popping. The slugs of lead were ricocheting around, and thank God for this crate he had found—

The scent of his own blood made him curse. Sonofabitch. She'd gotten him in the shoulder—of his right arm. His shooting arm.

And given the ache in his side, he was pretty sure he'd been hit somewhere else.

With a grimace, Assail got out his gun and waited for her to empty her clip. She was coming forward, closing in—and she had switched to Spanish, her fury more like a Wagner symphony than any kind of speech.

Then came the pause he was looking for.

With a quick shift, he leaned out for a glance into the warehouse proper.

She was smart. She had stepped behind another of the large crates that dotted the interior to exchange clips.

When she reemerged, he had a brief impression of her—long dark hair, dark eyes, just like Ricardo's, and, Marisol was right, the faces were shaped the same.

And then he shot her.

In the chest.

The impact sent her reeling back, her gun going off in a spray as she tripped off her feet and fell to the ground.

In any other circumstance, he would have closed in and made sure to finish the job, but his shot had been clean and he'd nailed her a good one—more the point, Marisol was in that departing Mercedes and she was all that mattered to him.

In spite of his injuries, he closed his eyes. Tried to calm himself. Breathed deeply so he could dematerialize . . .

SIXTY

As the Mercedes skidded out onto the road, Sola pounded on the door with her fists. "Let me out of this fucking car!"

The instant shots had rung out, she had leapt for the exit—only to find herself locked inside. And then there had been a roar and a lurch, the car's powerful engine thrown into gear and flooded with gas, her weight thrown back and to the far side.

The cursing scream that rose up in her throat could not be denied. And she didn't even try to hold it in.

Assail had been a sitting duck. Why had they let him go in there alone?

"Let me out!"

Done with the yelling, she went for the nine millimeter she'd been given, outing it. And then she put the muzzle to the back of the driver's skull and snarled, *"I said, let me the fuck out."*

They were speeding along the empty city streets, blowing through red lights and stop signs, getting farther and farther away from that warehouse. From Assail.

Oh, God, he could be dead—

"I swear to Christ, I will shoot you!"

"No," Vishous said in a bored tone. "You won't—"

To prove her fucking point, she shifted the muzzle ever so slightly to the right and pulled the trigger three times—blowing out the entire front windshield, the safety glass spidering and then falling back into the front seat in sheets because of their velocity.

"I sure as fuck will!" she hollered at the top of her lungs.

Suddenly, the world was in a blender, the vampire punching the brakes and wrenching the wheel to the side, sending them into a screeching one-eighty. No, three-sixty.

Sola ripped her finger off her trigger as she marble-in-a-jar'd around in the backseat. And then things moved so fast, she had no idea what happened.

Somehow, by the time the sedan lurched to a halt, her gun had been taken from her and Vishous was pointing it right in her face.

He was furious, his white eyes so angry, they threw shadows as he panted.

As cold air from the shot-out windshield replaced the warmth from the heater, and she smelled gasoline and burned rubber, the vampire lit into her.

"You are *really. Fucking. Lucky,*" he yelled—before seeming to force himself to calm down. At least temporarily. "That Fritz likes taking care of this car and will think that replacing that piece of glass is a treat. Because if he didn't, Assail or no Assail, I'd be *drilling you full of holes right now, sweetheart!*"

Sola panted along with him, her arms splayed out, her body half on, half off the seat. Between heaving inhales, she No-More-Wire-Hannnnnnnnnger'd him back: "Don't. Call. Me. *Sweeeetheeeeeeeeeeart!*"

Black slashing brows popped up in surprise.

And then Vishous let out a crack of laughter. "Yeah," he said as he lowered the gun. "I do like you. You can stay—"

At that moment, impossibly, Assail appeared from out of thin air, his body seeming to materialize in the bright illumination of the headlights.

"Assail!"

With the doors locked, she didn't even try them. She shoved the vampire behind the wheel out of the way and dove through the massive hole she'd created, her palms getting scratched on the glass, her head banging into something, her feet scrambling for purchase as she propelled herself out onto the Mercedes's hood.

Squeaking, slipping, crying, she leapt off the car and nearly tackled Assail.

The moment she made contact with his body, she realized she didn't care what the fuck he was. Man, male, human, vampire, she just really didn't give a shit.

He had been a mystery when she had first met him. Then a source of incredible sexual attraction. After that, she had run, and not just from the life she had been leading, but from him, too. She had been so scared by the love she had found.

And when she had come back, and nearly lost him, she'd discovered home.

"You're alive," she croaked against his chest. "Oh, God, you're alive!"

His arms came around her with hesitation, as if he weren't quite sure whether to believe his good fortune. But then he was holding her like he never wanted to let her go.

Pulling back, she put her hands to his face and looked into his moonlight eyes. "I don't care," she said. "I don't care, I don't care, I don't care. I just don't want to be without you. I love you, however you are—"

He didn't let her finish. He kissed her so deep, he took her breath away.

Sola had no idea what the future was going to bring. How this was all going to work. Whether she had lost her damn mind.

But she was smart enough to know that when fate sent you true love, no matter what form it took, you needed to accept the gift.

Besides, at least now her grandmother would start talking to her again—

As she dropped her hands to his shoulders, she frowned and broke their contact. Looking down, she saw blood on his fine overcoat.

"You're bleeding," she said.

"I love you," he replied.

"No, wait, you're bleeding . . ." She pointed at him—and noticed more blood on him. "You're bleeding!"

"You were right. It was Benloise's sister. I think she got me a couple of times—"

Sola jumped back and punched him in the chest with both palms. "Are you even kidding me! I told you not to go in there alone! I told you she'd recognize you! Are you out of your mind!"

As he doubled over with a curse and grabbed for his injured shoulder, she switched to Spanish and kept yelling at him, her adrenaline overload coming out verbally and then some.

Vishous got out, came over, and just shook his head ruefully, like seeing a male who was full of lead slugs getting slashed and burned by his significant other was just the normal course of business. He even lit a cigarette, like he knew they were going to be there for a while.

Eventually, he cut in. "How about we take this show back on the road, huh? The human cops are out this time of night, and not just to eat donuts—"

The sound of a cell phone going off cut through her tirade.

With a frown, Assail reached into his inner coat pocket and took out that burner. "It's her," he said tightly.

"Speakerphone," Vishous ordered. "If you don't mind."

Assail complied, and Sola stopped breathing just so she could focus on the female voice that came over the connection.

"If you're answering this," the woman said in well-articulated, only slightly accented English, "I can guess you somehow survived."

"I am well enough," Assail said, "and you?"

"I was better prepared than you thought. Kevlar is the new black, haven't you heard?"

"Thank you ever so kindly for the update. I shall have to remember that."

"Just so we are clear, I will kill you. I will find you, and I will kill you, and I will settle the score you started."

"Such ambition. You are your brother's sister, after all. But I think you will find that I have tricks up my sleeve and friends in very low places. You might reconsider the goal given what the prize is going to look like for you."

"I am not afraid."

"You should be."

"I will see you soon."

"I look forward to it."

As the call was ended, Sola became abruptly aware that Assail was weaving on his feet—which had a pool of blood around them.

And then the male lurched . . . and fell to the ground.

SIXTY-ONE

ome two hours later, Assail was out of surgery and in one of the training center's inpatient rooms—and he was awake, and smiling. He was fairly certain he had been smiling all the way through the stitch-up process, where, according to Doc Jane, he'd needed a repair for a collapsed lung, a leaky bowel, and something else that didn't matter to him.

There was an IV in his arm, which he'd been told was pumping meds into him, but he was floating on a bubble of such happiness, it could have been saline solution and the stuff would have been like morphine.

The only thing that could make him feel better was if his female—

Right on cue, the door opened wide. But it was not his Marisol; it was his other female.

"Mrs. Carvalho," he called out, even though her hearing was perfectly fine and the room no larger than ten by twelve. "Do come in."

Marisol's grandmother was smiling just as he was. "We stay, then. She told me. We stay with you. We stay here in Caldwell."

As the older woman came forward, Assail frowned as he caught sight, over her short stature, of an argument out in the corridor. Mari-

sol and Vishous were standing nose to nose, as if they were in disagreement about something—and he knew well that thrust of his woman's
chin: The Brother might have been bigger, stronger, and a vampire.

But he was going to lose whatever it was.

Assail refocused on her grandmother. "What are they arguing about?"

Mrs. Carvalho made a dismissive motion. "I no care. I only care that
we are here. My granddaughter not so stupid after all."

"That she is definitely not." He motioned for the elderly woman to
sit at the foot of his bed. "How are you feeling?"

"I am perfect. I live a hundred more years."

"Good. That's what I want to hear."

As a flicker of unease went through him, he considered how long he
was going to be alive as opposed to the humans in his life. But maybe . . .
miracles happened. Who knew what the future held? He had heard
stories of Mary and Jane being saved.

He would have to find a way for Marisol and her grandmother to be
similarly blessed.

"So," Mrs. Carvalho announced, "you come home next night they
say. We go to church then. Midnight mass. All house. Cousins and
Markcus."

"Yes, madam. As you wish."

Mrs. Carvalho took his hand in hers and gave him a little pat. "You
good boy. And then you convert—"

"Vovó," Marisol said as she entered. "He does not have to convert—"

"For you," Assail told his female's grandmother, "I will do anything.
If you want a Catholic in me, then you shall have it."

Marisol came over and kissed him on the lips. "Suck-up," she whispered.

"I have to be in good with the in-laws, as you call them."

"Listen," Marisol said, "I'm going to take Vovó back to the house, if
it's okay."

"I have to cook for those men," Mrs. Carvalho said gravely. "They
too thin. They no eat unless I make the food."

"You need to take it easy, *Vovó*."

The *pshhht* was quick and declarative, and then Mrs. Carvalho was onto her feet and heading off. "I go make my bed. I leave—"

"*Vovó*, this is a hospital. You don't have to make—" Marisol shut up as a glare came at her sure as the boxing of an ear. "Of course, *Vovó*. I'll be out in a minute to help you."

When they were alone, Assail reached up and touched her face. "My love."

She kissed his palm. "I'm so glad . . . well. You know."

"I know." He grew serious. "Listen, Ghisele is going to come in in a little bit and I'm going to . . ."

"Jane explained it to me."

"There is nothing sexual at all in it."

"I understand." She smiled. "Save the sex for me, okay?"

"Always," he growled.

"I'll be back as soon as I can. You rest."

"I love you. Always and forever."

"I love you, too, Assail." She leaned in and kissed him. Then ran her tongue across the points of his canines. "Man, I am so turned on—"

Before he could help himself, he snatched ahold of the nape of her neck and yanked her to his mouth. After he kissed her hard, he set her back so he could meet her eyes.

As the scent of her arousal flared, he knew she was staring at his fangs as they descended from the roof of his mouth.

"I will never hurt you with them," he said in a guttural voice. "Ever. But if you want them—"

"I do," she breathed. "I want you to do . . . whatever you do."

Without thinking about it—and even though the door was not locked and there were people around—he took her hand and pulled it under the sheets. Placing her palm on his erection, he rolled his hips.

She took over from there. As they kissed, and his hand found her breast through her fleece, she stroked him.

It did not take long. And even though his fresh stitches stung as he worked with her rhythm, the pleasure was so great, he started coming almost immediately—and he didn't stop.

He didn't ever want to stop.

"I love you," he said on a groan, "and I can't wait to be inside you again."

"Me, too. God . . . me, too . . ."

It was about an hour later when Sola caught a ride to her car with Vishous in the van they used to run her grandmother back home. Assail's cousins and Markcus had been overjoyed at the reunion, and the three males had fallen in line with marching orders to go to the supermarket.

All was well in the world.

And about to be even better, Sola thought as she got out. "Thanks for the ride."

"I do not like this."

"You've made that amply clear," she said dryly.

At that moment, his cell phone went off, and talk about perfect timing. In case it was about Assail, though, she waited.

The vampire cursed. "Goddamn it. Another attack."

"What?"

"Nothing. You just lucked out, though. I've got to go handle this—otherwise, I'd be going with you."

"I told you, this has to be a solo flight. It's the principle of the thing."

The vampire just shook his head. "You have that phone I gave you, true?"

She patted her parka. "Yup."

"When you're ready, assuming you live through this, call me and I'll get you back into the training center."

"Thank you." She cleared her throat. "I mean that. And you know, I'm sorry about the windshield."

"No, you're not."

She laughed. "Fine. I'm not. But will you let me pay for the damage?"

"Never." He looked over at her. "Just don't get yourself killed and we'll call it even. Assail won't make it without you."

"I won't make it without him. So don't worry, I'm not going to fuck up the good thing I got going."

With that, she closed the passenger-side door. And as she went to her car, she became so relaxed, she floated over the pavement sure as if her feet did not touch the ground.

Then again, she was in the zone with this one.

Revenge . . . was a dish best served calmly.

SIXTY-TWO

ome eight hundred miles to the south, on a tract of land that was serene and largely uninhabited, emissaries from the King arrived at a destination that knocked their socks off.

As Saxton, the King's solicitor, re-formed, he looked around and took a deep, easing breath. "Oh, this is beautiful."

His beloved mate, Ruhn, materialized beside him and echoed his sentiments. "This is . . . astounding."

They each reached for the other's hand at the same time—and then they stayed where they were, letting the gracious landscape sink in. Up ahead, under a fat moon in a balmy sky, a lovely old white house sat at the culmination of an allée of live oaks. With porches on both the first and second floors, and black shutters, and a hip roof, it was a Southern lady of gracious extraction.

"So he knows we're coming?" Ruhn said.

"Well . . . I wouldn't go that far, precisely."

When Saxton went to walk forward, his love pulled him back. "Murhder does not know we're here?"

"I sent him a letter."

"And his response was?"

"I didn't actually get one."

Ruhn was largely a placid and loving soul, a gentle giant with a heart of gold who had lived through more pain and suffering than Saxton could ever understand.

The male was not a pushover, however. And as those caramel eyes narrowed, Saxton held up his free hand. "We have to do this. It's the law."

Ruhn's eyes returned to the house's lineup of darkened windows. "I don't like this."

"I have to inform him of the inheritance. Come, let us approach."

They walked straight up the center of the allée, and as they proceeded, Saxton had to wonder why anyone ever volunteered to sit through Caldwell's winters. If he didn't have his position with the King, he would most certainly spend time down here.

Although . . . their old farmhouse was incredibly quaint, with its cheery fires in the fireplaces, and cozy quilts to cuddle under—and the opportunity for Ruhn to play plumber under that faulty kitchen sink.

There was nothing better than a male who knew how to deal with pipes—

Twin red laser beams hit both of them in the chest—directly at sternum height—and froze them in their tracks.

There were only two things in the world that would make that sort of optical effect. And one had to assume that nobody would be bothering with a laser pointer this late at night . . . toward two strangers who, technically, were not invited to be on the premises.

On the second floor, a light came on, illuminating a tremendous shadow that stood in what was an open window.

"You're trespassing," came a low, evil voice. "And I don't like people on my land."

Saxton cleared his throat as both he and Ruhn lifted their hands. "We come in peace. We are here to see Murhder."

There was a long pause. "You're the one that sent the letter."

"Yes. I am Saxton. I am Wrath, son of Wrath, sire of Wrath's solici-

tor. This is my mate, Ruhn. We have arrived here to inform him that he
has come into an inheritance—"

"I don't want it."

Saxton glanced down at his own chest. "Would you consider lowering your weapons? This is a bit unsettling."

"No, I won't. And I don't want anyone's money."

"Then will you kindly sign the documents I sent in my letter re-
nouncing it—"

"My signature is no good."

Saxton recoiled. "Why?"

"I'm insane. Haven't you heard. The insane cannot consent, we do
not legally exist."

Excellent point. But let us not get hung up on technicalities, Saxton
thought to himself.

He took a deep breath. "Forgive me, but you do not sound crazy."
Although the male was threatening to shoot two perfectly innocent
people—so how balanced could he be? "And I am required to see this
through. It's my job."

There was a long period of silence. "Tell your King that I will sign
those papers, but only if he sees me personally. I want to meet with
him. I think it's about time."

"Once again, forgive me, but this is not a matter usually handled in
such a fashion. The King doesn't—"

"Those are my terms. You know where to find me. If Wrath will see
me, I will sign the papers. Now go. Before I decide to indulge my need
for target practice."

Saxton measured the sheer heft of the shadow in the window. Backlit as the male was, there was no telling what the face looked like—
although he was fairly certain that the hair was long, and yes, the size of
the body was definitely that of a Brother.

Saxton bowed low. "I will inform the King of your preference, and
I shall be back in touch. Perhaps if you would like to give me a number
where I can—"

"I am old-fashioned. I prefer parcel post—or FedEx, I believe is what you used. You can communicate with me that way. Now get off my property."

Saxton glanced at his love. "Let us go, the now," he said under his breath.

"Yes," Ruhn agreed readily.

As the two of them dematerialized for the first leg of the trip back to Caldwell, Saxton's only thought was that this did not bode well.

This did not bode well, at all.

SIXTY-THREE

It took Sola, relatively speaking, no time at all to get to West Point, and as she parked her car down by the water and got out, she remembered another trip here in the dark, on a different cold night. That previous visit to Ricardo's house, that other infiltration, that bid to claim what was properly owed to her, had set everything else in motion: her abduction, Assail's actions on her behalf . . . her introduction to the training center.

And here she was, doing a full circle for closure.

Just as she had before, she stuck to the low-slung stone wall as she proceeded up the incline of the long, ascending front lawn. Unlike before, she wasn't on skis or wearing white to blend into the snowy landscape. It didn't matter; she moved fast, and the cloud cover over the moon gave her a pass.

As she approached Ricardo's mansion, she noted where the lights were glowing: A couple in his master suite, but there were ones on in the lower level as well.

She had her gun out the entire time. And she'd screwed the suppressor on.

She knew a couple of different ways to break into the house, and mentally reviewed her options. She didn't have her grappling gear with her, which was perhaps an oversight on her part. No matter, though. She would make this work and get her job done.

When she arrived at the apex, she had to cross over the side lawn to get to the corner of the mansion, and she did not enjoy being without cover—but she made it and flattened her back against a wall between two arching windows.

There was no way of knowing how many people were inside. Or where they were located. Assail had told her that Vitoria had been in the warehouse alone, but that did not mean she didn't have guards at her home base.

And of course she would stay here. She was Ricardo's sister. She would have standards, and no hotel, not even with the best accomodations and most attentive maids, could rival this estate.

Sola shifted her position to the corner of the house, and leaned around to visualize the back of the—

There was a pattern of illumination cast onto the snowpack, all of the windows of the mansion's promenade throwing a row of yellow light squares onto the ground. And way down, at the far side, a figure came out of the kitchen and headed in Sola's direction.

She stepped free of her position, but stuck to the shadows as she assessed the person.

It was Vitoria. Long dark hair down, face free of makeup, a silk robe falling to her slippered feet. She was holding a porcelain teacup, as if she couldn't sleep and had gone down to fix herself something soothing.

Lavender and rose hips, perhaps?

Sola lifted her gun and tracked Vitoria with the muzzle.

If this were the movies, she would break in and chase the woman around the grand house, the drama culminating in some kind of shootout where they each accused the other of crimes against blood and love—perhaps she'd get herself wounded and have to heroically drive herself back to Caldwell.

But this was not Hollywood.

Sola was as mortal as her target was, and she didn't know enough about what kind of bees' nest she was going to stir up as soon as she pulled her trigger. What she was clear on was that this woman needed to die, tonight, and she had a good shot in another seven feet, six feet . . . five feet . . .

More than anything, Sola wanted to eliminate the threat and just get back to her grandmother and the male she loved safely.

In one piece. No leaks.

As Vitoria walked along, she was stirring a silver spoon in circles, her eyes downcast.

So she never saw it coming. Didn't hear the shot, either.

But when that old-fashioned glass broke right next to her, she looked up in alarm.

Sola got the bitch right between the eyes.

It was the hole-in-one kill shot, the one-in-a-million, the if-it-ever-was-going-to-go-like-that-tonight-is-the-night shot.

No need to double tap that shit.

The woman pinwheeled her arms, dropping the porcelain cup, stumbling, falling . . . grabbing on to the nearest thing she could.

Which happened to be the bronze statue of a ballet dancer done by Degas.

The very statue that Sola had shifted one inch out of position on its base, as payback for Ricardo stiffing her for what she'd been owed for watching Assail.

It seemed like poetic justice that the sister took that piece of art down with her—right on top of her, as a matter of fact. So if she hadn't already been in the process of dying, the impact would surely have killed her.

As the clatter rang out, Sola took off, her gun by her side, head ducked. Now, if her good luck streak held, she'd make it down to the car without trouble and head back to Caldwell.

But no matter what happened, she had made sure her male was safe. Because that was what real women did.

Real women didn't wait for their dragon slayers to come save them. They were true partners—and good with a gun on their own.

Booyah.

SIXTY-FOUR

As dawn arrived, Jane came back to the Pit and found her *hellren* at his computers. The instant V sensed her, he looked up and held his arms wide.

"There she is," he said.

She went to him with light feet and a lighter heart. "Soooooo, I guess Sola and Assail worked things out, huh?"

"Yeah." He reached up and threaded his fingers through her short hair. "You were great in the OR with him. Real mastery. I was so fucking impressed."

"You say the sweetest things."

"Sit in my lap?"

"Always—" She frowned as she moved around and caught sight of a video on one of his monitors. "What is that—wait . . . that's you!"

"I know." V shook his head and toggled the mouse so it replayed the clip. "We got problems."

Jane leaned in closer and watched as the images that were dark and fuzzy—but not *that* dark and fuzzy—moved around: two males fighting something that . . . didn't seem there at all; one falling to the ground as the shadow disappeared; V and Rhage appearing out of thin air; V crouching down by the civilian injured on the ground.

He paused the thing. "I don't want you to see what happens after the civilian dies. I already told you."

Yes, she thought. V had had to kill him. Just as the poor male was turning into whatever they turned into.

"This footage is on the Web," he said with resignation. "And it's going viral."

"How can you stop it?"

"I'm working on that right now." He cursed. "Which reminds me. I didn't want to get involved, but we got a half-breed out there who's about to go through the change. I'm no Good Samaritan, but it's dawning on me—as I watch this—that the last thing we need is her showing up in a medical crisis because she's going through her transition. I think we're going to have to go get her."

"Oh, God. The poor thing. Of course, bring her here." Jane shook her head. "She may not live."

"But at least we won't have more documentation. We don't need that shit. And I already stripped her memories—she was on to us, posting on this blog of hers. It's supposed to be all taken down now, but yeah, she's still doing it. At least I know where she lives. There isn't time before sunlight comes, but at nightfall, I'll go get her, even if she doesn't like it."

Jane traced the tattoos on his temple with her fingertips. "Good. I'll help in any way I can."

"You always do." He smiled a little—which for her Vishous was like anybody else breaking out into a clown grin. "Hey. You wanna go have sex."

Jane laughed. "Yes. I do."

"OhmyfuckingGodthatisSOtherightanswer."

As he stood up, he took her with him, carrying her down the hall as if she weighed nothing—except then he stopped for some reason.

Turning in his arms, she smiled and looked at the floor. "Hey, Boo. What are you doing here?"

The household's black cat meowed up to her, as if in greeting, and then pawed like it wanted to be let into the tunnel.

"I think he wants to go down into—"

"I got it," V said tightly as he leaned to the wall and released the lock on the door. "Go on, there—that's it."

As the cat disappeared, he shut things up and refocused. "Now. Where were we?"

"How'd Boo get in here?"

"I, ah . . . I let it in."

"You don't like cats."

"I know." He kept going. "Now let's concentrate on us."

When they got to their room, he kicked the door shut and threw her on the bed. Then he loomed over her like he wanted to eat her.

"You are so fucking hot," he growled.

She eyed the enormous bulge in his leathers. "You are not so bad yourself."

Except he stayed where he was. Clearing his throat, he said, "I think I'm going to get rid of the penthouse. You know, too many bad memories there."

Jane stared up at him for a moment. "You love it there."

"With you, yeah. But whatever. I don't want you to ever wonder, you know. Ever."

Her smile was slow and she held her arms out to him. "Come here."

Vishous joined her, lying half on and half off her body. As his diamond eyes met hers, she felt no hesitation at all.

"I trust you," she said.

V blinked a number of times—as if he were having a moment—and then he pressed his lips to her own with a smile.

"I love you, too, Jane Whitcomb. Forevermore."

SIXTY-FIVE

Assail did not sleep. At all. Even as the post-feeding loginess settled in, he was wide fucking awake.

Because he figured out what Marisol and Vishous had been arguing about. He knew *exactly* what the subject had been, and why V had been so cranked off, and why his Marisol had, as always, absolutely refused to budge.

He looked across the wall at the clock and tried not to freak out that she had been gone nearly two hours. "Goddamn it—"

The door opened, and as his female stood between the jambs, he was at once overjoyed and ready to yell at her.

"I know what you did," he said sharply. "You went to Benloise's house, didn't you. You went to see his sister."

Marisol at least had the grace to look sheepish. "Now, Assail—"

"Don't you 'now, Assail' me! You could have gotten yourself killed!"

"Didn't we just do this, with different pronouns," she muttered as she forced the door closed faster than its hinges appreciated. "And she was going to kill you—if we stay in Caldwell, she would have found you and—"

"Is she dead," he demanded tightly.

"Yes. Someone is going to find her with a bronze statue on her head and a shattered teacup about six feet from the body in the rear promenade of her brother's house." Marisol put her hand up. "And, I was a good little assassin—I didn't go in. I had a clean shot and I took it and made it count. Then I left and now I'm home, and we are never speaking of this again. You took care of Ricardo for me, I took care of his sister for you, and now we are both out of that life for good. Vishous and his people are going to have to buy all those bullets from somebody else. They're not stupid. They'll figure it out."

Assail crossed his arms over his chest. "I do not approve."

"Which was why I didn't ask you."

She sidled up to the bed, taking off her parka. Then her fleece. Then her . . .

As her naked breasts made a stunning appearance, and his sex punched out in an erection that could have jacked up the back of a car, he forgot all about being upset.

Which was not fair.

"You're trying to distract me," he complained as she started to take off her pants. "You're . . . oh, God . . ."

No panties. She wasn't wearing panties.

"Is it working," she said with a slow turn back toward the door.

"Fuck," he breathed as she sashayed over and locked things. "Yes."

"Good. That was the plan."

Assail didn't waste any goddamn time. He shoved the light blankets down, yanked up his hospital johnny, and then she was up on the bed straddling him.

"I love you," she said as she kissed him. "And I didn't take any chances. In and out. The job was done safely, I swear."

Just as she lowered herself onto his arousal, he thought he never would have imagined him and the love of his life having such a factual conversation about murdering someone. Then again, who else did he think he'd end up with?

Only a strong female, with a will of her own and the skills to match, would ever capture his heart.

And Marisol Maria Rafaela Carvalho, a.k.a. Sola Morte, was that female exactly.

"I love you," he said with a groan as they became one.

And then he stopped thinking altogether, and just reveled in the feeling. Surely there were going to be obstacles to surmount and conflicts to be resolved—and he was going to have to find something productive to do with himself.

But if he had learned one thing, in his four hundred years of existence?

With love . . . all things are possible.

ACKNOWLEDGMENTS

With immense gratitude to the readers of the Black Dagger Brotherhood!

Thank you so very much to Kara Welsh and everyone else at Ballantine—these books are truly a team effort.

With love to Team Waud—you know who you are. This simply could not happen without you.

None of this would be possible without: my loving husband, who is my adviser and caretaker and visionary; my wonderful mother, who has given me so much love I couldn't possibly ever repay her; my family (both those of blood and those by adoption); and my dearest friends.

And as always, with love and devotion, to my WriterDog II, Naamah.

ABOUT THE AUTHOR

J. R. WARD is the #1 *New York Times* bestselling author of more than thirty novels, including the Black Dagger Brotherhood series, the Black Dagger Legacy series, and The Bourbon Kings. There are more than fifteen million copies of her novels in print worldwide, and they have been published in twenty-six different countries around the world. She lives in the South with her family.

JRWard.com
Facebook.com/jrwardbooks
Twitter: @JRWard1

ABOUT THE TYPE

This book was set in Garamond, a typeface originally designed by the Parisian type cutter Claude Garamond (c. 1500–61). This version of Garamond was modeled on a 1592 specimen sheet from the Egenolff-Berner foundry, which was produced from types assumed to have been brought to Frankfurt by the punch cutter Jacques Sabon (c. 1520–80).

Claude Garamond's distinguished romans and italics first appeared in *Opera Ciceronis* in 1543–44. The Garamond types are clear, open, and elegant.

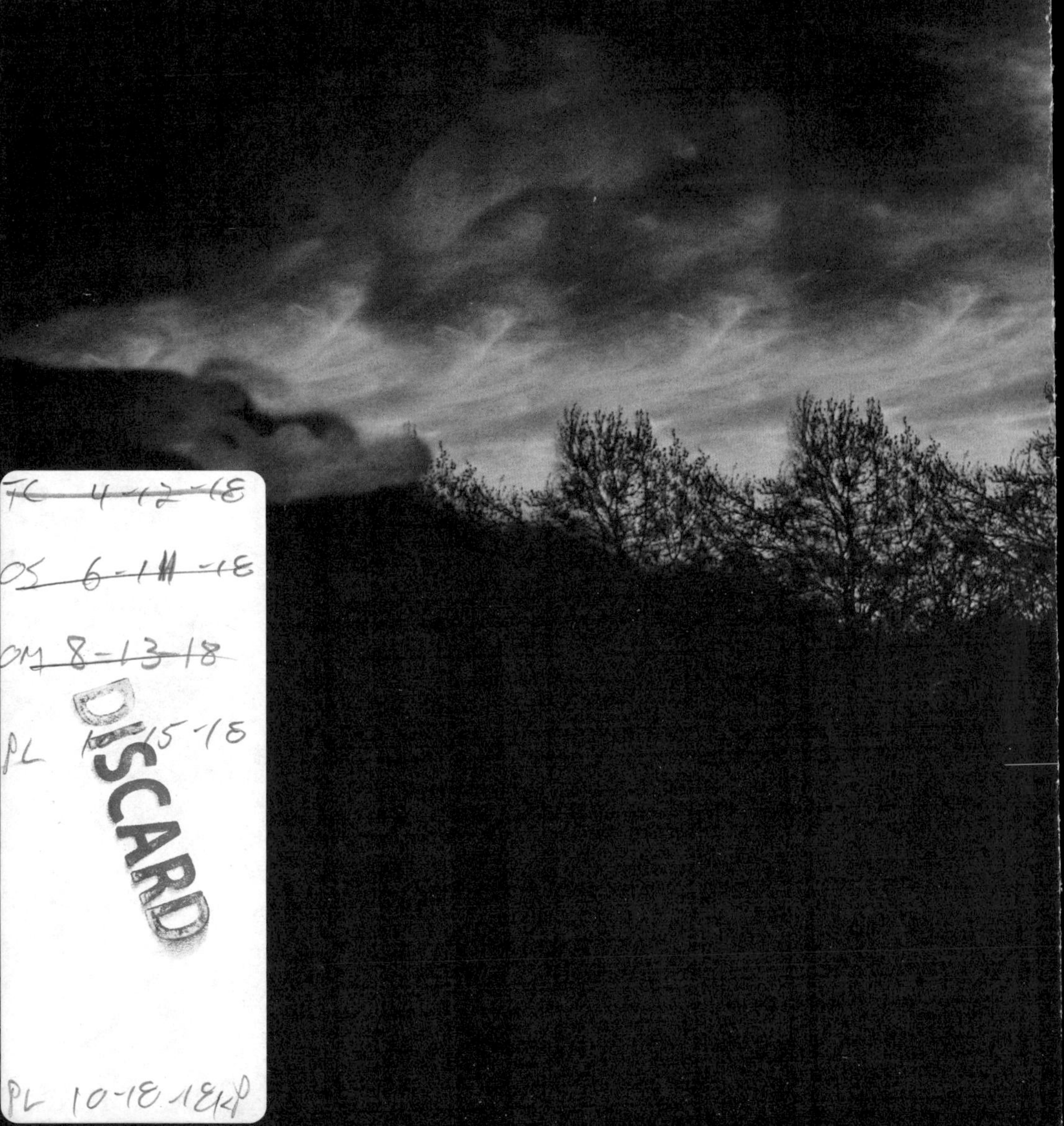